OUR ANCESTORS

Italo Calvino was born in Cuba in 1923, and grew
up in Italy. He was an essayist and journalist and a
member of the editorial staff of Einaudi in Turin.
His other novels include *Invisible Cities* and *The
Castle of Crossed Destinies*. In 1973 he won the
prestigious Premio Feltrinelli. He died in 1985.

ALSO BY ITALO CALVINO

ITALO CALVINO

Our Ancestors

THREE NOVELS
The Cloven Viscount
Baron in the Trees
The Non-Existent Knight

TRANSLATED FROM THE ITALIAN BY
Archibald Colquhoun

WITH AN INTRODUCTION BY THE AUTHOR

VINTAGE BOOKS
London

Published by Vintage 1998

21

Il Visconte Dimezzato copyright © Giulio Einaudi editore, S.A., Torino 1951
The Cloven Viscount English translation copyright © William Collins Sons &
Company Ltd., London and Random House Inc., New York 1962
Il Barone Rampante copyright © Giulio Einaudi editore, S.A., Torino 1957
The Baron in the Trees English translation copyright ©
William Collins Sons & Company Ltd. 1959
Il Cavaliere Inesistente copyright © Giulio Einaudi editore, S.A., Torino 1959
The Non-existent Knight English Translation copyright © William Collins Sons
& Company Ltd., London and Random House Inc., New York 1962

First published in Italian under the titles *Il Visconte Dimezzato, Il Barone
Rampante* and *Il Cavaliere Inesistente*.

First published in Great Britain by Martin Secker & Warburg in 1980

Vintage
Random House, 20 Vauxhall Bridge Road,
London SW1V 2SA

www.vintage-classics.info

Addresses for companies within The Random House Group Limited can be
found at: www.randomhouse.co.uk/offices.htm

The Random House Group Limited Reg. No. 954009

A CIP catalogue record for this book
is available from the British Library

ISBN 9780099430865

Penguin Random House is committed to a sustainable future for
our business, our readers and our planet. This book is made from
Forest Stewardship Council® certified paper.

Printed and bound in Great Britain by Clays Ltd, Elcograf S.p.A.

Introduction
by the author

There are two different words in English, novel and romance, for what in Italian is always called a *romanzo*. But although we have only a single word for them in Italian, the difference between the two kinds is felt. The three tales collected in this volume are what I think should be called romances in English. In the fifties, however, what was expected from Italian literature in general, and from me in particular, was novels. This is why they raised eyebrows when they appeared in Italy. From my first published works I was thought a 'realistic' writer; indeed, a 'neo-realistic' one, the term then in use, taken from the cinema. I was surprised, too, because I had written *Il Visconte Dimezzato* almost for fun, as a *divertissement* which I thought would slip by unnoticed, and I was not prepared for the outcry that greeted it or the fact that it would be thought a shocking turnabout on my part.

The fact is that after my first novel, written in 1946, and my first short stories, which told of picaresque adventures in an Italy of wartime and postwar upheaval, I had made efforts to write the realistic-novel-reflecting-the-problems-of-Italian-society, and had not managed to do so. (At the time I was what was called a 'politically committed writer'.) And then, in 1951, when I was twenty-eight and not at all sure that I was going to carry on writing, I began doing what came most naturally to me – that is, following the memory of the things I had loved best since boyhood. Instead of making myself write the book I *ought* to write, the novel that was expected of me, I conjured up the book I myself would have liked to read, the sort by an unknown writer, from another age and another country, discovered in an attic.

Among the writers I have always read and, willy-nilly, have taken as a model is R. L. Stevenson. This is because Stevenson himself wrote the books he would have liked to read, because he, who was so delicate an artist, imitated old adventure stories and then relived them himself. To him, writing meant translating an invisible text containing the quintessential fascination of all adventures, all mysteries, all conflicts of will and passion scattered throughout the books of hundreds of writers; it meant translating them into his own precise and almost impalpable prose, into his own rhythm which was like that of dance-steps at once impetuous and controlled. (Stevenson's admirers are a chosen few in all literatures; J. L. Borges is the most eminent of them.)

Another of my models was the *conte philosophique*, chiefly Voltaire's *Candide*. What drew me to it also was its precision, lightness and rhythm and my own liking for the eighteenth century. Then there were the German Romantics, not all of them but some stories by some writers: Chamisso, Hoffmann, Arnim, Eichendorff.

Of course these were not my only literary sources. For *Baron in the Trees* there was a nineteenth-century Italian novelist who died young and deserves to be known outside Italy, Ippolito Nievo, 1831–61. *The Non-Existent Knight* pretends to be yet another version of the romances of chivalry in the medieval cycle of Charlemagne's paladins. These had a literary and popular success that in Italy continued much longer than it did in any other country, and continues in our own time in the Sicilian puppet theatre.

But what I mean is that through all these literary filters I may have managed to express myself far better than if I had started off from my own experience. Hidden behind those screens, I could write more freely. What about? I wrote, of course, about the only thing I had to speak of: my relationship with the problems of my own time and my own life.

My own experience appears in the three stories; to start with, in their landscape. Although they take place in imaginary countries (the *Knight* in the arbitary geography of the chivalric poems), they breathe the air of the Mediterranean which I had breathed throughout my life. Much of Italian literature has regional roots. I have always tried to avoid what seems to me a regressive local feeling, but my own history starts from a very particular place. My home was in San Remo, on the Riviera which was discovered and loved by the English in the last century, and which building development in the postwar years has now made unrecognizable. As I lived in San Remo throughout infancy, childhood and youth until the age of twenty-five, without moving from the coast and the mountains that dominate it, and as my father's family had lived there for centuries, it is natural when I tell imaginary stories set in an imaginary country that this country should be like the Riviera where I grew up. So the Ligurian landscape, where trees have almost disappeared today, in the *Baron* is transformed into a kind of apotheosis of vegetation.

What the three stories have in common is the fact that they had a very simple, very obvious image or situation as their point of departure: a man sliced in half, the two halves of whom continue living on their own; a boy who climbs up into the trees and refuses to come down, and ends by spending the rest of his life there; an empty suit of armour that persuades itself it is a man and carries on through its own will-power. The tale is born from the image, not from any thesis which I want to demonstrate, and the image is developed in a story according to its own internal logic. The story takes on meanings, or rather, around the image extends a network of meanings that are always a little uncertain, without insisting on an unequivocal, compulsory interpretation. More than anything else it is a case of moral themes suggested by the central image, and developed in the secondary stories. In the *Viscount*, these are themes of incompleteness, bias, the lack of human fullness; in the *Baron*, themes of isolation, distance, difficulties in relationships with others; in the *Knight*, themes of empty forms and the concrete nature of living, awareness of being in the world and building one's own destiny, or else lack of involvement altogether. I will give no more than these very general points because the reader must interpret the stories as he will, or else not interpret them at all and read them simply for enjoyment – which would fully satisfy me as a writer. So I agree to the books being read as existential or as structural works, as Marxist or neo-Kantian, Freudianly or Jungianly;

but above all I am glad when I see that no single key will turn all their locks.

The *Viscount* was written in 1951, the *Baron* in 1957, and the *Knight* in 1959. References to the intellectual climate of the years in which they were written can be found in them all: in the *Viscount*, dislike of the divisions of the Cold War, which affected the rest of us as well; in the *Baron*, the problem of the intellectual's political commitment at a time of shattered illusions; in the *Knight*, criticism of the 'organization man' in a mass society. I would say, in fact, that the *Knight*, in which references to the present seem most remote, says something that touches our present situation most closely of the three.

I have thought that this trilogy might help to provide a family tree for contemporary man. And so I have republished the three books in a single volume entitled *Our Ancestors*: in order to guide my readers round a portrait gallery where they may recognize some of their own features, and tics, and obsessions.

Translated by Isabel Quigly

Our Ancestors

The Cloven Viscount

I

There was a war on against the Turks. My uncle, the Viscount Medardo of Terralba, was riding towards the Christian camp across the plain of Bohemia, followed by a squire called Kurt. Storks were flying low, in white flocks, through the thick still air.

'Why all the storks?' Medardo asked Kurt. 'Where are they flying?'

My uncle was a new arrival, just enrolled to please ducal neighbours involved in that war. After fitting himself out with a horse and squire at the last castle in Christian hands he was now on his way to report at Imperial headquarters.

'They're flying to the battlefields,' said the squire glumly. 'They'll be with us all the way.'

The Viscount Medardo had heard that in those parts a flight of storks was thought a good omen; and he wanted to seem pleased at the sight. But in spite of himself he felt worried.

'What can draw such birds to a battlefield, Kurt?' he asked.

'They eat human flesh too nowadays,' replied the squire, 'since the fields have been stripped by famine and the rivers dried by drought. Vultures and crows have now given place to storks and flamingos and cranes.'

My uncle was then in his first youth; the age in which feelings all confused, rush, not yet sifted, into good and bad; the age in which every new experience, macabre and inhuman too, is palpitating and warm with love of life.

'What about the crows then? And the vultures?' he said. 'And the other birds of prey? Where have they gone?' He was pale, but his eyes glittered.

The squire, a dark-skinned soldier with heavy moustaches, never raised his eyes. 'There are so many plague-ridden bodies that the plague got 'em too,' and he pointed his lance at some black bushes, which a closer look revealed as made not of branches, but of feathers and dried claws from birds of prey.

'One can't tell which died first, bird or man, or who tore the other to bits,' said Kurt.

To escape the plague exterminating the population entire families had taken to the open country, where death had caught them. Over the bare plain were scattered tangled heaps of men's and women's corpses, naked, covered with plague boils and, inexplicably at first, with feathers, as if these skinny legs and ribs had grown black feathers and wings. These were carcasses of vultures mingled with human remains.

The ground was now scattered with signs of past battles. Their progress slowed, for the two horses kept jibbing and rearing.

'What's the matter with our horses?' Medardo asked the squire.

'Signore,' he replied, 'horses hate nothing more than the stink of their own guts.'

The patch of plain they were crossing was covered with horses' carcasses, some supine with hooves to the sky, others prone with muzzles dug into the earth.

'Why all these fallen horses round here, Kurt?' asked Medardo.

'When a horse feels its belly ripped open,' explained the squire, 'it tries to keep its guts in. Some put bellies on the ground, others turn on their backs to prevent them dangling. But death gets 'em soon all the same.'

'So mostly horses die in this war?'

'Turkish scimitars seem made to cleave their bellies at a stroke. Farther on we'll see men's bodies. First it's horses, then riders. But there's the camp.'

On edges of the horizon rose pinnacles of the highest tents, the standards of the Imperial army, and smoke.

As they galloped on, they saw that those fallen in the last battle had nearly all been taken off and buried. There were just a few limbs, fingers in particular, scattered over the stubble.

'Every now and again I see a finger pointing our way,' said my uncle Medardo. 'What does that mean?'

'May God forgive them, but the living chop off the fingers of the dead to get at their rings.'

'Who goes there?' said a sentinel in a cloak covered in mould and moss like a tree-bark exposed to the north wind.

'Hurrah for the Holy Imperial crown!' cried Kurt.

'And down with the Sultan!' replied the sentinel. 'Please, though, when you get to headquarters, do ask 'em to send along my relief, as I'm starting to grow roots!'

The horses were now at a gallop to escape the clouds of flies surrounding the camp and buzzing over heaps of excrement.

'Many's the brave man,' observed Kurt, 'whose dung is still on the ground when he's already in heaven,' and he crossed himself.

At the entrance they rode past a series of canopies, beneath which thick-set women with long brocade gowns and bare breasts greeted them with yells and coarse laughter.

'The pavilions of the courtesans,' said Kurt. 'No other army has such fine women.'

My uncle was riding with his head turned back to look at them.

'Careful, Signore,' added the squire, 'they're so foul and pox-ridden even the Turks wouldn't want them as booty. They're not only covered with lice, bugs and ticks, but even scorpions and lizards make their nests on them now.'

They passed by the field batteries. At night the artillerymen cooked their ration of turnips and water on the bronze parts of swivel-guns and cannons, burning hot from the day's firing.

Carts were arriving, full of earth which the artillerymen were passing through sieves.

'Gunpowder is scarce now,' explained Kurt, 'but the soil of the battlefields is so saturated with it that a few charges can be retrieved there.'

Next came the cavalry stabling, where, amid flies, veterinary surgeons were at work patching up hides with stitches, belts and plasters of boiling tar, as horses and doctors neighed and stamped.

Long stretches of infantry encampments followed. It was

dusk, and in front of every tent were sitting soldiers with bare feet in tubs of warm water. Used as they were to sudden alarms night and day, even at footbath time they kept helmet on head and pike tight in fist. Inside taller tents draped like kiosks could be seen officers powdering armpits and waving lace fans.

'That's not from effeminacy,' said Kurt, 'just the opposite; they want to show how they're at ease in the rigours of military life.'

The Viscount of Terralba was immediately introduced into the presence of the emperor. In his pavilion, amid tapestries and trophies, the sovereign was studying future battle plans. Tables were covered with unrolled maps and the emperor was busy sticking pins in them, taking these from a small pin cushion proffered by one of his marshals. By then the maps were so covered with pins that it was impossible to understand a thing, and to read them pins had to be taken out and then put back. With all this pinning and unpinning, the Emperor and his marshals, to keep their hands free, all had pins between their lips and could only talk in grunts.

At sight of the youth bowing before him, the sovereign let out a questioning grunt and then took the pins out of his mouth.

'A knight just arrived from Italy, your majesty,' they introduced him, 'the Viscount of Terralba, from one of the noblest families in the Genoese republic.'

'Let him be made lieutenant at once.'

My uncle clicked spurs to attention, while the emperor gave a regal sweep of the arm and all the maps folded in on themselves and rolled away.

Though tired, Medardo was late asleep that night. He walked up and down near his tent and heard calls of sentries, neighs of horses and broken speech from soldiers in sleep. He gazed up at the stars of Bohemia, thought of his new rank, of the battle next day, and of his distant home, of the rustling reeds in its brooks. He felt no nostalgia or doubt or apprehension.

Things were still indisputably whole as he was himself. Could
he have foreseen the dreadful fate awaiting him he might have
found it quite natural too, with all its pain. His eyes kept
straying towards the verges of the dark horizon where he
knew lay the enemy camp, and he hugged himself with crossed
arms in his certainty both of distant and differing realities, and
of his own presence amid them. He sensed the bloodshed in
that cruel war pouring over the earth in innumerable streams
and finally reaching him; and he let it lap him with no out-
rage or pity.

2

Battle began punctually at ten next morning. From high on
his saddle Lieutenant Medardo gazed over the broad array
of Christians ready for attack, and raised his face to the wind
of Bohemia, swirling with chaff like in some dusty barn.

'No, don't turn round, Signore,' explained Kurt, now a
sergeant, beside him. And to justify the peremptory phrase he
murmured: 'It's said to bring bad luck before battle.'

In reality he did not want the Viscount to feel discouraged,
for he knew that the Christian army consisted almost entirely
of the line drawn up there, and that the only reinforcements
were a few platoons of rickety infantry.

But my uncle was looking into the distance at a nearing
cloud on the horizon and thinking: 'There, that cloud is
Turks, real Turks, and these men here spitting tobacco are
veterans of Christendom, and this bugle now sounding is the
attack, the first attack in my life, and this roaring and shaking,
this shooting star plunging to earth and treated with languid

irritation by veterans and horses is a cannonball, the first enemy cannonball I've ever seen. May it not be the day when I'll say: and it's my last.'

Then, with bared sword, he was galloping over the plain, his eyes on the Imperial standard vanishing and reappearing amid the smoke, while friendly cannonballs rotated in the sky above his head, and enemy ones opened gaps in the Christian ranks and sudden umbrellas of earth. 'I'll see the Turks! I'll see the Turks!' he was thinking. There's no greater fun than having enemies and then finding out if they are like one thought.

Now he saw them, saw the Turks. Two came right up. With mantled horses, round little leather shields, black and saffron-striped robes. Turbaned, ochre-coloured faces and moustaches like someone at Terralba called 'Micky the Turk'. One of the two was killed and the other killed someone else. But now numbers of them were arriving and the fight got hand to hand. To see two Turks was to see the lot. They were soldiers, too, all in their own army equipment. Their faces were tanned and tough, like peasants. Medardo had seen as much as he wanted of them; he felt he might as well get back to Terralba in time for the quail season. But he had signed on for the whole war. So on he rushed, avoiding scimitar thrusts, until he found a short Turk, on foot, and killed him. Now he had got the way of it he looked round for a tall one on horseback. That was a mistake, for small ones were the most dangerous. They got right under horses with those scimitars and hamstrung them.

Medardo's horse stopped short with legs splayed. 'What's up?' said the Viscount. Kurt came up and pointed down-wards. 'Look there.' All its guts were hanging to the ground. The poor beast looked up at its master, then lowered its head as if to browse on its intestines, but that was only a last show of heroism; it fainted, then died. Medardo of Terralba was on foot.

'Take my horse, Lieutenant,' said Kurt, but did not manage to halt it, as he fell from the saddle, wounded by a Turkish arrow, and the horse ran away.

'Kurt!' cried the Viscount, and went to his squire groaning on the ground.

'Don't think of me, sir,' exclaimed the squire. 'Let's hope there's some schnapps in hospital. A can is due to every wounded man.'

My uncle Medardo flung himself into the mêlée. The fate of battle was uncertain. In the confusion it seemed the Christians were winning They had certainly broken the Turkish lines and turned some of their positions. My uncle, with other bold spirits, even got close up to the enemy guns as the Turks moved them to keep the Christians under fire. Two Turkish artillerymen were twisting round a cannon. With their slow movements, beards, and long robes, they looked like a pair of astronomers. My uncle said, 'I'll see to them.' In his enthusiasm and inexperience he did not know that cannons are to be approached only by the side or the breech. He leapt in front of the muzzle, with sword bared, thinking he would frighten the two astronomers. Instead of which they fired a cannonade right in his chest. Medardo of Terralba jumped into the air.

After dusk, when a truce came, two carts went gathering Christian bodies on the battlefield. One was for the wounded and the other for the dead. A first choice was made on the spot. 'I'll take this one, you take that.' Where it looked as if something was saveable, they put the man on the cart of wounded; where there was nothing but bits and pieces they went on the cart of dead, for decent burial; and those who hadn't even a body were left for the storks. In the last few days, as losses were growing, orders had been given to be liberal about wounded. So Medardo's remains were considered those of a wounded man and put on that cart.

The second choice was made in hospital. After battles the field hospital was an even ghastlier sight than the battle itself. On the ground were long rows of stretchers with poor wretches in them, and all around swarmed doctors, clutching forceps, saws, needles, amputated joints and balls of string. From body to body they went, doing their very best to bring every one back to life. A saw here, a stitch there, leaks plugged, veins turned inside out like gloves and put back with more string than blood inside, but patched up and shut. When a patient died whatever good bits he still had in him went to patching up another, and so on. What caused most confusion were intestines; once unrolled they just couldn't be got back.

Pulling away the sheet, there lay the Viscount's body, horribly mutilated. It not only lacked an arm and leg, but the whole thorax and abdomen between that arm and leg had been swept away by the direct hit. All that remained of the head was one eye, one ear, one cheek, half a nose, half a mouth, half a chin and half a forehead; the other half of the head was just not there. The long and short of it was that exactly half of him had been saved, the right part, perfectly preserved, without a scratch on it except for that huge slash separating it from the left-hand part, which had been blown away.

How pleased the doctors were! 'A fine case!' If he didn't die meanwhile, they might even have a try at saving him. And they gathered round, while poor soldiers with an arrow in the arm died of blood poisoning. They sewed, kneaded, stuck; who knows what they got up to. The fact is that next day my uncle opened his only eye, his half mouth, dilated his single nostril and breathed. The strong Terralba constitution had pulled him through. Now he was alive and cloven.

3

When my uncle made his return to Terralba I was seven or eight years old. It was late, after dusk, in October, with a cloudy sky. We had been working on the vintage that day and on the grey sea over the vine rows we saw approaching the sails of a ship flying the Imperial flag. At every ship we saw then we used to say: 'There's Master Medardo back,' not because we were impatient for his return but in order to have something to wait for. This time we guessed right; and that evening we were sure, where a youth called Fiorfiero, who was pounding at the grapes on top of the vat, cried, 'Ah, look down there!' It was almost dark and down in the valley we saw a row of torches being lit on the mule path; then when the procession passed the bridge we made out a litter borne by hand. There was no doubt; it was the Viscount returning from the wars.

The news spread through the valley; people gathered in the castle courtyard, retainers, domestics, vintagers, shepherds, men-at-arms. The one person missing was Medardo's father, old Viscount Aiolfo, my grandfather, who had not been down to the courtyard for ages. Weary of worldly cares, he had renounced his prerogatives in favour of his only son before the latter left for the wars. Now his passion for birds, which he raised in a huge aviary within the castle, was beginning to exclude all else; the old man had recently had his bed taken into the aviary too, and there he shut himself, never to leave it night or day. His meals were handed through the grille of the cage together with the bird seed, which Aiolfo shared. And he spent his hours stroking pheasants and turtle doves, as he awaited his son's return.

Never had I seen so many in the courtyard of our castle; the days were long past, and but tales then, of fêtes and feuds with neighbours. For the first time I realized how ruined were the walls and towers, and how muddy the yard where we now foddered goats and filled troughs for pigs. As they waited, all were discussing in what state the Viscount Medardo would return; rumours had reached us some time before of grave wounds inflicted by the Turks, but no one quite knew yet if he was mutilated or sick or only scored by scars; at the sight of the litter we prepared for the worst.

Now the litter was set on the ground, and from the blackness within came the glitter of a pupil. Sebastiana, his old nurse, made a move towards it, but from the dark came a raised hand with a sharp gesture of refusal. Then the body in the litter was seen to give angular and convulsive movements, and before our eyes Medardo of Terralba jumped to the ground, leaning on a crutch. A black cloak and hood covered him from head to foot; the right-hand part was thrown back, showing half his face and body close against the crutch, while all on the left seemed hidden and wrapped in edges and folds of that ample drapery.

There he stood looking at us, we around him in a circle, without anyone saying a word; but maybe he was not looking at us out of that fixed eye at all, and just wanted to go off on his own. A gust of wind blew from the sea and a broken branch on top of a fig tree groaned. My uncle's cloak waved, and the wind bellowed it out, stretched it taut like sail; it seemed almost to be passing through the body as if that body was not there at all, and the cloak empty, like a ghost's. Then on looking closer we saw that it was clinging to him like a standard to its pole, and this pole was a shoulder, an arm, a side, a leg, all leaning on the crutch. The rest was not there at all.

Goats looked at the Viscount with fixed inexpressive stares, each from a different direction, but all tight against each other, their backs arranged in an odd pattern of right angles. Pigs, more sensitive and quick-witted, screamed and fled, bumping flanks against each other. And we could no longer hide our terror; 'Oh, my dear boy,' cried old Sebastiana and raised her arms. 'You poor little thing!'

My uncle, annoyed at making such an impression, advanced the point of his crutch on the ground and with a hop began pushing himself towards the castle entrance. But sitting cross-legged on the steps of the great gate were the litter bearers, half-naked men with gold earrings and crests and tufts of hair shaven heads. They straightened up and one man with plaits who seemed their leader said, 'We're waiting for our pay.'

'How much?' asked Medardo, almost laughing.

The man with the plaits said, 'You know the tariff for carrying a man in a litter ...'

My uncle pulled a purse from his belt and threw it tinkling at the bearer's feet. The man quickly weighed it in a hand, and exclaimed, 'But that's much less than we'd agreed on, Señor.'

Medardo, as the wind raised the edges of his cloak, said, 'Half.'

He brushed past the litter bearer with little jumps on his single foot and went up the stairs, through the great open gate giving on to the interior of the castle, pushed his crutch at both the heavy doors which shut with a clang, and then, as the wicket-gate remained open, banged that too and so vanished from our eyes. From inside we went on hearing the alternating tap of foot and crutch, moving down passages towards the wing of the castle where lay his private apartments, and the banging and bolting of doors there too.

His father stood waiting behind the grille of the bird-cage. Medardo had not even paused to greet him; he shut himself into his rooms alone, and refused to show himself or reply even to Sebastiana who knocked and sympathized for a long time.

Old Sebastiana was a big woman dressed in black and veils, her red face without a wrinkle except for one almost hiding her eyes; she had given milk to all the males of the Terralba family, gone to bed with all the older ones, and closed the eyes of all the dead ones. Now she went to and fro between the apartments of the two self-imposed prisoners, not knowing what to do to help them.

Next day, as Medardo gave no more sign of life, we went back to our vintaging, but there was no gaiety and among the vines we talked of nothing but his fate, not because we were so fond of him but because the subject was fascinating and strange. Only Sebastiana stayed in the castle, listening attentively to every sound.

But old Aiolfo, as if foreseeing that his son would return so glum and fierce, had already trained one of his dearest birds, a shrike, to fly up to the castle wing in which were Medardo's apartments, then empty, and enter through the little window of his rooms. That morning the old man opened the birdcage door to the shrike, followed its flight to his son's window, then went back to scattering bird seed to magpies and tits, imitating their chirps.

A little later he heard the thud of something flung against the windows. He leant out; there on the pediment was the shrike, dead. The old man took it up in the palms of his hands

and saw that a wing was broken off as if someone had tried to
tear it, a claw wrenched off as if by two fingers, and an eye
gouged out. The old man held the shrike tight to his breast
and began to sob.

That same day he took to his bed, and attendants on the
other side of the cage saw that he was very ill. But no one could
go and take care of him, as he had locked himself inside and
hidden the keys. Birds flew around his bed. Since he had taken
to it they had all refused to settle or stop fluttering their
wings.

Next morning, when the nurse put her head into the bird-
cage, she realized that the Viscount Aiolfo was dead. The birds
had all perched on his bed, as if it were a floating tree trunk
in the midst of sea.

4

After his father's death Medardo began leaving the castle.
Sebastiana was the first to notice when one morning she found
his doors flung open and his rooms deserted. A group of
servitors was sent out through the countryside to follow the
Viscount's traces. The servitors, hastening along, passed under
a pear tree which they had seen the evening before loaded with
tardy, still unripe, fruit. 'Look up there,' said one of the men;
they stared at pears hanging against a whitish sky, and the
sight filled them with terror. For the pears were not whole,
but in halves, cut longways, and each still hanging on its own
stalk; all there was of every pear was the right side (or left
according to which way one looked, but they were all on the
same side) and the other half had vanished, cut or maybe
eaten.

'The Viscount has passed by here!' said the servitors.

Obviously, after being shut up without food for so long, he had felt hungry that night and climbed up the first tree he saw to eat pears.

As they went the servitors met half a frog on a rock, still alive and jumping with the vitality of frogs. 'We're on the right track!', and on they went. But they soon lost it, for they missed half a melon among its leaves, and had to turn back until they found it.

So they passed from fields to woods and saw a mushroom cut in half, an edible one, then another, a poisonous red boletus, and as they went deeper into the wood kept finding every now and again mushrooms sprouting from the ground on half a leg and with only half an umbrella. These seemed divided by a neat cut, and of the other half not even a spore was to be seen. They were fungi of all kinds, puff-balls, ovules and toadstools; and as many were poisonous as eatable.

Following this scattered trail, the servitors came to an open space called the Nun's Field, with a pool in the middle of the grass. It was dawn and on the edge of the pool stood Medardo's slim figure wrapped in his black cloak and reflected in the water, on which floated white, yellow, dun coloured fungi. They were the halves which he had carried off, scattered now on that transparent surface. On the water the mushrooms looked whole, and the Viscount was gazing at them; the servitors hid by the other verge of the pool and did not dare say a thing, but just stared at the floating mushrooms, until suddenly they realized that those were actually edible ones only. Where were the poisonous ones? If he had not flung them into the pool, whatever could he have done with them? Back the servitors set off through the woods at a run. They did not have to go far because on the path they met a child carrying a basket, and inside it were all the poisonous halves.

That child was myself. One night I was playing alone around the Nun's Field giving myself frights by jumping out from behind trees, when I met my uncle hopping along by moonlight over the field on his one leg, with a basket on his arm.

'Hallo, Uncle!' I shouted; it was the first time I had a chance of calling him that.

He seemed vexed at the sight of me. 'I'm out for mushrooms,' he explained.

'And have you got any?'

'Look,' said my uncle and we sat down on the edge of the pool. He began choosing among the mushrooms, flinging some in the water, and dropping others in the basket.

'There you are,' said he, giving me the basket with the ones he had chosen. 'Have them fried.'

I wanted to ask him why the basket only contained halves of mushrooms, but I realized that the question would have been disrespectful and ran off after thanking him warmly. I was just going to fry them for myself when I met the group of servitors, and heard that all my halves were poisonous.

Sebastiana, the nurse, when I told her the story, said, 'The bad half of Medardo has returned. Now I wonder about this trial today.

That day there was to be a trial of a band of brigands arrested the day before by the castle constabulary. The brigands were from our estates and so it was for the Viscount to judge them. The trial was held and Medardo sat sideways on his chair chewing a fingernail. The brigands appeared in chains; the head of the band was the youth called Fiorfiero who had been the first to notice the Viscount's litter while pounding grapes. The injured parties appeared: they were a group of Tuscan knights who were passing through our woods on their way to Provence when they had been attacked and robbed by Fiorfiero and his band. Fiorfiero defended himself saying that those knights had come poaching on our land and he had stopped and disarmed them as poachers, since the constabulary had done nothing about them. It should be said that at the time assaults by brigands were very common, and laws were clement. Also our parts were particularly susceptible in turbulent times and our people would join brigand bands. As for poaching, it was about the lightest crime imaginable.

But Sebastiana's apprehensions were well founded. Medardo condemned Fiorfiero and his whole band to die by hanging,

as criminals guilty of armed rapine. But since those robbed
were guilty of poaching he condemned them to die on the
gibbet too. And to punish the constables who had appeared
too late and not prevented either brigands or poachers from
misbehaving, he decreed death by hanging for them too.
There were about twenty altogether. This cruel sentence produced consternation in us all, not so much for the Tuscan
gentry whom no one had seen until then, as for the brigands
and constables who were generally well liked. Master Pietrochiodo, packsaddle-maker and carpenter, was given the job of
making the gibbet; he was a most conscientious worker who
took great pains in all he did. With great sorrow, for two of
the condemned were his relations, he built a gibbet ramifi-
cating like a tree, whose nooses all rose together and were
manoeuvred by a single winch. It was such a big and ingenious
machine that it could have hanged simultaneously even more
people than those now condemned; the Viscount took advantage of this to hang ten cats alternating with every two criminals. The rigid corpses and cats' carcasses hung there for three
days, and at first no one had the heart to look at them. But
soon people noticed what a really imposing sight they were,
and our own judgements and opinions began to vary, so that
we were even sorry when it was decided to take them down
and dismantle the big machine.

5

For me those were happy times, wandering through woods with
Dr Trelawney in search of fossil traces. Dr Trelawney was
English; he had reached our coasts after a shipwreck, astride
a ship's barrel. All his life he had been a ship's doctor and

made long and perilous journeys, among them ones with the famous Captain Cook, though he had seen nothing of the world since he was always under hatches playing cards. On being shipwrecked among us he had soon acquired a taste for a wine called *cancarone*, the harshest and heaviest in our parts, and now could not do without it, so that he always had a full water-flask of it slung over his shoulder. He had stayed on at Terralba and become our doctor; but he bothered little about the sick, only about his scientific researches, which kept him on the go – and me with him – through fields and woods by day and night. First came a cricket's disease caught by one cricket in a thousand and doing no particular harm; Dr Trelawney wanted to examine them all and find the right cure. Next there were signs of the time when our lands were covered by sea; and we would load up with pebbles and flints which, according to the doctor, had been fish in their time. Finally, his last great passion; wills-o'-the-wisp. He wanted to find a way of catching and keeping them, and with this aim in view we would spend nights wandering about our cemetery, waiting for one of those vague lights to go up among the mounds of earth and grass, when we would try to draw it towards us, make it follow us and then capture it without it going out, in various receptacles with which we experimented: sacks, flasks, strawless demijohns, braziers, colanders. Dr Trelawney had settled in a shack near the cemetery which had once been the grave-digger's in times of pomp and war and plague when a man was needed on the job full-time. There the doctor had set up his laboratory, with test-tubes of every shape to bottle the wisps, and nets, like fishing ones, to catch them; and retorts and crucibles in which he examined the why and wherefore of those pale little flames coming from the soil of cemeteries and the exhalations of corpses. But he was not a man to remain for long absorbed in studies; he would break off and come out, and then we would go hunting together for new phenomena of nature.

I was free as air since I had no parents and belonged to the category neither of servants nor masters. I was part of the Terralba family only by tardy recognition, but did not bear

their name and no one had bothered to give me any education.
My poor mother had been the Viscount Aiolfo's daughter and
Medardo's elder sister, but she had besmirched the family
honour by eloping with a poacher who was my father. I was
born in a smuggler's hut in rough scrub by the woods; and
shortly afterwards my father was killed in some squabble, and
pellagra put an end to my mother who had stayed in that
wretched hut all alone. Then I was brought into the castle,
as my grandfather Aiolfo took pity on me, and grew up under
the care of the chief nurse, Sebastiana. I remember that when
Medardo was still a boy and I was a small child he would
sometimes let me take part in his games as if we were of equal
rank; then the distance between us grew and I dropped to
the level of a servant. Now in Dr Trelawney I found a companion such as I had never had.

The doctor was sixty but about as tall as me; he had a lined
face like an old chestnut, under tricorne and wig; his legs, with
gaiters halfway up his thighs, looked long and disproportionate
as a cricket's, due also to his long strides; he wore a dove-
coloured tunic with red facings, and slung across it the bottle
of *cancarone* wine.

His passion for wills-o'-the-wisp made him take long night
marches to the cemeteries of nearby villages, where at times
were to be seen flames finer in colour and size than those in
our abandoned cemetery. But it was bad for us if our stalking
was found out by locals; once we were mistaken for sacrilegious
thieves and followed for miles by a group of men armed with
forks and tridents.

It was a rocky part scored by torrents; I and Dr Trelawney
hopped from rock to rock, but heard the infuriated peasants
getting closer behind. At a place called Grimace's Leap was a
small bridge of tree trunks straddling a deep abyss. Instead of
crossing over, the doctor and I hid on a ledge of rock on the
abyss's very edge, just in time as the peasants were right on our
heels. They did not see us, and yelling, 'Where are the swine?'
rushed straight at the bridge. A crack, and they were flung
screaming into the torrent far below. Trelawney's and my
terror for our own skins changed to relief at danger escaped,

and then to terror again at the awful fate that had befallen our pursuers. We scarcely dared lean over and peer down into the darkness where the peasants had vanished. Then raising our eyes we looked at the remains of the little bridge; the trunks were still firmly in place, but they were broken in half as if sawn through; that could be the only explanation for thick wood giving way with such a clean break.

'There's the hand of *you know who* in this,' said Dr Trelawney, and I understood.

Just then we heard a quick clatter of hooves and on the verge of the precipice appeared a horse and a rider half wrapped in a black cloak. It was the Viscount Medardo, who was contemplating with his frozen triangular smile the tragic success of his trap, unforeseen perhaps by himself; he must certainly have wanted to kill us two off; instead of which, as it turned out, he had saved our lives. Trembling, we saw him gallop off on that thin horse, which went leaping away over the rocks as if born of a goat.

At that time my uncle always went round on horseback; he had got our saddle-maker Pietrochiodo to make him a special saddle with a stirrup to which he could hitch himself, while the other had a counterweight. A sword and crutch was slung by the saddle. And so the Viscount galloped about, wearing a plumed hat with a great brim which half vanished under a wing of the ever fluttering cloak. Wherever the sound of his horse's hooves was heard everyone took to his heels even more than when Galateo the leper passed, and bore off their children and animals and feared for their plants, as the Viscount's wickedness spared no one and could burst at any moment into the most unforeseen and incomprehensible actions.

He had never been ill so never needed Dr Trelawney's care; I don't know how the doctor would have dealt with such an eventuality as he did his very best to avoid ever hearing my uncle mentioned. When he heard people talking about the Viscount and his cruelty Dr Trelawney would shake his head and curl a lip with a mutter of 'Oh, oh, oh ... zzt, zzt, zzt!' It seemed that from the medical point of view my uncle's case aroused no interest in him; but I was beginning to think that he had become a doctor only from family pressure or for his own convenience, and did not care a rap about the science of it. Perhaps his career as ship's doctor had been due only to his ability at card games, which made the most illustrious navigators, particularly Captain Cook himself, contend for him as partner.

One night Dr Trelawney was fishing with a net for wills-o'-the-wisp in our ancient cemetery when his eyes fell on Medardo of Terralba pasturing his horse amongst the tombs. The doctor was much confused and alarmed, but the Viscount came nearer and asked him, in the defective pronunciation of his halved mouth; 'Are you looking for night butterflies, Doctor?'

'Oh, m'lord,' replied the doctor in a faint voice. 'Oh, not exactly butterflies, m'lord ... Wills-o'-the-wisp, you know, wills-o'-the-wisp ...'

'Ah, wills-o'-the-wisp, eh? I've often wondered about their origin too.'

'They have been the subject of my modest studies for some time, m'lord ...' said Trelawney, encouraged by his benevolent tone.

Medardo twisted his angular half face into a smile, the skin taut as a skull's. 'You deserve all assistance in your studies,' he said to him. 'A pity that this cemetery is so abandoned, and thus no good for wills-o'-the-wisp. But I promise you that I'll see about helping you as much as I can tomorrow.'

Next day was the one allocated for administering justice, and the Viscount condemned a dozen peasants to death, because according to his computation they had not handed over the whole proportion of crops due from them to the castle. The dead men were buried in earth of the common grave, and the cemetery blossomed every night with wills-o'-the-wisp. Dr Trelawney was terrified by this help, useful as it was to his studies.

With all these tragic developments Master Pietrochiodo was producing greatly improved gibbets. Now they were real masterpieces of carpentry and mechanics, as also were the

racks, winches and other instruments of torture by which the
Viscount Medardo tore confessions from the accused. I was
often in Pietrochiodo's workshop, as it was a fine sight to watch
him at work with such ability and enthusiasm. But a sorrow
always weighed on the saddler's heart. The scaffolds he was
constructing were for innocent men. 'How can I manage to get
orders for work as delicate, but with a different purpose? What
new mechanisms could I enjoy making more?' But finding
these questions coming to no conclusions, he tried to thrust
them out of his mind and settle down to making his instruments as fine and ingenious as possible.

'Just forget the purpose for which they're used,' he said to
me, 'and look at them as pieces of mechanism. You see how
fine they are?'

I looked at that architecture of beams, criss-cross of ropes,
links of capstans and pulleys, and tried not to see tortured
bodies on them, but the more I tried the more I found myself
thinking of them, and said to Pietrochiodo: 'How can I forget?'

'How indeed, my lad,' replied he. 'How d'you think I can,
then?'

But with all their agonies and terrors, those days had times
of delight. The loveliest hour was when the sun was high and
the sea golden and the chickens sang as they laid their eggs
and from the lane came the sound of the leper's horn. The
leper would pass every morning to collect alms for his companions in misfortune. He was called Galateo, and round his
neck he wore a hunting horn whose sound warned us from a
distance of his arrival. Women would hear the horn and lay
out eggs or melons or tomatoes and sometimes a little rabbit
on the edge of the wall; and then they would run off and hide,
taking their children, for no one should be out in the open
when a leper goes by: leprosy can be caught from a distance
and it's dangerous even to look at a leper. Preceded by notes
on his horn, Galateo would come slowly along the deserted
lanes, with a high stick in his hand and a long tattered robe
touching the ground. He had long towy yellow hair and a

round white face already eaten away by leprosy. He gathered up the gifts, put them in his knapsack, and called his thanks towards the houses of the hidden peasants in honeyed tones that always included some jolly double meaning.

Leprosy was very prevalent in districts near the sea in those days, and near us was a village called Pratofungo inhabited only by lepers, for whom we were bound to produce gifts which Galateo gathered up. When anyone from seaboard or country caught leprosy, they left relatives and friends and went to Pratofungo to spend the rest of their lives waiting for the disease to devour them. There were rumours of great jollifications to greet each new arrival; from afar songs and music were to be heard coming from the lepers' houses till nightfall.

Many things were said of Pratofungo, although no healthy person had ever been there; but all rumours were agreed in saying that life there was a perpetual party. Before becoming a leper colony the village had been a great place for prostitutes and visited by sailors of every race and religion; and the women there, it seemed, still kept the licentious habits of those times. The lepers did no work on the land, except for a vineyard of strawberry grapes whose juice kept them the whole year round in a state of simmering tipsiness. The lepers spent most of their time playing strange instruments of their own invention, such as harps with little bells attached to the string, and singing in falsetto, and painting eggs with daubs of every colour as if for a perpetual Easter. And so, whiling away the time with sweet music, their disfigured faces hung round with garlands of jasmine, they forgot the human community from which their disease had cut them off.

No local doctor had ever taken on the care of the lepers, but when Trelawney settled amongst us some hoped that he might dedicate his lore to healing that running sore in our locality. I shared the same hopes too in my childish way; for some time I had been longing to get into Pratofungo and attend those lepers' parties: and had the doctor done any experimenting with his drugs on those wretches he might have allowed me to accompany him into the village sometimes. But none of this ever happened; as soon as he heard Galateo's horn Dr Trelawney ran off at full speed and no one seemed more afraid of contagion than he. Sometimes I tried to question him on the nature of the disease, but he would make evasive or muted replies, as if the very word 'leper' put him out .

Actually I can't think why we were so determined to think of him as a doctor; he was very attentive to animals, particularly small ones, to stones or natural phenomena; but human beings and their infirmities filled him with dismay and disgust. He had a horror of blood, he would only touch the sick with the tips of his fingers, and when faced with serious cases plunged his nose in a silk bandanna dipped in vinegar. He was shy as a girl and blushed at the sight of a naked body; if it was a woman's he would stutter and keep his eyes lowered. In all his long journeys over the oceans he never seemed to have known women. Luckily for us in those times births were matters for midwives and not doctors: otherwise I wonder how he would have coped.

Into my uncle's head now came the notion of arson. At night all of a sudden a wretched peasant's haystack would burn, or a tree cut for fuel, or a whole wood. Then we would spend the whole night passing buckets of water from hand to hand in order to put out the flames. The victims were always poor unfortunates who had fallen out with the Viscount, either because of one of his increasingly severe and unjust orders or because of the dues he had doubled. From burning other things he then began setting fire to houses; it was thought that he came up close at night, threw burning brands on roofs and then rushed off on horseback; but no one ever managed to catch him in the act. Once two old people died; once a boy had his brains fried. The peasants grew to hate him more and more. His most stubborn enemies were some families of Huguenots who were living in huts up on Col Gerbido; their men kept guard in turn all night to prevent fires.

Without any plausible reason one night he even went under the houses of Pratofungo, whose roofs were thatched, and threw burning brands at them. A characteristic of lepers is to feel no pain when scorched, and had they been caught by the flames in their sleep they would never have woken again. But as the Viscount galloped away he heard a tune on a violin from the village behind him; the inhabitants of Pratofungo were still up and intent on their fun. They all got a little scorched, but felt no ill effects and amused themselves in their own way. The fire was soon put out; and their homes, perhaps because so impregnated with leprosy, suffered little damage from the flames.

Medardo's evil nature even turned him against his own personal property, the castle itself. A fire went up in the servants' wing and spread amid the loud shrieks of those imprisoned there, while the Viscount was seen galloping off into the country. It was an attempt on the life of his nurse and foster-mother Sebastiana. With the stubborn bossiness that women think to maintain over those they have seen as children, Sebastiana was constantly reproving the Viscount for his every misdeed, even when all were convinced that his nature forced him to acts of insane and irreparable cruelty. Sebastiana was pulled out from the burning walls in a very bad state and had to stay in bed for days to heal her burns.

One night the door of the room in which she was lying opened and the Viscount appeared by her bed.

'What are those marks on your face, nurse?' said Medardo, pointing at her burns.

'Marks of your sins, son,' said the old woman calmly.

'Your skin is all speckled and scored; what ails you, nurse?'

'My ails are nothing, son, compared to those awaiting you in hell unless you mend your ways.'

'You must get well soon; I would not like to hear of you going round with this disease on you.'

'I'm not out for a husband, that I need bother about my looks. A good conscience is enough for me. I only wish you could say the same.'

'And yet your bridegroom is waiting to bear you off with him, you know!'

'Do not deride old age, my son, you who've had your youth ruined.'

'I do not jest. Hark, nurse; there is your bridegroom playing beneath your window ...'

Sebastiana listened and from outside the castle heard the sound of the leper's horn.

Next day Medardo sent for Dr Trelawney.

'Suspicious marks have appeared on the face of our old servant, I don't know how,' he said to the doctor. 'We're all afraid it's leprosy. Doctor, we entrust ourselves to the light of your knowledge.'

Trelawney bowed and stuttered.

'M'duty, m'lord ... at your orders as always, m'lord ...'

He turned, slipped out of the castle, got himself a small barrel of *cancarone* and vanished into the woods. He was not seen again for a week. When he got back Sebastiana had been sent to the leper village.

One evening at dusk she left the castle, veiled and dressed in black, with a bundle on her arm. She knew that her fate was sealed; she must take the road to Pratofungo. Leaving the room where she had been kept till then, the passages and stairs were deserted. Down she went, across the courtyard, out into the country; all was deserted, everyone at her passage withdrew and hid. She heard a hunting horn sounding a low call on two notes only: on the path ahead of her was Galateo with the mouthpiece of his instrument raised to the sky. With slow steps the nurse advanced; the path went towards the setting sun; Galateo moved far ahead of her; every now and again he stopped as if gazing at the bumble bees amid the leaves, raised his horn and played a sad note; the nurse looked at the flowers and banks that she was leaving, sensed behind hedges the presence of people avoiding her, and walked on. Alone, a long way behind Galateo, she reached Pratofungo, and as the village gates closed behind her harps and violins began to play.

Dr Trelawney had disappointed me a lot. Not having moved a finger to prevent old Sebastiana being condemned to the leper colony – though knowing that her marks were not those of leprosy – was a sign of cowardice, and for the first time I felt a sense of aversion from the doctor. On top of this he had not taken me with him when he ran off into the woods, though knowing how useful I would have been as hunter of squirrels and finder of raspberries. Now I no longer enjoyed going with him for wills-o'-the-wisp as before, and often went round alone, on the lookout for new companions.

The people who most attracted me now were the Huguenots upon Col Gerbido. They were people who had escaped from France where the King had those who followed their religion cut into small pieces. While crossing the mountains they had lost their books and sacred objects, and now had neither bibles to read from nor Mass to say nor hymns to sing nor prayers to recite. Suspicious, like all those who have passed through persecutions and live amid people of a different faith, they had refused to accept any religious book or listen to any advice on how to conduct their rites. If someone came looking for them saying he was a fellow-Huguenot, they were frightened he might be a Papal agent in disguise and shut themselves in silence. So they had set to work cultivating the harsh lands of Col Gerbido, and overworked, men and women, from before dawn till after dusk, in the hope of illumination by Grace. Inexpert in what constituted sin, they multiplied their prohibitions lest they made mistakes, and were reduced to giving each other constant severe glances in case the least gesture betrayed a blameworthy intention. With confused memories of theological disputations they avoided naming God or using any other religious expression for fear of sacrilege. So they followed no rites and probably did not even dare formulate thoughts on matters of faith, though preserving an air of grave absorption as if these were constantly in their minds. But with time the rules of their agricultural labours had acquired a value equal to those of the Commandments, as also the habits of thrift to which they were forced, and the women's abilities at housekeeping.

They were all one great family, with lots of grandchildren and in-laws, all tall and knobbly, and they worked the land always formally dressed in buttoned black, the men in wide-brimmed hats and the women in white kerchiefs. The men

wore long beards and always went round with slung blunder-
busses, but it was said that none of them had ever fired a shot
except at sparrows, as it was forbidden by the Commandments.

From chalky terraces with a few stunted vines and scrappy
crops would rise the voice of old Ezekiel, for ever shouting
with fists raised to the sky, his white goatee beard atremble,
eyes rolling under his tubular hat. 'Famine and plague!
Famine and plague!' he would yell at his family bent over
their work. 'Hoe harder, Jonah! Tear at the weeds, Susanna!
Spread that manure, Tobias!' and give out thousands of orders
and reproofs in the bitter tone of one addressing a bunch of
inept wasters: every time, after shouting out the innumerable
things they must do to prevent the land going to ruin, he
would begin doing them himself pushing away the others
around, still shouting 'Famine and plague!'

His wife on the other hand never shouted, and seemed,
unlike the others, secure in a secret religion of her own, which
was fixed to the smallest details but never mentioned by so
much as a single word to anyone. She would just stare, her
eyes all pupils, and only say, through set lips, 'D'you think
that's right, sister Rachel? D'you think that's right, brother
Aaron?' for the rare smiles to vanish from her family's mouths
and their grave intent expressions to return.

One evening I arrived at Col Gerbido while the Huguenots
were praying. Not that they pronounced any words or joined
hands or knelt; they were standing in a row in the vineyard,
men on one side and women on the other, with old Ezekiel at
the end, beard on chest. They looked straight in front of them,
with clenched hands hanging from long knobbly arms, but
though they seemed absorbed they had not lost awareness of
what was going on around them; and Tobias put out a hand
and tweaked a caterpillar off a vine, Rachel crushed a snail
with her nailed boot, and Ezekiel himself suddenly took off
his hat to frighten sparrows on the crops.

Then they intoned a psalm. They did not remember the
words, only the tune, and even that not well, and often some-

one went off tone or maybe they all were the whole time, but they never stopped and on finishing one verse started another, always without pronouncing any words.

I felt a tug at my arm; it was little Esau signing me to be quiet and come with him. Esau was the same age as me; he was old Ezekiel's last son; the only look he had of his parents was their hard tense expression, with a sly malice of his own. We went off on all fours through the vineyard, with him saying: 'They'll be at it another half-hour, you see. Come and look at my lair.'

Esau's lair was secret. He used to hide there so that his family could not find him and send him to look after goats or take snails off the crops. He would spend entire days there doing nothing, while his father went searching and calling for him throughout the countryside.

Esau gave me a pipe and told me to smoke it. He lit one for himself and drew great mouthfuls with an enthusiasm I had never seen in a boy. It was the first time I had smoked; it soon made me feel sick and I stopped. To pull me together Esau drew out a bottle of Grappa and poured me a glass which made me cough and wrung my guts. He drank it as if it were water.

'It takes a lot to get drunk,' he said.

'Where did you find all these things you have here in your lair?' I asked him.

Esau made a gesture of clawing the air: 'Stolen!'

He had put himself at the head of a band of Catholic boys who were sacking the country round; they not only stripped the trees of fruit, but went into houses and hen coops. And they swore stronger and more often even than Master Pietrochiodo; they knew every swear-word, Catholic and Huguenot, and exchanged them freely.

'There's a lot of other sins I commit too,' he explained to me. 'I bear false witness, I forget to water the beans, I don't respect father and mother, I come home late. Now I want to commit every sin there is; even the ones people say I'm not old enough to understand.'

'Every sin?' I asked him. 'Killing too?'

He shrugged his shoulders. 'Killing's not in my line now, it's no use.'

'My uncle kills and has people killed just for fun, they say,' I exclaimed, just for something to counterbalance Esau.

Esau spat. 'A mug's game,' he said.

Then it thundered and outside the lair it began to rain.

'They'll be on the lookout for you at home,' I said to Esau. Nobody was ever on the lookout for me, but I had seen other boys being sought by parents, particularly in bad weather, and I thought that was something important.

'Let's wait for it to stop,' said Esau. 'And have a game of dice.'

He pulled out the dice and a heap of money. I had no money, so I gambled my whistles, knives and catapults, and lost the lot.

'Don't let it get you down,' said Esau eventually. 'I cheat, you know.'

Outside, thunder, lightning and torrential rain. Esau's cave was flooding. He salvaged his pipes and other things and said, 'It'll pour all night; better run and shelter at home.'

We were soaked and muddy when we reached old Ezekiel's hut. The Huguenots were sitting around the table by a flickering candle, and trying to remember episodes from the Bible, taking great care to recount it as something which they thought they had once read, of uncertain meaning and truth.

'Famine and plague!' Ezekiel shouted, and banged a fist on the table so hard it put out the light just when his son Esau appeared in the doorway with me.

My teeth began chattering. Esau shrugged his shoulders. Outside all the thunder and lightning seemed to be unloading on Col Gerbido. As they were rekindling the light the old man with raised fists enumerated his son's sins as the foulest ever committed by any human being; but he only knew a small part of them. The mother nodded mutely, and all the other sons and sons-in-law and daughters-in-law and grandchildren listened chins on chest and faces hidden in their hands. Esau was chewing away at an apple as if the sermon did not concern him. What with the thunder and Ezekiel's voice I was trembling like a reed.

The diatribe was interrupted by the return of the men on guard, sacks over heads, all soaking wet. The Huguenots kept guard all night long in turns, armed with muskets, scythes and pitchforks, to prevent the prowling incursions of the Viscount, now their declared enemy.

'Father! Ezekiel!' said these Huguenots, ''tis a night for wolves. For sure the Lame One won't come. May we return home, father?'

'Are there no signs of the Maimed One?' asked Ezekiel.

'No, father, except for the smell of burning left by the lightning. 'Tis not a night for the Bereft One.'

'Stay here and change your clothes then. May the storm bring peace to the Sideless One and to us.'

The Lame One, the Maimed One, the Bereft One and the Sideless One were some of the appellations given by the Huguenots to my uncle; never once did I hear them call him by his real name. These remarks showed a kind of intimacy with the Viscount, as if they knew a great deal about him, almost as if he were an old enemy. They would exchange brief phrases accompanied by winks and laughs; 'Ha ha! The Maimed One ... Just like him, ha ha! The Half-Deaf One ...' as if to them all Medardo's dark follies were clear and fore-seeable.

They were talking thus when a fist was heard knocking at the door in the storm. 'Who knocks in this weather?' said Ezekiel. 'Quick, open.'

They opened the door, and there was the Viscount standing on his one leg on the threshold, wrapped in a dripping cloak, his plumed hat soaked with rain.

'I have tied up my horse in your stall,' said he. 'Give me hospitality too, please. It's a bad night for the traveller.'

All looked at Ezekiel. I had hidden myself beneath the table lest my uncle should discover that I frequented this enemy house.

'Sit down by the fire,' said Ezekiel. 'In this house a guest is always welcome.'

Near the threshold was a heap of sheets, the kind used for stretching under trees to gather olives; there Medardo lay down and went to sleep.

In the dark the Huguenots gathered round Ezekiel. 'Father, we have the Lame One in our hands now!' they whispered to each other. 'Must we let him go? Must we let him commit other crimes against innocent folk? Ezekiel, has the hour not come for the Buttockless One to pay the price?'

The old man raised his fists to the ceiling, 'Famine and plague!' he shouted, if someone can be said to shout who scarcely emits a sound but does it with all his strength. 'No guest has ever been ill-treated in our house. I myself will mount guard to protect his sleep.'

And with his musket at the ready he took his place by the sleeping Viscount. Medardo's eye opened, 'What are you doing there, Master Ezekiel?'

'I protect your sleep, guest. You are hated by many.'

'That I know,' said the Viscount. 'I do not sleep at the castle as I fear the servants might kill me as I lie.'

'Nor do they love you in my house, Master Medardo. But tonight you will be respected.'

The Viscount was silent for some time, and then said, 'Ezekiel, I wish to be converted to your religion.'

The old man said nothing.

'I am surrounded by men I do not trust,' went on Medardo, 'I should like to rid myself of the lot and call the Huguenots to the castle. You, Master Ezekiel, will be my minister. I will declare Terralba to be Huguenot territory and we will start a war against the Catholic princes. You and your family shall be the leaders. Are you agreed, Ezekiel? Can you convert me?'

The old man stood there straight and motionless, his big chest crossed by the bandolier of his gun. 'Too many things have we forgotten in our religion,' said he, 'for me to dare convert anyone. I will remain in my own territory, according to my own conscience, you in yours with yours.'

The Viscount raised himself on his elbow. 'You know, Ezekiel, that I have not yet reported to the Inquisition the presence of heretics in my domains? And that your heads

sent as a present to our bishop would at once bring me back
to favour with the Curia?'

'Our heads are still on our necks, sir,' said the old man.
'But there is something else far more difficult to tear from
us.'

Medardo leapt to his foot and opened the door. 'Rather
would I sleep under that oak tree there than in the house of
enemies.' And off he hopped into the rain.

The old man called the others. 'Sons, it was written that
the Lame One was to come to visit us. Now he's gone; the way
to our house is clear. Do not despair, sons; one day perhaps a
better traveller will pass.'

All the bearded Huguenots and the quiffed women bowed
their heads.

'And even if no one comes,' added Ezekiel's wife, 'we will
stay at our posts.'

At that moment a streak of lightning rent the sky, and thunder made the tiles and the stones of the wall quiver. Tobias
shouted, 'The lightning has struck the oak tree. It is burning!'

They ran out with their lanterns and saw the great tree
carbonized halfway down, from tip to roots, and the other
half intact. Far off under the rain they heard a horse's hooves,
and by a lightning flash caught a glimpse of the cloaked figure
of its thin rider.

'Father, you have saved us,' said the Huguenots. 'Thank
you, Ezekiel.'

The sky cleared to the east and it was dawn.

Esau called me aside. 'You see what sillies they are!' he
whispered. 'Look what I've done meanwhile,' and he showed
me a handful of glittering objects. 'I took all the gold studs
on the saddle while the horse was tied in the stall. You see
what sillies they are, not to have thought of it.'

I did not like Esau's ways, and those of his relations I found
oppressive. So I preferred being on my own and going to the
shore to gather limpets and catch crabs. While I was on top
of a little rock trying to corner a small crab, in the calm water

below me I saw the reflection of a blade above my head and fell into the sea from fright.

'Catch hold of this,' said my uncle, for it was he who had come up behind me. And he tried to make me grasp his sword by the blade.

'No, I'll do it by myself,' I replied, and clambered up on to a crag separated by a limb of water from the rest of the rocks.

'Are you out for crabs?' said Medardo, 'I'm out for baby octopuses,' and he showed me his catch. They were big brown and white baby octopuses. And although they had been cut in two with a sword, they were still moving their tentacles.

'If only I could halve every whole thing like this,' said my uncle, lying face down on the rocks and stroking the convulsive halves of octopuses, 'so that everyone could escape from their obtuse and ignorant wholeness. I was whole and all things were natural and confused to me, stupid as the air; I thought I was seeing all and it was only the outside rind. If you ever become a half of yourself, and I hope you do for your own sake, my boy, you'll understand things beyond the common intelligence of brains that are whole. You'll have lost half of yourself and of the world, but the remaining half will be a thousand times deeper and more precious. And you also would find yourself wanting everything to be halved like you, as there's beauty and knowledge and justice only in what's been cut to shreds.'

'Uh, uh!' I kept on saying, 'What a lot of crabs there are here!' and I pretended to be interested only in my catch, so as to keep as far as possible from my uncle's sword. I did not return to land until he had moved off with his octopuses. But the echo of his words went on disturbing me and I could find no escape from this frenzy of his for halving. Wherever I turned, Trelawney, Pietrochiodo, the Huguenots, the lepers, we were all under the sign of the halved man, he was the master whom we served and from whom we could not succeed in freeing ourselves.

6

Hitched to the saddle of his high-jumping horse, Medardo of Terralba would be out early, up and down bluffs, leaning over precipices to gaze over a valley with the eye of a bird of prey. So it was he saw Pamela in the middle of a field with her goats.

Said the Viscount to himself: 'Now with all my acute emotions there is nothing corresponding to what whole people call love. If an emotion so silly is yet so important to them, then whatever may correspond in me will surely be very grand and awesome.' So he decided to fall in love with Pamela, as she lay, plump and barefoot, in a simple pink dress, face downwards in the grass, dozing, chatting to the goats and sniffing flowers.

But thoughts thus coldly formulated should not deceive us. At the sight of Pamela, Medardo had sensed a vague stirring of the blood, something not felt for ages, and such reasoning had been a refuge in a kind of alarmed flurry.

On her way home at midday Pamela noticed that all the daisies in the fields had only half their petals and the other half had been stripped off. 'Dearie me!' she said to herself, 'of all the girls in the valley, that this should happen to me!' For she realized that the Viscount had fallen in love with her. She picked all the half-daisies, took them home and put them among the pages of her Massbook.

That afternoon she went to the Nun's Field to pasture her ducks and let them swim in the pond. The field was covered with white parsnip blossoms, but these flowers had also suffered the fate of the daisies, as if part of each had been cut away with a snip of scissors. 'Dearie, oh dearie me!' she said to herself, 'So it's myself he wants!' and she gathered the halved parsnip blossoms in a bunch, to slip them into the frame of the mirror over her chest of drawers.

Then she put it out of her mind, tied her plaits round her

head, took off her dress and had a bathe in the pond with her ducks.

That evening as she went home the fields were full of dandelion flowers. And Pamela saw that they had lost their fluff on only one side, as if someone had lain on the ground and blown just on one side, or with only half a mouth. Pamela gathered some of those halved white spheres, breathed on them and their soft fluff floated away. 'Dear, oh dearie dear!' said she to herself. 'He wants me, he really does. How will it all end?'

Pamela's cottage was so small that once the goats had been let on to the first floor and the ducks on to the ground floor there was no more room. It was surrounded by bees all around, for they also kept hives. And the subsoil was so full of ants that a hand put down anywhere came up all black and swarming ... Because of this Pamela's mother slept in the haystack, her father in an empty barrel and Pamela in a hammock slung between a fig and an olive tree.

On the threshold Pamela stopped. There was a dead butterfly. A wing and half the body had been crushed by a stone. Pamela let out a shriek and called her father and mother.

'Who's been here?' said Pamela.

'Our Viscount passed by a short time ago,' said her father and mother. 'He said he was chasing a butterfly that had stung him.'

'When has a butterfly ever stung anyone?' said Pamela.

'We've been wondering too.'

'The truth is,' said Pamela, 'that the Viscount has fallen in love with me and we must be ready for the worst.'

'Uh, uh, don't get a swollen head now, don't exaggerate,' answered the old couple, as old folk are apt to answer when the young don't do the same to them.

Next morning when Pamela reached the stone on which she usually sat when pasturing her goats, she let out a cry. It was all smeared with ghastly remains; half a bat and half a jellyfish, one oozing black blood and the other shiny matter, one with a wing spread and the other with soft, gelatinous edges. The goat-girl realized that this was a message. It meant, 'rendezvous on the seashore tonight'. Pamela took her courage in both hands and went.

By the sea she sat on pebbles and listened to the rustle of white-flecked waves. Then came a clatter on the pebbles and Medardo galloped along the shore. He stopped, unhitched, got off his saddle.

'Pamela, I have decided to fall in love with you,' he said to her.

'And is that why,' exclaimed she, 'you're taking it out on all these creatures of nature?'

'Pamela,' sighed the Viscount, 'we have no other language in which to express ourselves but that. Every meeting between two creatures in this world is a mutual rending. Come with me, for I know about that, and you'll be safer than with anyone else; for I do harm as do all, but the difference between me and others is that I have a steady hand.'

'And will you tear me in two as you have the daisies and the jelly-fish?'

'I don't know what I'll do with you. Certainly my having you will make possible things I never imagined. I'll take you to the castle and keep you there and no one else will ever see you and we'll have days and months to realize what we should do and to invent new ways of being together.'

Pamela was lying on the sand and Medardo had knelt beside her. As he spoke he waved his hand all round her, but without touching her.

'Well, first I must know what you'll do to me. You can give me a sample now and then I'll decide whether to come to the castle or not.'

The Viscount slowly drew his thin bony hand near to Pamela's cheek. The hand was trembling and it was not clear if it was stretched to caress or to scratch. But it had not yet touched her when he suddenly drew it back and got up.

'It's at the castle I want you,' he said, hitching himself back on to his horse. 'I'm going to prepare the tower you will live in. I leave you another day to think it over, then you must make up your mind.'

So saying he spurred off along the beach.

Next day Pamela climbed up the mulberry tree as usual to gather fruit, and heard a moaning and fluttering among the branches. She nearly fell off from fright. A cock was tied on a branch by its wings and being devoured by great hairy blue caterpillars; a nest of those evil insects that live on pines had settled right on top.

This was another of the Viscount's ghastly messages, of course. Pamela's interpretation was, 'tomorrow at dawn in the wood'.

With the excuse of gathering a sackful of pine cones Pamela went up into the woods, and Medardo appeared from behind a tree trunk leaning on his crutch.

'Well,' he asked Pamela, 'have you made up your mind to come to the castle?'

Pamela was lying stretched out on pine needles. 'I've made up my mind not to go,' she said, scarcely turning. 'If you want me, come and meet me here in the woods.'

'You'll come to the castle. The tower where you're to live is ready and you'll be its only mistress.'

'You want to keep me prisoner there and then get me burnt in a fire maybe or eaten up by rats. No, no. I told you; I'll be yours if you like but here on these pine needles.'

The Viscount had crouched down near her head. In his hand he had a pine needle, which he brought close on her neck and passed all round it. Pamela felt goose-flesh come over her, but lay still. She saw the Viscount's face bent over her, that profile which remained a profile even when seen from the front, and that half set of teeth bared in a scissors-like smile. Medardo clutched the pine needle in his fist and broke it. He got up. 'I want you shut in the castle, yes, shut in the castle!'

Pamela realized she could risk it, so she waved her bare feet in the air and said: 'Here in the wood I wouldn't say no; I wouldn't do it all shut up – not if I were dead.'

'I'll get you there!' said Medardo, putting his hand on the shoulder of his horse which had come up as if it were passing there by chance. He leapt on the saddle and spurred off down a forest track.

That night Pamela slept in her hammock swung between

olive and fig, and in the morning, horrors! She found a little bleeding carcass in her lap. It was half a squirrel, cut as usual longways, but with its fluffy tail intact.

'Poor me!' said she to her parents. 'This Viscount just won't leave me alone.'

Her father and mother passed the carcass of the squirrel from hand to hand.

'But,' said her father, 'he's left the tail whole. That may be a good sign.'

'Maybe he's beginning to be good ...' said her mother.

'He always cuts everything in two,' said her father, 'but the loveliest thing on a squirrel, he respects that ...'

'Maybe that's what the message means,' exclaimed her mother, 'he'll respect what's good and beautiful about you.'

Pamela put her hands in her hair. 'What things to hear from my own father and mother! There's something behind this; the Viscount has spoken to you ...'

'Not spoken,' said her father. 'But he's let us know that he wants to visit us and will take an interest in our wretched state.'

'Father, if he comes to talk to you open up the hives and set the bees on him.'

'Daughter, maybe Master Medardo is growing gooder ...' said the old woman.

'Mother, if he comes to talk to you, tie him to the ant heap and leave him there.'

That night the haystack where the mother slept caught fire and the barrel where the father slept came apart. In he morning the two old folk were staring at the remains when the Viscount appeared.

'I must apologize for alarming you last night,' said he, 'but I didn't quite know how to approach the subject. The fact is that I am attracted to your daughter Pamela and want to take her to the castle. So I wish to ask you formally to hand her over to me. Her life will change, and so will yours.'

'You can imagine how pleased we'd be, Signore!' said the old man. 'But if you knew what a character my daughter has! Why she told us to set the bees from the hives on you ...'

'Think of it, Signore ...' said the mother, 'why she told us to tie you to our ant heap ...'

Luckily Pamela came home early that day. She found her father and mother tied and gagged, one on the beehive, the other on the ant heap. And it was lucky that the bees knew the old man and the ants had other things to do than bite the old woman. So Pamela was able to save them both.

'You see just how good the Viscount's got, eh?' said Pamela.

But the two old people were plotting something. Next day they tied up Pamela and locked her in with the animals; then they went off to the castle to tell the Viscount that if he wanted their daughter he could send down for her as they on their side were ready to hand her over.

But Pamela knew how to talk to her creatures. The ducks pecked her free from the ropes, and the goats butted down the door. Off Pamela ran, taking her favourite goat and duck. She set up house in the wood, living in a cave known only to her and to a child who brought her food and news.

That child was myself. Life was fine with Pamela in the woods. I brought her fruit, cheese and fried fish and in exchange she gave me cups of goat's milk and duck's eggs. When she bathed in pools and streams I stood guard so that no one should see her.

Sometimes my uncle passed through the woods, but he kept at a distance, though showing his presence in his usual grim way. Sometimes a shower of stones would graze Pamela and her goat and duck; sometimes the trunk of a pine tree on which she was leaning gave way, mined at its base by blows of a hatchet; sometimes a spring would be fouled by the remains of slaughtered animals.

My uncle had now taken to hunting with a crossbow, which he succeeded in manoeuvring with his one arm. But he had got even grimmer and thinner, as if new agonies were gnawing at that remnant of a body of his.

One day Dr Trelawney was going through the fields with me when the Viscount came towards us on horseback and nearly ran him down. The horse stopped with a hoof on the Englishman's chest. My uncle said, 'Can you explain, Doctor?

I have a feeling as if the leg I've not got were tired from a long walk. What can that mean?'

Trelawney was confused and stuttered as usual, and the Viscount spurred off. But the question must have struck the doctor, who began thinking it over, holding his head in his hands. Never had I seen him take such an interest in a case of human ills.

7

Around Pratofungo grew bushes of mint and hedges of rosemary, and it was not clear if these were wild or the paths of some herb garden. I used to wander round them breathing in the laden air and trying to find some way of reaching old Sebastiana.

Since Sebastiana had vanished along the track leading to the leper village I realized more often that I was an orphan. And I despaired of ever getting news of her. I asked Galateo, calling out to him from the top of a tree I had climbed when he passed; but Galateo was no friend of children who used sometimes to throw live lizards at him from treetops, and he only gave me jeering and incomprehensible replies in that treacly, squeaky voice of his. Now longing to enter Pratofungo went with a yearning to see the old nurse again, and I was for ever meandering around the odoriferous bushes.

Once from a tangle of thyme rose a figure in a light-coloured robe and straw hat, which walked off towards the village. It was an old leper, and wanting to ask him about the nurse I got close enough for him to hear me without shouting and said: 'Hey, there, sir leper!'

But at that moment, perhaps woken by my words, right by

me rose another figure who sat up and stretched. His face was all scaly like dried bark, and he had a sparse woolly white beard. He took a whistle out of his pocket and blew a jeering blast in my direction: I realized then that the sunny afternoon was full of lepers lying hidden in the bushes; now very slowly they began rising to their feet in their light-coloured robes and walking against the sun towards Pratofungo, holding musical instruments or gardening tools with which they set up a great din. I had drawn away from the bearded man but nearly bumped right into a noseless leper combing his hair among the laurels, and however much I went jumping off through the undergrowth I kept on running into other lepers and began to realize that the only direction I could move was towards Pratofungo, whose thatched roofs stuck over with eagles' feathers were now quite close at the foot of the slope.

Only now and again did the lepers pay me any attention, with winks of the eye and notes of the mouth organ; but I felt that the real centre of that march was myself, and that they were accompanying me to Pratofungo as if I were a captured animal. The house walls in the village were painted mauve and at a window a half-dressed woman with mauve marks on face and breast was calling out: 'The gardeners are back!' and playing on a lyre. Other women now appeared at windows and balconies waving tambourines and singing, 'Gardeners, welcome back!'

I was being very careful to keep in the middle of the lane and not touch anyone; but I found myself at a kind of crossroads, with lepers all round me, men and women, sitting out on the thresholds of their houses, in faded rags showing tumours and intimate parts, their hair stuck with hawthorn and anemone blossoms.

The lepers were holding a little concert, to all appearances in my honour. Some were bending their violins towards me with exaggerated scrapes of the bow, others made frogs' faces as soon as I looked at them, others held out strange puppets that moved up and down on strings. The concert was made up of these varying and discordant gestures and sounds, but there was a kind of jingle they kept on repeating: 'Stainless was he, till he went on to blackberry.'

'I'm looking for my nurse, old Sebastiana,' I shouted. 'Can you tell me where she is?'

They burst out laughing in a knowing malicious way.

'Sebastiana!' I called, 'Sebastiana! Where are you?'

'There, child,' said a leper, 'now be good, child,' and he pointed to a door.

The door opened and out came a woman with an olive skin, maybe a Moor, half-naked and tattooed with eagles' wings, who began a licentious dance. I did not quite understand what happened next; men and women flung themselves on each other and began what I afterwards realized was an orgy.

I was making myself as small as possible when suddenly through the groups appeared old Sebastiana.

'Foul swine!' she cried. 'Have some regard for an innocent soul at least.'

She took me by a hand and drew me away while they went on chanting, 'Stainless was he, till he went on to blackberry!'

Sebastiana was wearing a light-coloured mauve robe like a nun's and already had a few marks blotching her unlined cheeks. I was happy at finding the nurse, but in despair as she had taken me by the hand and must have given me leprosy. I told her so.

'Don't worry,' replied Sebastiana. 'My father was a pirate and my grandfather a hermit. I know the virtues of every herb against ours and the Moors' diseases. They sting themselves here with marjoram and mallow; but I quietly make my own decoctions from borage and water-cress which prevent my getting leprosy as long as I live.'

'What about those marks on your face, nurse?' asked I, much relieved but still not quite convinced.

'Greek resin. To make them think I have the leprosy too. Come here now and I'll give you a drink of my piping hot tisane, for one can't take too many precautions when going about places like these.'

She had taken me off to her home, a shack a little apart, clean, with washing hung out to dry; and there we talked.

'How's Medardo? How's Medardo?' she kept on asking me, and every time I spoke she interrupted with 'Ah the rascal! Ah the rapscallion! In love forsooth! Ah poor girl! And here, you can't imagine what it's like here! What they waste! To think of all the things we deprive ourselves to give Galateo, and what they do with them! That Galateo is a good for nothing, anyway! A bad lot, and not the only one! What they get up to at night! And by day, too! Those women! Never have I seen such shameless hussies! If they'd only mend their clothes! Filthy and ragged! Oh, I told them so to their faces ... And d'you know their answer ... ?'

Delighted with this visit to the nurse off I went next day to fish for eels. I set my line in a pool of the stream and fell asleep as I waited. I don't know how long my sleep lasted; a sound awoke me. I opened my eyes, saw a hand raised over my head, and in the hand a red hairy spider. I turned and there was my uncle in his black cloak.

I gave a start of terror, but at that moment the spider bit my uncle's hand and scuttled off. My uncle put his hand to his lips, sucked the wound a bit and said, 'You were asleep and I saw a poisonous spider climbing down on to your neck from that branch. I put my hand out and it stung me.'

Not a word did I believe; at least three times he had made attempts on my life in ways like that. But the spider had certainly bitten his hand, and the hand was swelling.

'You're my nephew,' said Medardo.

'Yes,' I replied in slight surprise, for it was the first time he gave any sign of recognizing me.

'I recognized you at once,' he said; then added, 'Ah, spider! I only have one hand and you want to poison that! But better my hand than this child's neck.'

I had never known my uncle speak like that. The thought went through my mind that he was telling the truth and maybe had gone good all of a sudden, but I at once put it aside; lies and intrigue were a habit with him. Certainly he seemed much changed, with an expression that was no longer tense and cruel but languid and drawn, perhaps from fear and pain at the bite. But his clothes, dusty and oddly cut, were also different, and helped to give that impression; his black cloak was a bit tattered, with dry leaves and chestnut husks sticking to the ends; his suit too was not of the usual black velvet but of threadbare fustian, and the leg was no longer encased in a high leather boot but in a blue and white striped woollen stocking.

To show I was not curious about him I went to see if any eel had taken a bite at my line. There were no eels, but slipped over the hook was a golden ring with a diamond in it. I pulled it up and saw that the stone bore the Terralba crest.

The Viscount's eye was following me, and he said, 'Don't be surprised. As I passed I saw an eel wriggling on the hook and felt so sorry for it I freed it; then thinking of the loss I'd caused the fisherman by my action, I decided to repay him with my ring, the last thing of value I possess.'

I stood there open-mouthed with amazement. Medardo went on, 'I didn't know at the time that the fisherman was you. Then I found you asleep on the grass and my pleasure at seeing you quickly turned to alarm at that spider coming down on you. The rest you already know.' And so saying he looked sadly at his swollen purple hand.

All this might have been just a series of cruel deceptions; but I thought how lovely a sudden conversion of his feelings would be, and the joy it would also bring Sebastiana and Pamela and all the people suffering from his cruelty.

'Uncle,' said I to Medardo, 'wait for me here. I'll rush off to Nurse Sebastiana who knows all about herbs and get her to give me one to heal spiders' bites.'

'Nurse Sebastiana ...' said the Viscount, as he lay outstretched with his hand on his chest, 'How is she nowadays?'

I did not trust him enough to tell that Sebastiana had not caught leprosy and all I said was, 'Oh, so-so. I'm off now,' and away I ran, longing more than anything else to ask Sebastiana what she thought of these strange developments.

I found the nurse still in her shack. I was panting with

running and impatience, and gave her a rather confused account, but the old woman was more interested in Medardo's bite than in his acts of goodness. 'A red spider d'you say? Yes, yes, I know just the right herb ... Once a woodman had his arm swell up ... He's gone good you say? Oh well, he always was in a way, if one knew how to take him ... Now where did I put that herb? Just make a poultice with it ... Yes, Medardo's always been a scatter-brain, ever since he was a child ... Ah here's the herb, I'd put a little bag of it in reserve ... Yes, he always was; when he got hurt he'd come and sob to his nurse ... Is it a deep bite?'

'His left hand is all swollen up,' said I.

'Oh, oh, you silly boy ...' laughed the nurse. 'The left hand ... Where's Master Medardo's left hand? He left it behind in Bohemia with those Turks, may the devil take them, he left it there, with the whole left half of his body ...'

'Oh yes, of course,' I exclaimed. 'And yet ... he was there, I was here, he had his hand turned round like this ... How can that be?'

'Can't you tell left from right any more?' said the nurse. 'And yet you learnt when you were five ...'

I just couldn't make it out. Sebastiana must be right, but I remembered exactly the opposite.

'Well, take him this herb, like a good boy,' said the nurse, and off I ran.

Panting hard, I reached the brook, but my uncle was no longer there. I looked around; he had vanished with that swollen, poisoned hand of his.

That evening I was wandering among the olives. And there he was, wrapped in his black mantle, standing on a bank leaning against a tree trunk. His back was turned and he was looking out over the sea. I felt fear coming over me again, and with an effort managed to say in a faint voice, 'Uncle, here is the herb for the bite ...'

The half face turned at once and contracted into a ferocious sneer.

'What herb, what bite?' he cried.

'The herb to heal ...' I said. But the sweet expression of

before had vanished, it must have been a passing moment's; perhaps it was slowly returning now in a tense smile, but that was obviously put on.

'Ah yes ... fine ... Put it in the hollow of that tree trunk ... I'll take it later then,' he said.

I obeyed and put my hand in the hollow. It was a wasps' nest. They all flew at me. I began to run, followed by the swarm, and flung myself into the stream. By swimming underwater I managed to put the wasps off my track. Raising my head I heard the Viscount's grim laugh in the distance.

Another time too he managed to deceive me. But there were many things I did not understand, and I went to Dr Trelawney to talk to him about them. In his sexton's hut, by the light of a lantern, the Englishman was crouched over a book of human anatomy, very rare for him.

'Doctor,' I asked him, 'have you ever heard of a man bitten by a red spider coming through unharmed?'

'A red spider, did you say?' The doctor started. 'Who had another bite from a red spider?'

'My uncle the Viscount,' I said. 'And I'd brought him a herb from Sebastiana, and from being good, as it seemed before, he became bad again and refused my help.'

'I have just tended the Viscount for a red spider's bite on his hand,' said Trelawney.

'Tell me, Doctor; did you find him good or bad?'

Then the doctor described to me what had happened.

After I left the Viscount sprawled on the grass with his swollen hand Dr Trelawney had passed that way. He noticed the Viscount and, seized with fear as always, tried to hide among the trees. But Medardo had heard his footsteps and got up and called, 'Who's there?'

The Englishman thought, 'If he finds it's me hiding from him there's no knowing what he won't do,' and ran off so as not to be recognized. But he stumbled and fell into a pool in the stream. Although he had spent his life on ships, Dr Trelawney did not know how to swim, and was threshing about in the middle of the pool shouting for help. Then the Viscount said, 'Wait for me,' went on to the bank and got into the water, swung by his aching hand on a protruding tree root and stretched out until the doctor could seize his foot. Long and thin as he was, he acted as a rope for the doctor to reach the bank.

There they are both safe and sound, with the doctor stuttering, 'Oh oh, m'lord ... thank you indeed, m'lord ... How can I ...?' and he sneezes right in the other's face, as he's caught a cold.

'Good luck!' says Medardo. 'But cover yourself, please,' and he puts his cloak over the doctor's shoulders.

The doctor protests, more confused than ever. And the Viscount exclaims, 'Keep it, it's yours.'

Then Trelawney notices Medardo's swollen hand.

'What bit you?'

'A red spider.'

'Let me tend it, m'lord.'

And he takes him to his sexton's hut, where he does up the hand with medicines and bandages. Meanwhile the Viscount chats away with him, all humanity and courtesy. They part with a promise to see each other soon and reinforce their friendship.

'Doctor!' I said after listening to his tale, 'the Viscount whom you tended, shortly afterwards went back to his cruel madness and roused a whole nest of wasps against me.'

'Not the one I tended,' said the doctor with a wink.

'What d'you mean, Doctor?'

'I'll tell you later. Now not a word to anyone. And leave me to my studies, as there are difficult times ahead.'

And Doctor Trelawney took no more notice of me; back he went to that unusual reading of a treatise on human anatomy. He must have had some plan or other in his head, and for all the following days remained reticent and absorbed.

Now news of Medardo's double nature began coming from various sources. Children lost in the woods were approached to their terror by the half-man with a crutch who led them home by the hand and gave them figs and flowers and sweets; poor widows were helped across brooks by him; dogs bitten by snakes were tended, mysterious gifts were found on thresholds and window-sills of the poor, fruit trees torn up by the wind were straightened and put back into their sockets before their owners had put a nose outside the door.

At the same time, though, appearances of the Viscount half wrapped in his black cloak were also a signal for dire events. Children were kidnapped and later found imprisoned in caves blocked by stones; branches broke off and rocks rolled on to old women; newly ripe pumpkins were slashed to pieces from wanton malice.

For some time the Viscount's crossbow had been used only against swallows, and in such a way as not to kill but only wound and stun them. But now were seen in the sky swallows with legs bandaged and tied to splints, or with wings stuck together or waxed; a whole swarm of swallows so treated were prudently flying about together, like convalescents from a bird hospital; and there was an incredible rumour that Medardo was their doctor.

Once a storm caught Pamela in a wild and distant spot, together with her goat and duck. She knew that nearby was a cave, very small, a kind of hollow in the rock, and towards that she went. Sticking out of it she saw a tattered and patched boot. Inside was huddling the half-body wrapped in its black cloak. She was just going to run away, but the Viscount had already seen her, came out under the pouring rain and said to her; 'Come, girl, take refuge here.'

'No, I'm not taking any refuge there,' said Pamela, 'as there's scarcely room for one, and you want to squeeze up to me.'

'Don't be alarmed,' said the Viscount, 'I will stay outside and you take ease in there, with your goat and your duck too.'

'The goat and duck can get wet.'

'They'll take refuge too, you'll see.'

Pamela, who had heard tell of strange impulses of goodness by the Viscount, said to herself, 'We'll just see,' and crouched down inside the cave, tight against her goat and duck. The Viscount stood up in front and held his cloak there like a tent so that neither goat nor duck got wet either. Pamela looked at the hand holding the cloak, remained for a moment deep in thought, began looking at her own hands, compared them with each other, then burst into a roar of laughter.

'I'm glad to see you so jolly, girl,' said the Viscount. 'But why are you laughing, if I may ask?'

'I'm laughing because I've understood what is driving all my fellow villagers quite mad.'

'What is that?'

'That you are in part good and in part bad. Now it's all obvious.'

'Why's that?'

'Because I've realized that you are the other half. The Viscount living in the castle, the bad one, is one half. And you're the other, who was thought lost in the war but has now returned and it's a good half.'

'That's nice of you. Thank you.'

'Oh, it's the truth, not a compliment.'

Now this was Medardo's story, as Pamela heard it that evening. It was not true that the cannon ball had blown part of his body to bits; it had split him in two halves. One was found by the army stretcher bearers, the other remained buried under a pyramid of Christian and Turkish corpses and was not seen. Deep in the night through the battlefield passed two hermits, whether faithful to the true religion or necromancers is not certain. They, as happens to some in wars, had been reduced to living in the no-man's-land between two battlefields, and maybe, according to some nowadays, were trying to worship at the same time the Christian Trinity and the Allah of Mohammed. In their peculiar piety these hermits, on finding Medardo's halved body, had taken him to their den, and there, with balsams and unguents prepared by themselves, tended and saved him. As soon as his strength was re-established the wounded man had bidden farewell to his saviours, and supported on his crutch moved for months and years throughout all the nations of Christendom in order to return to his castle, amazing people along the way by his acts of goodness.

After having told Pamela his story, the good half of the Viscount asked the shepherd girl to tell him hers. Pamela explained how the bad Medardo was laying siege to her and how she had fled from home and was now wandering in the woods. At Pamela's account the good Medardo was moved, his pity divided between the goat girl's persecuted virtue, the bad Medardo's hopeless desolation, and the solitude of Pamela's parents.

'As for them,' said Pamela, 'my parents are just a pair of old rogues. There's no point in your pitying them.'

'Oh, but just think of them, Pamela, how sad they'll be in their old home at this hour, without anyone to look after them and work the fields and do out the stall.'

'It can fall on their heads, can the stall, for all I care!' said Pamela. 'I'm beginning to realize that you're a bit too soft, and instead of attacking that other half of yours for all the swinish things he does, you seem almost to pity him as well.'

'Of course I do! I know what it means to be half a man, and of course I pity him.'

'But you're different; you're a bit daft too, but good.'

Then the good Medardo said, 'Oh, Pamela, that's the good thing about being halved; that one understands the sorrow of every person and thing in the world at its own incompleteness. I was whole and I did not understand, and moved about deaf and unfeeling amid the pain and sorrow all round us, in places where as a whole person one would least think to find it. It's not only me, Pamela, who am a split being, but you and everyone else too. Now I have a fellowship which I did not understand, did not know before, when whole; a fellowship with all the mutilated and incomplete things in the world. If you come with me, Pamela, you'll learn to suffer with everyone's ills, and tend your own by tending theirs.'

'That sounds all very fine,' said Pamela, 'but I'm in a great pickle with that other part of you being in love with me and my not knowing what he wants to do with me.'

My uncle let fall his cloak, as the storm was over.

'I'm in love with you too, Pamela.'

Pamela jumped out of the cave, 'What fun! There's the

sign of the whale in the sky and I've a new lover! This one's halved too, but has a good heart.'

They were walking under branches still dripping, through paths all mud. The Viscount's half mouth was curved in a sweet, incomplete smile.

'Well, what shall we do?' said Pamela.

'I'd say you ought to go back to your parents, poor things, and help them a bit in their work.'

'You go if you want to,' said Pamela.

'I do indeed want to, my dear,' exclaimed the Viscount.

'I'll stay here,' said Pamela, and stopped with her duck and goat.

'Doing good together is the only way to love.'

'A pity. I thought there were other ways.'

'Goodbye, my dear. I'll bring you some honey cake.'

And he hopped off on his stick along the path.

'What d'you say, goatee? What d'you say, duckling dear?' exclaimed Pamela when alone with her pets. 'Why must all these oddities come to *me*?'

8

Once the news had got round that the Viscount's other half had reappeared, things at Terralba became very different.

In the morning I accompanied Dr Trelawney on his round of visits to the sick; for the doctor was gradually returning to the practice of medicine and was realizing how many ills our people suffered, their fibre undermined by the long famines of recent times – ills which he had not bothered about before.

We would go round the country lanes and find the signs

of my uncle having preceded us. My good uncle, I mean, the one who every morning not only went the rounds of the sick, but also of the poor, the old, of whoever needed help.

In Bacciccia's orchard the ripe pomegranates were each tied round with a piece of rag. From this we understood that Bacciccia had toothache. My uncle had wrapped up the pomegranates in case they fell off and squashed now that their owner's ills were preventing him coming out and picking them himself; but it was also a signal for Dr Trelawney to pay the sick man a visit and bring his pincers.

Prior Cecco had a sunflower on his terrace, but in starved soil so that it never flowered. That morning we found three chickens tied on the railing there, all pecking grain as fast as they could and unloading their white excrement into the sunflower pot. We realized that the Prior must have diarrhoea. My uncle had tied up the chickens there to manure the sunflower, and also to warn Dr Trelawney of his urgent case.

On old Giromina's steps we saw a row of snails moving up towards the door; they were big snails of the kind that are eaten cooked. This was a present from the woods brought by my uncle to Giromina, but also a sign that the old woman's heart disease had got worse and that the doctor should enter quietly lest he gave her a fright.

All these methods of communication were used by the good Medardo so as not to alarm the sick by too brusque a request for the doctor's help, but also so that Trelawney should get some notion of the case to be treated before entering, and thus overcome his reluctance to set foot in the houses of others and to approach sick whose ills he did not know.

Suddenly throughout the valley ran the alarm, 'The Bad 'Un! The Bad 'Un's coming.'

It was my uncle's bad half who had been seen riding in the neighbourhood. Then everyone ran to hide, Dr Trelawney first, with me behind.

We passed by Giromina's, and on the steps was a streak of cracked snails, all slime and bits of shell.

'He's passed this way! Quick!'

On Prior Cecco's terrace the chickens were tied to the pan where tomatoes had been laid out to dry, and were ruining the lot.

'Quick!'

In Bacciccia's orchard the pomegranates had all been squashed on the ground and empty rag ends hung from the branches.

'Quick!'

So we spent our lives between doing good and being frightened. The Good 'Un (as my uncle's left half was called in contrast to the Bad 'Un who was the other) was now considered a saint. The maimed, the poor, women betrayed, all those with troubles went to him. He could have profited by this to become Viscount himself. Instead of which he went on being a vagabond, going round half-wrapped in his ragged black cloak, leaning on his crutch, his blue and white stocking full of holes, doing good both to those who asked him and to those who thrust him harshly from their doors. No sheep that broke a leg in a ravine, no drunk drawing a knife in a tavern, no adulterous wife hurrying to her lover by night, but found him appearing as if dropped from the sky, black and thin and sweetly smiling, to help and advise, prevent violence and sin.

Pamela was still in the woods. She had made herself a swing between two pine trees, then another firmer one for the goat and a lighter one for the duck, and she spent hours swinging herself to and fro with her pets. But at fixed times the Good 'Un would come hobbling through the pine trees with a bundle tied to his shoulder. It held clothes to be washed and mended which he gathered from lonely beggars, orphans and sick, and he got Pamela to wash them, thus giving her a chance to do good too. Pamela, who was getting bored with always being in the wood, washed the clothes in the brook, and he helped her. Then she hung them all to dry on the ropes of her swings, while the Good 'Un sat on a stone and read Tasso's *Jerusalem Freed*.

Pamela took no notice of the reading and lay taking it easy on the grass, delousing herself (for while living in the woods she had got a few on her), scratching herself with a plant whose literal name was 'bum-scratch', yawning, dangling stones in her bare toes, and looking at her legs which were pink and plump as ever. The Good 'Un, without ever raising his eye from the book, would go on declaiming octave after octave with the aim of civilizing the rustic girl's deportment.

But she, unable to follow the thread, and bored, was quietly inciting the goat to lick the Good 'Un's half-face and the duck to perch on the book. The Good 'Un started back and raised the book which shut up: at that very moment the Bad 'Un appeared at a gallop among the trees, brandishing a great scythe against the Good 'Un. The scythe's blade fell on the book and cut it neatly in half lengthways. The back part remained in the Good 'Un's hand, and the rest fluttered through the air in a thousand half pages. The Bad 'Un vanished at a gallop; he had certainly tried to scythe the Good 'Un's half-head off, but the goat and duck had appeared just at the right moment. Pages of Tasso with their white margins and halved verses flew about in the wind and came to rest on pine branches, on grass, on water in the brook. From the top of a hillock Pamela looked at the white flutter and cried, 'How lovely!'

A few leaves reached a path along which Dr Trelawney and I were passing. The doctor caught one in the air, turned it over and over, tried to decipher those verses with no head or tail to them and shook his head; 'But I can't understand a thing ... tzt ... tzt ...'

The Good 'Un's reputation even reached the Huguenots, and old Ezekiel was often seen standing on the highest terrace of the yellow vineyard, gazing at the stony mule path up from the valley.

'Father,' one of his sons said to him, 'I see you are looking down into the valley as if awaiting someone's arrival.'

''Tis man's lot to wait,' replied Ezekiel 'and the just man's to wait with trust, the unjust man's with fear.'

'Is it the Lame-One-on-the-other-foot that you are waiting for?'

'Have you heard him spoken of?'

'There's nothing else but the Half-Man spoken of down in the valley. Do you think he will come up to us here?'

'If ours is the land of those who live in the right, and he is one who lives in the right, there is no reason why he should not come.'

'The mule path is steep for one who has to do it on a crutch.'

'There was a one-footed man who found himself a horse to come up with!'

Hearing Ezekiel talk, the other Huguenots had appeared from among the vines and gathered around him. And hearing an allusion to the Viscount they quivered silently.

'Father Ezekiel,' they said, 'that night when the Thin One came and the lightning burnt half the oak tree, you said that maybe one day we would be visited by a better traveller.'

Ezekiel nodded and lowered his beard to his chest.

'Father, the one talked of now is as much a cripple as the other, his opposite in both body and soul; kind as the other was cruel. Could he be the visitor whom your words announce?'

'It could be every traveller on every road,' said Ezekiel, 'and so he too.'

'Then let's all hope that it be he!' said the Huguenots.

Ezekiel's wife came forward with her eyes fixed before her, pushing a wheelbarrow full of vine twigs. 'We always hope for everything good,' said she, 'but even if he who hobbles over these hills is but some poor soldier mutilated in the war, good or bad in soul, we must continue every day to do right and to cultivate our land.'

'That is understood,' replied the Huguenots. 'Have we indeed said anything that meant the contrary?'

'Then, if we are all agreed,' said the woman, 'we can go back to our hoes and pitchforks.'

'Plague and famine!' burst out Ezekiel. 'Who told you to stop work, anyway?'

The Huguenots scattered among the vine-rows to reach their tools left in the furrows, but at that moment Esau, who, as his father was not looking, had climbed up the fig tree to eat the early fruit, cried, 'Down there! Who's arriving on that mule?'

A mule was in fact coming up the slope with a half-man tied to the crupper. It was the Good 'Un, who had bought an old nag just as she was about to be drowned since she was so far gone it was not worth sending her to the slaughterhouse.

'Anyway I'm only half a man's weight,' he said to himself, 'and the old mule might still bear me. And with my own mount I can go farther and do more good.' So his first journey was up to pay a visit to the Huguenots.

The Huguenots greeted him all lined up, standing stiffly to attention, singing a psalm. Then the old man went up to him and greeted him like a brother. The Good 'Un dismounted and answered these greetings ceremoniously, kissing the hand of Ezekiel's wife as she stood there grim and frowning. He asked after everyone's health, put out his hand to stroke the tousled head of Esau, who drew back, interested himself in everyone's trouble, made them tell the story of their persecutions, was touched, deprecating. They talked of course without dwelling on religious controversy, as if it were a sequence of misfortunes imputable to the general wickedness of man. Medardo passed over the fact that the persecutions were by the Church to which he belonged, and the Huguenots on their part did not launch out any affirmations of faith, partly also for fear of saying things that were theologically mistaken. So they ended up by making vague charitable speeches, disapproving of all violence and excess. All were agreed, but on the whole it was a bit chilling.

Then the Good 'Un visited the fields, commiserated with them on the bad crops, and was pleased to hear that, if nothing else, they had a good crop of rye.

'How much d'you sell it for?' he asked.

'Three *scudi* the pound,' said Ezekiel.

'Three *scudi* the pound? But the poor of Terralba are dying of hunger, my friends, and cannot buy even a handful of rye! Perhaps you don't know that hail has destroyed the rye crop in the valley, and you are the only ones who can preserve many families from famine?'

'We do know that,' said Ezekiel. 'And this is just why we can sell our rye well ...'

'But think of the help it would be for those poor people if you lowered the price ... Think of the good you can do ...'

Old Ezekiel stopped in front of the Good 'Un with arms crossed, and all the Huguenots imitated him.

'To do good, brother,' he said, 'does not mean lowering our prices.'

The Good 'Un went over the fields and saw aged Huguenots like skeletons working the soil in the sun.

'You have a bad colour,' he said to an old man with his beard so long he was hoeing it into the ground. 'Don't you feel well?'

'As well as someone can feel who hoes for ten hours at the age of seventy with only thin soup in his belly.'

' 'Tis my cousin Adam,' said Ezekiel, 'an exceptional worker.'

'At your age you must rest and nourish yourself,' the Good 'Un was just saying, but Ezekiel dragged him brusquely away.

'All of us here earn our bread the hard way, brother,' said he in a tone that admitted of no reply.

When he first got off his mule the Good 'Un had insisted on tying it up himself, and asked for a sack of fodder to refresh it after the climb. Ezekiel and his wife had looked at each other, as according to them a mule like that needed only a handful of wild chicory; but it was at the warmest moment of greeting the guest, and they had the fodder brought. Now though, thinking it over, old Ezekiel felt he really could not let that old carcass of a mule eat up the little fodder they had, and out of his guest's earshot he called Esau and said; 'Esau, go quietly up to the mule, take the fodder away, and give it something else.'

'A decoction for asthma?'

'Maize husks, chick-pea pods, what you like.'

Off went Esau, took the sack from the mule and got a kick which made him walk lame for a time. To make up for this he had the remaining fodder to sell on his own account, and said that the mule had finished the lot.

It was dusk. The Good 'Un was in the middle of the fields

with the Huguenots and they no longer knew what to say to each other.

'We still have a good hour of work ahead of us, guest,' said Ezekiel's wife.

'Well then, I'll leave you.'

'Good luck to you, guest.'

And back the good Medardo went on his mule.

'A poor creature mutilated in the wars,' said the woman when he had gone. 'What a number there are around here! Poor wretches!'

'Poor wretches indeed,' agreed the whole family.

'Plague and famine!' old Ezekiel was shouting as he went over the fields, fists raised at botched work and damage from drought. 'Plague and famine!'

9

Often in the mornings I used to go to Pietrochiodo's workshop to see the ingenious carpenter's constructions. He lived in growing anguish and remorse, since the Good 'Un had been visiting him at night, reproving him for the tragic purpose of his inventions, and inciting him to produce mechanisms set in motion by goodness and not by an evil urge to torture.

'What machine should I make then, Master Medardo?' asked Pietrochiodo.

'I'll tell you. For example you can ...' and the Good 'Un began to describe a machine which he would have ordered were he the Viscount instead of his other half, and to help out his explanation he traced some involved designs.

Pietrochiodo thought at first that this machine must be an organ, a huge organ whose keys would produce sweet music, and was about to look for suitable wood for the pipes when from another conversation with the Good 'Un he got his ideas more confused, as it seemed that Medardo wanted not air but wheat to pass through the pipes! In fact it was to be not only an organ but a mill grinding corn for the poor, and also possibly an oven for baking. Every day the Good 'Un improved his idea and covered more and more paper with plans, but Pietrochiodo could not manage to keep up with him; for this organ-cum-mill-cum-bakery was also to draw up water from wells, so saving donkeys' work, and to move about on wheels serving different villages. While on holidays it was to hang suspended in the air with nets all round, catching butterflies.

The carpenter was beginning to doubt whether building good machines was not beyond human possibility when the only mechanism which could function really practically and exactly seemed to be gibbets and racks. In fact as soon as the Bad 'Un explained to Pietrochiodo an idea for a new mechanism, the carpenter found that a way of doing it occurred to him immediately; and he would set to work and find every detail coming out perfect and irreplaceable, and the instrument when finished a masterpiece of ingenious technique.

The torturing thought came to the carpenter, 'Can it be in my soul, this evil which makes only my cruel machines work?' But he went on inventing other tortures with great zeal and ability.

One day I saw him working on a strange instrument of execution, with a white gibbet framed in a wall of black wood, and a rope, also white, running through two holes in the wall at the exact place of the noose.

'What is that machine, Master?' I asked him.

'A gibbet for hanging in profile,' he said.

'Who have you built it for?'

'For one man who both condemns and is condemned. With half of his head he condemns himself to capital punishment, and with the other half he enters the noose and breathes his last. I want to arrange it so one can't tell which is which.'

I realized that the Bad 'Un, feeling the popularity of his

good half growing, had arranged to get rid of him as soon as possible.

In fact he called his constables and said: 'A low vagabond has been infesting our estates and sowing discord for far too long. By tomorrow the criminal must be captured and brought here to die.'

'Lordship, it will be done,' said the constables, and off they went. Being one-eyed the Bad 'Un had not noticed that when answering him they had winked at each other.

For it should be told that a palace plot had been hatching in those days and the constabulary were part of it too. The aim was to imprison and suppress the reigning half-Viscount and hand castle and title over to the other half. The latter however knew nothing of this. And that night he woke up in the hayloft where he lived and found himself surrounded by constables.

'Have no fear,' said the head constable. 'The Viscount has sent us to murder you, but we are weary of his cruel tyranny and have decided to murder him and put you in his place.'

'What do I hear? Has this been done? I ask you: the Viscount, you have not already murdered him, have you?'

'No, but we certainly will in the course of the morning.'

'Thanks be to Heaven! No, do not stain yourself with more blood, too much has been shed already. What good could come of rule born of crime?'

'No matter; we'll lock him in the tower and not bother any more about him.'

'Do not raise your hands against him or anyone else, I beg you! I too am pained by the Viscount's arrogance; yet the only remedy is to give him a good example, by showing ourselves kind and virtuous.'

'Then we'll have to murder you, Signore.'

'Ah no! I told you not to murder anyone.'

'What can we do then? If we don't suppress the Viscount, we must obey him.'

'Take this phial. It contains a few drops, the last that remain to me, of the unguent with which the Bohemian hermits healed me and which till now has been most precious to me at a change of weather, when my great scar hurts. Take it to the Viscount and say merely: "Here is a gift from one who knows what it means to have veins that end in plugs!"'

The constables took the phial to the Viscount, who condemned them to be hanged. To save the constables the other plotters planned a rising. They were clumsy, and let out news of the revolt, which was suppressed with bloodshed. The Good 'Un took flowers to the graves and consoled widows and orphans.

Old Sebastiana was never moved by the goodness of the Good 'Un. When about his zealous enterprises he would often stop at the old nurse's shack and visit her, always full of kindness and consideration. And every time she would preach him a sermon. Perhaps because of her maternal instinct, perhaps because old age was beginning to cloud her mind, the nurse took little account of Medardo's separation into two halves; she would criticize one half for the misdeeds of the other, give one advice which only the other could follow and so on.

'Why did you cut the head off old Granny Bigin's chicken, poor old woman, which was all she had? You're too grown-up now to do such things ...'

'Why d'you say that to me, nurse? You know it wasn't me...'

'Oho! Then just tell me who it was?'

'Me, but—'

'There you see!'

'But not me here ...'

'Ah, because I'm old you think I'm soft too, do you? When I hear people talk of some rascality I can tell at once if it's one of yours. And I say to myself; I swear Medardo's hand is in that...'

'But you're always mistaken ...'

'I'm mistaken, am I ... ? You young people tell us old folk that we're mistaken ...! And what about you? You went and gave your crutch to old Isodoro ...'

'Yes, that was me ...'

'D'you boast of it? He used it for beating his wife, poor woman ...'

'He told me he couldn't walk because of gout ...'

'He was pretending ... And you at once go and give him your crutch ... Now he's broken it on his wife's back and you go round on a twisted branch ... You've no head, that's what's the matter with you! Always like this! And what about that time when you made Bernardo's bull drunk with grappa ...'

'That wasn't ...'

'Oho, so it wasn't you! That's what everyone says; but it's always the Viscount isn't it?'

The Good 'Un's frequent visits to Pratofungo were due, apart from contagion (also due, apparently, to the mysterious cures then dedicating himself to helping the poor lepers. Immune from contagion (also due, apparently to the mysterious cures of the hermits) he would wander about the village informing himself minutely of each one's needs, and not leave them in peace until he had done every conceivable thing he could for them. Often he would go to and fro on his mule between Pratofungo and Dr Trelawney's, for advice and medicines. The doctor himself had not the courage to go near the lepers, but he seemed, with the good Medardo as intermediary, to be beginning to take an interest in them.

But my uncle's intentions went further; he was not only proposing to tend the bodies of the lepers but their souls too. And he was for ever among them, moralizing away, putting his nose into their affairs, being scandalized, and preaching. The lepers could not endure him. Pratofungo's happy licentious days were over. With this thin figure on his one leg, black-dressed, ceremonious and sententious, no one could have fun without arousing public recriminations, malice and back-biting. Even their music, by dint of being blamed as futile, lascivious and inspired by evil sentiments, grew burdensome, and those strange instruments of theirs became covered with dust. The leper women, deprived of their revels, suddenly found themselves face to face with their disease and spent their evenings sobbing in despair.

'Of the two halves the Good 'Un is worse than the Bad
'Un,' they began to say at Pratofungo.

But it was not only among the lepers that admiration for
the Good 'Un was decreasing.

'Lucky that cannonball only split him in two,' everyone was
saying. 'If it had done it in three, who knows what we'd have
to put up with!'

The Huguenots now kept guard in turns to protect themselves from him too, as he had now lost respect for them and
would come up at all hours spying out how many sacks were
in their granaries, and preaching to them about their prices
being too high and spreading this around, so ruining their
business.

Thus the days went by at Terralba, and our sensibilities
became numbed, as we felt ourselves lost between an evil and a
virtue equally inhuman.

10

There is never a moonlight night but wicked notions writhe
like serpents' nests in evil souls, and charitable ones sprout
lilies of renunciation and dedication. So Medardo's two halves
wandered, tormented by opposing furies, amid the crags of
Terralba.

Then each came to a decision on his own, and next morning
set out to put it into practice.

Pamela's mother was just about to draw water when she
stumbled into a snare and fell into the well. She hung on a
rope and shrieked 'Help!'; then, in the circle of the well-
head, against the sky she saw the silhouette of the Bad 'Un,
who said to her, 'I just wanted to talk to you. This is what I've

decided: your daughter Pamela is often seen about with a halved vagabond. You must make him marry her; he has compromised her now and if he's a gentleman he must put it right. That's my decision: don't ask me to explain more.'

Pamela's father was taking a sack of olives from his grove to the oil press, but the sack had a hole in it, and a dribble of olives followed him along the path. Feeling his burden grown lighter, the old man took the sack from his shoulders and realized it was almost empty. But behind him he saw the Good 'Un, gathering up the olives one by one and putting them in his cloak.

'I was following you in order to have a word and had the good fortune of saving your olives. This is what is in my heart. For some time I have been thinking that the unhappiness of others, which I desire to help, is perhaps increased by my very presence. I intend to leave Terralba. But I do so only if my departure will give peace back to two people – to your daughter who sleeps in a cave while a noble destiny awaits her, to my unhappy right part who should not be left so lonely: Pamela and the Viscount must be united in matrimony.'

Pamela was training a squirrel when she met her mother, who was pretending to look for pine cones.

'Pamela,' said her mother, 'the time has come for that vagabond called the Good 'Un to marry you.'

'Where does that idea come from?' said Pamela.

'He has compromised you and he shall marry you. He's so kind that if you tell him so he won't say no.'

'But how did you get such an idea in your head?'

'Quiet: if you knew who told me you wouldn't ask so many questions; it was the Bad 'Un in person told me, our most illustrious Viscount!'

'Oh dear!' said Pamela dropping the squirrel in her lap. 'I wonder what trap he's preparing for us.'

Soon afterwards she was teaching herself to hum through a blade of grass when she met her father, who was pretending to look for wood.

'Pamela,' said her father, 'it's time you said "yes" to the Viscount, the Bad 'Un, on condition you marry in church.'

'Is that your idea or someone else's?'

'Wouldn't you like to be Viscountess?'

'Answer my question.'

'All right. Imagine, it was told me by the best hearted man in all the world, the vagabond they call the Good 'Un.'

'Oh, that one has nothing else to think of. You wait and see what I arrange!'

Ambling through the thickets on his gaunt horse, the Bad 'Un thought over his stratagem; if Pamela married the Good 'Un then by law she would be wife to Medardo of Terralba, his wife, that is. By this right the Bad 'Un would easily be able to take her from his rival, so meek and unaggressive.

Then he met Pamela, who said to him, 'Viscount, I have decided that we'll marry if you are willing.'

'You and who?' exclaimed the Viscount.

'Me and you, and I'll come to the castle and be the Viscountess.'

The Bad 'Un had not expected this at all, and thought, 'Then it's useless to arrange all the play-acting of getting her married to my other half; I'll marry her myself and that'll be that.'

So he said, 'Right.'

Pamela said, 'Arrange things with my father.'

A little later Pamela met the Good 'Un on his mule.

'Medardo,' she said, 'I realize now that I'm really in love with you and if you wish to make me happy you must ask for my hand in marriage.'

The poor man, who had made that great renunciation for love of her, sat open-mouthed. 'If she's happy to marry me, I can't get her to marry the other one any more,' he thought, and said, 'My dear, I'll hurry off to see about the ceremony.'

'Arrange things with my mother, do,' she said.

All Terralba was in a ferment when it was known that Pamela was to marry. Some said she was marrying one half, some the other. Her parents seemed to be trying to confuse things on purpose. Up at the castle everything was certainly being polished and decorated for a great occasion. And the Viscount had a suit of black velvet made with a big puff on the sleeve and another on the thigh. But the vagabond had also had his poor mule brushed up and mended his clothes at elbow and knee. In church all the candelabras were aglitter.

Pamela said that she would not leave the wood until the moment of the nuptial procession. I did the commissions for her trousseau. She sewed herself a white dress with a veil and a long train and made up a circlet and belt of lavender sprigs. As she still had a few yards of veil over, she made a wedding robe for the goat and a wedding dress for the duck, and so ran through the woods followed by her two pets, until the veil got torn in the branches and her train gathered every pine needle and chestnut husk drying along the paths.

But the night before the wedding she was thoughtful and slightly alarmed. Sitting at the top of a bare hillock with her train wrapped round her feet, her lavender circlet all awry, she propped her chin on her hand and looked round sighing at the woods.

I was always with her, for I was to act as page, together with Esau, who was, however, not to be found.

'Who will you marry, Pamela?' I asked her.

'I don't know,' she said. 'I really don't know what might happen. Will it go well? Will it go ill?'

Every now and again from the woods rose a kind of guttural cry or a sigh. It was the two halved swains who, prey to the excitement of the vigil, were wandering through glades and defiles in the woods, wrapped in their black cloaks, one on his bony horse, the other on his bald mule, moaning and sighing in anxious imaginings. And the horse leaped over ledges and landslides, and the mule clambered over slopes and hillsides, without their two riders ever meeting.

Then at dawn the horse, urged to a gallop, was lamed in a ravine; and the Bad 'Un could not get to the wedding in time. The mule on the other hand went slowly and carefully and the Good 'Un reached the church punctually, just as the bride arrived with her train held by me and by Esau, who had finally been dragged down.

The crowd was a bit disappointed at seeing that the only bridegroom to arrive was the Good 'Un leaning on his crutch. But the marriage was duly celebrated, bride and groom said yes and the ring was passed and the priest said: 'Medardo of Terralba and Pamela Marcolfi, I hereby join you in holy matrimony.'

Just then from the end of the nave, supporting himself on his crutch, entered the Viscount, his new slashed velvet suit dripping and torn. And he said, ' 'Tis I am Medardo of Terralba and Pamela is my wife.'

The Good 'Un swayed up face to face with him. 'I am the Medardo whom Pamela has married.'

The Bad 'Un flung away his crutch and put his hand to his sword. The Good 'Un had no option but do the same.

'On guard!'

The Bad 'Un lunged forward, the Good 'Un went into defence, but both of them were soon rolling on the floor.

They agreed that it was impossible to fight balanced on one leg. The duel must be put off so they'd be better prepared.

'D'you know what I'll do?' said Pamela. 'I'll go back to the woods.' And away she ran from the church, with no pages any longer holding her train. On the bridge she found the goat and duck waiting, and they trotted along beside her.

The duel was fixed for dawn next day in the Nun's Field. Master Pietrochiodo invented a kind of leg in the shape of a compass which, fixed to the halved men's belts, would allow them to stand upright and move and even bend their bodies backwards and forwards while the point stayed firmly in the ground. Galateo the leper, who had been a gentleman when in health, acted as umpire; the Bad 'Un's seconds were Pamela's father and the chief constable, the Good 'Un's two Huguenots. Dr Trelawney stood by to lend his services, and arrived with a huge roll of bandages and a demijohn of balsam as if to tend a battlefield. A lucky thing for me as, since he needed my help to carry all those things, I could watch the fight.

It was a greenish dawn; on the field the two thin black duellists stood still with swords at the ready. The leper blew his horn; it was the signal; the sky quivered like taut tissue, dormice in their lairs dug claws into soil, magpies with heads under wings tore feathers from their sides and hurt themselves, worms' mouths ate their own tails, snakes bit themselves with their own teeth, wasps broke their stings on stones, and everything turned against itself; frost lay in puddles, lichen turned to stone and stone to lichen, dry leaves to mould, and trees were filled by thick hard sap. So man moved against himself, both hands armed with swords.

Once again Pietrochiodo had done a masterly job; the compass legs made circles on the field and the duellists flung themselves into assaults of clanking metal and thudding wood, into feints and lunges. But they did not touch each other. At every lunge the sword's point seemed to go straight at the adversary's fluttering cloak, and each seemed determined to make for the part where there was nothing, that is the part where he should have been himself. Certainly if instead of half duellists there had been two whole ones, they would have wounded each other again and again. The Bad 'Un fought with fury and ferocity, yet never managed to launch his attacks just where his enemy was; the Good 'Un had correct mastery, but never did more than pierce the Viscount's cloak.

At a certain point they found themselves sword-guard to sword-guard; the points of their wooden legs were stuck in the ground like stakes. The Bad 'Un freed himself with a start and was just losing his balance and rolling to the ground, when he managed to give a terrific swing, not right on his adversary but very close; a swing parallel to the edge interrupting the Good 'Un's body, and so near that it was not clear at once if it was this side or the other. But soon we saw the body under the cloak go purple with blood from head to groin, and there was no more doubt. The Good 'Un swayed, but as he fell, in a last wide almost pitiful movement he too swung his sword very near his rival, from head to abdomen, between the point where the Bad 'Un's body was not and where it might have been. Now the Bad 'Un's body also spouted blood along the whole length of the huge old wound; the lunges of both had burst all their vein-ends and reopened the wound which had divided them in two. Now they lay face to face, and the blood which had once been one man's alone was now again mingling in the field.

Aghast at this sight I had not noticed Trelawney, then I realized that the doctor was jumping up and down with joy on his grasshopper's legs, clapping his hands and shouting, 'He's saved, he's saved! Leave it all to me.'

Half an hour later we bore back one single wounded man on a stretcher to the castle. Bad and Good 'Un had been tightly bound together; the doctor had taken great care to get all guts and arteries of both parts to correspond, and then a mile of bandages had tied them together so tightly that he looked more like an ancient embalmed corpse than a wounded man.

My uncle was watched night and day as he lay between life and death. One morning, looking at that face crossed by a red line from forehead to chin and on down the neck, it was Sebastiana who first said: 'There. He's moved.'

A quiver was in fact going over my uncle's features, and the doctor wept for joy at seeing it transmitted from one cheek to the other.

Finally Medardo shut eyes, lips; at first his expression was lopsided; he had one eye frowning and the other supplicating, a forehead here corrugated and there serene, a mouth smiling in one corner and gritting its teeth in the other. Then gradually it became symmetrical again.

Dr Trelawney said, 'Now he's healed.'

And Pamela exclaimed, 'At last I'll have a husband with everything complete.'

So my Uncle Medardo became a whole man again, neither good nor bad, but a mixture of goodness and badness, that is apparently not dissimilar to what he had been before the halving. But having had the experience of both halves each on its own, he was bound to be wise. He had a happy life, many children and a just rule. Our lives too changed for the better. Some might expect that with the Viscount entire again a period of marvellous happiness would open; but obviously a whole Viscount is not enough to make all the world whole.

Now Pietrochiodo built gibbets no longer, but mills; and Trelawney neglected his wills-o'-the-wisp for measles and chickenpox. Amid all this fervour of wholeness I felt myself growing sadder and more deficient. Sometimes one who considers himself incomplete is merely young.

I had reached the threshold of adolescence and still hid among the roots of the great trees in the wood to tell myself stories. A pine needle could represent a knight, or a lady, or a jester; I made them move before my eyes and became rapt in interminable tales about them. Then I would be overcome with shame at these fantasies and ran off.

A day came when Dr Trelawney left me too. Into our bay one morning sailed a fleet of ships flying the British flag and anchored offshore. The whole of Terralba went to the seashore to look at them, except me, who did not know. The gunwales and rigging were full of sailors carrying pineapples and tortoises and waving scrolls with maxims on them in Latin and English. On the quarter-deck, amid officers in tricorne and wig, Captain Cook fixed the shore with his telescope, and as soon as he sighted Dr Trelawney gave orders for him to be signalled by flag, 'Come on board at once, doctor, as we want to get on with that game of cards.'

The doctor bade farewell to all at Terralba and left us. The sailors intoned an anthem 'Oh, Australia!' and the doctor was hitched on board astride a barrel of *cancarone*. Then the ships drew anchor.

I was deep in the wood telling myself stories and had seen nothing. When I heard later I began running towards the seashore crying, 'Doctor! Doctor Trelawney! Take me with you! Doctor, you can't leave me here!'

But already the ships were vanishing over the horizon and I was left behind, in this world of ours full of responsibilities and wills-o'-the-wisp.

Baron in the Trees

to Paloma

I

It was on 15 June 1767 that Cosimo Piovasco di Rondò, my brother, sat among us for the last time. And it might have been today, I remember it so clearly. We were in the dining-room of our house at Ombrosa, the windows framing the thick branches of the great holm oak in the park. It was midday, the old traditional dinner hour followed by our family, though by then most nobles had taken to the fashion set by the slug-gard Court of France of dining halfway through the afternoon. A breeze was blowing from the sea, I remember, rustling the leaves. Cosimo said: 'I told you I don't want any, and I don't!' and pushed away his plateful of snails. Never had we seen such disobedience.

At the head of the table was the Baron Arminio Piovasco di Rondò, our father, wearing a long wig over his ears in the style of Louis XIV, out of date like so much else about him. Between me and my brother was the Abbé Fauchelefleur, almoner of the family and tutor of us two boys. We were facing our mother, the Baroness Corradina di Rondò, nicknamed the Generalessa, and our sister Battista, a kind of pseudo-nun. At the other end of the table, opposite our father, sat, dressed in Turkish robes, the Cavalier Avvocato Enea Silvio Carrega, lawyer, administrator and hydraulic engineer of our estates, and our natural uncle, being the illegitimate brother of our father.

A few months before, Cosimo having reached the age of twelve and I of eight, we had been admitted to the parental board; I had benefited by my brother's promotion and been moved up prematurely, so that I should not be left to eat alone. 'Benefited' is perhaps scarcely the word; for really it meant the end of our carefree life, Cosimo's and mine, and we regretted the meals in our little room, alone with the Abbé Fauchelefleur. The Abbé was a dry, wrinkled old man, with a reputation as a Jansenist; and he had in fact escaped from his native land, the Dauphiné, to avoid trial by the Inquisition. But the rigour of character for which he was so often praised, the severe mental

discipline that he imposed on himself and others, was apt to
yield before a deep-rooted urge towards apathy and indolence,
as if his long meditations with eyes staring into space had but
brought on him a great weariness and boredom, and in every
little difficulty now he had come to see a fate not worth opposing. Our meals in the Abbé's company used to begin, after many
a prayer, with ordered ritual, silent movements of spoons, and
woe to anyone who raised his eyes from his plate or made the
slightest sucking noise with the soup; but by the end of the
first dish the Abbé was already tired, bored, looking into space
and smacking his lips at every sip of wine, as if only the most
fleeting and superficial sensations could get through to him;
by the main dish we were using our hands, and throwing pear
cores at each other by the end of the meal, while the Abbé every
now and again let out one of his languid, '... *Oooo bien! ...
Oooo alors.*'

Now, at table with the family, up came surging the intimate
grudges that are such a burden of childhood. Having our father
and mother always there in front of us, using knives and forks
for the chicken, keeping our backs straight and our elbows
down, what a strain it all was! – not to mention the presence of
that sister of ours, Battista. So began a series of scenes, spiteful
exchanges, punishments, pinpricks, until the day when Cosimo
refused and snails and decided to separate his fate from ours.

These accumulating family resentments I myself only noticed
later; then I was eight, everything seemed a game, the struggle
between us boys and grown-ups was the usual one all children
play, and I did not realize that my brother's stubbornness hid
something much deeper.

Our father the Baron was a bore, it's true, though not a bad
man: a bore because his life was dominated by conflicting
ideas, as often happens in periods of transition. The movement
of the times makes some people feel a need to move themselves,
but in the opposite direction, away from the road; so, with
things stirring all round him, our father had set his heart on
regaining the lapsed title of Duke of Ombrosa, and thought of
nothing but genealogies and successions and family rivalries and
alliances with grandees near and far.

Life at our home was a constant dress rehearsal for an appearance at court, either the Emperor of Austria's, King Louis's, or
even the mountain court of Turin. When, for instance, a turkey
was served, our father would watch carefully to see if we carved
and boned it according to royal rules, and the Abbé scarcely
dared touch a morsel lest he made some error of etiquette, for,
poor man, he had to put up with our father's rebukes too. And
we saw now a deceitful side of the Cavalier Carrega; he would
smuggle away whole legs under the folds of his Turkish robe,
to munch them up bit by bit later, at his ease, hidden in the
vineyard; and we could have sworn (although we never succeeded in catching him in the act, his movements were so quick)
that he came to table with a pocketful of stripped bones, which
he left on the table in place of the hunks of turkey he whisked
away. Our mother, the Generalessa, did not worry us, as even
when serving herself at table she used brusque military manners, *'So! Noch ein wenig! Gut!'* and no one found fault with
her: she held us not to etiquette, but to discipline, supporting
the Baron with parade-ground orders, *'Sitz ruhig!* And clean
your nose!' The only person really at ease was Battista, the
nun of the house, who would sit shredding her chicken with
minute concentration, fibre by fibre, using some sharp little
knives, rather like surgeon's scalpels, which she alone had. The
Baron, who should have held her up to us as an example, did
not dare look at her, for, with her staring eyes under the
starched wings, her narrow teeth set tight in her yellow rodent's
face, she frightened him too. So it can be seen why our family
board brought out all the antagonisms, the incompatibilities,
between us, and all our follies and hypocrisies too; and why it
was there that Cosimo's rebellion came to a head. That is why
I have described it at some length – and anyway it is the last
set table we shall find in my brother's life, that's sure.

It was also the only place where we would meet the grown-
ups. The rest of the day our mother spent in her apartments,
doing lace and embroidery and petit-point; for in truth it was
only in these traditionally womanly occupations that the
Generalessa could vent her warrior's urge. The lace and embroidery was usually in designs of geographical maps; stretched

over cushions or tapestry, our mother would scatter them with pins and tiny flags, showing the disposition of battles in the Wars of Succession, which she knew by heart. Or she would embroider cannons, with the trajectories from the muzzle and the line of flight and the signs of anglings, for she was highly competent in ballistics, and also had at her disposal the entire library of her father the General, with treatises on military lore and atlases and tables of fire. Our mother was a von Kurtewitz – Konradine, daughter of General Konrad von Kurtewitz, who, twenty years before, had commanded the Empress Maria Teresa's troops which had occupied our area. A widower, the General had taken her round with him from camp to camp; there was nothing romantic about that, for they travelled well equipped, put up at the best castles, with a suite of servants, and she had spent her days making lace on a cushion. All the stories people told of her going into battle with him were legends: she had always been an ordinary little woman with a rosy face and a snub nose, in spite of that inherited zest for things military, which was perhaps a way of keeping her end up with her husband.

Our father was one of the few nobles in our parts who had taken sides with the Imperialists in that war; he had greeted General von Kurtewitz with open arms, put our retainers at his disposal, and even shown his great devotion to the Imperial cause by marrying Konradine; all this with an eye to that duchy, he was considerably put out when the Imperial troops soon moved on, as usual, and the Genoese came down on him for taxes. But he had gained an excellent wife, the Generalessa, as she began to be called after the death of her father on the Provence expedition, when Maria Teresa sent her a golden collar on a cushion of brocade; a wife with whom he nearly always got on, even if she, born and bred in camps, thought of nothing but armies and battles and criticized him for being just a wretched landowner.

But at heart they were still living in the times of the Wars of Succession, she with her artillery, he with his genealogical trees; she dreaming of a career for us boys in some army, no matter which, he, on the other hand, seeing us married to a

Grand-duchess and Electress of the Empire ... With all this, they were excellent parents, but so preoccupied that Cosimo and I were left almost to ourselves during our childhood. Who can say if that was a good thing or a bad? Cosimo's life was so much out of the ordinary, mine so conventional and modest, and yet our childhood was spent together, both indifferent to the manias of adults, both trying to find paths unbeaten by others.

We clambered about the trees (those early innocent games come back to me now as a first initiation, an omen; but who could even have thought it then?), we followed the mountain streams, jumping from rock to rock, exploring caves on the seashore, sliding down the marble banisters of the house. It was one of these slides that caused a first serious rift between Cosimo and our parents, for he was punished, unjustly, he declared, and since then harboured a grudge against the family (or society? or the world in general?) which was to express itself later in his decision on that fifteenth of June.

We had already, as a matter of fact, been warned against sliding down the marble banisters, not from fear of our breaking a leg or an arm, for that our parents never worried about, which was – I think – why we never broke anything; but in case in our gathering momentum we knocked over the busts of ancestors placed by our father on the banisters at the turn of every flight of stairs. Cosimo had, in fact, once brought down a bishop, a great-great-great uncle, mitre and all; he was punished, and since then had learnt to brake just before reaching the turn of a flight and jumping off within a hair's breadth of running into a bust. I learnt this trick too, for I copied all he did, except that I, ever more prudent and modest, jumped off halfway down, or slid the rest bit by bit, with constant little brakes. One day he was flying down the banisters like an arrow when who should be coming up but the Abbé Fauchelefleur, meandering from stair to stair, with his breviary open in front of him and his gaze fixed on space like a hen's. If only he had been half-asleep as usual! But no, he was in one of those sudden moods, that occasionally came over him, of extreme attention and awareness. He saw Cosimo, and thought; banisters, bust, he'll hit it, they'll blame me too (at every escapade of ours he used to be blamed too for not keeping us in order), and he flung himself on the banister to catch my brother. Cosimo banged into the Abbé, dragged him down the banisters too (the old man was just skin and bone), found he could not brake, and hit with double force the statue of our ancestor Cacciaguerra Piovasco, the Crusader. They all landed in a heap at the foot of the stairs, the Crusader in smithereens (he was plaster), the Abbé and him. Followed endless recriminations, a beating, and lock-up on bread and cold soup. And Cosimo, who felt innocent because the fault had not been his but the Abbé's, came out furiously with the phrase: 'A fig for all your ancestors, Father!' a pre-announcement of his mission as a rebel.

Our sister felt the same at heart. She too, though the isolation in which she lived had been forced on her by our Father after that affair of the Marchesino della Mella, had always been a rebellious and lonely soul. What happened with the Marchesino, none of us ever really knew. How, as the son of a family hostile to ours, had he ever got into the house? And why? It could only be to seduce, nay to rape, our sister, said my father in the long quarrel which ensued between the families. We boys, in fact, could never succeed in picturing that spotty simpleton as a seducer, least of all of our sister, who was certainly much stronger than him, and famous for beating the stable hands at competitions in elbow-power. And then, why was it he who shouted for help, not her? And how did the servants who rushed to the scene, led by our father, come to find him with his knee-breeches torn to strips as if by the talons of a tiger? The della Mella family refused even to admit that their son had made an attempt on Battista's virtue or to agree to a marriage between them. So our sister was eventually confined to the house, dressed up as a nun, though without taking any vows even as a tertiary, in view of her rather dubious vocation.

Her gloom only left her in the kitchen. She was a really excellent cook, for she had the primary gifts in the culinary art, diligence and imagination, and when she took a hand no one ever knew what surprise might appear at table; once she made some *pâté* toast, really exquisite, of rats' livers; this she never told us until we had eaten them and pronounced them good; and some grasshoppers' claws, crisp and sectioned, laid on an open tart in a mosaic; and pigs' tails roasted as if they were little cakes; and once she cooked a complete porcupine with all its quills, who knows why, probably just to give us all a shock at the raising of the dish cover, for even she, who usually ate everything however odd that she had prepared herself, refused to taste it, though it was a baby porcupine, rosy and certainly tender. In fact, most of these peculiar dishes of hers were thought out just for effect, rather than for any pleasure in making us eat disgusting food with her. These dishes of Battista's were works of the most delicate animal or vegetable jewellery; cauliflower heads with hares' ears set on a collar of fur; or a pig's head from whose mouth stuck a scarlet lobster as if putting out its tongue, and the lobster was holding the pig's tongue in its pincers as if they had torn it out. And finally the snails; she had managed to behead I don't know how many snails, and the heads, those soft little equine heads, she had inserted, I think with a toothpick, each in a wiremesh; they looked, as they came on the table, like a flight of tiny swans. Even more revolting than the sight of this dish was the thought of Battista zealously preparing them, of those thin hands of hers tearing the little creatures to pieces.

It was as a protest against this macabre fantasy of our sister's that my brother and I were incited to show our sympathy with the poor tortured creatures, and our disgust, too, for the flavour of cooked snails – a revolt really against everything and everybody; and it was from this, not surprisingly, that stemmed Cosimo's gesture and all that followed after.

We had devised a plan. When the Cavalier brought home a basket full of eatable snails, these were put into a barrel in the cellar, so they should starve, or eat only bran and so be purged. On moving the planks covering these barrels an inferno was revealed; snails moving up the staves with a languor which was already a presage of their death agony, amid remnants of bran, streaks of opaque clotted slime and multicoloured excrement, mementoes of the good old days of open air and grass. Some of them were right outside their shells with heads exten-

ded and horns waving, some all curled up in themselves, showing a diffident pair of antennae; others were grouped like village
gossips, others shut and sleeping, others dead with their shells
upside down. To save them from meeting that sinister cook,
and to save us from her administrations too, we made a hole in
the bottom of the barrel, and from there traced as hidden a
train as we could, with bits of chewed grass and honey, behind
barrels and various tools in the cellar, to draw the snails towards a little window giving on to a neglected grass-grown path.

Next day we went down into the cellar to see results, and
inspected the walls and passage by candlelight – 'One here! ...
And another there! ... And just see where this one got to!'
Already there was an almost continuous line of snails moving
from the barrel over the flagstones and walls towards the little
window, following our trail. 'Quick, snaily-wailies! Hurry up,
out!' we could not help shouting at them, seeing the creatures
moving along so slowly, deviating now and again in languid
circles over the rough cellar walls, attracted by occasional fly-
droppings and mildew; but the cellar was dark and cluttered;
we hoped no one would notice them, and that they would all
have time to escape.

Also that restless creature our sister Battista used to spend
the nights wandering round the house in search of mice, holding a candelabra, with a musket under her arm. That night she
went down into the cellar, and the candlelight shone on a lost
snail on the ceiling, with its train of silvery slime. A shot rang
out. We all jumped in our beds, but soon dropped our heads
back on to the pillows, used as we were to the night hunts of
our resident nun. But Battista, having destroyed the snail and
brought down a hunk of plaster with her instinctive shot, now
began to shout in that strident voice of hers: 'Help! They're all
escaping! Help!' Servants hurried to her half dressed, our
father armed with a sabre, the Abbé without his wig; the Cavalier did not even find out what was happening, but ran off into
the woods to avoid the fuss and went to sleep in a haystack.

Everyone began hunting the snails all over the cellar by
the light of torches – no one with any real will, but just out of
self-respect, so as not to admit being disturbed for nothing.

They found the hole in the barrel, and at once realized we had made it. Our father came and seized us from bed, with the coachman's whip. Then, our backs, buttocks and legs covered with violet weals, we were locked into the squalid little room used as a prison.

They kept us there three days, on bread, water, lettuce, beef, rinds and cold soup (which, luckily, we liked). Then, as if nothing had happened, we were brought out for our first family meal at midday on that fifteenth of June; and what should the kitchen superintendent, our sister Battista, have prepared for us but snail soup and snails as a main course! Cosimo refused to touch even a mouthful. 'Eat up or we'll shut you in the little room again!' I yielded and began to chew the wretched molluscs (a cowardice on my part which had the effect of making my brother feel more alone than ever, so that his leaving us was also partly a protest against me for letting him down; but I was only eight years old, and then how can I compare my own strength of will, particularly as a child, to the super-human tenacity which my brother showed throughout his life?).

'Well?' said our father to Cosimo.

'No, and no again!' exclaimed Cosimo, and pushed his plate away.

'Leave the table!'

But Cosimo had already turned his back on us all and was leaving the room.

'Where are you going?'

We saw him through the windows climbing up the holm oak. He was dressed up in the most formal clothes and head-dress, as our father insisted on his appearing at table in spite of his twelve years of age; powdered hair with a ribbon in the queue, tricorne, lace stock and ruffles, green tunic with pointed tails, flesh-coloured stockings, rapier, and long white leather gaiters halfway up his legs, the only concession to a mode of dressing more suitable to our country life. (I, being only eight, was exempted from powdered hair except on gala occasions, and from the rapier, which I should have liked to wear.) So he climbed up the knobbly old tree, moving his arms and legs along the branches with the sureness and speed which came to him from years of practice together, he and I.

I have mentioned that we used to spend hours and hours on the trees, and not for utilitarian motives as most boys do, who go up only in search of fruit or birds' nests, but for the pleasure of getting over difficult parts of the trunks and forks, reaching as high as we could, and finding a good perch on which to pause and look down at the world below, to call and joke at those passing by. So I found it quite natural that Cosimo's first thought, at that unjust attack on him, was to climb up on the holm oak, to us a familiar tree which spread its branches to the height of the dining-room windows, through which he could show his proud offended air to the whole family.

'*Vorsicht! Vorsicht!* Now he'll fall down, poor little thing!' anxiously exclaimed our mother, who would not have turned a hair at seeing us under cannon fire, but was in agony meanwhile at our games.

Cosimo climbed up to the fork of a big branch where he could settle comfortably and sat himself down there, his legs dangling, his arms crossed with hands tucked under his elbows, his head buried in his shoulders, his tricorne hat tilted over his forehead.

Our father leant out of the window-sill. 'When you're tired of being up there, you'll change your ideas!' he shouted.

'I'll never change my ideas,' exclaimed my brother from the branch.

'You'll see as soon as you come down!'

'Then I'll never come down again!' And he kept his word.

2

Cosimo was up on the holm oak. The branches spread out, high bridges over the earth. A slight breeze blew; the sun shone. It shone among the leaves so that we had to shade our eyes with our hands to see Cosimo. From the tree Cosimo looked at the world; everything, seen from up there, was different, which was fun in itself. The alley took on a new aspect, and so did the flower-beds, the hortensias, the camellias, the iron table for coffee in the garden. Farther away the tops of the trees thinned out and the kitchen garden merged into little terraced fields, propped by stone walls; the middle distance was dark with olive trees, and beyond that the village of Ombrosa thrust up roofs of slate and faded brick, and down on the port showed the tops of battlements. In the background was the sea, with a high horizon, on which a boat was slowly sailing.

And now out into the garden, after their coffee, came the Baron and the Generalessa. They stood looking at a rose bush, pretending not to take any notice of Cosimo. They were arm-in-arm first, then soon drew apart to discuss and gesture. But I moved under the holm oak as if I were playing on my own, though really to try and attract Cosimo's attention; he was still feeling resentful about me, and stayed up there looking away into the distance. I stopped and crouched down under a bench so as to go on watching him without being seen.

My brother sat there like a sentinel. He looked at everything, and everything looked at him. A woman with a basket was passing between the lemon trees. Up the path came a muleteer holding the mane of his mule. The two never set eyes on each other; at the sound of the metal-shod hoofs the woman turned round and moved towards the path but did not reach it in time. She broke into song then, but the muleteer had already passed the turn; he listened, cracked his whip and said 'Aaah!' to the mule; nothing more. Cosimo saw it all.

Now along the path passed the Abbé Fauchelefleur with his open breviary. Cosimo took something from the branch and dropped it on his head; he was not sure what it was, a little spider perhaps, or a piece of bark; anyway, it did not hit him. Cosimo then began to search about with his rapier in a hole of the trunk. Out came a furious bee, he chased it away with a wave of his tricorne and followed its flight with his eyes until it settled on a pumpkin plant. From the house, speedy as ever, came the Cavalier, hurried down the steps into the gardens and vanished among the rows of vines; Cosimo climbed on to a higher branch to see where he went. There was a flutter of wings among the leaves, and out flew a blackbird. Cosimo was rather sorry it had been up there all that time without his noticing it. He looked against the sun for others. No, there were none.

The holm oak was near an elm: their two crests almost touched. A branch of the elm passed a foot or so above a branch of the other tree; it was easy for my brother to pass and so reach the top of the elm, which we had never explored as it had a high trunk with no branches reachable from the ground. From the elm, by a branch elbow-to-elbow with the next tree, he passed on to a carob, and then to a mulberry tree. So I saw Cosimo swing from one branch to another, high above the garden.

Some branches of the big mulberry tree reached and over-lapped the boundary wall of our property, beyond which lay the gardens of the Ondarivas. Although neighbours, we knew none of the Ondariva family, Marquises and Nobles of Ombrosa, as for a number of generations they had enjoyed certain feudal rights claimed by our father, and the two families were separated by mutual antipathy, just as our properties were separated by a high fortress-like wall, put up by either our father or the Marquis, I am not sure which. To this should be added the jealous care which the Ondarivas took of their garden, full, it was said, of the rarest plants. In fact, the grandfather of the present Marquis had been a pupil of the botanist Linnaeus, and since his time all the family connections at the Courts of France and England had been set in motion to send the finest botanical rarities from the colonies; for years boats had landed at the port of Ombrosa sacks of seeds, bundles of

cuttings, potted shrubs and even entire trees with huge wrappings of sacking round the roots; until the garden – it was said
– had become a mixture of the forests of India and the
Americas, and even of New Holland.

All that we were able to see were some dark leaves, growing
over the garden wall, of a newly imported tree from the American colonies, the *magnolia*, from whose black branches sprang
a pulpy white flower. Cosimo, on our mulberry, reached the
corner of the wall, balanced on it for a step or two and then,
holding on by his hands, jumped down on to the other side,
amid the flowers and leaves of the magnolia. Then he vanished
from sight; and what I am about to tell, as also much else in
this account of his life, he described to me afterwards, or I have
put together from a few scattered hints and guesses.

Cosimo was on the magnolia. Although the branches were
very close together, this was an easy tree to manoeuvre on for
a boy so expert in all trees as my brother; and the branches held
his weight, although they were slender and of soft wood, so that
the points of his shoes tore white wounds on the black bark;
he was enveloped in the fresh scent of leaves, turned this way
and that by the wind in pages of contrasting greens, dull one
moment and glittering the next.

But the whole garden was scented, and although Cosimo
could not yet see it clearly, because of all the thick trees, he was
already exploring it by smell, and trying to discern the source
of the various aromas which he already knew from their being
wafted over into our garden by the wind: and these seemed
an integral part of the mystery of the place. Then he looked at
the branches and saw new leaves, some big and shining as if
running water were constantly flowing over them, some tiny
and feathered, and tree trunks either all smooth or all scaly.

There was a great silence. A flight of little wrens went up,
chirping. And now a faint voice could be heard singing: '*O la-la
... O la ba-la-nçoire ...*' Cosimo looked down. From the branch
of a big tree nearby was dangling a swing, and on it was sitting
a little girl of about ten years old.

She was a blonde little girl, with hair combed high in an
odd style for a child, and a green dress which was also too grown

up; its skirt, as it rose with the swing, was swirling with petti-
coats. The girl had her eyes half closed and her nose in the air
as if used to giving orders, and she was eating an apple in little
bites, bending her head down towards her hand, which had to
hold the apple and balance her on the rope of the swing at the
same time; and every time the swing reached the lowest point
of its flight she would give herself little pushes on the ground
with the end of her tiny shoes, blow out bits of apple peel and
sing 'O la-la-la ... O la ba-la-nçoire ...' as if she cared neither
for the swing, nor the song, nor (though perhaps a little more)
for the apple, and had other thoughts on her mind.

Cosimo dropped from the top of the magnolia to a lower
perch, and now had his feet set on each side of a fork and his
elbows leaning on a branch in front like a window-sill. The
flight of the swing was bringing the little girl up under his
nose.

She was not watching and did not notice. Then suddenly she
saw him there, standing on the tree, in tricorne and gaiters.
'Oh!' she said.

The apple fell from her hand and rolled away to the foot
of the magnolia. Cosimo drew his rapier, leant down from
the lowest branch, skewered the apple and offered it to the girl,
who had meanwhile made a complete turn on the swing and was
up there again. 'Take it, it's not dirty, only a little bruised on
one side.'

The fair little girl now seemed to be regretting she had shown
so much surprise at the sudden appearance of this unknown
boy on the magnolia, and put on her disdainful air again with
her nose in the air. 'Are you a thief?' she said.

'A thief?' exclaimed Cosimo, offended; then he thought it
over; the idea rather pleased him. 'Yes, I am,' he said, doffing
his tricorne at her. 'Any objection?'

'And what have you come to steal?'

Cosimo looked at the apple which he had skewered on the
point of his rapier, and suddenly realized he was hungry, as
he had scarcely touched a thing at table. 'This apple,' said he,
and began to peel it with one side of his rapier, which, in spite
of family orders, he kept very sharp.

'Then you're a fruit thief,' said the girl.

My brother thought of the rabble of poor urchins from Ombrosa, who scrambled over walls and hedges sacking orchards, boys he had been taught to despise and avoid; and for the first time he thought how free and enviable their life must be. Well now: he might become like them, and live as they did, from now on. 'Yes,' he said. He cut the apple into slices and began eating it.

The fair girl broke into a laugh which lasted a whole flight of the swing, up and down. 'Oh, go on! The boys who steal fruit! I know them all! They're all friends of mine! And they go round barefoot, in shirt sleeves and tousled hair, not gaiters and powder!'

My brother went as red as the apple peel. To be laughed at not only for his powdered hair, which he didn't like at all, but also for his gaiters, which he liked a lot, to be considered inferior in appearance to a fruit thief, to boys he had despised till a moment before, and above all to find that this girl who seemed quite at home in the Ondariva gardens was a friend of all the fruit thieves but not of his, all this made him feel annoyed, jealous and ashamed.

'O la-la-la ... In gaiters and powder!' hummed the little girl on the swing.

For a moment his pride was stung. 'I'm not a thief like the boys you know!' he shouted. 'I'm not a thief at all! I only said that to frighten you; if you really knew who I was you'd die of fright! I'm a brigand, a terrible brigand!'

The little girl went on flying through the air under his nose, almost as if wanting to graze him with the point of her shoes. 'Oh, nonsense. Where's your musket? Brigands all have muskets! And catapults! I've seen them! They've stopped our coach five times on the way here from the castle!'

'But not the chief! I'm the chief! The chief of the brigands doesn't carry a musket! Only a sword!' and he held out his little rapier.

The little girl shrugged her shoulders. 'The chief brigand,' she said, 'is a man called Gian dei Brughi, and he always brings me presents at Christmas and Easter!'

'Ah!' exclaimed Cosimo di Rondò, seized by a wave of family rancour, 'then my father's right when he says that the Marquis of Ondariva is the protector of all the brigands and smugglers around.'

The girl swept down to the ground and instead of giving herself a push, braked with a quick little stamp of the foot, and jumped off. The empty swing leapt back into the air on its ropes. 'Get down from there at once! How dare you come on to our land!' she exclaimed, pointing a furious finger at the boy.

'I haven't and I won't come on to it,' answered Cosimo with equal warmth, 'I've never set foot on your land, and I wouldn't for all the gold in the world!'

Then the girl very calmly took up a fan lying on a wicker chair, and though it was not very hot, began fanning herself and walking up and down. 'Now,' she said in a steady voice, 'I'll call the servants and have you taken and beaten! That'll teach you to trespass on our land!' She was constantly changing tone, this girl, putting my brother out every time.

'Where I am isn't land and isn't yours!' proclaimed Cosimo, and felt tempted to add: 'And I'm Duke of Ombroso too, and lord of the whole area,' but he held himself back, as he did not want to repeat things his father was always saying now that he had quarrelled with him and run away from his table; he did not want to and did not think it right; also those claims to the dukedom had always seemed just obsessions to him; why should he, Cosimo, now start boasting of being a duke? But he did not want to contradict himself and so went on saying whatever came into his head. 'This isn't yours,' he repeated, 'because it's the ground that's yours, and if I put a foot on it I would be trespassing. But up here, I can go wherever I like.'

'Oh, so it's all yours, up there...'

'Yes! It's all mine up here,' and he waved vaguely towards the branches, the leaves against the sun, the sky. 'On the branches it's all mine. Tell 'em to come and fetch me, and just see if they can!'

Now, after all that boasting, he half expected her to begin jeering at him in some way. Instead of which she seemed suddenly interested. 'Ah yes? And how far does it reach, this property of yours?'

'As far as I can get on the trees, here, there, beyond the wall, in the olive groves, up the hill, the other side of the hill, the wood, the Bishop's land ...'

'As far as France?'

'As far as Poland and Saxony,' said Cosimo, who knew nothing of geography but the names he had heard from our mother when she talked of the Wars of Succession. 'But I'm not selfish like you. I invite you into my property.' Now they were calling each other by the familiar *tu*; it was she who had begun.

'And whose is the swing, then?' said she, sitting down and opening her fan.

'The swing's yours,' pronounced Cosimo, 'but as it's tied to this tree, it depends on me. So, when you're touching the earth with your feet you're in your property, when you're in the air you're in mine.'

She gave herself a push and flew off, her hands tight on the ropes. Cosimo jumped from the magnolia on to the thick branch which held the swing, seized the ropes from there and began pushing her himself. The swing went higher and higher.

'Are you frightened?'

'No, not me. What's your name?'

'Mine's Cosimo ... And yours?'

'Violante but they call me Viola.'

'They call me Mino, too, as Cosimo's an old man's name.'

'I don't like it.'

'Cosimo?'

'No, Mino.'

'Ah ... you can call me Cosimo.'

'Wouldn't think of it! Listen, you, we must get things straight.'

'How d'you mean?' exclaimed he, who found everything she said disturbed him.

'What I say! I can come up into your property and be an honoured guest, d'you see? I come and go as I please. You, though, are sacred and untouchable while you stay in the trees, on your property, but as soon as you set a foot on the soil of my garden you become my slave and I put you in chains.'

'No, I'm not coming down into your garden or into mine either ever again. It's all enemy territory to me. You come up with me, and your friends who steal fruit, and perhaps my brother Biagio too, though he's a bit of a coward, and we'll make an army in the trees and bring the earth and the people on it to their senses.'

'No, no, not at all. Just let me explain how things are. You have the lordship of the trees, all right? But if you touch the earth just once with your foot, you lose your whole kingdom and become the humblest slave. D'you understand? Even if a branch breaks under you and you fall, it's the end of you!'

'I've never fallen from a tree in my life!'

'No, of course not, but if you do fall, if you do, you change into ashes and the wind'll carry you away.'

'Fairy tales. I'm not coming down to the ground because I don't want to.'

'Oh, what a bore you are!'

'No, no, let's play. For instance, can I come on to the swing?'

'Yes, if you manage to sit on it without touching the ground.'

Near Viola's swing was another one, hanging on the same branch, but pulled up by a knot in the ropes so it should not bump against the other. Cosimo let himself down from the branch by gripping one of the ropes, an exercise he was very good at as our mother had made him do a lot of gymnastics, reached the knot, undid it, stood up on the swing and to give himself impetus bent down on his knees and rocked the weight of his body to and fro. So he got higher and higher. The two swings moved in opposite directions, at the same height now, and passed each other halfway.

'But if you try sitting down and giving a push with your feet you'll go higher,' insinuated Viola.

Cosimo made a face at her.

'Come down and give me a push, now, do,' said she, smiling sweetly at him.

'No, I said I wouldn't come down at any cost ...' And Cosimo began to feel put out again.

'Do, please.'

'No.'

'Ah, hah! You nearly fell into the trap! If you'd set a foot on the ground you'd have lost everything!' Viola got off her swing and began giving little pushes to Cosimo's. 'Oh!' Suddenly she had snatched the seat of the swing on which my brother was standing and overturned it. Luckily Cosimo was holding tight to the ropes. Otherwise he would have dropped to the ground like a sausage.

'Cheat!' he cried, and clambered up again on the two ropes, but going up was much more difficult than coming down, particularly with the fair-haired girl maliciously pulling the ropes as hard as she could.

Finally he reached the big branch, and got astride it. With his lace jabot he wiped the sweat on his forehead. 'Ah! Ah! You didn't get me!'

'Very nearly.'

'But I thought you were a friend!'

'You thought!' and she began fanning herself again.

'Violante!' broke in a sharp female voice at that moment. 'Who are you talking to?'

On the white flight of steps leading to the house had appeared a tall, thin lady, with a very wide skirt; she was looking through a *lorgnette*. Alarmed, Cosimo drew back into the leaves.

'With a young man, *ma tante*,' said the little girl, 'who was born on the top of a tree and is under a spell so he can't set foot on the ground.'

Cosimo, scarlet in the face, asked himself if the little girl was talking like that to make fun of him in front of her aunt, or to make fun of the aunt in front of him, or just to continue the game, or because she did not care a rap about either him or the aunt or the game and he saw he was being watched through the *lorgnette*, whose owner had approached the tree and was gazing at him as if he was some strange parrot.

'*Uh, mais c'est un des Piovasques, ce jeune homme, je crois. Viens, Violante.*'

Cosimo bridled with shame; the way the aunt recognized him so easily without even asking herself why he was there and at once called the girl away firmly though not severely, the way

Viola followed her aunt's call docilely without even turning round, it all suggested that they considered him of no importance, a person who scarcely existed. And so that extraordinary afternoon of his looked like fading into a cloud of self-pity.

Then suddenly the girl made a sign to her aunt, the aunt lowered her head, and the child whispered in her ear. The aunt pointed her *lorgnette* at Cosimo again. 'Well, young man,' she said, 'would you care to take a dish of chocolate with us? Then we too can get to know you,' and here she gave a sideways glance at Viola, 'as you're already a friend of the family.'

Cosimo sat there staring round-eyed at aunt and niece. His heart was beating fast. Here he was being invited by the Onda-rivas of Ombrosa, the most powerful family in the neighbourhood, and the humiliation of a moment before changed to triumph: he was getting his own back on his father by this invitation from enemies who had always snubbed them, and Viola had interceded for him, and he was now officially accepted as a friend of hers and would play with her in that garden so different from all other gardens. All this Cosimo felt, but an opposite, though confused emotion at the same time; an emotion made up of shyness, pride, loneliness and punctilio; and amid this contrast of feelings my brother seized the branch above him, climbed it, moved into the leafiest part, on to another tree, and vanished.

3

It was endless, that afternoon. Every now and again we heard a plop, a rustle, as often in gardens, and ran out hoping that it was him, that he had decided to come down. But no, I saw a quiver on the top of the magnolia, Cosimo appeared from the other side of the wall and climbed over.

I went up the mulberry to meet him. At seeing me he seemed put out; he was still angry with me. Sitting on a branch of the mulberry above me he began slicing off bits of bark with his rapier, as if he did not want to speak to me.

'The mulberry is easy,' I exclaimed, just for something to say. 'We'd never been on it before ... '

He went on whittling the branch with the blade, then said sourly: 'Well, did you enjoy the snails?'

I held out a basket. 'I've brought you some dried figs, Mino, and a slice of pie ...'

'Did *they* send you?' he exclaimed, still distant, but his mouth watering as he looked at the basket.

'No, I had to escape from the Abbé,' I said hurriedly. 'They wanted to keep me doing lessons all the afternoon, so I shouldn't get in touch with you, but the old man fell asleep! Mother's worried you might fall and wanted a search made for you, but since Father hasn't seen you on the holm oak any more he says you've come down and are hiding away brooding over your misdeeds, and we're not to worry.'

'I never came down!' said my brother.

'Have you been in the Ondariva garden?'

'Yes, but always from one tree to another, without ever touching the ground!'

'Why?' I asked. It was the first time I heard him announce this rule of his, but he had said it as if it were already understood between us, almost as if he wanted to reassure me that he had not broken it; so I did not dare persist in my questions.

Instead of answering me, he said: 'You know, it'd take days and days to explore that garden of the Ondarivas! If you saw the trees! From the American forests!' Then he remembered he was angry with me and so should not enjoy telling me of his finds. He cut off, brusquely: 'Anyway I won't take you there. You can go round here with Battista, from now on, or the Cavalier!'

'No, Mino, do take me!' I exclaimed. 'You mustn't blame me

about the snails, they were foul, but I just couldn't bear their scolding!'

Cosimo was munching the tart. 'I'll try you out,' he said. 'You've got to show me you're on my side, not on theirs.'

'Tell me what you want me to do then.'

'Get me some ropes, long strong ones, as I'll have to tie myself to get over some places up here: then a rowlock, and screws and nails ... big ones ...'

'What d'you want to make? A crane?'

'We'll need to get a lot of things up, we'll see later; planks, bamboo ...'

'You want to make a hut in a tree! Where?'

'If needs be. We'll choose the place later. Meanwhile you can leave the things for me there in that hollow oak. Then I'll let down the basket by the rope and you can put whatever I need in it.'

'But why? You talk as if you're going on hiding for a long time ... Don't you think they'll forgive you?'

He turned round, red in the face. 'What do I care if they forgive me or not? And I'm not hiding; I'm not afraid of anyone! What about you, are you afraid of helping me?'

Though I now realized that my brother was refusing to come down for the time being, I pretended not to understand this, so as to make him declare himself and say for instance: 'Yes, I want to stay in the trees till tea-time, or dusk, or supper, or till it gets dark,' something in fact which would show a limit, a proportion to his protest. Instead of which he said nothing of the kind, and I began to feel alarmed.

Calls came from down below. It was our father shouting, 'Cosimo! Cosimo!' and then, realizing already that Cosimo would not answer him, 'Biagio! Biagio!' he was calling me.

'I'll go and see what they want. Then I'll come and tell you,' said I hurriedly. This eagerness to keep my brother informed also, I must admit, coincided with a hurry to get away for fear of being caught confabulating with him on top of the mulberry and having to share the punishment he was certain to get. But Cosimo did not seem to see this shadow of cowardice in my face; he let me go, not without shrugging his shoulders to show how little he cared about what our father might have to say to him.

When I got back he was still there; he had found a good place to settle, on a lopped branch, and was sitting with his chin on his knees and his arms tight round his shins.

'Mino! Mino!' I called, clambering breathlessly up. 'They've forgiven you! They're waiting for you! There's tea on the table, and Father and Mother already sitting down and putting out slices of cake on the plates! And there's a cream and chocolate cake, but not made by Battista, you know! She must have shut herself in her room, green with rage! They stroked my hair and said: Go and tell poor Mino we'll make it all up and not mention it again! Quick, let's go!'

Cosimo was chewing a leaf. He did not move.

'Hey,' said he, 'try to fetch me a blanket, will you, without anyone seeing, and bring it to me. It must be cold, up here at night.'

'You're not going to spend the night in the trees!'

He did not answer. Chin on knees, he went on chewing the leaf and looking ahead. I followed his look, which went straight to the wall of the Ondariva garden, just where the white magnolia flower showed, with an eagle wheeling beyond it.

So we got to evening. The servants came and went laying the table; in the dining-room the candles were already lit. Cosimo must have been able to see all this from the tree, and Baron Arminio turned to the shadows outside the window and called: 'If you want to stay up there, you'll starve!'

That evening we sat down to supper without Cosimo for the first time. He was astride a high branch of the holm oak, sideways, so that we could see only his dangling legs; and we could only just see those if we leant out of the window and peered, for the room was brightly lit and it was dark outside.

Even the Cavalier felt it his duty to lean out and say something, but as usual he could not manage to express any opinion on the matter. All he said was: 'Oooh ... Strong wood ... It'll last a hundred years ...' and then a few words in Turkish, perhaps the one for holm oak; he seemed, in fact, to be talking about the tree and not my brother.

Our sister Battista, on the other hand, showed a kind of envy for Cosimo, as if, used to keeping the family on tenterhooks with her crazy whims, she had now been outdone at her own game; and she was endlessly biting her nails (she would bite them without raising a finger to her mouth, but lowering her head and raising her elbow with her hand upside down).

The Generalessa was reminded of some soldiers who had been on sentry duty in the trees round a camp either in Slavonia or Pomerania, and how they had sighted the enemy, and so avoided an ambush. This memory, quite suddenly, brought her out of her maternal preoccupations and back to her favourite military atmosphere, and now, as if she had finally succeeded in understanding her son's behaviour, she became calmer, almost proud. No one agreed with her except the Abbé Fauchelefleur, who listened with grave assent to her warlike tale and the parallel she drew from it, for he would have grasped at any argument to persuade himself that what was happening was natural and so clear his mind of responsibility and worry.

After supper we went off to sleep early, not changing our timetable even that night. By now our parents had decided that they would not give Cosimo the satisfaction of taking notice of him and would wait for exhaustion, discomfort and the cold night air to bring him to his senses. Everyone went up to their rooms. The candlelight opened golden eyes in the chinks of the blinds. What cosiness, what memories of warmth must have seeped from that house so known and near, to my brother in the night chill! I leant from the window of our room and made out his shadow bent over a hollow of the holm oak, between branch and trunk, wrapped in the blanket, and – I think – bound round with the rope to avoid falling.

The moon rose late and shone above the branches. In their nests slept the swallows, huddled up like him. The night, the open, the silence of the park was broken by hundreds of rustlings and distant sounds, and cut through by the wind. At times there was a remote murmur; the sea. From my window I listened to this dispersed breathing and tried to imagine it heard without the protection of the familiar background of the house from which he was only a few yards away, with only the night all round; the only friendly object to hold the rough bark of a tree, scored with innumerable little tunnels where the larvae slept.

I went to bed but did not put out the candle. Perhaps that light at the window of his own room would keep him company. We shared a room, with two little bunks in it. I looked at his, untouched, and at the darkness out of the window where he was, and turned over between the sheets feeling perhaps for the first time the pleasure of being naked, with bare feet, in a warm white bed, and seeming to sense at the same time the discomfort he must be in, tied up there in his rough blanket, his legs buttoned in his gaiters, without being able to turn round, with bones aching. It is something which has never left me since that night, the sense of good luck in having a bed, clean sheets, a soft mattress! And as that went through my mind, which had been fixed for so long and so completely on the person we all had on our minds, I dozed off and so fell asleep.

4

I don't know if it's true, the story they tell in books, that once upon a time a monkey left Rome and skipped from tree to tree till it reached Spain without once touching the ground. The only place so thick with trees in my day was the whole length, from end to end, of the gulf of Ombrosa and its valley right up to the mountain crests; the area was famous everywhere.

Nowadays, these parts are very different. It was when the French came that people began cutting the woods as if they were meadows that are scythed every year and grow again. They have never grown again. At first we thought it was something to do with the war, with Napoleon, with the period; instead of which it went on. Now the hillsides are so bare that it gives us a shock when we look at them, we who knew them before.

Anyway, in those days wherever one went there were always leaves and branches between us and sky. The only trees growing near the ground were the lemons, but even among them rose the twisted shapes of fig trees, arching their domes of heavy leaves over the orchards up towards the hills: there were the brown boughs of the cherry, the tender quince, peach, almond or young pear, the great plum, and sorb apples and carobs too, with an occasional mulberry or knobbly walnut. Where the orchards ended the olive groves began, silvery grey, a cloud anchored halfway up the hillsides. In the background, crouching between the port below and the rock above, was the village; and there, too, the roofs were feathery with the tops of trees: plane trees, and oaks too, haughty and detached, rioting – an orderly riot – where the nobles had built their villas and walled in their parks.

Above the olives began the woods. At one time the pines must have dominated the whole bay, for their needles and feathers still grew here and there down the slopes as far as the beaches, as did the larches too. The oaks then were thicker than they seem to me today, for they were the first, most valuable victims. Higher up, the pines gave way to chestnuts, which went on and on up the mountainsides as far as the eye could reach. This was the world of sap amid which we lived, we inhabitants of Ombrosa, almost without our noticing it.

The first to give any real thought to all this was Cosimo. He realized that, as the trees were so thick, he could move for several miles by passing from one branch to another, without ever needing to descend to earth. Sometimes a patch of bare ground forced him to make long detours, but he soon got to know all the necessary routes and came to measure distances by quite different estimates than ours, bearing always in mind the twisted trail he had to take over the branches. And where not even a jump would carry him on to the nearest branch, he began to use various tricks of his own: but all that I will describe later; so far we have only reached that first dawn when he woke up to find himself amid fluttering swallows on top of a holm oak, soaked in cold dew, sneezing, with bones aching, ants crawling over his legs and arms, and set out happily to explore the new world.

He reached the last tree of the park, a plane tree. Below him the valley swept away under a sky of wispy clouds and smoke curling up from the slate roofs of cottages hiding behind rocks like piles of stones; the figs and cherries formed another sky of leaves; lower down thrust out the grizzled branches of plums and peaches; everything was clear and sharp, even the grass, blade by blade, all except the soil with its crawling pumpkin leaves or dotted lettuces or fuzz of crops: it was the same on both sides of the V in which the valley opened, a high funnel over the sea.

Through this landscape was rippling a kind of wave, not visible or even, except now and then, audible, though what was gave a sense of disquiet; a sudden sharp cry, and then the faint crash of something falling and perhaps even the crack of a breaking branch, and more cries, different ones this time, of angry voices, converging on the place where the cry had come from before. Then nothing, a sense of nothingness, as if things were happening in a completely different part; and in fact the voices and sounds now began again but seemed to be coming from one or other side of the valley, always from where the jagged little leaves of the cherry trees were moving in the wind. And so Cosimo, with a part of his mind meandering on its own – while another part seemed to know and understand it all beforehand – found the thought crossing his mind: cherry trees talk.

He began moving towards the nearest cherry tree, or row, rather, of cherry trees, tall, of superb leafy green, thick with black cherries; but my brother had not yet trained his eye to distinguish at once exactly what was and what was not on branches. He paused; the sounds of before had gone. He was on the lowest boughs, and felt all the cherries above weighing down on him; he could not have explained why but they seemed to be converging on him, as if, in fact, he were on a tree with eyes instead of cherries.

Cosimo raised his face and an over-ripe cherry fell on his forehead with a plop! He strained his eyes to look up against the sun (which was growing stronger), and saw that the tree he was on and the ones nearby were full of perching little boys.

When they realized that they had been seen they were no longer silent, and called to each other in sharp though muted voices something that sounded like: 'Just look how he's dressed!' Then, parting the leaves in front of them, each climbed down from the branch he was on to one lower, towards the boy wearing the tricorne. They were bare-headed or in ragged straw hats, and some had their heads wrapped in sacking; they wore torn shirts and breeches; such of their feet as were not bare had strips of rag, and one or two of them had wooden clogs hung round their necks, taken off so as to climb better; they were the great band of fruit thieves from which Cosimo and I – in obedience to parental orders – had always kept as far away as possible. That morning, though, my brother seemed to be on the look-out for them, though with no very clear idea of what he expected from the meeting.

He stood still and waited as they climbed down towards him, throwing out, in strident whispers, remarks like 'What's he think he's up to, ay?' and spitting out an occasional cherry stone at him or flinging a worm or a blackbird's beak with a little swirl as if slinging a stone.

'Uuuh!' they exclaimed all of a sudden. They had seen the rapier dangling behind him. 'D'you see what he's got?' And more laughter. 'The ironmonger . . .'

Then they stopped and stifled their laughter as if something wildly funny was about to happen; two of the little urchins had very quietly moved on to a branch right above Cosimo and were lowering the top of an open sack down over his head (one of the filthy sacks that they must have used for their booty, and which when empty they arranged over their heads and shoulders like hoods). In a short time my brother would have found himself trussed into a sack without even knowing how, then tied up like a sausage so they could hit him to their heart's content.

Cosimo sensed the danger, or perhaps did not sense anything. Knowing they were jeering at his rapier, he drew it as a point of honour. As he brandished it, the blade grazed the sack, which with a twist he tore from the hands of the two little thieves and flung away.

It was a good move. The others gave an 'Oh!' of both disappointment and surprise, and began yelling insults in dialect at the two who had let their sack be taken: *'Cuiasse! Belinùi!'*

But Cosimo had no time to congratulate himself on his success. For suddenly there broke out another commotion, this time from the earth below; barking dogs, showers of stones and yells of 'You won't get away this time, you thieving little swine!'; and up came the tops of pitchforks. The urchins on the branches yanked up legs and elbows and hugged themselves. All that noise round Cosimo had aroused the fruit growers who had been on the watch.

It was an attack prepared in force. Tired of having their fruit stolen as it ripened, many of the small landowners and tenant farmers of the valley had banded together; for the only answer to the little boys' tactics of setting on an orchard all together, sacking and stripping it, then making off in the opposite direction, was to use similar tactics themselves; that is all to keep watch on an orchard where the boys were bound to come sooner or later, and catch them red-handed. Now the unmuzzled dogs were baying and champing with bared teeth at the foot of the cherry trees, while hay forks were brandished in the air. Three or four of the little thieves jumped to the ground just in time to have their backs pricked by the tridents and their bottoms bitten by the dogs, and rushed off screaming and lurching down the rows of vines. No more dared go down: they stayed quivering where they were, and Cosimo too. Then the fruit-growers began setting ladders against the trees and climbing up, preceded by points of pitchforks.

It took Cosimo some minutes to realize that there was no reason at all for him to be terrified because the band of urchins was, just as there was no reason at all for him to think that they were crafty and he wasn't. The fact that they were sitting still like bemused idiots was proof enough; why didn't they escape on to the trees around? My brother had got there by a certain route and so could make off by the same route; he pulled his tricorne down on his head, looked round for the branch which he had used as a bridge, passed from the last cherry tree on to a carob, then dangled from the carob, dropped on to a plum tree, and so away. The others, seeing him moving on the branches as if he were in the village square, realized that they must follow close behind him or never find his route again, and they followed his tortuous itinerary in silence, on all fours. Meanwhile he had got on to a fig tree, skirted a field, and swung down on a peach tree with such slender branches that his flock had to pass over it one at a time. The peach was just used to get a grip on the twisted trunk of an olive sprouting out of a wall; from the olive they jumped on to an oak stretching out a thick arm over the stream, and so reached the trees on the other side.

The men with pitchforks, who thought they had caught the fruit thieves at last, saw them hopping away through the air like birds. They followed, running among the barking dogs, but had to get round the field, then over the wall, then across the stream at a point where there was no bridge, lost time finding a ford, and saw the urchins running away in the distance.

They ran like human beings, with their feet on the ground. On the branches only my brother remained. 'Where's that pole-jumper with the gaiters got to?' they asked each other, not seeing him ahead still. They looked up: there he was clambering about the olives. 'Hey you, come down, we've shaken 'em off now!' But instead of coming down, he went leaping from bough to bough, from olive to olive, till he vanished from sight among the close-knit silvery leaves.

The band of little vagabonds, with sacks on their heads and canes in their hands, were now assaulting some cherry trees at the bottom of the valley. They were working methodically, stripping branch after branch, when, on the top of the highest tree, squatting with his legs crossed, flicking down bunches of cherries and popping them in the tricorne on his lap, who should they see but the boy with the gaiters! 'Hey, you, where've you come from?' they asked arrogantly. But they weren't too pleased, as he seemed to have come to steal their cherries.

My brother was now taking the cherries one by one from his tricorne and putting them in his mouth as if they were sweets. Then he would spit out the stones with a flick of the lips, taking care they did not mark his waistcoat.

'This cake-eater,' said one, 'what's he leaving for us? What's he come to bother us for? Why doesn't he go and eat the cherries in his own garden?' But they were a little abashed, since seeing that he was smarter at getting about the trees than any of them.

'Among cake-eaters,' said another, 'a smart one does crop up now and again by mistake; take the Sinforosa for instance ...'

At this mysterious name Cosimo pricked up his ears and, he did not know why, blushed.

'The Sinforosa let us down!' said another.

'But she was smart, she was, for a cake-eater herself, and this morning if she'd been there to sound her horn they wouldn't have caught us.'

'Even cake-eaters can come with us, of course, if they're on our side!'

(Cosimo now understood that 'cake-eater' meant an inhabitant of a villa, a noble, or at any rate someone of rank.)

'Listen you,' said one to him, 'let's get this straight; if you want to come with us, you pick the stuff with us and you teach us all the tricks you know.'

'And you let us into your father's orchards,' said another. 'They once shot at me there!'

Cosimo listened to them, half-absorbed in his own thoughts. Then he said: 'Tell me, who is the Sinforosa?'

Then all the ragamuffins scattered among the branches burst into roars and roars of laughter, so that one nearly fell off the cherry tree, and one flung himself back and held on to the branch by his legs, and another let himself dangle by his hands, shrieking with laughter all the time.

Such a row did they make that their pursuers were on their

heels again. In fact they must have been right underneath, the men and the dogs, for a loud barking arose and then up came the pitchforks again. Only this time, made canny by their recent set-back, they first occupied the trees around and climbed up them with ladders, and from there surrounded the band with tridents and rakes. On the ground the dogs, with all their men scattered about on trees, did not know at first where to make for and wandered round barking away with muzzles in the air. So the little thieves were able to jump quickly to the ground and run away in different directions among the confused dogs, and though one or two got a bite on a calf or a blow from a stone, most of them got away safe and sound.

On the tree remained Cosimo. 'Come down!' shouted the others as they made off. 'What are you doing? Sleeping? Jump down while it's clear!' But he gripped the branch with his knees and drew his rapier. From nearby trees the fruit-growers were thrusting out pitchforks tied on sticks to reach him, and Cosimo kept them off by brandishing his sword, till one got right at his chest and pinned him to the trunk.

'Stop!' called a voice, 'it's the young Baron of Piovasco! What are you doing up there, sir? How on earth did you get mixed up with that rabble?'

Cosimo recognized one of our father's labourers, Giuà della Vasca.

The pitchforks withdrew. Many of the group took off their hats. My brother also raised his tricorne with two fingers, and bowed.

'Hey, you down there, tie up the dogs!' shouted they. 'Let him get down! You can come down, sir, but be careful, it's a high tree! Wait a moment, we'll put up a ladder! Then I'll take him back home!'

'No, thank you, thank you,' said my brother. 'Don't put yourself out, I know the way, I know the way on my own!'

He vanished behind the trunk and reappeared on another branch, twirled round the trunk and reappeared on a branch higher up, vanished behind this and then only his feet were visible on an even higher branch, as there were thick leaves above; and then the feet jumped, and nothing more was seen.

'Where's he gone to?' said the men to each other, not knowing where to look, up or down.

'There he is!' He was at the top of another tree farther away, then vanished again.

'There he is!' He was at the top of still another tree, swaying as if in the wind, and jumping.

'He's fallen! No! There he is!' All that could be seen, above the waving green, was his tricorne and queue.

'What sort of master have you got?' the others asked Giuà della Vasca. 'A man or a wild animal? Or is he the devil in person?'

Giuà della Vasca was gasping. He crossed himself.

A song could be heard from Cosimo, a kind of symphonic call: 'Oh Sin-for-ro-saaa!'

5

The Sinforosa; gradually Cosimo picked up a lot about this personage from the chatter of the band. It was a name they had given to a little girl from one of the villas, who went about on a small white pony, had made friends with them and protected them for a time and even, dominating as she was, commanded them. She would ride the lanes and paths on her pony, tell them when she saw ripe fruit in an unguarded orchard, then follow their attack from horseback like an officer. Round her neck she wore a hunting horn, and while they were sacking the almond and pear trees she would be galloping up and down slopes from which she could see over the whole countryside, blowing her horn as soon as she noticed any suspicious movements which might mean discovery. At the sound, the urchins would jump off the trees and hide: so while the little girl was with them they had never once been surprised.

What happened afterwards was more difficult to understand; the Sinforosa's 'betrayal' seemed to have been twofold: partly her having invited them into her own garden to eat fruit and then getting them beaten up by her servants; and then her having made a favourite of one of them, a certain Bel-Lorè – who was still jeered at for it – and of another, called Ugasso, at the same time, and set them against each other; and later it transpired that the urchins had been beaten by her servants not when they were stealing fruit but after her dismissal of both rival swains, who had then allied against her; there was also talk of some cakes she had often promised and which were made with castor oil, when she finally gave them, so that they had tummy-aches for a week afterwards. One of these episodes or kind of episodes or all these episodes together had caused a break between the Sinforosa and the band, and now they talked of her with a bitterness mingled, however, with regret.

Cosimo listened eagerly to these stories, nodding as if every detail fitted into a picture he knew already, and finally decided to ask: 'But which villa does she come from, the Sinforosa?'

'What, you mean you don't know her? You're neighbours! The Sinforosa from the Ondariva villa!'

Even without this confirmation Cosimo had felt sure that the friend of the urchins was Viola, the girl of the swing. It was – I think – because she had said she knew all the fruit thieves around, that he had first begun looking out for the band. And yet from then on the urge inside him, vague though it still was, grew sharper. At one moment he found himself longing to lead the band in a raid on the Ondariva orchards, then to offer her his services against them (after, perhaps, inciting them to molest her so as to be able to defend her), then to do some acts of valour which would reach her ears indirectly. With all these ideas buzzing in his head he followed the band more and more distractedly; and when they left the trees and he was alone a veil of sadness would pass over his face, like a cloud over the sun.

Then he would suddenly jump up and, agile as a cat,

scramble over branches and across orchards and gardens, humming some tense little song between his teeth, his eyes set as if seeing nothing, balancing by instinct just like a cat.

We saw him pass various times, all absorbed, over the branches of our garden. 'There he is!' we would suddenly shout, for whatever we did he was still in the forefront of our minds, and we used to count the hours and days he had been up on the trees, and our father would say, 'He's mad! He has a devil in him!' and then attack the Abbé Fauchelefleur; 'The only thing is to exorcise him! What are you waiting for, you. I tell you, *mon Abbé*, what are you doing there with your hands crossed? He's got the devil in him, don't you realize, *sacré nom de Dieu!*'

The word 'devil' seemed to wake a precise chain of thought in the Abbé's mind; he shook himself out of his lethargy all of a sudden and launched into a most complicated theological discourse on how the presence of the devil should be properly understood, from which it was not clear if he was contradicting my father or just generalizing. He would make no pronouncement, in fact, on whether a relationship between the devil and my brother was to be considered possible or excluded *a priori*.

The Baron became impatient, the Abbé lost the thread, I was already bored. With our mother, on the other hand, the state of maternal anxiety, of fluid emotion, had consolidated, as every emotion tended to with her, into practical decisions and a search for concrete ways and means, as the preoccupations of a general should. She had found a rustic telescope, a long one, with a tripod; she would put her eye to it and so spend hours on the terrace of the villa continually regulating the lenses to keep the boy in focus among the leaves, even when we could have sworn he was out of range.

'Can you still see him?' our father would ask from the garden, where he was pacing up and down under the trees without ever succeeding in laying eyes on Cosimo, except when the boy was right above his head. The Generalessa would signal down that she could, and that we mustn't disturb her, as if she were following troops' movements from a height. Sometimes she obviously did not see him at all, but she had got a fixed idea, I don't know how, that he must appear in a given place and not elsewhere, and there she kept her telescope trained. Every now and again she must have admitted to herself that she had made a mistake; and then she would take her eye from the lenses and begin to examine a surveyor's map which she held open on her knees, with one hand to her mouth in a thoughtful attitude and another following the hieroglyphics on the map, until she had decided on the spot which her son must have reached, plotted the angles, and pointed her telescope on some treetop in that leafy sea, slowly moving the lenses into focus; and then from the gentle smile on her lips we would know she had seen him, that he was really there!

Next, she would take up some coloured flags which she had on a stool, and wave one and then the other in decisive, rhythmic movements, like signals. (This slightly annoyed me as I did not know that our mother had those flags and knew how to manage them, and I thought how lovely it would have been if she had taught us to play at flag-signalling before, when we were both small; but our mother never played and now it was too late.)

I must say, though, that in spite of all her tools of war, she remained a mother, with her heart in her mouth, and her handkerchief screwed in her hand; if asked, she might have said that she found acting the general a relief, or that working off her apprehensions as a general rather than a simple mother soothed her distress; for she was a sensitive woman, whose sole defence was that military style inherited from her von Kurtewitz forebears.

There she was, waving one of her flags and looking through her telescope, when suddenly her face lit up and she laughed. We realized that Cosimo had answered. How I don't know, by a wave of the hat perhaps, or a shape at a bough. Certainly from that moment our mother changed; she lost her apprehensions, and if her destiny as a mother was different from others, with a son so strange and lost to normal affections, she came to accept this strangeness of Cosimo's before any of the rest of us, as if placated by those greetings which from then onwards he would send her unexpectedly every now and again, by their silent exchange.

The strange thing was that our mother never deluded herself that Cosimo, now he had sent her a greeting, was thinking of ending his escape and returning among us. Our father, on the other hand, lived perpetually in this hope and at the slightest news about Cosimo would repeat: 'Ah yes? You've seen him? He's coming back?' But our mother, the most removed from Cosimo in a way, seemed the only one who managed to accept him as he was, perhaps because she did not try to give herself any explanation.

But let us return to that day. Peeping from behind our mother's skirts now appeared Battista, who very rarely went outside; holding up a plate with some soup in it and raising a spoon she cooed: 'Cosimo ... D'you want any?' But she got a slap from our father and went back indoors. Who knows what monstrous potage she had prepared! Our brother had vanished.

I yearned to follow him, above all now that I knew he was taking part in the escapades of the band of little ruffians, and to me he seemed to have opened the doors of a new kingdom, one to be looked at no longer with alarm and mistrust but with shared enthusiasm. I was constantly on the move between the terrace and a high dormer-window from which I could look over the tree tops, and from there, more with the ear than the eye, I would follow the scamperings of the band through the orchards, watch the tops of the cherry trees quiver, and every now and again a hand appear plucking and picking, a tousled or hooded head, and among the voices hear Cosimo's and ask myself: 'But how on earth did you get over there? You were in the park just a moment ago. Are you quicker than a lizard?'

They were on the red plum trees above the Upper Pool, I remember, when they heard the horn. I heard it too but took no notice, not knowing what it was. But they did! My brother told me that they stood rooted to the spot, and in their astonishment at hearing the horn again seemed to forget it was a signal of alarm: they just asked each other if they'd heard aright, if it was the Sinforosa again, riding round on her pony

to warn them of danger. Suddenly they scattered from the
orchard, not in a rush to escape, but to look for her and reach
her.

Only Cosimo remained, his face red as fire. But as soon as he
saw the urchins running and realized they were running to her,
he began to leap from branch to branch himself, risking his neck
at every move.

Viola was on a curving slope of the lane, sitting still, one hand
with the reins on the pony's crupper, the other brandishing a
small whip. As she looked down on the little boys she brought
the point of the whip to her mouth and began chewing it. Her
dress was blue, the horn gilt and hanging on her neck by a
chain. The boys had all stopped together and were also chewing, at plums or fingers or scabs on their hands and arms, or
corners of sacking. And slowly from their chewing mouths, as if
overcoming some inner disquiet and not from any real feeling,
almost as if wanting to be contradicted, they began to mouth
phrases under their breaths, in rhythm, like a song: 'What have
you ... come to do ... Sinforosa ... back you go ... now you
are ... our friend no more ... ah, ah, ah ... ah, betrayer.'

Above, the branches burst apart and there, in a high fig tree
appeared the head of Cosimo, panting, surrounded by leaves.
From down below, with that little whip in her hand, she swept
him and the others with the same look. Cosimo did not budge;
still with his tongue out he stuttered: 'D'you know I've never
been down from the trees since then?'

Undertakings such as these should be left mute and mysterious; once declared or boasted about they are apt to seem
pointless and even petty. So my brother had scarcely pronounced those words when he wished he had not said them; it
did not seem to matter any more, and he even found himself
wanting to come down and have done with the whole business.
All the more when Viola slowly took her whip out of her
mouth and said, softly:

'*Haven't* you now? You clever little thing!'

From the flea-ridden urchins came rumbles of laughter, then
their mouths opened and they broke into roars and screams till
their bellies ached, and Cosimo went into such a paroxysm of

rage on the fig tree that the brittle wood gave way, and a branch cracked under his feet. Cosimo fell like a stone.

He fell with his arms wide open, making no effort to stop himself. That was the only time, to tell the truth, during his whole life in the trees of this world, that he had neither will nor instinct to grip hold of something. But a corner of his coat caught and stuck on a low branch; Cosimo found himself hanging in the air with his head down, a foot or so from the ground.

The blood in his head came from the same force which was making him blush scarlet. And his first thought on turning his eyes up and catching sight the wrong way round of the screaming boys, who were now seized by a general frenzy of somersaulting in which one by one they appeared right side up as if gripping the ground above an abyss, and the little blonde girl prancing up and down on her beribboned little pony, his one thought was that it was the first time he had ever actually spoken of being on the trees and that it would also be the last.

With a jerk he drew himself back on to the branch and got astride it. Viola had now calmed down her pony and did not seem to have noticed what had been happening. Cosimo immediately forgot his confusion. The girl brought the horn to her lips and blew the deep call of alarm. At the sound the urchins (who – as Cosimo commented later – seemed to be sent by Viola's presence into a wild state of agitation, like hares under a full moon) went rushing off in flight. They let themselves be drawn off like that, as if by instinct, though realizing she had done it as a game and doing it as a game themselves, running down the slope imitating the call of the horn with her galloping in front on her short-legged pony.

They were blundering along so blindly that every now and again they found her no longer ahead. Eventually she shook them off by galloping away from the path, and left them behind. Where was she going? Along she galloped through the olive groves, dropping down the valley in gradually broadening slopes; she looked for the tree on which Cosimo was perched at that moment, galloped right round it, and was off again. A moment later there she was at the foot of another olive, with my brother's head appearing above the leaves. And so, in lines as twisted as the branches of the olives themselves, down the valley they went together.

When the little thieves noticed, and saw how the two of them were linked from branch to saddle, they all began whistling together, a spiteful whistle of derision; and whistling louder and louder, went off towards their village of Porta Capperi.

The girl and my brother remained chasing each other alone among the olives, but Cosimo was mortified to notice that when the rabble vanished Viola's enjoyment of the game seemed to fade and boredom to set in. The suspicion came to him that she was doing all this on purpose to anger the others, and at the same time the hope came that she would continue even if only to anger him; certainly she seemed to need the anger of others in order to make herself feel more precious. (All things scarcely more than sensed by the boy Cosimo then; in reality I imagine he was scrambling over the rough barks without realizing anything much, like an owl.)

Suddenly, round a bluff they were assailed by a sharp little hail of gravel. The girl put her head down behind the pony's neck for protection and made off; my brother, in full view, up on the turn of a branch, remained under fire. But the little stones reached him too glancingly up there to hurt much, except for one or two on the forehead and ears. The little ruffians whistled and laughed, shouting: 'Sin-fo-ro-sa is a bitch,' as they ran away.

The urchins reached the village, Porta Capperi, with its green cascades of caper plants down the walls. From the hovels around came the cry of mothers. But the mothers shouted at their children not to get them home, but for coming home to supper instead of finding themselves something to eat elsewhere. Around Porta Capperi, in huts and wattle-shacks, broken-down carts, and tents, were huddled the poorest folk of Ombrosa, so poor that they were kept outside the town gates and away from the fields, people who had drifted there from distant places from which they had been thrust by the famine and poverty on the increase in every State. It was dusk, and dishevelled women with babies at their breasts were fanning at smoky stoves; beggars lying in the open were bandaging their

sores, and others playing at dice with raucous shouts. The gang
of fruit-thieves now scattered among the squabbles and smoke
of frying, got a slapping from their mothers, scuffled among
themselves in the dust. And already their rags had taken on
the colour of all the other rags, and their birdlike gaiety was
muted into that dense rubbish-heap of humanity. So that, on
the appearance of the fair girl at the gallop and of Cosimo on
the trees nearby, they just raised intimidated eyes, then slunk
off and tried to lose themselves amid the dust and fire smoke, as
if between them a wall had suddenly gone up.

For the two of them all this was just a moment, a glance. Then
Viola left behind her the smoke from the shacks mingling with
the evening shades and the cries of women and children, to
gallop among the pines on the beach.

Beyond was the sea. A faint clatter of stones. It was dark. The
clatter became a hammer: the pony racing along struck sparks
against the pebbles. From the low twisted branches of a pine
tree my brother looked at the clear-cut shadow of the fair girl
cross the beach. From the black sea rose a wave with a faint
crest, it curled higher, advanced all white, broke and grazed
the shadow of the horse and girl racing at full speed; Cosimo on
the pine tree found his face wet with salty spray.

6

Those first days of Cosimo's on the trees were without aim or
purpose, and were dominated entirely by the desire to know
and possess his new kingdom. He would have liked to explore
it to its extreme limits, to study all the possibilities it offered
him, to discover it plant by plant and branch by branch. I say,

he would have liked to, but in fact we found him continuously returning above our heads, with the busy quick movements of a wild animal, which always seems, even when squatting and still, to be on the point of jumping away.

Why did he return to our park? Seeing him twisting about on a plane tree or an ilex within the range of our mother's telescope, one would have said that the impulse urging him, his dominating passion, was always to scare us off, make us worried or angry. (I say us, because I had not yet managed to understand how his mind was working; when he needed something, the alliance with me could never, it seemed, be put in doubt; at other times he went over my head as if he had not even seen me.)

But really he was only passing by us. It was the wall of the magnolia tree which attracted him, it was there that we saw him vanish again and again, even when the fair little girl could not have been up or when the group of governesses and aunts had made her go to bed. In the Ondariva gardens the branches spread out like the tentacles of extraordinary animals, and the plants on the ground opened up stars of fretted leaves with the green skins of reptiles, and waved feathery yellow bamboos with a rustle like paper. From the highest tree Cosimo, in his yearning to enjoy to the utmost the different greens and different light and different silence, would drop his head upside down, so that the garden became a forest, a forest not of this earth but a new world.

Then Viola appeared. Cosimo would see her suddenly giving herself a push on the swing, or in the saddle of the pony, or hear from the end of the garden the deep note of the hunting horn.

The Marchese and Marchesa of Ondariva had never really worried about their daughter's wanderings. When she was about on foot, she had all her aunts following behind; as soon as she mounted the saddle she was free as air, for the aunts did not go out riding and could not see where she went. And her intimacy with those urchins was too inconceivable even to cross their minds. But they had immediately noticed the little baron clambering about the branches and were on the lookout for him, though with a certain air of superior contempt.

Our father, on the other hand, linked his bitterness at Cosimo's disobedience to his aversion of the Ondarivas, almost as if wanting to blame them, as if it were they who were attracting his son into their garden, entertaining him, and encouraging him in that rebellious game of his. Suddenly he decided to organize a round-up to capture Cosimo, not on our land, but while actually in the Ondariva gardens. Almost as if to underline his aggressive intentions towards our neighbours, he decided not to lead the round-up himself (this would have meant presenting himself personally to the Ondarivas and asking them to restore his son – which, however unjustified, would have been a dignified link between noblemen), but to send a group of servitors under the orders of the Cavalier Enea Silvio Carrega.

Armed with ladders and ropes these came to the gates of the Ondariva villa. The Cavalier fluttered about in robe and skullcap, excusing himself and asking if they could enter. At first the Ondariva servants thought that ours had come about certain trailing plants which grew over into their garden; then, at the Cavalier's confused phrases, 'We want to catch ... to catch ...' as he tacked to and fro looking up among the branches, they asked, 'But what have you lost, a parrot?'

'The son, the eldest son, the heir,' said the Cavalier hurriedly, putting a ladder against an Indian chestnut and beginning to climb up it himself. Among the branches was Cosimo, dangling his legs with a carefree air. Viola, just as carefree, was bowling a hoop along the paths. The servants offered the Cavalier ropes with which to capture my brother, how none of them exactly knew. But Cosimo, before the Cavalier had got halfway up the ladder, was already on top of another tree. The Cavalier had the ladder moved, and the same thing happened four or five times, each time with the Cavalier ruining a bush and Cosimo passing in a couple of jumps on to a nearby tree. Suddenly Viola was seen being surrounded by aunts and governesses, then led into the house and shut in so as not to be present at this scene. Cosimo broke off a branch, brandished it in both hands and swished it in the air.

'But why can't you go into your own wide park to conduct this hunt, my dear sirs?' asked the Marchese of Ondariva, appearing solemnly on the flight of steps from the villa, in dressing-gown and skull-cap, which made him look strangely like the Cavalier. 'I ask the whole family of Piovasco di Rondò!' And he made a wide circular gesture which embraced the young baron on the tree, his illegitimate uncle, our servants, and everything of ours beyond the wall.

At this point Enea Silvio Carrega changed his tone. He trotted up to the Marchese and, fluttering about as if nothing was happening, began to talk to him about the fountains in the basin nearby and how he had got the idea of a much higher and more effective jet which would also serve, by changing a rosette, to water the lawns. This was a new proof of our illegitimate uncle's unpredictable and untrustworthy nature; he had been sent there by the Baron with a definite mandate, and with orders to treat the neighbours firmly; why, then, start a friendly chat with the Marchese as if wanting to ingratiate himself? The Cavalier only seemed to show talents as a conversationalist when it happened to suit him, and at the very moment when people were counting on his stubbornness of character. The extraordinary thing was that the Marchese listened to him, began asking him questions and eventually took him off to examine all the fountains and jets, both of them were dressed the same, both in long robes, both so much the same height that they might have been mistaken for each other, with behind them walking all our servants and theirs, some carrying ladders, which they did not know what to do with.

Meanwhile Cosimo was climbing undisturbed on to the trees near the windows of the villa, trying to find beyond the curtains the room in which Viola had been shut. He discovered it, finally, and threw a twig against the pane.

The window opened and the face of the little blonde girl appeared.

'It's all your fault I am locked in here,' she said, and shut the window again, pulling the curtain.

*

When my brother was taken by one of his wild moods, it really was something to worry about. We saw him running (if the word running has any sense when referring not to the earth's surface but to a series of irregular supports at different heights, with empty air between) and any moment it seemed he might lose his footing and fall, which never happened. He jumped, moved with rapid little steps on a sloping branch, leant over and suddenly swung on to a higher branch, and in four or five of these precarious zigzags vanished from sight.

Where did he go? That time he ran and ran, from ilex to olive to beech, till he was in the wood. There he paused, panting. Under him spread a field. A slight breeze was moving in a wave over the thick tufts of grass, with subtle shades of green. Over it flew those impalpable feathery balls of flowers called *Saffioni*. In the middle stood an isolated pine tree, unreachable, with oblong cones. Tree-creepers, swift little birds with stippled purple wings, were perching on the thick clusters of pine needles, some askew with their tails up and their beaks down, pecking at worms and pine nuts.

That urge to enter into a difficult element which had taken my brother on to the trees was still working inside him unsatisfied, making him long for a more intimate link, a relationship which would bind him to each leaf and chip and tuft and twig. It was the love which the hunter has for living things and which he can only express by aiming his gun at them; Cosimo could not yet recognize it and was trying to satisfy it by probing deeper.

The wood was thick and impracticable. Cosimo had to open his way through by hacking with his rapier, and gradually he forgot his fixation, all taken up as he was by the practical problems to be faced one by one, and by a fear (which he did not want to recognize but which was there) of drawing too far away from familiar places. So, clearing his way on through the thick greenery, he reached a point where he saw two yellow eyes fixed on him between the leaves right ahead. Cosimo brought up his rapier, moved a branch aside and let it fall slowly back into place. Then he heaved a sigh of relief, and laughed at the fear he had felt; he had seen who those yellow eyes belonged to, a cat.

But the sight of the cat, just glimpsed in moving the branch, stuck in his mind, and a moment later Cosimo found himself trembling with fear again. For that cat, outwardly in every way the same as every other cat, was a terrible and terrifying cat, enough to make one scream just to look at. It was difficult to say exactly what was so terrifying about it; it was a kind of tabby, bigger than any other tabby, but that did not mean anything; it was terrible with its straight whiskers like hedgehogs' quills, with the breath which one could sense almost more by sight than by ear coming from between a double row of teeth sharp as claws; its tautly pricked up ears were two flames of tension, covered by deceptively soft hair; the fur, all standing on end, swelled around the neck in a yellow ring from which spread stripes quivering over its flanks as if it were being stroked; the neck in a position so unnatural it seemed impossible to hold: all this that Cosimo had caught sight of in the second before he dropped the branch back to its proper place was in addition to what he had not had time to see but could imagine; the great tufts of hair around the paws masking the tearing strength of the claws, ready to spring at him; and what he could still see; the yellow irises with the rolling black pupils fixed on him between the leaves; and what he heard; the breathing growing heavier and hoarser; it all made him realize that he was face to face with the savagest wildcat in the woods.

All the twitter and flutter of the woods were silent. And then it leapt, the wildcat, but not at the boy, an almost vertical leap which astounded more than terrified Cosimo. The terror came afterwards, at seeing the animal on a branch right above his head. It was there, crouching, he could see the belly with its long whitish fur, the tense paws with their claws in the wood, the arched back. 'Fff . . . fff . . .' it was hissing, ready to drop right on him. Cosimo, with a quick manoeuvre that was purely in-stinctive, moved on to a lower branch. 'Fff . . . fff . . .' hissed the wildcat, and at each of the fff's it jumped, to one side and another, and was on a branch above Cosimo again. My brother repeated his manoeuvre, but found himself astride the lowest branch of the tree. The jump to the ground beneath was of some height, but not so high that he would not have preferred to jump down rather than wait for what the animal would do, as soon as it had stopped making that ominous mixture of wheeze and growl.

Cosimo raised a leg, on the very point of jumping to the ground, but two instincts in him clashed – the natural one to save himself and the stubborn one never to leave the trees at any cost – and he tightened his legs and knees on the branch; the cat thought this, with the boy wavering, was the moment to spring; it came down at him with fur on end, claws out, and that wheeze: Cosimo could think of nothing better than shut his eyes and bring up his rapier, a stupid move which the cat easily avoided; then it was on him, sure of bearing him down with it under its claws. One caught Cosimo on the cheek, but instead of falling, tied as he was to the branch by the knees, he swung round upside down. Quite the opposite to what the cat was expecting, who found itself thrown out of balance, and falling itself. It tried to save itself by plunging its claws into the branch, and to do so had to twist round in the air; an instant, but enough for Cosimo, in a sudden victorious thrust, to plunge his rapier deep into its belly.

He was saved, covered in blood, with the wild beast stuck on his rapier as on a spit, and cheek torn from under the eye to the chin by a triple slash. He was screaming with pain and victory and frenziedly clinging to the branch, to the rapier, to the body of the cat, in that desperate moment which comes to one who wins for the first time and realizes the agony of victory, realizes too that now he is bound to continue on the road he has chosen and will not be granted any evasion through failure.

So I saw him arriving over the trees, covered with blood down to his waistcoat, his queue in disorder under the battered tricorne, holding by the neck that dead wildcat which now seemed just a cat like any other.

I ran to the Generalessa on the terrace. 'Lady mother,' I shouted, 'he's wounded!'

'*Was?* Wounded? How?' She was already pointing her telescope.

'Wounded so he looks wounded!' I exclaimed, and the Generalessa seemed to understand my definition, for following him with the telescope as he came jumping on quicker than ever, she said: *'Es ist wahr.'*

At once she began to prepare lint and bandages and balsams as if for first aid to a battalion, and handed them all over for me to take to him, without the hope even occurring to her that he might decide to return home for doctoring. I ran into the park with the parcel of bandages and stood waiting under the last mulberry tree by the wall of the Ondarivas, for he had already vanished up the magnolia.

He made a triumphant appearance in the Ondariva garden with the dead animal in his hands. And what should he see in the space in front of the villa? A coach ready to leave, with servants loading luggage on to racks, and, amid a cluster of severe, black-robed governesses and aunts, Viola in travelling-dress embracing the Marchese and Marchesa.

'Viola!' he shouted, raising the cat by its neck, 'where are you going?'

All the people round the coach raised their eyes to the branches, and at the sight of him, lacerated, bleeding, with that mad air and that dead animal in his hands, began making gestures of disgust: *'Ici de nouveau! Et arrangé de cette façon!'* And as if swept by a sudden gust of rage all the aunts began to push the girl towards the coach.

Viola turned round with her nose in the air and an air of contempt and boredom which might have been meant for Cosimo as well as her relations, gave a quick glance at the trees (surely in reply to his question), said: 'They're sending me to school!' and turned round to get into the coach. She had not deigned to look either at him or his trophy.

The carriage door was already shut, the coachman was on the box, and Cosimo, still unable to take in this departure, was trying to attract her attention and make her understand that he had dedicated that bloodthirsty victory to her, but could only explain by shouting: 'I've killed a cat!'

The whip gave a crack, the coach started off amid waving of handkerchiefs by the aunts, and from the door came: 'How clever of you!' from Viola, whether of enthusiasm or denigration was not clear.

This was their farewell. And in Cosimo, tension, pain from his wounds, disappointment at not getting any glory from his victory, despair at that sudden departure, all surged up in him and he broke into violent sobs, shrieking and screaming and tearing at the twigs.

'*Hors d'ici! Hors d'ici! Polisson sauvage! Hors de notre jardin!*' shrieked the aunts, and all the Ondariva servants came running up with long sticks and threw stones to drive him away.

Still sobbing and screaming, Cosimo flung the dead cat in the faces of whoever was below. The servants took the animal up by its neck and flung it on a rubbish heap.

When I heard that our little neighbour had left, I hoped for a time that Cosimo might come down. I don't know why, I linked with her, or partly with her, my brother's decision to stay up in the trees.

But he did not even mention it. I climbed up to take him bandages and lint, and he himself tended the scratches on his face and arms. Then he asked for a fishing-rod with a hook. He used it to fish up the dead cat, from an olive tree over the Ondarivas' rubbish heap. He skinned it, cured the fur as best he could, and made a cap of it. It was the first of the fur caps which we were to see him wear his whole life through.

7

The last attempt to capture Cosimo was made by our sister Battista. It was her initiative, of course, done without consulting anyone, in secret, as she did things. She went out at night, with a pailful of glue and a rope ladder, and painted a carob tree over with glue from top to toe. It was a tree on which Cosimo used to perch every morning.

In the morning, stuck to the carob tree were swallows beating their wings, bats all wrapped in sticky mess, night-butterflies, leaves borne by the wind, a squirrel's tail, and some braid torn off Cosimo's tunic. Who knows if he had sat on a branch and managed to free himself, or if instead – more probably, as I had not seen him wear the jacket for some time – he put that piece of braid there on purpose to pull our legs. Anyway, the tree remained hideously daubed with glue and then dried up.

All of us, even our father, began to be convinced that Cosimo would never return. Since my brother had been jumping on trees all over Ombrosa, the Baron had not dared show himself in public, for fear the ducal dignity might be compromised. Every day he became gaunter and paler, how much due to paternal anxiety and how much to dynastic worries I do not know; but the two were now fused, for Cosimo was his eldest son, the heir to the title, and if it is difficult to imagine a Baron jumping about on trees like a grasshopper, it seems still more unsuitable for a Duke, even though a boy, and this conduct by the heir was certainly no support for the contested title.

They were useless preoccupations, of course, for the people of Ombrosa just laughed at our father's pomposity; and the nobles living around thought him mad. By now these nobles had taken to living in pleasantly sited villas rather than in their feudal castles, and this already tended to make them behave more like private citizens, avoiding unnecessary bothers. Who gave a thought any more to the ancient Dukedom of Ombrosa? The pleasant thing about Ombrosa was that it was no one's and yet everyone's; with certain rights to the Ondarivas, lords of almost all the land there, but a free Commune for some time, tributary of the Republic of Genoa; we did not have to worry about our inherited lands and about others we had bought for nothing from the Commune at a moment when it was heavily in debt. What more could anyone ask? There was a small society of nobles living around, with villas and parks down to the sea, all of whom lived a pleasant life visiting each other and hunting; life cost little; they had certain advantages over those who were at court, having none of the worries, duties and expenses of nobles with a royal family, a capital, politics to think of. But feeling himself a dethroned potentate, our father did not enjoy this life at all, and had eventually broken off all relations with the nobles of the neighbourhood (our mother, being a foreigner, had never had any at all, one could say); this had its advantages, as by seeing no one we both saved money and concealed our penury.

With the people of Ombrosa we had better relations; you know what they are like, rather crude, thinking of nothing but business; at that period, with the habit of sugared lemonade spreading among the richer classes, lemons were beginning to sell well; and they had planted lemon groves everywhere and restarted the port ruined by the incursions of pirates many years before. Situated between the Republic of Genoa, the fiefs of the King of Sardinia, the Kingdom of France and episcopal lands, they trafficked with all and worried about none, except for tributes owed to Genoa which made them sweat every time they fell due, and caused riots every year against the tax-gatherers of the Republic.

When these disturbances about taxes broke out, the Baron of Rondò always imagined that he was going to be approached with an offer of the ducal coronet. He would appear in the Piazza, and offer himself to the people of Ombrosa as their protector, but every time he had to make a quick get-away under a hail of rotten lemons. Then he would say that a conspiracy had been mounted against him; by the Jesuits, as usual. For he had got it into his head that there was a life-and-death struggle between him and the Jesuits, and that the Society thought of nothing but plotting his ruin. In fact there had been some difference of opinion between them about the ownership of an orchard which was contested between our family and the Society of Jesus; after some tension the Baron, being then on good terms with the Bishop, had managed to get the Father Provincial removed from the diocese. Since that time our father was certain that the Society was sending agents to make attempts on his life and rights; he on his part tried to enrol a militia of faithful to liberate the Bishop, whom he considered had fallen prisoner of the Jesuits; and he offered asylum and protection to any Jesuit who declared himself persecuted, which was why he had chosen as our spiritual father that semi-Jansenist with his head in the clouds.

There was only one person our father trusted, and that was the Cavalier. The Baron had a weakness for this illegitimate brother of his, as if he were an only son in misfortune; and I don't know if we realized it, but there must certainly have been, in our attitude towards the Cavalier Carrega, a touch of jealousy at our father being fonder of that fifty-year-old brother of his than of either of us boys. Anyway, we were not the only ones to look at him askance; the Generalessa and Battista pretended to respect him but really could not bear him; under that subdued exterior he did not care a fig about any of us, and may have hated us all, even the Baron to whom he owed so much. The Cavalier spoke so little that at certain times he might have been thought either deaf and dumb or incapable of understanding our language; I don't know how he had managed once to practise as a lawyer, and if he had been so abstracted before his time with the Turks. Perhaps he had also been a person of intellect, if he had learned from the Turks all those calculations of hydraulics, the only job he was now capable of applying himself to, exaggeratedly praised by my father. I never knew much about his past, nor who his mother had been, nor what his relations had been in youth with our grandfather (who must surely have been fond of him too, as he had made him into a lawyer and granted him the title of Cavalier) nor how he had come to be in Turkey. It was not even certain if it was in Turkey itself that he had spent so long, or in some barbarian state, Tunis, Algiers; anyway it was a Mohammedan country, as it was said that he had become a Mohammedan too. So many things were said of him; that he had held important appointments, been a high dignitary of the Sultan, Hydraulic Adviser to the Divan or something of the kind, before falling into disgrace due to a palace plot or a woman's jealousy or a gambling debt, and been sold as a slave. It was known that he was found in chains rowing with the slaves in an Ottoman galley captured

by the Venetians, who freed him. In Venice he had lived more
or less as a beggar until he had got into some other trouble, a
fight, I think (though who could he fight with, a man so mild,
heaven only knows) and ended in prison again. He was bought
out by our father through the good offices of the Republic of
Genoa, and returned to us, a little bald man with a black
beard, very downcast, half dumb (I was a child but the scene
that evening left an impression on my mind), togged up in
clothes that were far too big for him. Our father imposed him
on everyone as a person in authority, named him administrator,
and allotted him a study which was filled more and more with
disordered papers. The Cavalier wore a long robe and a skull-
cap in the shape of a fez, as many nobles and bourgeois did then
in their studies; only he was, to tell the truth, very rarely in his
study, and was seen going round dressed like that outside in the
country too. Eventually he also appeared at table in those
Turkish robes, and the strange thing was that our father,
usually such a stickler for rules, seemed to tolerate it.

In spite of his duties as administrator, the Cavalier scarcely
ever exchanged a word with bailiffs or tenants or peasants, given
his timid temperament and difficulty in talking; and all the
practical cares, the giving of orders, the keeping of people up
to the mark, in fact fell on our father. Enea Silvio Carrega kept
the account books, and I do not know if our affairs were going
so badly because of the way in which he kept them, or if his
accounts went so badly because of our affairs. He would also
make calculations and drawings of irrigation schemes, and fill a
big blackboard with lines and figures, and words in Turkish
writing. Every now and again our father shut himself up in the
study with him for hours (they were the longest periods the
Cavalier ever spent there) and after a short time the angry
voice of the Baron, and the loud sounds of a quarrel, would
come from behind the closed door, but the voice of the Cavalier
could scarcely ever be heard. Then the door would open and
the Cavalier appear wrapped in the folds of his robe, with
the skull-cap stuck on the top of his head, go towards a french
window with his quick little steps and out into the park and
garden. 'Enea Silvio! Enea Silvio!' shouted our father, run-

ning behind, but his half-brother was already between the rows of vines, or among the lemon groves, and all that could be seen was the red fez moving stubbornly among the leaves. Our father would follow, calling; after a little we saw them returning, the Baron always talking and waving his arms, and the little Cavalier hobbling along beside him, his fists clenched in the pockets of his robe.

8

In those days Cosimo often challenged men on the ground to competitions, usually in aiming, partly to try out his capacities and discover just what he could manage to do up there on the tree-tops. The urchins he challenged to quoits. One day they were among the shacks of the vagabonds and down-and-outs near Porta Capperi, with Cosimo playing them at quoits from a dried and leafless ilex tree, when he saw a horseman approaching, a tall, rather bowed man, wrapped in a black cloak. He recognized his father. The rabble dispersed, while the women stood looking on from the thresholds of their shacks.

The Baron Arminio rode right up under the tree. The sunset was red. Cosimo stood among bare branches. They looked straight at each other. It was the first time since the dinner of the snails that they found themselves like that, face to face. Many days had passed, things had changed, both of them knew that the snails had no bearing now, nor did the obedience of sons or the authority of fathers; that all the many logical and sensible things which could be said would be out of place; yet they had to say something.

'You're making yourself a figure of fun!' began the father, bitterly. 'Really worthy of a gentleman!' (He called him by the formal *voi*, as he did for the most serious reprimands, but the use of the word now had a sense of distance, of detachment.)

'A gentleman, my lord father, is such whether he is on earth or on the tree-tops,' replied Cosimo, and at once added: 'If he behaves with decency.'

'An excellent maxim,' admitted the Baron gravely. 'And yet only a short time ago you were stealing plums from one of our tenants.'

It was true. My brother had been seen in the act. What was he to reply? He smiled, but not haughtily or cynically, a shy smile, and blushed.

The father smiled too, a melancholy smile, and for some reason or other blushed too.

'You're making common cause with the worst little ruffians in the area!' he said then.

'No, my lord father, I'm on my own, and each acts for himself,' said Cosimo firmly.

'I ask you to come down to earth,' said the Baron in a calm, rather faint voice, 'and to take up the duties of your station!'

'I have no intention of obliging you, my lord father,' said Cosimo. 'I am very sorry.'

They were ill at ease, both of them, bored. Each knew what the other would say. 'And what about your studies? Your devotions as a Christian?' said the father. 'Do you intend to grow up like an American savage?'

Cosimo was silent. These were thoughts he had not yet put to himself and had no wish to. Then he exclaimed: 'Just because I'm a few yards higher up does it mean that good teaching can't reach me?'

This was an able reply too, though it diminished, in a way, the range of his gesture; a sign of weakness.

His father realized this and became more pressing. 'Rebellion cannot be measured by yards,' he said. 'Even when a journey seems no distance at all, it can have no return.'

Now was the moment for my brother to produce some other noble reply, perhaps a Latin tag, but at that instant none came into his mind, though he knew so many by heart. Instead he suddenly got bored with all this solemnity, and shouted: 'But

I can spray water farther from the trees,' a phrase without much meaning, but which cut the discussion off short.

As though they had heard the phrase, a shout went up from the urchins round Porta Capperi. The Baron of Rondò's horse shied, the Baron pulled the reins and wrapped himself in his cloak, ready to leave. Then he turned, drew an arm out of his cloak, pointed to the sky which had suddenly become overcast with black clouds, and examined: 'Be careful, son, there's Someone who can spray water on us all!' and spurred away.

The rain, long awaited in the countryside, began to fall in big scattered drops. Among the hovels there was a scattering and running of urchins hooded in sacks and singing in dialect: '*Ciêuve! Ciêuve! L'Aiga va pe êuve!*' Cosimo vanished through leaves drooping with water, which poured showers on his head at a touch.

As soon as I realized it was raining, I began to worry about him. I imagined him soaking wet, cowering against a tree trunk without ever managing to avoid the oblique rain. And I knew that a storm would not make him return. So I hurried off to our mother. 'It's raining! What will Cosimo do, lady mother?'

The Generalessa shook the curtain and looked out at the rain. She was calm. 'The worst nuisance from heavy rain is the mud. Up there he's away from that.'

'But will he find enough shelter in the trees?'

'He'll withdraw to his tents.'

'Which, lady mother?'

'He'll have had the foresight to prepare them in time.'

'But don't you think I'd better go and find him to give him an umbrella?'

As if the word 'umbrella' had suddenly torn her from her observation post and flung her back into maternal preoccupations, the Generalessa began saying: '*Ja, ganz gewiss!* And a bottle of apple syrup, well heated, wrapped in a woollen sock! And some oilcloth, to stretch over the branches and stop the wet coming through ... But where'll he be now, poor boy ...! Let's hope you manage to find him ...'

Loaded with parcels I went out into the rain, under an

enormous green umbrella, holding under my arm another umbrella, shut, for Cosimo.

I gave our particular whistle, but the only answer was the endless patter of the rain on the trees. It was dark; once outside the garden precincts I did not know my way and put my feet haphazard on slippery stones, spongy grass, puddles, whistling all the time and tipping the umbrella back to send the sound upwards, so that the rain whipped my face and washed the whistle from my lips. My idea was to go towards some public lands full of tall trees where I thought he might possibly have taken refuge, but in that darkness I got lost and stood there clutching the umbrellas and packages, with only the bottle of syrup wrapped in its woollen sock to give me a little warmth.

Then, among the trees, high in the darkness above, I saw a light which could not be coming from either moon or stars. And at my whistle I seemed to hear his in reply.

'Cosimooo!'

'Biagiooo!' came a voice through the rain from up on the tops.

'Where are you?'

'Here . . . I'm coming towards you, but hurry up as I'm getting wet!'

We found each other. Wrapped in a blanket, he came down on to the low fork of a willow to show me how to climb up, through complicated interlacing branches, as far as a beech tree with a high trunk, from which came that light. I gave him the umbrella and some of the parcels at once, and we tried to struggle up with the umbrellas open, but it was impossible and we got wet all the same. Finally I reached the place he was leading me to; but I saw nothing except for a faint light that seemed to be coming from the flaps of a tent.

Cosimo raised one of those flaps and let me in. By the light of a lantern I saw I was in a kind of little room, covered and enclosed on every side by curtains and carpets, crossed by the trunks of the beech-tree, with a floor of stakes, all propped on thick branches. At that moment it seemed a palace to me, but soon I began to realize how unstable it was, for already the two of us being inside was upsetting the balance and Cosimo at once had to get down to repairing leaks. He also opened and put out the two umbrellas I had brought to cover two yawning holes in the roof; but the water was pouring in from various other points and we were both soaked and as cold as if we'd stayed outside. However, such a quantity of blankets was amassed there that we were able to bury ourselves under them, leaving only our heads outside. The lantern sent out an uncertain spluttering light, and the branches and leaves threw intricate shadows on the roof and walls of that strange construction. Cosimo drank the apple syrup in great gulps, gasping 'Puah! Puah!'

'It's a nice house,' said I.

'Oh, it's only provisional,' replied Cosimo hurriedly. 'I've got to think it out better.'

'Did you build it all yourself?'

'Of course, who d'you think? It's secret.'

'Can I come here?'

'No, or you'll show someone else the way.'

'Father said he's giving up the search for you.'

'This must be a secret all the same.'

'Because of those boys who steal? But aren't they your friends?'

'Sometimes they are and sometimes they aren't.'

'And the girl on the pony?'

'What's that to do with you?'

'I meant she's your friend, isn't she, and you play together, don't you?'

'Sometimes we do and sometimes we don't.'

'Why sometimes you don't?'

'Because I may not want to or she may not want to.'

'And her, would you let her up here?'

Cosimo, frowning, was trying to spread a straw mat over a branch. 'Yes. If she came, I'd let her up,' he said gravely.

'Doesn't she want to?'

Cosimo flung himself down. 'She's left.'

'Say,' I whispered, 'are you engaged?'

'No,' answered my brother and shut himself in a long silence.

*

Next day the weather was fine, and it was decided that Cosimo would begin taking lessons again with the Abbé Fauchelefleur. How was not said. Simply and rather brusquely, the Baron asked the Abbé ('—instead of just standing there looking at the flies, *mon Abbé* ...') to go and find my brother wherever he might be and get him to translate a little Virgil. Then, fearing he had put the Abbé in too embarrassing a position, he tried to ease his task, and said to me: 'Go and tell your brother to be in the garden in half an hour for his Latin lesson.' This he said in as natural a tone as he could, the tone which he intended to keep from then on; even with Cosimo on the trees everything must continue as before.

So the lesson took place. They sat, my brother astride an oak branch, his legs dangling, and the Abbé on the grass beneath, on a stool, intoning hexameters in chorus. I played around there and then wandered off for a short time. When I got back, the Abbé was on the tree. With his long thin legs in their black stockings he was trying to hitch himself on to a fork and Cosimo was helping him by an elbow. They found a comfortable position for the old man, and together construed a difficult passage, bending over the book. My brother seemed to be showing great diligence.

Then I don't know what happened, why the pupil made off; perhaps because the Abbé felt restless up there and began staring into the void as usual; the fact is that suddenly only the black figure of the old priest was left crouched up in the branches, with his book on his knees, looking at a white butterfly flying by and following it with an open mouth. When the butterfly vanished, the Abbé suddenly realized he was there alone on the tree and felt frightened. He clutched the trunk and began shouting '*Au secours! Au secours!*' until people came with a ladder and he very slowly calmed down and descended.

9

In fact, Cosimo, despite that escape of his which had upset us all so much, lived almost as closely with us as he had before. He was a solitary who did not avoid people. In a way, indeed, he seemed to like them more than anything else. He would squat above places where peasants were digging, turning manure, or scything the fields, and call out polite greetings. They would raise their heads in surprise and he at once tried to show them where he was, for he had got over the pastime we had so often indulged in when we had been together on the trees *before,* of cocking snooks and making faces at passers-by. At first the peasants were rather confused at seeing him covering such distances all on branches, and did not know whether to greet him by doffing their hats as they did to gentry or to shout at him as they did to urchins. Then they got into the habit of chatting with him about their work or the weather, and seemed to find the game he was playing up there no better and no worse than so many other games they had seen the gentry play.

He would sit for whole half-hours watching their work from the trees and asking questions about seeds and manure which it had never occurred to him to do when he'd been on the ground, prevented then by shyness from ever addressing a word to villagers or servants. Sometimes he would point out if the furrow they were digging was going straight or crooked; or if the tomatoes in a neighbour's field were already ripe; sometimes he would offer himself for little commissions such as going to tell the wife of a scyther to bring a whetstone, or warning them to turn off the water into an orchard. And if, when he was moving around with these messages for the peasants, he happened to see a flight of sparrows settling on a field of corn, he would shout and wave his cap to scare them away.

In his solitary turns around the woods, encounters with humans were memorable though rare, for they were with folk whom people like us never used to meet. In those times a variety of wanderers used to camp in the forests: charcoal-burners, tinkers, glass-cutters, families driven far from their homes by famine, to earn their bread by these unstable jobs. They would set up their workshops in the open, and erect shacks made of branches to sleep in. At first they were rather alarmed by the boy covered in fur passing over their heads, particularly the women who took him for a hobgoblin; then he became friends with them, and spent hours watching them work, and in the evening when they sat around the fire he would settle on a branch nearby, to hear the tales they told.

In a glade covered with beaten cinders the charcoal-burners were the most numerous. They would shout '*Hura! Hota!*' as they were from Bergamo and their speech was impossible to understand. They were the strongest and most self-enclosed, a corporation ramifying throughout the woods, with links of blood and friendship and revenge. Cosimo would sometimes act as messenger between one group and another, pass on news, and arrive full of commissions.

'The men under the Red Oak have told me to tell you *Hanfa la Hapa Hota'l Hoc!*'

'Tell 'em *Hegn Hobet Ho de Hot!*'

He would remember the mysterious aspirated syllables, and try to repeat them, as he tried to repeat the twitter of the birds which woke him in the morning.

By now the news had spread that a son of the Baron of Rondò had been up in the trees for months; yet our father tried to keep it secret from strangers. There came to visit us, for instance, the Count and Countess of Estomac, on their way to France, where they had estates in the bay of Toulouse. I do not know what self-interest lay beneath this visit; claims to certain rights, or the confirmation of a parish to their son, who was a bishop, for which they needed the agreement of the Baron of Rondò; and our father, as can be imagined, built on this alliance a castle of projects for his dynastic pretensions on Ombrosa.

. There was a dinner of agonizing boredom, endless ceremonial, and bowing and scraping all round. The guests had with them a young son, a bewigged little fop. The Baron presented his sons, that is me alone, and added: 'My daughter Battista, poor girl, lives such a retired life, is so very pious, that I don't know if you'll be able to see her,' and at that moment she appeared, looking very silly in a nun's wimple covered all over with ribbons and frills, a powdered face, and mittens. It should be emphasized that since that business of the young Marchese della Mella she had never once set eyes on a young man, apart from page-boys and village lads. The young Count of Estomac bowed; she broke into hysterical laughter. The Baron, who had already crossed off his daughter as a non-starter, now began to mill new possibilities over in his mind.

But the old Count made a show of indifference. He asked: 'Have you not got another son, Monsieur Arminio?'

'Yes, the eldest,' said our father, 'but, by bad luck, he's out shooting.'

He had not lied, as at that period Cosimo was always in the woods with his gun, after hares and thrushes. The gun was one I had got for him, it was the light one Battista had used against the mice and which for some time she – having given up that particular sport – had abandoned on a nail.

The Count began to ask about the game thereabouts. The Baron in his replies kept to generalities, as, taking no interest in the world around him, he did not know how to shoot. I now interrupted the conversation, though I had been forbidden to say a word when grown-ups were talking.

'And what does anyone as young as you know about it?' asked the Count.

'I go and fetch the game my brother brings down, and take them up the ...' I was just saying when our father interrupted me.

'Who asked you to say anything? Go and play.'

We were in the garden, it was evening and still light, being summer. And now over the plane trees and oaks Cosimo came calmly along, with his cap of cat's fur on his head, his gun slung on one shoulder, a spear on the other, and his legs in gaiters.

- 'Hey, hey!' exclaimed the Count, getting up and moving his head to see better, much amused. 'Who's that? Who's that on the trees?'

'What? What? I really don't know ...' began our father, and instead of looking in the direction where the other was pointing, looked in the Count's eyes as if to assure himself he could see well.

Cosimo meanwhile had reached a point right above them, and was standing on a fork with legs splayed out.

'Ah, it's my son, yes, Cosimo, just a boy, you see, to give us a surprise he's climbed up there ...'

'Is he your eldest son?'

'Yes, yes, of the two boys he's the eldest, but only by a little, you know, they're still children, playing ...'

'But he must be a bright lad to go over branches like that. And with that arsenal on him ...'

'Eh, just playing,' and with a terrible effort at lying which made him go red all over he called: 'What are you doing up there? Eh? Will you come down? Come and greet our Lord Count here!'

Cosimo took off his cat's fur cap, and bowed. 'My respects, Lord Count.'

'Ah, ah, ah!' laughed the Count, 'fine, fine! Let him stay up there, let him stay up there, Monsieur Arminio! A very clever boy at getting about trees!' and he laughed.

And even that little monkey of a Count kept on repeating: 'C'est original, ça c'est très original!'

Cosimo sat down there on the fork, our father changed the subject and talked on and on in the hope of diverting the Count's attention. But every now and again the Count raised his eyes and there my brother always was, up that tree or another, cleaning his gun, or greasing his gaiters, or as night was coming on, donning his flannel shirt.

'Oh, but look! He can do everything up there, that boy can! What fun! Ah, I'll tell them about it at Court, the very first time I go there! I'll tell my son the bishop! I'll tell my aunt the princess!'

My father could scarcely control himself any longer. And he had another worry on his mind; he could not see his daughter around, and the young Count had vanished too.

Cosimo had gone off on one of his tours of exploration, and

now came panting back. 'She's given him the hiccups! She's given him the hiccups!'

The Count looked worried. 'Oh, that's unfortunate. My son suffers a lot from hiccups. Do go, like a good boy, and see what's happening. Tell 'em to come back.'

Cosimo went jumping off, and came back panting more than ever. 'They're holding each other. She wants to put a live lizard under his shirt to get rid of his hiccups! He doesn't want her to!' And off he skipped for another look.

So we spent that evening at home, not so very different in truth from others, with Cosimo percolating through our lives from up on the trees; but that time we had guests, and as a result the news of my brother's behaviour spread over the Courts of Europe, to the great shame of our father. Quite a baseless shame, for the Count of Estomac took away a favourable impression of our family, and as a result our sister Battista became engaged to the little Count.

10

The olives, because of their tortuous shapes, were comfortable and easy routes for Cosimo, patient trees with rough, friendly barks on which to pass or pause, in spite of the scarcity of thick branches and lack of variety in shape. On a fig tree, though, as long as he was careful that a branch bore him, he could move about for ever; Cosimo would stand under the pavilion of leaves, watching the sun diffusing through the network of twigs and branches, the gradual swell of the green fruit, smelling the scent of flowers budding in the stalks. The fig tree seemed to absorb him, impregnate him with its gummy texture and the buzz of hornets; after a little Cosimo would begin to feel he was becoming a fig himself, and move away, uneasy. On the hard sorb apple or the mulberry he was all right; a pity they were so rare. Or the nut ... sometimes seeing my brother lose himself in the endless spread of an old nut tree, like some palace of many floors and innumerable rooms, I found a longing coming over me to imitate him and go and live up there too; such is the strength and certainty that a tree has in being a tree, its stubbornness in being hard and heavy expressed even in its leaves.

Cosimo would spend happy hours, too, amid the undulating leaves of the ilex (or holm oak, as I have called them when describing the ones in our park, perhaps influenced by our father's stilted language) and he loved its peeling bark from which, when preoccupied, he would pick off a piece with his fingers, not from any desire to do harm, but to help the tree in its long travail of rebirth. Or he would peel away the white bark of a plane tree, uncovering layers of old yellow mildew. He also loved the encrusted trunks like the elm, with the tender shoots and clusters of little jagged leaves and twigs growing out of the whorls; but it wasn't an easy tree to move about on as the branches grow upwards, slender and thickly covered, leaving little foothold. In the woods he preferred beeches and oaks; as on pines the very close-knit branches, brittle and thick with pine cones, left him no space or support; and the chestnut, with its prickly leaves, husks and bark, and its high branches, seemed made on purpose to avoid.

These sympathies and antipathies Cosimo came to recognize in time – or to recognize consciously; but already in those first days they had begun to be an instinctive part of him. Now it was a whole different world, made up of narrow curved bridges in the emptiness, of knots or peel or scores roughening the trunks, of lights varying their green according to the veils of thicker or scarcer leaves, trembling at the first quiver of the air on the shoots or moving like sails with the bend of the tree in the wind. While down below our world lay flattened, and our bodies looked quite disproportionate and we certainly understood nothing of what he knew up there – he who spent his nights listening to the sap germinating from cells, the circles marking the years inside the trunks, the mould enlarging its patches quivering under the north wind, the birds asleep in their nests quivering then resettling their heads in the softest down of their wings, and the caterpillar waking, and the chrysalis opening. There is the moment when the silence of the countryside composes itself in the eardrum into a toccata of sounds, a croaking and squeaking, a swift rustle in the grass, a plop in the water, a patter between soil and stones, and high above all the call of the cicada. The sounds draw each other on, and the ear eventually distinguishes more and more of them – just as to fingers unwinding a ball of wool every yarn shows itself interwoven with threads that seem progressively subtler and more impalpable. The frogs meanwhile continue their croaking in the background without changing the flow of sounds, just as light does not vary from the continuous winking of stars. But at every rise or fall of the wind, every sound changed and was renewed. All that remained in the depth of the eardrum was a vague murmur: the sea.

Winter came, Cosimo made himself a fur jacket. He sewed it from the fur of various animals he had hunted: hares, foxes, martens and polecats. On his head he always wore that cap of wildcat's fur. He also made himself some goatskin breeches with leather knees. As for shoes, he eventually realized that the best footgear for the trees was slippers, and he made himself a pair of some skin or other, perhaps badger.

So he defended himself against the cold. It should be said that in those days the winters in our parts were mild, and never had the freezing cold of nowadays which they say was loosed from its lair in Russia by Napoleon and followed him all the way here. But even so, spending the winter nights out in the open could not have been much fun.

For night Cosimo eventually found a fur sleeping-bag best; no more tents or shacks; a sleeping-bag with fur inside, hung on a branch. He got inside, the outside world vanished and he slept tucked up like a child. If there was an unusual sound in the night, from the mouth of the bag emerged the fur cap, the barrel of the gun, then his round eyes. (They said that his eyes had become luminous in the dark like a cat's or owl's; but I never noticed it myself.)

In the morning, on the other hand, when the jackdaw croaked, from the bag would come a pair of clenched fists; the fists rose in the air and were followed by two arms slowly widening and stretching, and in the movement drawing out his yawning face, his shoulders with a gun slung over one and a powder-horn over another, his slightly bandy legs (they were beginning to lose their straightness from his habit of always moving on all fours or in a crouch). Out jumped these legs, they stretched too, and so, with a shake of the back and a scratch under his fur jacket, Cosimo, wakeful and fresh as a rose, was ready to begin his day.

He went to the fountain, for he had a hanging fountain of his own, invented by himself, or rather made with the help of nature. There was a stream which at a certain place dropped sheer in a cascade, and nearby grew an oak, with very high branches. Cosimo, with a piece of scooped-out poplar, a couple of yards long, had made a kind of gutter which brought the water from the cascade to the branches of the oak tree, where he could drink and wash. That he did wash is sure, for I have seen him doing so a number of times; not much and not even every day, but he did wash; he also had soap. With the soap, when he happened to feel like it, he would also wash his linen; he had taken a tub up on to the oak tree on purpose. Then he would hang the things to dry on ropes from one branch to another.

In fact he did everything on the trees. He had also found a way to roast on a spit the game he caught, without ever coming down. This is what he did; he would light a pine cone with a flint and throw it to the ground on a spot already arranged for a fire (I had set this up, with some smooth stones); then he would drop twigs and dried branches on it, regulating the flame with a poker tied on a long stick in such a way that it reached the spit, which was hanging from two branches. All this called for great care, as it is easy to provoke a fire in the woods. And the fireplace was set on purpose under the oak tree, near the cascade from which he could draw all the water he wanted in case of danger.

Thus, partly by eating what he shot, partly by bartering with the peasants for fruit and vegetables, he managed very well, so that we no longer needed to send any food out to him from the house. One day we heard that he was drinking fresh milk every morning; he had made friends with a goat, which went and climbed up an easy fork on an olive tree a foot or two from the ground; actually it did not climb up properly, it just put up its two rear hoofs, so that he could come down on to the fork with a pail and milk it. He had a similar arrangement with a chicken, a red Paduan, a very good layer. He had made it a secret nest in the hole of a trunk, and on alternate days he would find an egg, which he drank after making two holes in it with a pin.

Another problem: his daily duties. At the beginning he did them wherever he happened to be, here or there it didn't matter, the world was big. Then he realized this was not very nice. So he found, on the banks of a torrent called the Merdanzo, an alder tree leaning over a most suitable and secluded part of the water, with a fork on which he could seat himself comfortably. The Merdanzo was a dark torrent, hidden among the bamboos, with a quick flow, and the villages nearby threw their slops into it. So the young Piovasco di Rondò lived a civilized life, respecting the decencies of his neighbour and himself.

But he lacked a necessary complement to his huntsman's life; a dog. There was I, flinging myself among the thorns and bushes, searching for a thrush, a snipe or a quail, which had fallen after being shot in mid-air, or even looking out for wolves when, after a night on the prowl, one of them would stop with its long tail extended just outside the bushes. But only rarely could I escape to join him in the woods; lessons with the Abbé, study, serving Mass, meals with my parents kept me back; the hundred and one duties of family life to which I submitted myself, as at bottom the phrase which was always being repeated all round me: 'One rebel in a family is enough,' had a certain sense and left its mark on my whole life.

So Cosimo almost always went hunting alone, and to recover the game (except in rare cases such as a nightingale whose dry brown wings caught and hung on a branch as it fell) he used a kind of fishing-tackle; rods with string, and hooks; but he did not always succeed in reaching it, and sometimes a woodcock ended black with ants in the bottom of a gully.

I have spoken up to now of shooting-dogs. For Cosimo then only did the kind of shooting which meant spending mornings and nights crouched on his branch, waiting for a thrush to pause on some exposed twig, or a hare to appear in the open space of a field. If not he wandered about at hazard, following the songs of the birds, or guessing the most probable tracks of the animals. And when he heard the baying of hounds behind a hare or a fox, he knew he must avoid them, for these were not animals for him, a solitary casual hunter. Respectful of the rules as he was, when from his observation post he noticed or could aim at some game chased by the hounds of others, he would never raise his gun. He would wait for the huntsman to arrive panting along the path, with ears cocked and eyes bleared, and point out to him the direction the animal had gone.

One day he saw a fox on the run: a red streak in the middle of the green grass, whiskers erect, dripping saliva; it crossed the field and vanished into the undergrowth. And behind: 'Uauauaaa!' – the hounds.

They arrived at a gallop, their noses to the ground, twice found themselves without the smell of a fox in their nostrils and then turned away at a right angle.

They were already some way off when with a howl of 'Ui, ui,' cleaving through the grass with leaps that were more a fish's than a dog's, came a kind of dolphin; it was swimming along sniffing with a nose sharper and ears droopier than a bloodhound's. From behind it seemed a fish, propelled by fins, or web feet, legless and very long. It came out into the open; a dachshund.

It must have tagged on to the hounds and been left behind, young as it was, almost a puppy. The sound of the hounds was now a 'Buaf' of annoyance as they had lost the scent, and their compact course was changing into a scattered snuffling all over an open field, too impatient to find the lost scent again to make a real search for it, and losing their impetus, so that already one or two of them were taking the opportunity of raising their legs against a stone.

The dachshund, panting hard, trotting along with its nose in the air in unjustified triumph, finally reached him. It was still unjustifiably triumphant, and gave a cunning howl: 'Uia! Uia!'

The hounds snarled at once 'Aurrch!' left their search for the fox's scent a minute and went towards the dachshund with mouths open ready to bite; 'Ggghrn!' Then they quickly lost interest again, and ran off.

Cosimo followed the dachshund, which was now moving about haphazard, and the dog, wavering with a distracted nose, saw the boy on the tree and wagged its tail. Cosimo felt sure that the fox was still hidden nearby. The hounds were scattered a long way off, they could be heard every now and again from the opposite slope barking in a broken and aimless way, urged on by the muted voices of the hunters. Cosimo said to the dachshund: 'Go on! Go on! Look!'

The puppy flung itself about sniffing hard, and every now and again turned its face up to look at the boy. 'Go on! Go on!'

Now he could not see it any more. He heard a crashing among the bushes, then, suddenly: 'Auauauaaa! Iai! Iaia!' It had raised the fox!

Cosimo saw the animal run out into the field. But could he fire at a fox raised by someone else's dog? Cosimo let it pass and did not shoot. The dachshund lifted its snout towards him, with the look of dogs when they do not understand and are not sure whether they should understand, and flung its nose down again, behind the fox.

'Iai, iai, iai!' The fox made a complete round. There, it was coming back. Could he fire or couldn't he? He didn't. The dachshund turned a sad eye up at him. It was not barking any more, its tongue was drooping more than its ears, it was exhausted, but it still went on running.

The dachshund's raising of the fox had amazed both hounds and hunters. Along the path was running an old man with a ponderous arquebus. 'Hey,' called Cosimo, 'is that dachshund yours?'

'A plague on you and all your family!' shouted the old man who must have been a bit cracked. 'Do we look like people who hunt with a dachshund?'

'Then whatever it puts up, I can shoot,' insisted Cosimo, who really wanted to do the right thing.

'Shoot at your guardian angel for all I care!' replied the other, as he hurried off.

The dachshund chased the fox back again to Cosimo's tree. Cosimo shot at it and hit it. The dachshund was his dog; he called it Ottimo Massimo.

Ottimo Massimo was no one's dog, it had joined the pack of hounds from youthful enthusiasm. But where had it come from? To discover this, Cosimo let it lead him.

The dachshund, its belly grazing the ground, crossed hedges and ditches; then it turned to see if the boy up there was managing to follow its tracks. So unusual was its route that Cosimo did not realize at once where they had got to. When he understood, his heart gave a leap; it was the garden of the Ondarivas.

The villa was shut, the shutters pulled to; only one, in a bay-window, was banging in the wind. More than ever the garden had the look of a forest from another world. And along the alleys now overgrown with weeds and the bush-laden flower-beds, Ottimo Massimo moved happily, as if at home, chasing butterflies.

It vanished into a thicket and came back with a ribbon. Cosimo's heart gave another leap. 'What is it, Ottimo Massimo? Eh? Whose is it? Tell me?'

Ottimo Massimo wagged its tail.

'Bring it here, Ottimo Massimo!'

Cosimo came down on to a low branch and took from the dog's mouth a faded piece of ribbon which must have been one of the ribbons on Viola's hair, just as that dog must have been Viola's dog, forgotten there in the last move of the family. In fact, Cosimo now seemed to remember it the summer before, as still a puppy, peeping out of a basket in the arms of the fair-haired girl; perhaps they had just that moment brought it to her as a present.

'Search, Ottimo Massimo!' The dachshund threw itself among the bamboos; and came back with other mementoes of her, a skipping rope, a torn eagle-feather, a fan.

At the top of the trunk of the highest tree in the garden, my brother carved with the point of his rapier the names *Viola and Cosimo* and then, lower down, certain that it would give her pleasure even if he called it by another name, *Ottimo Massimo, dachshund.*

From that time on, whenever we saw the boy on the trees we could be sure he was looking for the dachshund. Ottimo would trot along belly to ground. He had taught it how to search, stop, and bring back game, the jobs every hunting-dog does, and there was no woodland creature that they did not hunt together. To bring him the game, Ottimo Massimo would clamber with two paws as high up the trunk as it could; Cosimo would lean down, take the hare or the partridge from its mouth and stroke it. These were all their confidences, their celebrations. But between the two on the ground and branches ran a continual dialogue, an understanding of monosyllabic baying and clicks of tongue and finger. That necessary presence which man is for a dog and a dog for a man, never betrayed either; and different though they were from all other men and dogs in the world, they could still call themselves happy, as man and dog.

11

For a long time, the whole period of his adolescence, hunting was Cosimo's world. And fishing too, for he would wait for eels and trout with a line in the torrent pools. Sometimes he seemed almost to have developed instincts and senses different from ours, as if those skins he had made into clothes corresponded to a total change in his nature. Certainly the continual contact with the barks of trees, his eyes trained to the movement of a leaf, a hair, a scale, to the range of colours of his world, and then the various greens circulating through the veins of leaves like blood from another world, all those forms of life so far removed from the human as the stem of a plant, the beak of a thrush, the gill of a fish, those borders of the wild into which he was so deeply urged, might have moulded his mind, made him lose every semblance of man. Instead of which, however many new qualities he acquired from his community with plants and his struggles with animals, his place – it always seemed to me – was clearly with us.

But even quite unintentionally, he found certain habits becoming rarer, and finally abandoned – such as following High Mass at the church of Ombrosa. For the first months he tried to do so. Every Sunday, as we came out of the house – the whole family dressed up ceremonially – we would find him on the branches, he too rigged in an attempt at ceremonial dress, such as his old tunic, or his tricorne instead of the fur cap. We would set off, and he would follow us over the branches. So we reached the porch, with all the people of Ombrosa looking at us (soon even my father became used to it and his embarrassment decreased), we all walking with measured step, he jumping in the air – a strange sight, particularly in winter, with the trees bare.

We would enter the cathedral and sit at our family pew, while he stayed outside, kneeling on an ilex beside one of the aisles, just at the height of a big window. From our pew we would see, through the windows, the shadows of the branches and, in the middle, Cosimo's with hat on chest and head bowed. By agreement between my father and one of the sacristans, that window was kept half-open every Sunday, so that my brother could attend Mass from his tree. But as time went by we saw him there no more. The window was closed as it made a draught.

Many things which would have been important to him before were now so no longer. In the spring our sister got engaged.

Who would have thought it, only a year before? The Count and Countess of Estomac came with the young Count and there were great celebrations. Our house was lit up in every room, the whole local nobility were invited, and there was dancing. Did anyone remember Cosimo, then? Well, we did think of him, all of us. Every now and again I looked out of the window to see if he was coming; and our father was sad, and in that family celebration his thoughts must have gone out to him who was excluded from it; and the Generalessa, who was ordering the whole party about as if she were on a parade ground, was only trying to work off her thoughts about her absent son. Perhaps even Battista, pirouetting away, unrecognizable out of her nunnish robes, wearing a wig which looked like marzipan and a *grand panier* decorated with corals made up for her by some local dressmaker, even she was thinking of him, I could have sworn.

And he was there, unseen – I heard about it afterwards – in the shadows, on the top of a plane tree, in the cold, watching the brightly lit windows, the rooms he knew so well, festooned for the party, the bewigged dancers. What thoughts could have crossed his mind? Did he regret our life a little? Was he thinking how brief was the step which separated him from a return to our world, how brief and how easy? I have no idea what he thought, what he wanted, up there. I only know that he stayed for the whole of the party, and even beyond it, until one by one the candelabras were put out and not a lit window remained.

So Cosimo's relations with the family, either good or bad, continued. In fact, they became closer with one member of it – whom he only really now got to know – the Cavalier Enea Silvio Carrega. This vague, elusive little man, of whom nobody ever knew where he was and what he was doing, Cosimo discovered to be the only one of the whole family who had a great number of hobbies and was more or less competent in all of them.

He would go out, sometimes in the hottest hour of the afternoon, with his fez stuck on the top of his head, shambling along in his long robe to the ground, and vanish almost as if he had been swallowed up by a crevice in the earth or fields, or the stones in the walls. Cosimo, too, who passed his time always on the watch (or rather it was not a pastime now, it was his natural state, as if his eye had to embrace a horizon wide enough to understand all), would suddenly lose sight of him. Sometimes he used to start running from branch to branch towards the place where the old man vanished, without ever succeeding in finding where he had gone. But one sign always reappeared in the area where he was last seen; flying bees. Eventually Cosimo was convinced that the presence of the Cavalier was linked with the bees, and that in order to find him he would have to follow their flight. But how could he? Around each flowering plant was a scattered buzz of bees; he must not let himself be distracted into isolated and secondary routes, but follow the invisible airy way in which the coming-and-going of bees was growing thicker and thicker, until he reached a dense cloud rising like smoke from behind a bush. There behind were the beehives, one by one or in rows on a table, and concentrated over them, with bees buzzing all round him, was the Cavalier.

Beekeeping was in fact one of our uncle's secret activities; secret to a point only, for he himself every now and again would bring to the table a gleaming honeycomb fresh from the hive; but this activity of his took place outside the boundaries of our property, in places which he evidently did not want us to know about. It must have been a precaution on his part, to prevent the profits of this personal industry of his from passing through the family accounts, or – since the man was certainly not a miser, and anyway could not expect much of a profit from such small quantities of honey and wax – in order to have something in which the Baron, his brother, could not poke his nose, or pretend to be guiding him; or again in order not to mingle the few things which he loved, such as beekeeping, with the many which he did not love, such as administration.

Anyway, the fact remained that our father had never allowed him to keep bees near the house, as the Baron had an unreasonable fear of being stung; when by chance he happened to come across a bee or a wasp in the garden he would run along the alleys, looking ridiculous, thrusting his hands into his wig as if to protect himself from the pecks of an eagle. Once, as he was doing this, his wig slipped, the bee dislodged by the movement bumped against him and plunged its sting into his bald pate. For three days he tended his head with pieces of cloth soaked in vinegar, for he was that kind of man, very proud and strong in serious matters, but frenzied by a slight scratch or pimple.

And so Enea Silvio Carrega had scattered his beehives all over the valley of Ombrosa; various owners had given him permission to keep a beehive or two on a strip of their land in return for a little honey, and he was always going the rounds from one to the other, working at the beehives with movements that might have been by bees' feelers instead of hands, which, in order not to be stung, he had thrust into long black gloves. On his face, under his fez, he wore a black veil which either stuck to him or blew out at every breath. He used to wave about an instrument that scattered smoke, so as to chase the insects away while he was searching in the beehive. The whole scene, the buzz of bees, the veils and clouds of smoke, all seemed to Cosimo a spell which the old man was trying to cast so as to vanish, be obliterated, flown off and then be reborn elsewhere, in another time or another place. But he was not much of a magician, as he always reappeared just the same, though sometimes sucking a bitten thumb.

It was spring. One morning Cosimo saw the air vibrating with a sound he had never heard, a buzz growing at times almost into a roar, and a curtain of what looked like hail, which instead of falling was moving in a horizontal direction and turning and twisting slowly around, but following a kind of denser column. It was a great mass of bees; and around was greenery and flowers and sun; and Cosimo, he did not understand why, felt himself gripped by a wild and savage exultation. 'The bees are escaping! Cavalier! The bees are escaping!' he shouted, running along the trees searching for Carrega.

'They're not escaping, they're swarming,' said the voice of the Cavalier, and Cosimo saw he had sprung up like a mushroom below him and was making signs for him to be quiet. Then suddenly the old man ran off and vanished. Where had he gone to?

It was the period of swarms. A group of bees was following a queen bee outside the old hives. Cosimo looked around. Now the Cavalier reappeared from the kitchen door with a saucepan and ladle in his hand. He banged the ladle against the saucepan and raised a very loud ding-dong which resounded in the eardrums and died away in a long vibration, so disturbing that it made Cosimo want to stop up his ears. The Cavalier was following the swarm of bees, hitting these bronze instruments at every three steps. At each bang the swarm seemed seized by shock, made a rapid dip and turn, and its buzz lowered, its line of flight got more uncertain. Cosimo could not see well, but it seemed to him that the whole swarm was now converging towards a point in the wood and not going beyond it. And Carrega went on banging his pots.

'What's happening, Cavalier? What are you doing?' my brother asked him, coming up closer.

'Quick!' hissed the other. 'Go to the tree where the swarm has stopped, but be careful not to move it till I arrive!'

The bees were making for a pomegranate tree. Cosimo reached it and at first saw nothing, then suddenly realized that what looked like a big cluster of fruit hanging from a branch was in fact all made up of bees sticking to each other, with more and more coming along to make it bigger.

Cosimo stood at the top of the pomegranate, holding his breath. Beneath him the bunch of bees, and the bigger it became the lighter it seemed, as if it were hanging by a thread, or even less, by the claws of an old queen-bee; it was all thin tissue, with rustling wings spreading diaphanous greys over the black and yellow stripes on bellies.

The Cavalier came leaping up, holding a big pot in his hand. He held it under the cluster of bees. 'Hey,' he whispered to Cosimo. 'Give the tree a little shake.'

Cosimo made the pomegranate quiver very slightly. The swarm of bees broke off like a leaf and fell into the pot, over which the Cavalier put a plank. 'There we are.'

So between Cosimo and the Cavalier there arose an understanding, a collaboration which could have been almost called friendship, if friendship did not seem too excessive a term for two people who were both so unsociable.

My brother and Enea Silvio also came together, eventually, on the subject of hydraulics. That may seem odd, for one living on trees must find it rather difficult to have anything to do with wells and channels, but I have mentioned the kind of hanging fountain which Cosimo had made from a length of scooped-out poplar bringing water from a cascade to the fork of an oak. Now the Cavalier, though apparently so vague, noticed everything to do with moving water over the whole countryside. From above the cascade, hidden behind a privet hedge, he had watched Cosimo pull out his water-conductor from between the branches of the oak (where he kept it when he did not use it, following the habit of hiding everything which primitive people have and which had immediately become his), prop it on a fork of the tree on one side and on some stones in the bank on the other, and drink.

At this sight something seems to have taken wing in the Cavalier's head; he was swept by a rare moment of euphoria. He jumped out of the bush, clapped his hands, gave two or three skips as if with a rope, splashed the water, and nearly jumped into the cascade and flew down the precipice. And he began to explain the idea he had had to the boy. The idea was confused and the explanation very confused; the Cavalier normally spoke in dialect, from modesty rather than ignorance of the language, but in these sudden moments of excitement he would pass from dialect to Turkish without noticing it, and not another word of his could be understood.

To cut the story short: his idea was a hanging aqueduct, with a conducting pipe held up by branches of trees, which would reach the bare slope of the valley opposite and irrigate it. Cosimo supported the project at once, and suggested a refinement: using pierced tree trunks at certain points for the water to sprinkle over the crops like rain: this sent the Cavalier almost into ecstasy.

He rushed off back to his study, and filled pages and pages with plans. Cosimo took to working on this idea too, for everything that could be done on trees pleased him, and gave he felt, a new importance and authority to his position up there; and in Enea Silvio Carrega he seemed to have found an unexpected colleague. They made appointments on certain low trees; the Cavalier would climb up with a triangular ladder, his arms full of rolls of drawings; and they would discuss for hours the ever more complicated developments of their aqueduct.

But it never reached a practical stage. Enea Silvio grew tired, his discussions with Cosimo became rarer, and after a week he must have forgotten all about it. Cosimo did not regret it; he had soon realized it would become just a tiresome complication in his life and nothing else.

In the field of hydraulics it was clear our uncle could have achieved much. He had a bent for it, a particular turn of mind necessary to that branch of knowledge; but he was incapable of putting his projects into practice; he would waste more and more time, until every plan ended in nothing, like badly channelled water which after a little meandering is sucked up by porous earth. The reason perhaps was this, that while he could dedicate himself to beekeeping on his own, almost in secret, without having to cope with anyone, producing every now and again just a present of a honeycomb which no one had asked him for, this work of irrigation, on the other hand, meant considering the interests of this man or that, following the opinions and the orders of the Baron or of whoever else commissioned the work. Timid and irresolute as he was, he would never oppose himself to the will of others, but would soon dissociate himself from the work and leave it.

He could be seen at all hours in the middle of a field among men armed with stakes and spades, he with a sliderule and the rolled sheet of a map, giving orders to excavate a channel and measuring the ground out by his paces, which being very short must have lengthened things very much. He would get the men to begin scooping in one place, then in another, then call a halt, then start taking measurements again. Night fell and the work was suspended. Next day he could be very rarely induced to start work at the point they'd left off. And then for a week he was nowhere to be found. His passion for hydraulics was made up of aspirations, impulses, yearnings. It was a memory he had in his heart of the lovely, well-irrigated lands of the Sultan, of orchards and gardens in which he must have been happy, the only really happy time of his life; and to those gardens of Barbary or Turkey he would be continually comparing our countryside at Ombrosa, and so felt an urge to correct it, to try to identify it with the landscape in his memory, and being a specialist in hydraulics, he concentrated in that his desire for change, continually came up against a different reality and was continually disappointed.

He also practised water divining, not openly, though, for those were still times when that strange art could be considered witchcraft. Once Cosimo found him in a field twirling and holding a forked stick. That must have been just an experiment too, as nothing came out.

Understanding the character of Enea Silvio Carrega was a help to Cosimo; it made him understand a lot about loneliness, which was to be of use to him later in life. I should say that he always carried with him the strange image of the Cavalier, as a warning of what can happen to a man who separates his own fate from others, and he managed never to be like him.

12

Sometimes Cosimo used to be woken in the night by cries of 'Help! Brigands! Quick!'

Off he would hurry through the trees towards the place from which the cries were coming. This might turn out to be some peasant cottage, with a half-naked family outside tearing their hair.

'Help, help, Gian dei Brughi has just come and taken our whole earnings from the crop!'

People crowded up.

'Gian dei Brughi? Was it him? Did you see him?'

'Yes, it was! It was! He had a mask on his face and a long pistol, and he had two masked men behind him and was ordering 'em about! It was Gian dei Brughi!'

'And where is he? Where did he go?'

'Oh, catch Gian dei Brughi? He might be anywhere, by now!'

Or the shouts might be coming from a passer-by left in the middle of the road robbed of everything, horse, purse, cloak and baggage. 'Help! Thief! Gian dei Brughi!'

'Which way did he go? Tell me!'

'He jumped out of there! Black, bearded, musket at the ready, I'm lucky to be alive!'

'Quick! Let's follow him! Which way did he go?'

'That way! No, perhaps this! He was running like the wind!'

Cosimo was determined to lay eyes on Gian dei Brughi. He would go through the length and breadth of the wood behind hares or birds, urging on the dachshund, 'Go on, to it, Ottimo Massimo!' What he longed for was to track down the bandit in person, and not to do or say anything to him, just to look someone so renowned in the face. But he never succeeded in meeting him, even by prowling all night. 'That means he hasn't been out tonight,' Cosimo would say to himself; but in the morning, on one side or other of the valley, he would find groups of people standing on their doorsteps or a turn of the road commenting on the new robbery. Cosimo would hurry up and listen with bated breath to their stories.

'But you're always on the trees in the woods,' someone said to him. 'Surely you must have seen Gian dei Brughi?'

Cosimo felt very ashamed. 'But ... I don't think so ...'

'How could he have seen him?' asked another. 'Gian dei Brughi has hiding-places no one can find, and uses paths not a soul knows about!'

'With that reward on his head, whoever gets him can spend the rest of their lives in comfort!'

'Yes, indeed! But those who do know where he is have as many accounts with justice as he has, and if they say a word they'll go straight to the gibbet themselves!'

'Gian dei Brughi! Gian dei Brughi! But d'you think he really does all these crimes himself?'

'Of course, he's got so much to account for that even if he managed to get out of ten thefts, he'd still be hanged for the eleventh!'

'He's been a brigand in all the woods along the coast!'

'He's even killed a gang leader of his, in his youth!'

'He's been banished by the bandits themselves!'

'That's why he's taken refuge in our area.'

'As we're so easy-going here!'

Cosimo would go and talk over every new incident with the charcoal-burners. Among the people camped in the wood, there were in those times a whole breed of shabby wanderers; tinkers, men who covered chairs in straw, rag-and-bone merchants, people who went round houses and planned in the morning the theft they would commit that night. More than a workshop, they used the wood as a secret refuge, a hiding-place for their booty.

'D'you know, Gian dei Brughi attacked a coach last night!'

'Ah yes? Well, maybe ...'

'He stopped the galloping horses by grasping their bits!'

'Well, either it wasn't him or those horses were grasshoppers...'

'What's that you're saying? Don't you believe it was Gian dei Brughi?'

'Ha, ha, ha!'

When he heard them talk of Gian dei Brughi like that Cosimo did not know if he was on his head or his heels. He moved about the wood and went and asked another encampment of gypsies.

'Tell me, d'you think that job on the carriage last night was Gian dei Brughi's?'

'Every job is Gian dei Brughi's, when it succeeds. Didn't you know?'

'Why, when it succeeds?'

'Because when it doesn't, it means it really is Gian dei Brughi's!'

'Ha, ha! That bungler!'

Cosimo could not understand at all. 'D'you mean Gian dei Brughi's a bungler?'

The others then hurriedly changed their tone. 'No, no, of course not, he's a brigand who frightens everyone!'

'Have you seen him yourself?'

'Us? Has anyone ever seen him?'

'But are you sure he exists?'

'What a thing to say! Sure he exists? Why, even if he didn't exist—'

'If he didn't exist?'

'—it wouldn't make any difference. Ha, ha, ha!'

'But everyone says ...'

'Sure, what should they say; that it's Gian dei Brughi who steals and robs everywhere, that terrible brigand! We'd just like to see anyone doubting that!'

'And you, boy, you don't doubt it, do you?'

Cosimo began to realize that the fear of Gian dei Brughi down in the valley changed, the farther one got into the woods, into an attitude of doubt and even of open derision.

So his longing to meet the brigand passed as he realized that the real experts did not bother about Gian dei Brughi at all. And it was just then that he did happen to come across him.

Cosimo was on a nut tree, one afternoon, reading. He had recently been taken by an urge for reading: to spend the whole day with a gun watching for a chaffinch gets boring in the long run.

Well, there he was reading Lesage's *Gil Blas*, holding his book in one hand and his gun in the other. Ottimo Massimo, who did not like seeing its master read, was wandering round in circles looking for excuses to disturb him; by barking, for instance, at a butterfly, to see if that would make Cosimo point his gun at it.

And then down the path from the mountain came running and panting a bearded, shabby, unarmed man, with two constables brandishing sabres and shouting behind him: 'Stop him! Stop him! It's Gian dei Brughi! We've caught him, at last!'

Now the brigand had gained a little on the constables, but he

was moving rather awkwardly as if afraid of mistaking the way
or falling into a trap, and so having them soon on his heels
again. Cosimo's nut tree did not offer much chance for anyone
to climb up it, but on his branch he had a rope which he always
took about with him for difficult parts. He flung one end on to
the ground and tied the other to the branch. The brigand saw
this rope falling almost on his nose and quickly clambered up,
thus showing himself to be one of those impulsive waverers or
wavering impulsives who always seem to be incapable of catching the right moment for doing anything and yet hit on it every
time.

The constables reached the spot. The rope had already been
pulled up and Gian dei Brughi was sitting by Cosimo among
the leaves of the nut tree. There was a fork in the path ahead.
The constables took one each, then met again, and did not
know where to go next. And then they bumped into Ottimo
Massimo, who was sniffling around there.

'Hey,' said one of the constables to the other, 'doesn't that
dog belong to the Baron's son, the one who's always up trees?
If the boy is around anywhere here, he might be able to tell us
something.'

'I'm up here!' Cosimo called out. But he did it not from the
nut tree where he had been before and where he had hidden
the brigand, but from a chestnut opposite, to which he had
quickly moved, so that the constables raised their heads at once
in that direction without beginning to look at the trees around.

'Good day, your lordship,' said they. 'You haven't by chance
seen the brigand Gian dei Brughi?'

'I didn't know who he was,' replied Cosimo, 'but if you're
looking for a little man, running, he took the road over there
by the torrent...'

'A little man? He's a great big man who frightens everyone...'

'Well, from up here everyone seems quite small...'

'Thank you, your lordship!' and they moved off towards the
stream.

Cosimo went back into the nut tree and began to read *Gil
Blas* again. Gian dei Brughi was still clinging to the branch, his
face, pale in the midst of red hair and dishevelled beard, stuck

all over with dried leaves, chestnut cones and pine needles. He was looking at Cosimo with a pair of green, round, stunned eyes; how ugly he was!

'Have they gone?' he decided to ask.

'Yes, yes,' said Cosimo affably. 'Are you the brigand, Gian dei Brughi?'

'How d'you know me?'

'Oh, just by reputation.'

'Are you the one who never comes down from the trees?'

'Yes. How do you know that?'

'Well, I hear of reputations too.'

They looked at each other politely, like two respectable folk meeting by chance who are pleased to find they are not unknown to each other.

Cosimo did not know what else to say, and began reading again.

'What are you reading?'

'Lesage's *Gil Blas.*'

'Is it good?'

'Oh yes.'

'Have you a lot more to read?'

'Why? Well, twenty pages or so.'

'Because when you've finished it, I'd like to ask if I can borrow it.' He smiled, rather confusedly. 'You know, I spend my days hiding and never know what to do with myself. If I only had a book every now and then, I say. Once I stopped a carriage, very little in it except for a book, and I took that. I brought it up with me, hidden under my jacket; I'd have given all the rest of the booty for that book. In the evening, lighting my lantern, I went to read it ... it was in Latin! I couldn't understand a word ...' He shook his head. 'You see, I don't know Latin ...'

'Oh well, Latin, that's difficult,' said Cosimo, feeling that in spite of himself he was taking on a protective air. 'This one is in French ...'

'French, Tuscan, Provençal, Spanish, I can understand them all,' said Gian dei Brughi, 'and even a bit of Catalan; *Bon dia! Bon nit! Esta la mar molt alborotada!*'

In half an hour Cosimo finished the book and lent it to Gian dei Brughi.

And so began the friendship between my brother and the brigand. As soon as Gian dei Brughi had finished a book, he would quickly return it to Cosimo, take another out on loan, hurry off to hide in his secret refuge, and plunge into reading.

Before, I used to get Cosimo books from the library of our house, and when he had read them he would give them back to me. Now, he began to keep them longer, as after he had read them he would pass them to Gian de Brughi, and they often came back with their covers stained, with marks of damp, streaks of snails, from the places the brigand had kept them.

Cosimo and Gian dei Brughi would arrange meetings on stated days on a certain tree, exhange the book and go off, as the wood was always being searched by police. This simple operation was very dangerous for both of them; for my brother too, who would certainly not have been able to justify his friendship with that criminal! But Gian dei Brughi was taken with such a longing to read that he would devour novel after novel, and, as he spent the whole day long reading, he would devour in one day certain tomes which my brother had spent a week over, and then he had to have another at once, and if it was not the day for their meeting he would rush all over the countryside searching for Cosimo, terrifying families in all the cottages and setting the whole police force of Ombrosa on the move.

Now, Cosimo, being always pressed by the brigand's demands, began to find that the books I got him were not enough, and he had to go and find other suppliers. He knew a Jewish bookdealer called Orbecche, who also got him works in a number of volumes. Cosimo would go and knock at his window from the branches of a carob tree, bringing him hares, thrushes and partridges he had shot, which he would exchange for books.

But Gian dei Brughi had his own special tastes; one could not give him just any book, or he would return it to Cosimo next day and have it changed. My brother was at the age in which people begin to enjoy more serious reading, but he was forced to go slowly, as Gian dei Brughi had brought him back the *Adventures of Telemachus*, warning him that if he gave him such a dull book another time he would saw the tree down from under him.

At this point Cosimo would have liked to separate the books which he wanted to read calmly on his own, from those which he got only to lend the brigand. But this was impossible, for he had to read these over too, as Gian dei Brughi became more exigent and difficult and before taking a book wanted Cosimo to tell him something about the plot and made a great fuss if he caught him out. My brother tried to pass him some light novels; and the brigand came back furiously asking if he'd taken him for a womanizer. Cosimo could never succeed in guessing what he would like or not.

In fact, with Gian dei Brughi always at him, reading, from being just Cosimo's pastime for half an hour, became his chief occupation, the aim of his entire day. And what with handling the books, judging them and acquiring them, getting to know of new ones, what with his reading for Gian dei Brughi and his own increasing need to read as well, Cosimo acquired such a passion for reading and for all human knowledge, that the hours from dawn to dusk were not enough for what he would have liked to read, and he, too, would go on by the light of a lantern.

Finally, he discovered the novels of Richardson. Gian dei Brughi liked these. Having finished one, he immediately wanted another. Orbecche would get Cosimo a whole pile of volumes. The brigand had enough to read for a whole month. Cosimo, having found peace again, plunged into the lives of Plutarch.

Gian dei Brughi, meanwhile, lying in his hiding-place, his dishevelled red hair full of dried leaves on his corrugated forehead, his green eyes growing pink in the effort to see, was reading and reading, moving his jaws in a frenzied spelling motion, holding up a finger damp with saliva ready to turn the page. This reading of Richardson seemed to bring out a disposition long latent in his mind; a yearning for the cosy habits of family life, for relations, for sentiments known in the past, a sense of virtue and of dislike for the wicked and vicious. Nothing round him interested him any more, or it filled him with disgust. He never came out of his nest now, except to run to Cosimo to exchange a volume, particularly if it was a novel in many volumes and he had got to the middle of the story. And so he lived in isolation, without realizing the storm of resentment gathering over his head, even among the inhabitants of the wood who had once been his confidants and accomplices but were tired now of a brigand so passive yet who had the whole of the local police force after him.

In the past, round him had gathered all the locals who had fallen foul of the police, even in small ways: petty thieves such as vagabonds and tinkers, or real criminals such as his bandit comrades. These people not only made use of his authority and experience for each of their thefts or raids, but also used his name as a cover, for it would go round from mouth to mouth and leave them unknown. And even those who did not take part in these operations drew advantage from their success, for the wood would fill with stolen goods and contraband of every kind, which had to be disposed of or resold, and all those who trafficked round there did good business. And then anyone who did a job of thieving on his own account unknown to Gian dei Brughi, would use that terrible name to frighten his victims and get more out of them; people lived in terror, thinking they saw Gian dei Brughi or one of his band in every evildoer they came across, and so loosened the strings of their purses.

These good times had lasted a long while; then gradually Gian dei Brughi found he could live on unearned income, and drew apart more and more. Things would all go on like this for ever, he thought, instead of which they changed, and his name no longer inspired the reverence it had before.

What use was he, Gian dei Brughi, now? With him tucked away somewhere, starry-eyed, reading novels, never doing a job, never getting any stuff, normal business in the woods was at a standstill, and what was more, the police were now always around looking for him and would take people off on the slightest suspicion. Add the temptation of the reward on Gian dei Brughi's head, and it's obvious the poor brigand's days were numbered.

Two other brigands, youths who had been his pupils and could not resign themselves to lose such a fine leader, decided to give him a chance to rehabilitate himself. They were called Ugasso and Bel-Lorè, and, as boys, had been in the band of fruit stealers. Now, as youths, they had become apprentice brigands.

So they went to see Gian dei Brughi in his cave. There he was, lying on the straw. 'Yes, who is it?' he muttered, without raising his eyes from the page.

'We've an idea to discuss, Gian dei Brughi.'

'Mmmmm ... what idea?' and he went on reading.

'Do you know where Costanzo the excise-man's house is?'

'Yes, yes ... eh? Who? What excise-man?'

Bel-Lorè and Ugasso exchanged an irritated look. If the brigand didn't take that cursed book from under his eyes, he wouldn't understand a single word they said. 'Do shut that book a moment, Gian dei Brughi, and listen to us.'

Gian dei Brughi seized the book with both hands and got up on to his knees, made as if to hold it against his chest while keeping it open at the mark, then the urge to go on reading was too much and, still holding it tight against him, he raised it enough to plunge his nose in again.

Bel-Lorè had an idea. He saw a cobweb with a big spider on it. Bel-Lorè raised the cobweb with the spider on top and threw it at Gian dei Brughi, between his book and his nose. And poor Gian dei Brughi had gone so soft he was even frightened of a spider. He felt the spider's legs tickling and the web sticking to his nose, and without even understanding what it was, gave a little yelp of disgust, dropped the book and began fanning his hands in front of his face, with staring eyes and dribbling mouth.

Ugasso swooped down and managed to seize the book before Gian dei Brughi could put a foot on it.

'Give me back that book!' said Gian de Brughi, trying to free himself from spider and web with one hand, and tear the book from Ugasso's hand with the other.

'No, listen to us first!' said Ugasso, hiding the book behind his back.

'I was just reading *Clarissa*. Do give it back! I'd just reached a bit . . .'

'Listen to us. Tonight we're to take a load of wood to the excise-man's house. In the sack, instead of wood there'll be you. When it's dark, you come out of the sack . . .'

'But I want to finish *Clarissa*!' He had managed to free his hands from the last remains of the cobweb and was struggling with the two youths.

'Listen to us . . . when it's dark, you come out of the sack, armed with pistols, get the excise-man to give you all the week's takings, which he keeps in the coffer at the head of the bed . . .'

'Do just let me finish the chapter . . . pl-e-ease.'

The two youths thought of the times when Gian dei Brughi used to plant a pair of pistols in the belly of anyone who dared contradict him. It gave them a twinge of nostalgia. 'Well, you take the bags of money, d'you understand?' They went on sadly. 'Bring 'em back to us, and we'll give you your book back, so's you can read to your heart's content. All right? You going?'

'No. It's not all right. I'm not going!'

'Ah, not going, aren't you . . . so you're not going . . . Well, we'll just see!' And Ugasso took a page towards the end of the book ('No!' screamed Gian dei Brughi), tore it out ('No, stop!'), crushed it up, and threw it in the fire.

'Ah! Swine! you can't do that! I shan't know how it ends!' And he ran after Ugasso to snatch the book.

'Are you going to the excise-man's then?'

'No! I'm not!'

Ugasso tore out another two pages.

'Stop! I haven't reached that yet! You can't burn them!'

Ugasso had already flung them in the fire.

'Swine! *Clarissa!* No!'

'Well, are you going?'

'I . . .'

Ugasso tore out another three pages and flung them in the flames.

Gian dei Brughi threw himself down with his head in his hands. 'I'll go,' he said. 'But promise you'll wait with the book outside the excise-man's.'

So the brigand was wrapped in a sack, with a band over his head. Bel-Lorè carried the sack on his shoulders. Behind came Ugasso with the book. Every now and again, when Gian dei Brughi by a jerk or groan inside the sack showed like regretting his bargain, Ugasso let him hear the sound of a page being torn out, and Gian dei Brughi would immediately be submissive and calm again.

By this method they took him as far as the excise-man's, dressed up as charcoal-burners, and left him there. Then they went and hid a short way off, behind an olive tree, waiting for him to do the robbery.

But Gian dei Brughi was in too much of a hurry, and came out of the sack before dark, when the place was still full of people.

'Up with your hands!' he called, but he wasn't the same man as before; he seemed to be seeing himself from the outside and felt a little ridiculous. 'Up with your hands, I said. Get against the wall, all of you ...'

Oh dear, he didn't believe it himself, he was just acting. 'Is this the lot?' He hadn't noticed that a child had escaped.

Well, there wasn't a minute to be lost on a job of that kind. Instead of which it lengthened out, the excise-man pretended to be stupid and not to be able to find the keys; Gian dei Brughi realized they were no longer taking him seriously, and felt rather pleased at this, deep down.

Finally, he came out, his arms loaded with bags of coins, and ran almost blindly towards the olive tree fixed as the meeting-place.

'Here's the lot! Now give me back *Clarissa*!'

Four – seven – ten arms flung themselves round him, gripped him from shoulder to ankle. He was raised up bodily and tied like a sausage. 'You'll see *Clarissa* behind bars!' and they took him off to prison.

The prison was a small tower beside the sea. A pine copse grew nearby. From the top of one of these pine trees, Cosimo could get quite near Gian dei Brughi's cell and see his face through the grille.

The brigand did not worry about his interrogation or trial. Whatever happened, his only worry was those empty days in prison without being able to read, with that novel left half finished. Cosimo managed to lay hands on another copy of *Clarissa* and took it up on the pine tree.

'What part did you get to?'

'The part where Clarissa is escaping from the brothel!' Cosimo turned over a few pages. 'Ah, yes, here we are. Well ...' and facing the grille on which he could see Gian dei Brughi's gripping hands, he began reading out loud.

The prosecution took a long time preparing its case. The brigand resisted the rack; it took days to make him confess each one of his innumerable crimes. So before and after the interrogations every day he would listen to Cosimo reading. When *Clarissa* finished, Cosimo saw he was rather sad, and it struck him that Richardson might be a little depressing to one shut up like that, so he decided to start on a novel by Fielding, whose plot and movement might give him back a sense of his lost liberty. That was during the trial, and Gian dei Brughi could think of nothing but the adventures of Jonathan Wild.

The day of execution came before the novel was finished. Gian dei Brughi made his last journey in the land of the living on a cart with a friar. Hangings at Ombrosa were from a high oak in the middle of the square. The whole population was standing round in a circle.

When his head went in the noose, Gian dei Brughi heard a whistle between the branches. He raised his face. There was Cosimo with a shut book.

'Tell me how it ends,' said the condemned man.

'I'm sorry to tell you, Gian,' answered Cosimo, 'that Jonathan ends hanged by the neck.'

'Thank you. Like me! Goodbye!' And he himself kicked away the ladder and so was strangled.

When the body ceased to twitch, the crowd went away. Cosimo remained till nightfall, astride the branch from which the hanged man was dangling. Every time that a crow came near to peck at the corpse's eyes or nose, Cosimo chased it away with a wave of his cap.

13

From this period in the brigand's company Cosimo had acquired a passion for reading and study which remained with him for the rest of his life. The attitude in which we now usually found him was astride a comfortable branch with a book open in his hand, or his back against a fork as if on a school bench, with a sheet of paper on a plank and an inkstand in a hole of the tree, writing with a long quill pen.

Now it was he who would go and look for the Abbé Fauchelefleur to give him lessons, to explain Tacitus or Ovid and the celestial bodies and the laws of chemistry. But the old priest, apart from a bit of grammar and a scrap of theology, was floundering in a sea of doubts and rifts, and at his pupil's questions he would open his arms and raise his eyes to the sky.

'*Mon Abbé*, how many wives can one have in Persia?' '*Mon Abbé*, who is the Savoyard Vicar?' '*Mon Abbé*, can you explain the systems of Linnaeus?' '*Alors ... Maintenant ... Voyons ...*' would begin the Abbé, then hesitate and go no further.

But Cosimo, who was devouring books of every kind, and spending half his time in reading and half in hunting to pay the bookseller's bills, always had some new story to tell him. Of Rousseau botanizing on his walks through the forests of Switzerland, or Benjamin Franklin trying to capture lightning with an eagle, of the Baron de la Hontan living happily among the Indians of America.

Old Fauchelefleur seemed to listen to all this with surprised attention, whether from real interest or only from relief at not having to teach himself, I don't know; and he would nod and interject a '*Non! Dites-Moi!*' when Cosimo turned to him and asked 'Do you know how it is that ... ?' or with a '*Tiens!*' '*C'est bien épatant!*' when Cosimo gave him a reply; and sometimes a '*Mon Dieu!*' which could be either from exultation at this new revelation of the greatness of God, or from regret at the omnipresence of Evil still rampant in the world under so many guises.

I was too much of a boy and Cosimo's only friends were

illiterate, hence his need to comment on the discoveries he kept on making in books found an outlet in this spate of questions and rejoinders to the old tutor. The Abbé, of course, had the gentle accommodating outlook that comes from a higher understanding of the vanity of all things; and Cosimo profited by it. Thus the relationship of pupil and teacher between the two was reversed. It was Cosimo who became the teacher and Fauchelefleur the pupil. And my brother was acquiring such strength of character that he even managed to drag the trembling old man behind him up on to the trees. He made him spend an entire afternoon with his thin legs dangling from a chestnut tree in the Ondariva gardens, contemplating the rare plants and the sunset reflected in the basins of the fountains and discussing monarchies and republics, the right and truth in various religions, Chinese rituals, the Lisbon earthquake, the bottle of Leyden, and the philosophy of Sensism

I was supposed to have my Greek lesson with him, and could not find the tutor. The whole family was alerted, the countryside was searched and even the fishing-pond dragged for him lest in a careless moment he had fallen in and got drowned. But back he came that evening, complaining of lumbago after all the hours he had spent sitting so uncomfortably.

It must not be forgotten, though, that this state of general passive acceptance by the old Jansenist alternated with momentary returns of his old passion for spiritual rigour. And if, while in a careless and yielding mood, he accepted without resistance any new or libertarian idea, such as the equality of all men before the law, or the honesty of primitive people, or the bad influence of superstitions, he would be assailed, a quarter of an hour later, by an excess of austerity and sustain with all his old urge for coherence and moral severity the ideas he had accepted so lightly just before. On his lips, then, the duties of free and equal citizens or the virtues of natural religion became hard and fast dogmatic rules, articles of fanatical faith, beyond which he could only see a black picture of corruption; to him, then, all the new philosophers were far too bland and superficial in their denunciation of evil, for the way of perfection was arduous and left no room for compromises or halfway measures.

To these sudden about-turns of the Abbé, Cosimo did not dare say a word, for fear of being criticized for incoherence and lack of rigour, and his proliferating thoughts would go arid as if they had suddenly wandered into some marble cemetery. Luckily the Abbé would soon tire of these tensions of the will, and sit there looking exhausted, as if this whittling away of every concept to its pure essence left him the prey of impalpable shadows; he would blink, give a sigh, turn the sigh to a yawn, and go back into his nirvana.

But between one and other of these habits of mind he was now spending his entire days following the studies being pursued by Cosimo, shuttle-cocking between the trees where Cosimo was perched and Orbecche's shop, ordering books from Amsterdam or Paris, and taking out those newly arrived. And thus came his disaster. For the rumour reached the Ecclesiastical Tribunal that there was a priest at Ombrosa who read all the most forbidden books in Europe. One afternoon the police appeared at our house with orders to inspect the Abbé's cell. Among his breviaries they found the works of Bayle, still uncut, but this was enough for them to put him between them and take him away.

It was a sad little scene, on that misty afternoon; I remember the dismay with which I watched it from the window of my room, and stopped studying the conjugation of aorist, as there would be no more lessons. Old Abbé Fauchelefluer went off down the alley between the two armed ruffians, raising his eyes towards the trees, and at a certain point he staggered as if he wanted to run to an elm tree and climb up it, but had not the strength. Cosimo was hunting in the woods that day and knew nothing of it all; so they did not even say goodbye.

We could do nothing to help him. Our father shut himself up in his room and refused all food for fear of being poisoned by the Jesuits. The Abbé spent the rest of his days between prison and monastery in continual acts of abjuration, until he died, after an entire life dedicated to the faith, without ever knowing what he believed in, but trying to believe firmly until the last.

*

Anyway, the Abbé's arrest had no effects on the progress of Cosimo's education. And from that period dates his correspondence with the major philosophers and scientists of Europe, to whom he wrote in the hope of their resolving his queries and objections, or perhaps just for the pleasure of discussion with superior minds and also the practice of foreign languages. It was a pity that all his papers, which he kept in a hollow tree trunk known only to himself, have never been found and must certainly by now be mouldy or nibbled away by squirrels; there would be letters among them in the handwriting of the most famous scholars of the century.

To keep his books Cosimo constructed a kind of hanging bookcase, sheltered as best he could from rain and nibbling mouths. But he would continuously change them around, according to his studies and tastes of the moment, for he considered books as rather like birds which it saddened him to see caged or motionless.

On the strongest of these bookcases were ranged the tomes of Diderot and D'Alembert's Encyclopaedia as they reached him from a bookseller at Leghorn. And though recently all his living with books had put his head rather in the clouds and made him less interested in the world around him, now on the other hand reading the Encyclopaedia, and beautiful words like *Abeille*, *Arbre, Bois, Jardin*, made him rediscover everything around him as if seeing them for the first time. Among the books he sent for there began also to figure practical handbooks, for example on tree culture, and he found himself longing for the moment when he could experiment with his new knowledge.

Human work had always interested Cosimo, but up till now his life in the trees, his constant movements and his hunting had been enough to satisfy his disconnected instinct, as if he were a bird. Now on the other hand he found coming over him a need to do something useful for his neighbour. And this too, if one analyses it, was something he had learnt from his friendship with the brigand; the pleasure of making himself useful, of doing some service indispensable to another.

He learnt the art of pruning trees, and offered his help to the fruit-growers in winter, when the trees stuck out an irregular maze of twigs and seemed to long for a change to more ordered forms so as to cover themselves with flowers and leaves and fruit. Cosimo was good at pruning and charged little; so every owner or tenant of an orchard around would ask for his help, and he could be seen, in the crystalline air of those early mornings, standing with legs apart on low bare branches, his neck wrapped in a scarf to his ears, raising his shears and, clip! clip! off flew secondary branches and twigs under his sure touch. He did the same in gardens with bushes planted for shade or ornament, which he would attack with a short saw, and in the woods, where instead of the woodsman's axe, whose only use was chopping down some ancient trunk completely, he would lop away with his swift hatchet only on the tops and upper branches.

In fact, his love for this arboreal element made him, as all real loves do, become forthright to the point of hurting, wounding and amputating so as to help growth and give shape. Certainly he was careful, when pruning and lopping, to serve not only the interests of the owner but also his own, being a traveller with a need to make his own routes more practicable; thus he would see that the branches which he used as a bridge between one tree and another were always saved and reinforced by the suppression of others. And so, these trees of Ombrosa which he had already found so benign, now, by taking thought, he helped to render more directly helpful, thus being at the same time a friend to his neighbour, to nature and to himself. The advantages of this wise work of his he was to appreciate above all at a much later period, when the shape of the trees made up more and more for his loss of strength. Then, with the advent of more careless generations, of improvident greed, of people who loved nothing, not even themselves, all was to change, and no Cosimo will ever walk on the trees again.

14

If the number of Cosimo's friends grew so did his enemies. The vagabonds of the wood, in fact, after Gian dei Brughi's conversion to a love of literature and subsequent fall, had taken against him. One night my brother was sleeping in his leather bag hung on an ash tree in the wood, when he was woken by the barking of the dachshund. He opened his eyes and saw a light; it came from down below, there was a fire at the bottom of the tree and the flames were already licking the trunk.

A fire in the wood! Who could have set it going? Cosimo was quite certain he had never struck his flint that night. So it must have been done by those ruffians! They wanted to set the wood alight in order to get firewood and at the same time not only arrange to catch Cosimo, but burn him alive.

At that moment Cosimo did not think of the danger which was threatening him so closely; his only thought was that the vast kingdom of paths and retreats which were his alone might be destroyed, and this was his only terror. Ottimo Massimo was already rushing away to avoid being burnt, turning around every now and again to give a desperate yelp; the fire was spreading in the undergrowth.

Cosimo did not lose heart. He had taken a variety of objects up on the ash tree which was then his refuge, and among these was a bottle full of barley water, to placate the summer thirst. He climbed to the bottle. Alarmed squirrels and bats were fleeing up the branches of the ash tree, and birds were flying away from their nests. He seized the bottle and was about to unscrew the cork and pour it over the trunk of the ash tree to save it from the flames, when he realized that the fire was already catching the grass, the dried leaves and bushes of the undergrowth and would soon catch all the trees around. He decided to take a risk: 'Let the ash burn! If I manage to wet the earth all round where the flames have not got to yet, I'll stop the fire!' And opening the top of the bottle he poured it down with a twisting, circular movement on to the farthest tips of fire, putting them out. And so the fire in the undergrowth found itself in the midst of a circle of damp grass and leaves, and could not expand any more.

From the top of the ash tree Cosimo jumped down on to a beech nearby; he was only just in time; the trunk eaten away by fire at the base crashed down in a great funeral pyre amid the vain squeaks of squirrels.

Would the fire be limited to that point? Already hundreds of sparks and little flames were flying around; certainly the slippery barrier of wet leaves would not prevent it spreading! 'Fire! Fire!' Cosimo began to shout at the top of his voice. 'Fire!'

'Who's there? Who's shouting?' replied voices. Not far from the spot was a charcoal-burner's site, and a group of men from Bergamo, friends of his, were sleeping in a shack nearby.

'Fire! Fire!'

Soon the whole mountainside was resounding with the cry. The charcoal-burners scattered over the woods shouted it to each other in their incomprehensible dialect. Along they came running from all directions. And the fire was subdued.

This first attempt at arson and the attack on his life should have warned Cosimo to keep clear of the wood. Instead of which he began going into the whole matter of controlling fires. It was the summer of a hot, dry year. In the coastal woods towards Provence a fire had been burning non-stop for a week. At night its gleam reflected on the mountainside like the last sunset. The air was dry, trees and bushes like tinder in the drought. The wind seemed to be urging the flames in our direction, where occasional fires, either by chance or on purpose, would break out, joining the rest in a single belt of flame along the whole coast. Ombrosa was stunned by the danger, as if it were a fortress with a straw roof attacked by enemy incendiaries. The sky itself was charged with fire; every night shooting stars would fly all over the firmament and we would wait for them to fall right on to us.

In those days of general dismay, Cosimo bought up a lot of barrels, filled them with water, and hoisted them up to the tops of the highest trees on dominating points. 'One never knows, but this sort of thing's been useful once.' Not content with this, he studied the courses of the streams crossing the woods, half dried up though they were, right back to where their springs sent out only a trickle of water. Then he went to consult the Cavalier.

'Oh, yes,' exclaimed Enea Silvio Carrega, clapping a hand to his forehead. 'Reservoirs! Dykes! We must make plans!' and he broke out into little cries and jumps of enthusiasm with the myriad ideas crowding in his mind.

Cosimo set him to work at calculations and drawings, and meanwhile approached the owners of the private woods, the tenants of the public woods, the woodcutters, the charcoal-burners. All together, under the direction of the Cavalier (or rather the Cavalier under all of them, forced to direct them and not let his thoughts wander), with Cosimo superintending the work from above, they formed reserves of water in such a way that they could get pumps to every point where a fire might break out.

But this was not enough; squads of men had to be organized to put the fires out, groups who in case of alarm knew how to organize themselves at once into chains to pass buckets of water from hand to hand and halt the fire before it spread. So there appeared a kind of militia which took turns on guard and night inspection. The men were recruited by Cosimo among the peasants and artisans of Ombrosa. And at once, as happens in every association, there grew up a corporate spirit, a sense of competition between the groups, and all felt capable of great things. Cosimo, too, felt a new strength and content; he had discovered his ability to bring people together and to put himself at their head; an aptitude which, luckily for himself, he was never called on to abuse, and which he used only a very few times in his life, always when there were important results to be carried out, and always with great success.

This he understood; that association renders men stronger and brings out each person's best gifts, and gives a joy which is rarely to be had by keeping to oneself, the joy of realizing how many honest decent capable people there are for whom it is worth giving one's best (while living just for oneself very often the opposite happens, of seeing people's other side, the side which makes one keep one's hand always on the hilt of one's sword).

So that was a good summer, the summer of the fires; there was a common problem which everyone had at heart to resolve, and each put it above every other personal interest, and all were repaid by the pleasure of finding themselves in agreement and mutual esteem with so many others.

Later Cosimo came to realize that when a problem in common no longer exists, associations are not as good as they were before, and it is better then to be a man alone and not a leader. But being a leader, meanwhile, he spent the nights all alone in the woods on sentry duty, up on a tree as he had always lived.

He had arranged a bell on the top of a tree which could be heard from a distance and give the alarm at the first glimmer of an incipient fire. By this system they managed to catch three or four fires in time when they first broke out, and save the woods. They were due to arson, and the culprits were found to be the two brigands Ugasso and Bel-Lorè, who were banished from the territory of the Commune. Rain set in at the end of August; the danger of fires had passed.

At that time one heard nothing but good said of my brother at Ombrosa. These favourable voices also reached our home: 'How nice he is!' 'He really does know about *some* things' – in the tone of people wanting to make an objective judgement on someone of a different religion or another political party, and trying to show themselves so open-minded that they can even appreciate ideas far removed from their own.

The reactions of the Generalessa to this news were brusque and summary. 'Are they armed?' she would ask, when they talked of the squads of guards against fires formed by Cosimo. 'Do they do manoeuvres?' For she was already thinking of the formation of an armed militia which could, in case of war, take part in military operations.

Our father, on the other hand, would listen in silence, shaking his head so that it was difficult to understand if all these items of news about his son were painful to him or bored him, or flattered him in some way as if his one longing was a chance to hope in him again. This last must have been the right explanation, as a few days later he mounted his horse and went to look for him.

It was an open place, where they met, with a row of saplings round. The Baron rode up and down the row two or three times, without looking at his son, though he had seen him. Jump by jump the boy moved down from the last tree until he got nearer and nearer. When he was facing his father he took off his straw hat (which took the place in summer of that cap of wildcat fur) and said: 'Good day, my lord father.'

'Good day, son.'

'Are you in good health?'

'Considering my years and sorrows.'

'I am pleased to see you so well.'

'That is what I want to say to you, Cosimo. I hear that you are busying yourself for the common good.'

'I hold dear the forest in which I live, lord father.'

'Do you know that part of the wood is our property, inherited from your poor grandmother, the late Lady Elizabeth?'

'Yes, my lord father. In the Belrio area there are thirty chestnuts, twenty-two ashes, eight pines, and a maple. I have copies of all the surveyors' maps, and it was as a member of a family owning woods that I tried to collect together all those with a common interest in preserving them.'

'Ah yes,' said the Baron, giving this answer a favourable reception. 'But,' he added, 'they tell me that it is an association of bakers, market-gardeners and blacksmiths.'

'Them too, lord father. Of all professions that are honest.'

'Do you realize that you could lead noble vassals with the title of Duke?'

'I realize that when I have more ideas than others, I give those others my ideas, if they want to accept them; and that to me is leading.'

'And to lead nowadays, d'you need to be on a tree?' was on the tip of the Baron's tongue to say. But what was the use of bringing that up again? He sighed, absorbed in his thoughts, then loosened the belt on which his sword was hanging. 'You are now eighteen years of age... It is time you considered your-self an adult... I no longer have long to live ...' and he held out the flat sword on his two hands. 'Do you remember you are the Baron of Rondò?'

'Yes, lord father, I remember my name.'

'Do you wish to be worthy of the name and title you bear?'

'I will try to be as worthy as I can of the name of man, and also of his every attribute.'

'Take this sword, my sword.' The Baron raised himself on his stirrups. Cosimo stooped down on the branch and the Baron managed to strap the belt round his waist.

'Thank you, lord father ... I promise I will make good use of it.'

'Farewell, my son.' The Baron turned his horse, gave a slight tug at the reins, and rode slowly away.

Cosimo stood there a moment wondering whether he ought not to salute him with the sword, then reflected that his father had given it to him as a defence not as an instrument of cere-mony, and he kept it sheathed.

15

It was at this time, when he began seeing a lot of the Cavalier, that Cosimo noticed something odd in his behaviour, or rather something different from usual, whether odder or less odd. It was as if that abstracted air of his no longer came from a wan-dering mind, but from a fixed and dominating thought. He would often, now, have talkative moments; and though before, unsociable as he was, he never set foot in the town, now on the other hand he was always down at the port, mingling with groups or sitting on the pavements with old sailors and boat-men, commenting on the arrival and departure of ships and the misdeeds of the pirates.

Off our coasts there still cruised the feluccas of the Barbary pirates, molesting our traffic. Nowadays it was petty piracy, no longer as in the days when an attack by pirates meant ending as a slave at Tunis or Algiers, or losing nose and ears. Now when the Mohammedans managed to overtake a sloop from Ombrosa, they only took the cargo: barrels of dried fish, rounds of Dutch cheese, bales of cotton and the like. Sometimes our ships were faster and would escape, firing a round of grapeshot at the felucca's rigging; and the Barbary sailors would reply by spitting, making lewd gestures and shouting insults.

In fact it was almost amiable piracy, and went on because the Pashas of those countries claimed certain credits from our merchants and shipowners, which they extorted as according to them they had not been properly treated, or even cheated, in some business deal or other. And so they tried to settle their accounts piecemeal by robbery while at the same time con-tinuing their commercial transactions, with constant bickering and bargaining. So it was to neither side's interest to come to a definite break; and navigation hereabouts went on full of hazards and risks, without ever degenerating to tragedy.

The story I am about to tell was narrated to me by Cosimo in a number of different versions; I am keeping to the one which had the most details and was also the least logical. My brother when describing his adventures certainly added many out of his own head, but I always try to give a faithful report of what he told me, as he is the only source.

Well, one night Cosimo, who since that watching for fires had got into the habit of waking up at all hours, saw a light coming down into the valley. He followed it silently over the branches with his cat's tread, and saw Enea Silvio Carrega walking along very quietly, in his fez and robe, holding a lantern.

What was the Cavalier, who usually retired to bed with the chickens, doing up at that hour? Cosimo followed some way behind. He was careful not to make any noise, knowing too that his uncle, when walking along so concentratedly, was as good as deaf and saw only a few inches in front of his nose.

By mule-paths and short cuts the Cavalier reached the edge of the sea, on a stretch of pebbly beach, and began to wave his lantern. There was no moon and nothing could be seen in the sea except moving foam on the nearest waves. Cosimo was on a pine tree a little way from the shore, as at that level the vegetation petered out and it was not so easy to get about on branches. Anyway, he could see quite clearly the old man in his high fez on the deserted beach, waving his lantern towards the dark sea; and then suddenly from that darkness another lantern replied, very near, as if it had been lit that minute, and there emerged, moving very fast, a little boat with a dark square sail and oars, a different boat from the ones of these parts, and came towards the shore.

By the quavering light of the lantern, Cosimo saw men with turbans on their heads; some remained on the boat and kept it to the beach with little strokes of the oars; others landed, and they had wide swelling red pantaloons, and gleaming scimitars tied to their waists. Cosimo was all eyes and ears. His uncle and the Berbers talked among themselves, in a language which he could not understand but which he felt he might have been able to, and must surely be the famous *lingua franca*. Every now and again Cosimo understood a word or two in his own language, which Enea Silvio would emphasize, mingling these with other incomprehensible words, and the words in Italian were the names of ships, well-known sloops and brigantines belonging to the shipowners of Ombrosa, plying between our port and others nearby.

It didn't need much imagination to realize what the Cavalier must have been saying! He was informing the pirates about the times of arrival and departure of the Ombrosa boats, and about the cargo they were carrying, their route, and the weapons they had on board. And now the old man must have told them everything he knew, for he turned round and hurried away, while the pirates climbed back on to their boat and vanished into the dark sea. From the rate they talked he realized that they must have done this often before. Who knows how long those

Berbers had been acting on information supplied by our uncle!

Cosimo stayed on the pine tree, incapable of tearing himself away from there, from the deserted shore. A wind was blowing, waves were gnawing at the beach. The tree groaned in all its joints and his teeth chattered, not from the cold air but from the chill of his discovery.

So that timid and mysterious old man who as boys we had always judged to be false and whom Cosimo had thought he had gradually learnt to appreciate and understand was now revealed as a miserable traitor, an ungrateful wretch willing to harm his own country which had taken him in when he was but drift-wood after a life of errors. Had he been swept to such a point of nostalgia for countries and people where he must have found himself, for once in his life, happy? Or did he nurture a deep rancour against the home in which every mouthful he ate must have been one of humiliation? Cosimo was divided between the impulse to rush off and denounce him as a spy and so save our merchants' cargoes, and the thought of the pain it would cause our father, because of the affection which linked him so in-explicably to his half-brother. Cosimo could already imagine the scene; the Cavalier manacled amid police between two rows of Ombrosans cursing him, and so being led to the square, having the noose put over his head, being hanged ... After that night of watching over the dead body of Gian dei Brughi, Cosimo had sworn to himself that he would never again be present at an execution; and now he had to be the judge of whether to condemn to death one of his own relations!

This thought tortured him the whole night long and the whole of next day too, as he moved endlessly from one branch to another, slipping, saving himself with his arms, letting him-self slither on the bark, as he always did when preoccupied. Finally he made his decision; a compromise: to terrify both the pirates and his uncle, and put a stop to their criminal dealings without the intervention of the law. He would perch on that pine tree at night, with three or four loaded guns (by now he had collected an entire arsenal for his various hunting needs). When the Cavalier met the pirates he would begin firing one musket after another, making the bullets whistle over their heads. On hearing that firing, pirates and uncle would each escape on their own. And the Cavalier, who was certainly not brave, at the chance of being recognized and the certainty that his meetings on the beach were now watched, would be sure to break off relations with the Berber crew.

So Cosimo waited on the pine tree for a couple of nights, his muskets at the ready. And nothing happened. The third night, down came the old man in his fez, trotting along the pebbles of the beach, waving his lantern, and again a boat approached, with sailors in turbans.

Cosimo had his finger ready on the trigger, but did not fire, for this time everything was different. After a short colloquy, two of the pirates landed and signalled towards the boat and the others began unloading cargo; barrels, bales, sacks, demi-johns, cases full of cheeses. There was not just one boat, but a number of them, all heavily loaded; and a row of porters in turbans began winding along the beach, preceded by our uncle, leading them with his hesitant steps to a cave among the rocks. There the Moors set down all those goods, certainly fruit of their latest piracies.

Why were they bringing this on shore? Later it was easy to reconstruct the circumstances. As the Berber felucca had to anchor in one of our ports (for some legitimate business, as was always going on between them and us in the middle of all their piracy) and therefore had to undergo a search by our customs, they had to hide their stolen goods in a safe place, so as to retrieve them on their return. In this way the men of the felucca would prove they had nothing to do with the latest robberies on the high seas, and strengthen their normal commercial relations with Ombrosa too.

All this background was clear afterwards. At that moment Cosimo did not stop to ask himself questions. There was a pirate treasure hidden in a cave, the pirates were re-embarking and leaving it there; it must be moved as soon as possible. The first idea that crossed my brother's mind was to go and wake the merchants of Ombrosa, who were presumably the legitimate owners of the stuff. But then he remembered his charcoal-burner friends starving in the woods with their families. He did not hesitate, but hurried off over the branches straight to where, around patches of grey beaten earth, the Bergamese were sleeping in rough shacks.

'Quick! Come on, all of you! I've found the pirates' treasure!'

From under the tents and branches of the shacks came puffing, shuffling, cursing and finally exclamations of surprise, questions. 'Gold? Silver?'

'I haven't seen properly ...' said Cosimo. 'From the smell, I'd say that there was a lot of stockfish and goat's cheese.'

At these words all the men of the woods sprang to their feet. Those of them who had muskets snatched them up, others hatchets, spits, spades, or stakes, but they all took some receptacle or other to put the stuff into, even broken charcoal-baskets and blackened sacks. A long procession started. 'Hurrah! Hurrah!' Even the women went down with empty baskets on their heads, and the boys all hooded in sacks, holding torches. Cosimo went ahead from land pine to olive, from olive to sea pine.

They were just about to turn the spur of rock with the cave opening beyond, when on top of a twisted fig tree appeared the white shadow of a pirate, who raised his scimitar and shouted the alarm. A few leaps, Cosimo was on a branch above him, and plunged his sword into the man's guts, till he slumped over the cliff.

In the cave a meeting of the pirate chiefs was taking place. (Cosimo, in all that coming and going of unloading, had not realized they had stayed behind.) Hearing the sentinel's cry they came out and found themselves surrounded by a hoard of men and women black with charcoal, hooded in sacks and armed with stakes. Baring their scimitars the Moors rushed forward to cut a way through. *'Hurrah! Hota! Inshallah!'* The battle began.

The charcoal-burners were superior in numbers, but the pirates better armed. It's well known, though, that for fighting scimitars there's nothing better than stakes. Ding! Ding! And the Damascene blades withdrew all jagged at the edges. Their muskets, on the other hand, thundered and smoked, but to no purpose. Some of the pirates (officers, as could be seen) had lovely muskets, chased all over; but the tinder had got damp in the cave and wouldn't spark. Now some of the charcoal-burners began stunning the pirate officers by hitting them over the head with stakes, to get their muskets away from them. But with those turbans, every blow on the Berber's head was muffled as if by cushions; it was better to kick them in the stomach, as their midriffs were bare.

Seeing that the one weapon in good supply was pebbles, the charcoal-burners began flinging them in handfuls. The Moors, then, began throwing the pebbles back. With this stone-throwing, the battle eventually took on a more orderly aspect, but as the charcoal-burners were trying to enter the cave, attracted more and more by the smell of stockfish coming out of it, and the Berbers were trying to escape towards their sloop still off-shore, there was no great contrast in aims between the two sides.

Then the Bergamese launched an assault to break into the cave. The Mohammedans were still resisting under hails of stones, when they saw the way to the sea was free. Why go on resisting, then? Better hoist sails and be off.

On reaching the boat, three pirates, all nobles and officers, unfurled the sails. With a leap from a pine tree on the beach, Cosimo flung himself on to the mast, gripped the pennant-bar at the top, and from up there, hanging on by the knees, unsheathed his sword. The three pirates raised their scimitars. My brother with slashes to right and slashes to left, kept all three at bay. The boat was still beached and wobbling now from side to side. At that moment the moon came out and glinted on the sword given by the Baron to his son and on the Mohammedan blades. My brother slipped down the mast and plunged his sword into the breast of a pirate who was dropping overboard. Up he went again, swift as a lizard, defending himself with two parries from the others' slashes, slid down once more and thrust the sword through a second pirate, went up, had a short skirmish with the third, slid down and transfixed him too.

The three Mohammedan officers were lying half in the sea with beards full of seaweed. The other pirates at the cave mouth were stunned with stones and blows from stakes. Cosimo was looking triumphantly around from the top of the mast, when from the cave, like a cat with its tail afire, leapt the Cavalier Carrega, who had been hiding there till now. He ran up the beach with head down, gave the boat one shove which floated it away from the beach, jumped in, seized the oars and began rowing as hard as he could out to sea.

'Cavalier! What are you doing! Are you mad?' said Cosimo, gripping the mast. 'Go back to shore! Where are we going?'

No answer. It was clear that Enea Silvio Carrega wanted to reach the pirate ship to save himself. Now his felony had been discovered once for all, and if he stayed on shore he would certainly end on the gibbet. So he rowed and rowed and Cosimo, though he still had his bared sword in his hand and the old man was disarmed and weak, was at a loss what to do next. At the bottom of his heart he didn't at all want to do his uncle any harm, and, another thing, to reach him he would have to come right down the mast, and this descent on to a boat was equivalent to descending to earth; the question whether he had not already deviated from his unspoken laws by jumping from a tree with roots to the mast of a boat, was too complicated to think out at that moment. So he did nothing and settled on top of the mast, one leg each side, moving off on the waves, while a slight wind swelled the sail, and the old man never stopped rowing.

He heard a bark. And started with pleasure. The dog Ottimo Massimo, which he had lost sight of during the battle, was crouching there at the bottom of the boat and wagging its tail as if nothing unusual was happening. Oh well, reflected Cosimo, there was not so very much to worry about; it was a family party, what with his uncle and his dog; and he was going on a boating trip, which after so many years of arboreal life was a pleasant diversion.

The moon shone on the sea. Now the old man was tiring. He was rowing with difficulty, sobbing and saying again and again: 'Ah, Zaira ... ah, Allah, Allah, Zaira ... *Inshallah* ... !' then he'd relapse into Turkish, repeating over and over again amid tears this woman's name which Cosimo had never heard.

'What are you saying, Cavalier? What's the matter with you? Where are we going?' he asked.

'Zaira ... Ah, Zaira ... Allah, Allah ...' exclaimed the old man.

'Who is Zaira, Cavalier? Do you think you are going to Zaira this way?' and Enea Silvio Carrega nodded his head, and mumbled Turkish amid his tears, and called that name out to the moon.

Cosimo's mind at once began to mill over suppositions about this Zaira. Perhaps the deepest mystery of that reserved and mysterious man was about to reveal itself. If the Cavalier hoped to join this Zaira by going towards the pirate ship, she must then be a woman out there, in those Ottoman lands. Perhaps the whole of his life had been dominated by nostalgia for that woman, perhaps she was the image of the lost happiness which he had expressed by raising bees and tracing irrigation channels. Perhaps she was a mistress, a wife whom he had left over there, in the gardens of those lands beyond the seas, or perhaps she was really his daughter, a daughter whom he had not seen since she was a child, to find whom he had tried for years to establish contact with one of the Turkish or Moorish ships that came to our parts, until finally he had got news of her. Perhaps he had learnt that she was a slave, and as a ransom they had suggested his passing information on the Ombrosan sloops. Or perhaps it was a price he had to pay in order to be readmitted among them and embarked for the country of Zaira.

Now, his intrigue discovered, he was forced to flee from Ombrosa, and now the Berbers could not refuse to take him with them and carry him back to her. In his panting snatches of talk were mixed accents of hope, of invocation, and also of fear; fear lest this was still not the right opportunity, or lest some mischance might still separate him from the creature for whom he yearned.

He was just getting to the end of his tether in rowing, when a shadow drew near, another Berber boat. Perhaps from the ship they had heard the sounds of battle on the shore, and were sending out scouts.

Cosimo slipped halfway down the mast, so as to hide behind

the sail, but the old man began to shout in *lingua franca* for them to fetch him and take him to the ship, stretching out imploring arms. His petition was granted; two janissaries in turbans, as soon as they were within reach, took him up by the shoulders, light as he was, and pulled him on to their boat. The boat on which Cosimo was got pushed away, the wind caught the sail, and so my brother, who had really felt he was done for this time, escaped discovery.

As the wind bore him away from the pirate boat, Cosimo heard voices raised as if in argument. A word said by the Moors, which sounded like 'Marrano!' and the old man's voice repeating faintly, 'Ah Zaira!' left no doubts as to the Cavalier's reception. Certainly they held him responsible for the ambush at the cave, for the loss of their booty and the deaths of their men, and were accusing him of treachery.... A last shout, a plop, then silence; and to Cosimo's mind came as clearly as if he heard it the sound of his father's voice shouting, 'Enea Silvio! Enea Silvio!' as he followed his half-brother over the country-side; and Cosimo hid his face in the sail.

He climbed the mast again, to see where the boat was going. Something was floating in the midst of the sea as if carried by a current, an object, a kind of buoy, but a buoy with a tail ... A ray of moonlight fell on it, and he saw that it was not an object but a head, a head stuck in a fez with a tassel, and he recognized the upturned face of the Cavalier looking up with his mouth open; but below the beard the whole of the rest was in the water and could not be seen, and Cosimo shouted: 'Cavalier! What are you doing? What are you doing? Why don't you get in? Catch hold of the boat! I'll help you in, Cavalier!'

But his uncle did not answer; he was floating, floating, looking up with that dismayed air as if he could see nothing. And Cosimo said: 'Hey! Ottimo Massimo! Throw yourself in the water! Take the Cavalier by the nape of the neck! Save him! Save him!'

The obedient dog plunged in, tried to get his teeth into the old man's nape, did not succeed, and took him by the beard.

'By the nape, I said, Ottimo Massimo!' insisted Cosimo, but the dog raised the head by the beard and pushed it to the edge of the boat, and then it could be seen that there was no nape of the neck any more; no body or anything, just a head; the head of Enea Silvio Carrega struck off by the stroke of a scimitar.

16

The first version of the Cavalier's end, as given by Cosimo, was very different. When the wind brought the boat to the shore with him clinging to the mast and Ottimo Massimo dragging the truncated head, he told the people who came hurrying to his call a very simple story (meanwhile he quickly transferred himself on to a tree with the help of a pole); that the Cavalier had been kidnapped by the pirates and then killed. Perhaps it was a version prompted by the thought of his father, who would be so struck down with sorrow at the news of his half-brother's death and the sight of that pathetic relic that Cosimo lacked the heart to load him with the revelation of the Cavalier's felony too. In fact, afterwards, when he heard of the deep gloom into which the Baron had fallen, he tried to make up an imaginary glory for our natural uncle, inventing a secret and astute intrigue against the pirates to which the Cavalier had dedicated himself for some time and whose discovery had brought him to his death. But this account was contradictory and full of gaps, also because there was something else that Cosimo wanted to hide, which was the disembarking of the stolen goods by the pirates in the cave and the intervention of the charcoal-burners. For, if the whole story had been known, the entire population of Ombrosa would have gone into the woods to take their merchandise back from the Bergamese, and treat them as robbers.

After a week or so, when he was certain that the charcoal-burners had disposed of the goods, he told of the assault on the cave, and anyone who went up to try and recuperate their property came back with empty hands. The charcoal-burners had divided it all up into equal parts: the stock fish fillet by fillet, and with the sausages and cheeses, and the whole of the rest they had made a great banquet which lasted all day.

Our father was very much aged, and sorrow for the loss of Enea Silvio had strange consequences on his character. He was taken by a mania to prevent any of his brother's work being lost, so he insisted on looking after the beehives himself, and set to work with great ceremony, though he had never before seen a bee-hive close to. For advice he turned to Cosimo, who had learnt something about them; not that he would ask him direct questions, but just draw the conversation on to apiculture, listen to what Cosimo said, and then repeat it as orders to the peasants in an irascible self-sufficient tone, as if it were all quite obvious. To the hives themselves he tried not to get too close for fear of being stung, but he was determined to conquer this reaction, and must have gone through agonies because of it. He also gave orders for certain water-courses to be dug, in order to carry out a project initiated by poor Enea Silvio; and had he succeeded it would have been an excellent thing, as his poor dear brother had never completed a single one.

This tardy passion of the Baron for practical affairs lasted only a short time, alas. One day he was busying himself nervously among the beehives and water-courses, when at some brusque movement of his, a swarm of bees made for him. He took fright, began to wave his hands about, overturned a bee-hive, and rushed off with a cloud of bees behind him. He ran blindly, fell into the channel which they were trying to fill with water, and was pulled out soaking wet.

He was put to bed. What with a fever from the stings, and another from the wetting, he was in bed a week; then he was more or less cured, but he went into such a decline that he never pulled up again.

He had lost any attachment to life and would stay in bed all day long. Nothing in his life had turned out as he hoped. No one mentioned the Dukedom any more. His eldest son spent his whole life on trees even now he was grown up; his half-brother had been murdered; his daughter was married far away into a family even more unpleasant than herself; I was too young to be anything of a companion; his wife too impulsive and hectoring. He began getting hallucinations that the Jesuits had taken over his house and would not allow him to leave his room, and so, bitter and bizarre as he had lived, he came to death.

Cosimo followed the funeral too, from one tree to another, but he could not enter the cemetery, as cypresses are too close-knit for any foothold. He watched the burial from beyond the cemetery wall and when we all flung a handful of earth on the coffin he threw down a small branch of leaves. We had all, I thought, been as far removed from my father as Cosimo was on the trees.

So now Cosimo was Baron of Rondò. There was no change in his life. He looked after the family interests, it is true, but always rather haphazardly. When the bailiffs and tenants wanted to find him they did not know where to look; and just when they least wanted him to see them, there he would be on a branch.

Partly in connection with estate matters, Cosimo was now more often seen in the town, perched on the big nut tree in the square or on the ilexes by the quays. The people treated him with great respect, called him 'Lord Baron', and he came to take on certain attitudes of an older man, as young men sometimes do, and sit there telling stories to groups of Ombrosans, clustered round the foot of the tree.

He would often describe our uncle's end, though never in the same way, and bit by bit he began to disclose the Cavalier's complicity with the pirates; but in order to assuage the immediate upsurge of indignation from all below he at once added the story of Zaira, almost as if Carrega had confided it to him before dying; and eventually he even moved them about the old man's sad end.

From complete invention, Cosimo, I believe, had arrived, by successive approximations, at an almost entirely truthful account of the facts. He told this two or three times; then finding his audience never tired of listening to the story and new listeners always coming and asking for details, he found himself making new additions, amplifying, exaggerating, introducing new characters and episodes, so that the tale got quite distorted and became even more of an invention than it had been at first.

Cosimo now had a public which would listen open-mouthed to everything he said. He began to enjoy telling stories about his life on the trees, and his hunting, and the brigand Gian dei Brughi, and the dog Ottimo Massimo. They all became material for tales that went on and on and on. (Many episodes in this account of his life are taken from what he would narrate at the request of his rustic audience, and I mention this to excuse myself if not all I write seems likely or conforming to a harmonious view of humanity and fact.)

For example, one of the idlers would ask: 'But is it true you have never once set foot off the trees, Lord Baron?'

And that would start Cosimo off. 'Yes, once, but by mistake. I climbed the horns of a stag. I thought I was passing on to a maple tree, and it was a stag escaped from the royal game preserve, standing still at that particular spot. The stag felt my weight on its horns and ran off into the wood. You can imagine the state I was in. Up there I felt things sticking into me all over; what with the sharp points of the horns, the thorns, the branches hitting my face ... The stag backed, trying to get rid of me. I held on tight ...'

There he would pause and wait till the others asked: 'And how did you get out of that, sir?'

And every time he would bring out a different ending. 'The stag raced on and on, reached the herd, most of which scattered at seeing it with a man on its horns, while some came up from curiosity. I aimed the gun I still had slung over my shoulder and brought down every deer I saw. I killed fifty of 'em ...'

'Have there ever been fifty deer round these parts?' asked one of those layabouts.

'It's extinct now, that breed. For those fifty deer were all female, d'you see? Every time my stag tried to get close to a female deer, I fired and the animal fell dead. The stag simply

did not know what to do next. Then ... then it suddenly decided to kill itself, rushed on to a high rock and flung itself
down. But I managed to cling on to a jutting pine tree, and here
I am!'

Or he would tell how a fight had started between two of the
stags with horns and at every clash he jumped from the horns
of one to the horns of the other, till at a particularly sharp butt
he found himself tipped on to an oak tree ...

In fact he was swept by that mania of the storyteller, who
never knows which stories are more beautiful; the ones that
really happened and the evocation of which recalls a whole
flow of hours past, of petty emotions, boredom, happiness, in-
security, vanity, and self-disgust, or those which are invented,
and in which he cuts out a main pattern, and everything seems
easy, then begins to vary it as he realizes more and more that he
is describing again things that had happened or been understood in lived reality.

Cosimo was still at the age when the wish to recount gives an
urge to living and one thinks one has not done enough living to
recount, and so off he would go hunting, and be away weeks,
then return to the trees in the square, dangling by the necks
pheasants, badgers and foxes, and tell the folk of Ombrosa new
tales, which from being true, became, as he told them, invented,
and from invented true.

But behind all this mania of his there was a deeper dissatisfaction, and in this need for listeners, a different lack. Cosimo did
not yet know love, and what is any experience without that?
What worth in risking life, when the real flavour of life is as yet
unknown?

Peasant girls and fish-vendors used to pass through the square
of Ombrosa, and young ladies in coaches, and Cosimo would
look them sharply over from the trees, unable to understand
why something that he was looking for was there in all of them,
and not there completely in any one of them. At night, when
the lights went on in the houses, and Cosimo was alone on the
branches with the yellow eyes of the owls, he would begin
dreaming of love. The couples who met behind bushes or amid

vines filled him with admiration and envy, and he would follow them with his eyes as they went off into the dark, but if they lay down at the foot of his particular tree, he would rush off covered with shame.

Then to overcome his shyness, he would stop and watch the loves of animals. In spring the world on the trees was a world of nuptials; the squirrels made love with squeals and movements that were almost human, the birds coupled with flapping wings; even the lizards slid off united, with their tails in tight knots; and the porcupines seemed to soften to sweeten their embraces. Ottimo Massimo, in no way put off by the fact that it was the only dachshund in Ombrosa, would court big sheepdogs, or wolfhounds, with brazen ardour, trusting to the natural sympathy it inspired. Sometimes it would return bitten all over; but a successful love affair was enough to repay all defeats.

Cosimo, like Ottimo Massimo, was the only example of a species. In his daydreams, he would see himself courting girls of exquisite beauty; but how could he meet love up on the trees? In his fantasies, he managed to avoid specifying where it would happen; on earth, or up in the element where he lived now: a place without a place, he would imagine; a world reached by going up, not down. Yes, that was it. Perhaps there was a tree so high that by climbing it, he would touch another world, the moon.

Meanwhile, as this habit of chattering in the square grew, he began to feel less and less satisfied with himself. And then, one market day, a man who came from the nearby town of Olivabassa exclaimed, 'Ah! so you've got your Spaniard too, I see!' and when asked what he meant replied: 'At Olivabassa there's a whole tribe of Spaniards living on the trees!' Cosimo could not rest till he made the journey through the woods to Olivabassa.

17

Olivabassa was a town in the interior. Cosimo reached it after two days' journey and many a dangerous passage over the less wooded parts of the route. Whenever he passed near any houses people who had never seen him before gave cries of surprise, and one or two of them even threw stones at him, so that he tried to move as unobserved as possible. But as he neared Olivabassa, he noticed that any woodman or ploughman or olive-picker who saw him showed no surprise at all, in fact the men even greeted him by doffing their hats as if they knew him, and said words which were certainly not in the local dialect and sounded strange in their mouths, such as '*Señor! Buenas dias Señor!*'

It was winter, the trees were partly bare. In Olivabassa a double row of elms and plane trees crossed the town. And my brother, as he came nearer, saw that there were people up on the bare branches, one, two, or even three to each tree, sitting or standing in grave attitudes. In a few jumps he reached them.

They were men in noble garb, plumed tricornes, big cloaks, and noble-looking women too, with veils on their heads, sitting on the branches in twos and threes, some embroidering, and looking down on to the road now and again with a little sideways jerk of the bosom and a stretch of their arms along the branch, as if at a window-sill.

The men bade him greetings that seemed full of rueful understanding: '*Buenas dias, Señor.*' And Cosimo bowed and doffed his hat.

One who seemed the most authoritative, a heavily-built man wedged in the fork of a plane tree from which he appeared unable to extricate himself, with a liverish complexion through which his shaved chin and upper lip showed black shadows in spite of his advanced years, turned to his neighbour, a pale gaunt man dressed in black and also with cheeks blackish in spite of shaving, and seemed to be asking who was this unknown man coming towards them across the trees.

Cosimo thought the moment had come to introduce himself.

He moved on to the stout gentleman's plane tree, bowed and said: 'The Baron Cosimo Piovasco of Rondò at your service.'

'*Rondos?*' exclaimed the fat man, '*Rondos? Aragones? Galiciano?*'

'No, sir.'

'*Catalan?*'

'No, sir. I am from these parts.'

'*Desterrado tambien?*'

The gaunt gentleman now felt it his duty to intervene and interpret, very bombastically, with: 'His Highness Frederico Alonso Sanchez y Tobasco asks if your lordship is also an exile, as we see you climbing about on branches.'

'No, sir. Or at least, not exile by anyone else's decree.'

'*Viaja usted sobre los arboles por gusto?*'

And the interpreter: 'His Highness Frederico Alonso is gracious enough to ask if it is for pleasure that your lordship uses this mode of travel.'

Cosimo thought a little, then replied: 'I do it because I think it suits me, not because I'm forced to.'

'*Feliz usted!*' exclaimed Frederico Alonso Sanchez, sighing. '*Ay de mi, ay de mi!*'

And the man in black began explaining, more bombastically than ever: 'His Highness deigns to say that your lordship is to be held fortunate in enjoying such a liberty, which we cannot but compare to our own restriction, endured, however, with resignation to the will of God,' and he crossed himself.

And so, from Prince Sanchez's laconic exclamations and a detailed account by the gentleman in black, Cosimo succeeded in reconstructing the story of this colony living on plane trees. They were Spanish nobles who had rebelled against King Charles III about certain contested feudal privileges, and been exiled with their families as a result. On reaching Olivabassa they had been forbidden to continue the journey; those parts, in fact, on account of an ancient treaty with His Catholic Majesty, could neither give hospitality nor even allow passage to persons exiled from Spain. The situation of those noble families was a very difficult one with which to cope, but the magistrates of Olivabassa, who wanted to avoid any trouble with foreign chancelleries but also had no aversion to these rich foreigners, came to an understanding with them; the letter of their treaty laid down that no exiles were to 'touch the soil' of their territory; they only had to be up on trees, and all was in order. So the exiles had climbed up on to the elms and plane trees, on ladders supplied by the commune, which were then taken away. They had been roosting up there for some months, putting their trust in the mild climate, the arrival soon of a decree of amnesty from Charles III, and Divine Providence. They were well supplied with Spanish doubloons and bought many supplies, thus giving trade to the town. To draw up the dishes they had installed a system of pulleys. And on other trees they had set up canopies under which they slept. In fact they had done themselves very comfortably, or rather, the people of Olivabassa had done them well, as it was to their advantage. The exiles, for their part, never moved a finger the whole day long.

It was the first time Cosimo had ever met other human beings living on trees, and he began to ask practical questions.

'And when it rains, what do you do?'

'Sacramas todo el tiempo, Señor.'

Then the interpreter, who was Father Sulpicio de Guadalete, of the Society of Jesus, an exile since his Order had been banned in Spain, explained: 'Protected by our canopies, we turn our thoughts to Our Lord, thanking Him for the little that suffices us ...'

'Do you ever go hunting?'

'Con el visco, Señor, alguna vez.'

'Sometimes one of us daubs a branch with glue, for amusement!'

Cosimo was never tired of finding out how they had resolved problems that he had had to deal with too.

'And washing, what d'you do about that?'

'Por lavar? Hay lavanderas!' said Don Frederico, with a shrug of the shoulders.

'We give our linen to the washerwomen of the village,' translated Don Sulpicio. 'Every Monday, to be exact, we drop the dirty clothes basket.'

'No, I meant washing your faces and bodies.'

Don Frederico grunted and shrugged his shoulders, as if this problem had never presented itself to him.

Don Sulpicio thought it his duty to interpret this: 'According to His Highness's opinion, these are matters private to each one of us.'

'And, I beg your pardon, but where d'you do your daily duties?'

'*Ollas, Señor.*'

And Don Sulpicio, in his modest tone, said: 'We use certain jars, in truth.'

Taking his leave of Don Frederico, Cosimo, with Father Sulpicio as guide, went on a round of visits to the other members of the colony, in their respective residential trees. All these *hidalgos* and ladies preserved, even in circumstances that were still of some discomfort, their usual manners and air of composure. Some of the men used horses' saddles to bestride the branches, and this appealed very much to Cosimo, who in all these years had never thought of such a system (stirrups – he noted at once – did away with the discomfort of having to keep the feet dangling, which brought on pins and needles after a bit). Others were pointing naval telescopes (one of them had the rank of admiral) which they probably only used to look at each other from one tree to another, in idleness and gossip. The ladies, old and young, all sat on cushions embroidered by themselves, sewing (they were the only ones doing anything at all) or stroking big cats. On those trees there were a great number of cats as also of birds (in cages – perhaps they were victims of the glue), except for some free pigeons which came and perched on the hand of some girl, and were sadly stroked.

In this arboreal drawing room Cosimo was received with grave hospitality. They offered him coffee, then at once began talking of the palaces they had left behind in Seville, or Granada, and of their possessions and granaries and stables, and invited him to visit them when they were reinstated in their honours. Of the King who had banished them they spoke in a tone that was both of fanatical aversion and devoted reverence, separating exactly the person with whom they had a family feud and the royal title from whose authority stemmed their own. Sometimes, on the other hand, they combined these two viewpoints in a single outburst; and Cosimo, every time that the conversation fell on their sovereign, did not know where to look.

Over all the gestures and discourses of the exiles there hung an aura of mourning and gloom, which corresponded in part to their natures, in part to a conscious determination, as sometimes happens to those struggling for a cause with a rather vague conviction which they try to eke out by an imposing bearing.

In the girls – who at a first glance all seemed to Cosimo a little hairy and greasy-skinned – there rippled a note of gaiety that was always reined in time. Two of these were playing at shuttlecock from one tree to another. Tic tac, tic tac, then a little scream; the shuttlecock had fallen into the road. A beggar from Olivabassa gathered it up and threw it back for a fee of two *pesetas*.

On the last tree, an elm, was an old man, called *El Conde*, without a wig, and plainly dressed. Father Sulpicio, as he drew near, lowered his voice and Cosimo found himself doing the same. *El Conde* was moving aside a branch with an arm every now and again and looking down over at the slope of the hill and a plain of bare green and gold merging into the distance.

Sulpicio murmured to Cosimo a story about a son held in King Charles's prisons and tortured. Cosimo realized that while all those *hidalgos* were in a way acting the exile, and every now and again having to recall and repeat to themselves why they were there, this old man was the only one really suffering. This gesture of moving the branch as if waiting for another land to appear, this plunging of his gaze deeper and deeper into the undulating distance as if hoping never to see the horizon, but to succeed, perhaps, in making out some place, alas, far too far away, were the first real signs of exile that Cosimo saw. And he understood, too, how much those other *hidalgos* must depend on *El Conde*'s presence, as being the only thing that held them together, gave them a reason. It was he, perhaps the poorest and certainly the least important of them back home, who told them what they should be suffering and hoping.

On his way back from these visits, Cosimo saw on an alder tree a girl whom he had not seen before. In a couple of leaps he joined her.

She was a girl with lovely eyes the colour of periwinkles, and sweet-smelling skin. She was holding a bucket.

'How is it that when I saw everyone I never saw you?'

'I was drawing water at the well,' and she smiled. From the bucket, which was a little askew, was dripping some water. He helped her to set it straight.

'So you get down from the trees?'

'No, there's a twisted old cherry tree growing over the wall of a courtyard. We drop our buckets from there. Come.'

They went along a branch, and climbed the wall of a court-yard. She went first as a guide over the cherry tree. Beneath was the well.

'Do you see, Baron?'

'How d'you know I'm a baron?'

'I know everything,' she smiled, 'my sisters told me of your visit at once.'

'Those girls playing shuttlecock?'

'Irena and Raimunda, yes.'

'The daughters of Don Frederico?'

'Yes.'

'And what's your name?'

'Ursula.'

'You're much better at getting about trees than anyone else here.'

'I've been on 'em since I was a child; at Granada we had huge trees in the *patio*.'

'Can you pick that rose?' At the top of a tree was flowering a rambling rose.

'A pity, no.'

'Right, I'll pick it for you,' he went off and came back with the rose.

Ursula smiled and held out her hands.

'I want to pin it on myself. Tell me where.'

'On my head, thank you,' and she guided his hands.

'Now tell me,' Cosimo asked, 'd'you know how to reach that walnut tree?'

'Can one?' She laughed. 'I'm not a bird.'

'Wait,' and Cosimo threw her the end of a rope. 'If you tie yourself to that rope, I'll swing you over.'

'No ... I'm afraid ...' but she was laughing.

'It's my system. I've been travelling like this for years, doing it all by myself.'

'*Mamma mia!*'

He ferried her over. Then he came himself. It was a young walnut tree, not big at all. They were very close. Ursula was still panting and red from her flight.

'Frightened?'

'No,' but her heart was beating hard.

'You haven't lost the rose,' and he touched it to set it straight.

So, close together in the tree, their arms were round each other at every move.

'Uh!' said she, and then, he first, they kissed.

So began their love, the boy happy and amazed, she happy and not surprised at all (nothing happens by chance to girls). It was the love so long awaited by Cosimo and which had now inexplicably arrived, and so lovely that he could not imagine how he had even thought it lovely before. And the thing newest to him was that it was so simple, and the boy at that moment thought it must be like that always.

18

The peach and walnut and cherry were in blossom. Cosimo and Ursula spent their days together on the beflowered trees. The spring even coloured with gaiety the funereal proximity of her relatives.

My brother soon made himself useful among the colony of exiles, teaching them various ways of moving from one tree to another, and encouraging the grandees to abandon, for a moment, their habitual composure and practise a little movement. He also threw across some rope bridges, which allowed the older exiles to pay each other visits. And so, during the year, almost, that he spent with the Spaniards, he gave the colony many devices invented by himself; water-tanks, ovens, bags of fur to sleep in. It was his joy in new inventions that made him help those *hidalgos* in their habits even though they in no way agreed with the opinions of his favourite authors; thus, seeing the desire of those pious persons to go regularly to confession, he scooped out a confessional from a tree trunk, in which the lanky Don Sulpicio could insert himself and through a little curtained grating listen to sins.

The pure passion for technical innovation, in fact, was not enough to save him from paying homage to accepted forms; ideas were needed. Cosimo wrote to Orbecche the bookseller to send him by the post from Ombrosa to Olivabassa some volumes that had arrived meanwhile. So he was able to read out loud to Ursula *Paul et Virginie* and *La Nouvelle Héloïse*.

The exiles would often hold meetings on a big oak tree, parliaments in which they drafted letters to their sovereign. At first these letters must always have had a tone of indignation, protest and threat, almost of ultimatum; but gradually one or another of them proposed formulas that were blander and more respectful, and eventually they drafted a petition in which they prostrated themselves humbly at His Gracious Majesty's feet and implored his forgiveness.

Then *El Conde* rose. All were silent. *El Conde*, looking up, began speaking in a low vibrant voice and said everything that he had in his heart. When he sat down again, the others were serious and mute. No one mentioned the petition any more.

Cosimo had by now become one of the community and took part in the discussions. And there, with ingenuous youthful fervour, he would explain the ideas of philosophers and the wrong-doings of sovereigns, and how States could be governed by justice and reason. But the only ones among them all to listen at all were *El Conde*, who though old, was always searching for new ways of understanding and acting, Ursula, who had read a few books, and a couple of girls who were rather more wide awake than the others. The rest of the colony had heads like leather soles, fit only to drive nails in.

In fact, *El Conde* now began to want to read books instead of spending his time brooding over the landscape. Rousseau he found a little crude; but he liked Montesquieu; it was a first step. The other *hidalgos* read nothing, though one or two of them secretly asked Father Sulpicio to get Cosimo to lend them *La Puelzella* to go off and read the more exciting passages. So, with *El Conde* chewing over his new ideas, the meetings on the oak tree took on another turn; there was even talk of going to Spain and starting a revolution.

At first Father Sulpicio did not sense the danger. He was not a man of great subtlety himself, and being cut off from all the hierarchy of his superiors he was no longer very up to date on poisons to the conscience. But as soon as he was able to reorder his ideas (or as soon, said others, as he received certain letters with the bishop's seal) he began to say that the devil had insinuated itself into that community of theirs and that they would bring a flash of lightning down on themselves which would burn up the trees with everyone on them.

One night Cosimo was awakened by a groan. He hurried towards it with a lantern and on *El Conde*'s oak tree saw the old man bound to the trunk with the Jesuit tightening the knots.

'Stop, Father! What are you doing?'

'The arm of the Holy Inquisition, son! Now it is for this wretched old man to confess his heresy and spit out the devil. Then it will be your turn.'

Cosimo drew his sword and cut the ropes. 'Take care, Father! There are other arms which serve reason and justice!'

The Jesuit drew a naked sword from his cloak. 'Baron of Rondò, for some time your family has had accounts to settle with my Order!'

'He was right, my poor old father,' exclaimed Cosimo, as the steel crossed, 'the Society does not forgive!'

They fought swaying about on the trees. Don Sulpicio was an excellent fencer, and my brother very often found himself in difficulties. They were at the third round when *El Conde* pulled himself together and began to call out. The other exiles woke, hurried to the spot, and interposed between the duellers. Sulpicio put his sword away at once, and as if nothing had happened at once began calling for calm.

An event so serious would have been impossible to silence in any other community, but not in that, considering their wish to reduce all thought in their heads to a minimum. So Don Frederico offered his good offices and a kind of reconciliation was arranged between Don Sulpicio and *El Conde*, which left everything as it had been before.

Certainly Cosimo had to be careful, and when he went about the trees with Ursula he was in constant fear of being spied on by the Jesuit. He knew that their relationship was worrying Don Frederico, for the girl was no longer allowed out with him. Those noble families, in truth, were brought up to very enclosed customs; but they were on the trees there, in exile, and did not worry so much about such things. Cosimo seemed to them a fine young man, with a title too, and one who knew how to make himself useful, and who stayed there with them from his own free will; and if there did happen to be a tenderness between him and Ursula and they often saw them going off among the trees looking for fruit and flowers, they shut an eye so as not to find anything to criticize.

Now, however, with Don Sulpicio putting pressure, Don Frederico could no longer pretend to know nothing. He called

Cosimo to an audience on his plane tree. At his side was the long black figure of Sulpicio.

'*Baron*, you are often seen about with my *niña*, they tell me.'

'She is teaching me to speak *vuestra idioma*, Your Highness.'

'How old are you?'

'About nineteen.'

'*Joven!* Too young! My daughter is of marrying age. Why do you go about with her?'

'Ursula is seventeen.'

'Are you thinking already to *casarte*?'

'To what?'

'My daughter teaches you Spanish badly, *hombre*. I say if you are thinking of choosing yourself a *novia*, to set up a home.'

Sulpicio and Cosimo both moved their hands forward. The conversation was taking a turn desired neither by the Jesuit nor, even less, by my brother.

'My home ...' said Cosimo and waved a hand towards the highest branches, and the clouds, 'my home is everywhere, everywhere I can climb to, upwards ...'

'*No es esto*,' and Prince Frederico Alonso shook his head. 'Baron, if you care to visit Granada when we return, you will see the richest fief in the Sierra. *Mejor que aquí*.'

Don Sulpicio could contain himself no longer. 'But, Highness, this young man is a follower of Voltaire ... He must not go about in your daughter's company ...'

'Oh, *es joven*, he's young, ideas come and go, *que se case*, let him marry and they'll change, now come to Granada, do.'

'*Muchas gracias a usted* ... I'll think it over ...' And Cosimo, twiddling his cap of cat's fur in his hands, withdrew with many a bow.

When he saw Ursula again he was very preoccupied. 'You know, Ursula, your father talked to me about you ... He broached certain subjects ...'

Ursula looked alarmed. 'You mean he doesn't want us to see each other any more?'

'No, not that ... When you are no longer exiled, he wants me to come with you to Granada ...'

'Ah, yes! How nice!'

'But, you see, though I love you, I've always lived on the trees, and I want to stay on them ...'

'Oh, Cosimo, we've got lovely trees too ...'

'Yes, but meanwhile I'd have to come down to earth for the journey, and once down ...'

'Don't worry now, Cosimo. We're exiles, anyway, for the moment and may so remain for the rest of our lives.'

And my brother ceased to think about it.

But Ursula had guessed wrong. Shortly afterwards a letter reached Don Frederico with the royal seal. By gracious clemency of His Catholic Majesty, the ban was revoked. The noble exiles could return to their own homes and their own fiefs. At once there was a great coming and going among the plane trees. 'We're returning! We're returning! Madrid! Cadiz! Seville!'

The news soon spread to the town. The inhabitants of Olivabassa arrived with ladders. Some of the exiles descended amid acclamations, others stayed to collect their luggage.

'But it's not over!' kept on saying *El Conde*. 'The Cortes will hear of it! And the Crown!' and as none of his companions in exile showed any desire to agree with him at that moment, and already the ladies were thinking only of their dresses which were now out of fashion and of their wardrobe to be renewed, he began to make speeches to the population of Olivabassa. 'Now we're going to Spain and then you'll see! We'll settle our accounts there. I and this young man here will get justice!' and he pointed to Cosimo. Cosimo, confused, made signs of disagreement.

Don Frederico, carried by many hands, had descended to earth. *'Baja, joven bizarro!'* he shouted to Cosimo. 'Come down, you strange young man! Come with us to Granada!'

Cosimo was crouching on a branch, his head in his hands.

And the Prince went on: 'What, no? You'll be as my own son!'

'The exile is over,' said *El Conde*. 'Finally we can put into operation what we have brooded on for so long! Why stay up there on the trees, Baron? There's no reason now.'

Cosimo stretched out his arms. 'I came up here before you, my lords, and here I will stay afterwards too!'

'You want to withdraw!' cried *El Conde*.

'No, to resist,' replied the Baron.

Ursula, who had been among the first to go down and was busy with her sisters filling a coach full of luggage, rushed towards the tree. 'Then I'll stay with you! I'll stay with you!' and she began running up the ladder.

Four or five of the others stopped her, tore her away, took the ladders from the trees.

'*Adios*, Ursula, be happy!' said Cosimo as they carried her forcibly to the coach, which then set off.

There was a gay barking. The dachshund, Ottimo Massimo, which had snarled with discontent all the time its master had been at Olivabassa, seemed finally happy again. It began to chase, just as a joke, the little cats left behind and forgotten on the trees, and they bristled their fur and hissed at it.

The exiles departed, some on horseback, some by coach. The road cleared. No one remained on the trees of Olivabassa but my brother. Stuck on the branches here and there was some feather or ribbon or scrap of lace fluttering in the wind, and a glove, a fringed parasol, a fan, a spurred boot.

19

It was a summer all full moons, croaking frogs, twittering chaffinches, when the Baron was seen at Ombrosa once again. He seemed restless as a bird too, hopping from branch to branch, frowning, inquisitive, indecisive.

Soon there began to circulate rumours that a certain Cecchina, on the other side of the valley, was his mistress. This girl certainly lived in an isolated house, with a deaf aunt, and an olive branch did pass near her window. The idlers in the square discussed whether she was or not.

'I saw them, her at the window-sill, he on the branch. He was flapping at her like a bat and she was doubled up with laughter!'

'Later on he jumps in!'

'Nonsense; he's sworn never to leave the trees for his whole life ...'

'Well, he's set the rule, he can also allow the exceptions ...'

'Eh, if we're getting on to exceptions ...'

'No, no; it's she who jumps out of the window on to the olive!'

'How do they set about it then? They must be very uncomfortable ...'

'I say, they've never touched each other. Yes, he courts her, or maybe it's her who's leading him on. But he'll never come down from up there ...'

Yes, no, he, she, jump, branch ... the discussions seemed endless. Betrothed youths and husband, now, reacted at once if their girls or wives as much as raised eyes towards a tree. The women, on their side, would chatter away as soon as they met; what were they talking about? Him.

Whether it was Cecchina or anyone else, my brother had got her without ever leaving his trees. Once I met him running over the branches with a mattress slung over his shoulder, as easily as he slung guns, ropes, hatchets, water-bottles or powder horns.

A certain Dorothea, a woman of the town, admitted to me that she had met him, on her own initiative, and not for money, but just to get an idea.

'And what idea did you get?'

'Eh! I'm quite satisfied ...'

Another, a certain Zobeide, told me she had dreamt of the 'man on the trees' (as they called him) and this dream was so detailed, so remarkably well informed, that I think she must have lived it in reality.

Well, I don't know how those stories got about, but Cosimo must certainly have had a fascination for women. Since he had been with the Spaniards he had begun to take more care of his appearance, and had stopped going round muffled in furs like a bear. He wore stockings and a tapered coat and a tall hat in the English fashion, shaved his beard and combed his wig. In fact, one could tell for sure now, from his dress, whether he was going off on an expedition of shooting or love.

The story goes that a mature and noble lady whose name I will not give, as she was of Ombrosa (her children and grand-children still live here and might be offended, but at that time is was a well known story), always used to go about in a coach, alone, with an old coachman on the box, and had herself driven over a part of the main road which passed through the wood. At a certain point she would say to the coachman: 'Giovita, the wood is simply chockful of mushrooms. Get down, will you, fill this and then come back,' and she would hand him a big basket. The poor man, racked with rheumatism, got down from the box, loaded the basket on his shoulders, went off the road and began searching among the ferns in the dew, and got deeper and deeper into the beechwood, bowing down under every leaf to find a *porcina* or a *fungis vescia*. Meanwhile the noble lady would vanish from the coach, as if swept up to heaven, into the thick boughs overhanging the road. No more is known, except that often people passing by would find the coach standing there empty in the wood. Then, as mysteriously as she had vanished, there was the noble lady sitting in the coach again, looking languid. Giovita would return, soaking, with a few mushrooms at the bottom of the basket, and they would set off again.

Many of these stories were told, one in particular about cer-tain Genoese dames who gave little parties for rich young men (I frequented them myself when I was a bachelor) and how these five ladies were suddenly taken with a whim to visit the Baron. A certain old oak tree, in fact, is still called the Oak of the Five Sparrows, and we old men know what that means. The tale comes from a certain Gè, a *zibib* merchant, a man whom one can credit. It was a fine sunny day, this Gè was out shooting in the wood, he reached the oak tree and what did he see? Cosimo had taken all five of them up on the branches, and there they were, one here and one there, enjoying the warm afternoon, quite naked, with their little umbrellas open so as not to catch the sun, and the Baron in the midst of them reading Latin verses, Gè could not make out whether by Ovid or Lucretius.

So many stories were told of him, and what truth there was in them I don't know; at that time he was rather reserved and coy about these things; but as an old man he would tell many stories, almost too many; most of them, though, so fantastic that he could not thread his way through them himself. The fact was that people got into the habit, when a girl was pregnant and no one knew who was responsible, of finding it easiest to blame him. Once a girl described how as she was going picking olives she felt herself raised up by two long arms like a monkey's ... shortly afterwards she had twins. Ombrosa became filled with bastards of the Baron, real or false. Now they are all grown up and some, it is true, do resemble him; but this could also have been due to suggestion, as when pregnant women saw Cosimo suddenly jumping from one branch to another, they were apt to get a turn.

Myself, I don't believe most of these stories, told to explain certain births. Nor do I know if he had relations with as many women as they say, but what is sure is that those who had known him preferred to be silent about him.

And then, if he did have so many women after him, how can one explain the moonlit nights when he wandered like a cat on the fig trees, plums and quinces around the village, in the orchards overlooking the outer circle of the houses of Ombrosa, and there lament, with sighs, or yawns, or groans, which, however much he tried to control and render into normal sounds, usually came out of his throat as wails or growls. And the people of Ombrosa, who knew his habits, were not even alarmed when they heard all this in their sleep; they would just turn in bed and say, 'There's the Baron out for a woman. Let's hope he finds one and we can sleep.'

Sometimes an old man, one of those who can't sleep and are quite glad to go to the window if they hear a noise, would look out into the orchard and see Cosimo's shadow among the branches of the fig trees, thrown on the ground by the moon. 'Can't you get to sleep tonight, your lordship?'

'No, the more I move around the more awake I feel,' Cosimo

would say, as if talking from his bed, with his face deep in the pillows, longing to feel his eyelids drop, while in fact he was hanging suspended there like an acrobat. 'I don't know what it is tonight, the heat, nerves; perhaps the weather is going to change, don't you feel it too?'

'Oh, I feel it, I feel it ... but I'm old, your lordship. You, on the other hand, have a pull at your blood ...'

'Yes, it does pull ...'

'Well, try and get it to pull a little farther away, lord Baron, as there's nothing here to give you any relief; only poor folk who have to wake at dawn and want to sleep now ...'

Cosimo did not answer, he just rustled away into the orchard. He always knew how to keep within decent limits, and on their side the people of Ombrosa always knew how to tolerate these vagaries of his; partly because he was always the Baron and partly because he was a different Baron from others.

Sometimes those animal calls of his reached other windows, ears more curious to listen; the scratch as a candle was lit, the sound of muffled laughter, of feminine murmurs in the shadows which he could not manage to catch and which were certainly jokes. Making fun about him or pretending to call, were apt to be taken as serious, as true love, for this night wanderer on the branches like a werewolf.

And now one of the more shameless girls would come to the window as if to see what was outside, still warm from the bed, her breasts showing, her hair loose, a white smile between her strong lips; and a dialogue would ensue.

'Who is it? A cat?'

And he: 'It's a man, a man.'

'A man miaowing?'

'No, sighing.'

'Why? What's up?'

'Something's up ...'

'What?'

'Come here and I'll tell you ...'

But he never got insults from the men, or any vendettas, signs – it seems to me – that he was never as dangerous as all that. Only once, mysteriously, was he wounded. The news spread one morning. The Ombrosa doctor had to clamber up on to the nut tree where he was moaning away. He had a leg full of grapeshot, the little ones used to shoot swallows with; they had to be taken out one by one with pincers. This hurt, but he soon recovered. It was never quite known how this had happened; he said that he had been hit by mistake while climbing a branch.

Convalescent, immobilized in the nut tree, he plunged into serious study. At that time he began to write a *Project for the Constitution of an Ideal State in the Trees*, in which he described the imaginary Republic of Arborea, inhabited by just men. He began it as a treatise on laws and governments, but as he wrote his impulse to invent complicated stories supervened and out poured a hodge-potch of adventures, duels and erotic tales, the latter inserted in a chapter on matrimonial rights. The epilogue of the book should have been this: the Author, having founded the perfect State in the tree-tops and convinced the whole of humanity to establish itself there and live there happily, came down to live on an earth which was now deserted. This is what it should have been, but the work remained incomplete. He sent a précis to Diderot, signing it simply: 'Cosimo Rondò, Reader of the Encyclopaedia.' Diderot thanked him with a short note.

20

I cannot say much of that period, because it was the time of my first journey into Europe. I was just twenty-one and could make whatever use I liked of the family patrimony, as my brother needed very little, as did my mother, who had been getting very much older recently, poor dear. My brother had asked to sign a Power of Attorney in my favour over all our possessions, on condition I gave him a monthly allowance, paid his taxes, and kept his affairs in order. All I had to do was to take over direction of the estate and choose myself a wife, and already I saw ahead of me that regulated and pacific life which, in spite of all the great upheavals of the century, I have succeeded, in fact, in living.

But before starting this, I allowed myself a period of travel. I also went to Paris, just in time to see the triumphant reception of Voltaire on his return there after many years, for the staging of one of his plays. But these are not the memoirs of my life, which would not be worth writing; I only mention this journey, because everywhere I went I was struck by the fame of the tree-borne man of Ombrosa, in foreign countries too. Once on an almanac I saw a drawing with the words beneath: *'L'homme sauvage d'Ombreuse (Rep Génoise). Vit seulment sur les arbres.'*

They had represented him all covered in leaves, with a long beard and queue, eating a locust. This figure was in the Chapter of Monsters, between the Hermaphrodite and the Siren.

When faced with this kind of fantasy I was usually careful not to reveal that the man was my brother. But I proclaimed it very loud when I was invited to a reception in honour of Voltaire in Paris. The old philosopher was in his armchair, surrounded by a court of ladies, gay as a cricket and prickly as a porcupine. When he heard I came from Ombrosa he addressed me thus:

'Is it near you, *mon cher Chevalier*, that there is that famous philosopher who lives on the trees *comme un singe*?'

And I, flattered, could not prevent myself replying: 'He's my brother, *monsieur, le Baron de Rondeau.*'

Voltaire was very surprised, perhaps partly at finding the brother of such a phenomenon apparently so normal, and began asking me questions, such as: 'But is it to be nearer the sky that your brother stays up there?'

'My brother considers,' answered I, 'that anyone who wants to see the earth properly must keep himself at a necessary distance from it,' and Voltaire seemed to appreciate this reply.

'Once it was only Nature which produced living phenomena,' he concluded. 'Now 'tis Reason.' And the old sage plunged back into the chatter of his theistic adorers.

Soon I had to interrupt my journey and return to Ombrosa, recalled by an urgent despatch. Our mother's asthma had suddenly got worse and the poor woman could no longer leave her bed.

When I crossed the threshold and raised my eyes towards our house I was sure I would see him there. Cosimo was crouching on a high branch of a mulberry tree just outside the sill of our mother's bedroom. 'Cosimo,' I called, but in a muffled voice. He made me a sign which meant both that our mother was rather better but still in bed, and that I should come up quietly.

The room was in shadow. My mother lay in bed with a pile of pillows propping up her shoulders and seemed larger than I had ever seen her. Around her were a few women of the house. Battista had not yet arrived, as the Count her husband, who was to accompany her, had been held back for the vintage. In the shadow of the room glowed the open window in which Cosimo was framed on the branch of a tree.

I bent down to kiss our mother's hand. She recognized me at once and put her hand on my head. 'Ah, so you have arrived, Biagio ...' She spoke in a faint voice when the asthma did not grip her throat too much, but clearly and with great feeling. What struck me, though, was hearing her addressing both of us, Cosimo and myself, as if he were at her bedside too. And Cosimo answered her from the tree.

'Is it long since I took my medicine, Cosimo?'

'No, only just a few minutes, Mother, wait before you take more, as it won't do you any good just now.'

At a certain point she said, 'Cosimo, give me a sliver of orange,' and I felt surprised. But I was even more surprised when I saw Cosimo stretching into the room through the window a kind of ship's harpoon and on it a sliver of orange which was put into our mother's hand.

I noticed that for all these little services she preferred to turn to him.

'Cosimo, give me my shawls.'

And he with his harpoon would search among the things thrown on an armchair, take up the shawls and hand them to her. 'Here they are, Mother.'

'Thank you, Cosimo, my son.' She always spoke as if he were only a yard or two away, but I noticed that she never asked him services which he could not do from the tree. In such cases she always asked either me or the women.

At night our mother could not sleep; Cosimo remained watching over her from the tree with a little lantern hanging on the branch so that she could see him also in the dark.

The morning was the worst time for her asthma. The only remedy was to try and distract her, and Cosimo played little tunes on a flute or imitated the song of the birds, or caught butterflies and then made them fly into the room, or made festoons of jonquils.

It was a day of sunshine. Cosimo with a reed began to blow soap bubbles from the tree and puff them through the window towards the sick woman's bed. Our mother saw those iridescent colours flying and filling the room and said: 'Oh, what games you are playing.' This made me think of when we were little children and she always disapproved of our games as being too futile and infantile, but now, perhaps for the first time, she was enjoying our games. The soap bubbles even reached her face, and she would explode them with a puff and a smile. A bubble even reached her lips and stayed there intact. We bent down over her. Cosimo let the reed fall. She was dead.

Mourning is followed sooner or later by happy events, it is the law of life. A year after our mother's death I became engaged to a girl from the local nobility. It was very difficult to bring my fiancée round to the idea of coming to live at Ombrosa; she was afraid of my brother. The thought that there was a man moving among the leaves who was watching every move through the windows, who would appear when least expected, filled her with terror, also because she had never seen Cosimo and imagined him as a kind of Indian savage. To exorcise this fear out of her head I arranged a luncheon in the open, under the trees, to which Cosimo was also invited. Cosimo ate above us on an ilex tree, with his dishes on a little tray, and I must say that although he was rather out of practice for meals in company he behaved very well. My fiancée was somewhat calmed, and realized that apart from his being on the trees he was a man just like all the others; but she still kept an invincible diffidence towards him.

Even when, after we had married, we settled down together in the villa at Ombrosa, she avoided as much as possible, not only any converse but even the sight of her brother-in-law, although he, poor man, every now and again would bring her bunches of flowers and rare furs. When children began to be born and grow up, she got it into her head that their uncle's proximity would have a bad influence on their education. She was not happy until we put in order the old castle on our estate at Rondò which had been uninhabited for a long time; and we began staying up there much more than at Ombrosa, so that the children should be away from bad influences.

Cosimo too began to notice the passing of time: a sign of this was the ageing of the dachshund Ottimo Massimo, which had lost its urge to join the bitches of the pack after the foxes or to try any more absurd love affairs with local mongrels. It was always lying down, as if its stomach was anyway so near the ground when standing that it was not worth while holding itself upright. And lying there splayed out from snout to tail at the foot of the tree on which Cosimo was, it would raise a tired look towards its master and scarcely wag its tail. Cosimo was becoming discontented; the sense of the passing of time made him feel a kind of dissatisfaction with life, spent for ever wandering up and down the same old trees. And nothing any longer gave him full contentment, neither hunting, fleeting affairs nor books. He himself did not know what he wanted; taken by one of these moods, he would clamber quickly over the tenderest and most fragile boughs as if searching for other trees growing upon the tops, so as to climb those too.

One day Ottimo Massimo was restless. There seemed to be a spring wind. The dog raised its snout, sniffed and then flung itself down again. Two or three times it got up, moved around and lay down again. Suddenly it began to run. It trotted along slowly, every now and again stopping to take breath. Cosimo followed on the branches.

Ottimo Massimo made towards the woods. It seemed to have a very precise direction in mind, because even when it stopped every now and again to lift a leg, it would stand there with tongue out looking at its master, then scratch itself and begin moving once more with certainty. It was moving into parts little frequented by Cosimo, in fact almost unknown to him, towards the shooting reserves of the Duke Tolemaico. The Duke Tolemaico was a broken-down old rake and certainly had not been out shooting for a very long time, but no poacher could set foot in his reserves as the gamekeepers were numerous and vigilant, and Cosimo, who had had dealings with them, preferred to keep away. Now Ottimo Massimo and Cosimo were plunging deeper and deeper into the Duke's game reserves, but neither one nor the other thought of chasing the precious game; the dog trotted along following some secret call of its own, and the Baron was gripped by an impatient curiosity to discover where on earth the dog was going.

So the dachshund reached a point in which the forest ended and there was an open field. Two stone lions crouched on pillars were holding up a coat of arms. Beyond them should have begun a park, a garden, a more private part of the Tolemaico estate; but there was nothing except for those two stone lions with the field beyond, an immense field of short green grass, whose boundaries faded away in the distance against a background of black oak trees. The sky was lightly covered with clouds. No bird sang.

This field, for Cosimo, was a sight which filled him with discomfort. Having always lived in the thickness of the vegetation at Ombrosa, certain of being able to reach any place by his own routes, the Baron only had to see in front of him an empty and impassable space, bare under the sky, to feel a sense of vertigo.

Ottimo Massimo rushed into the field, and began running

along at full tilt as if it had become young again. From the ilex where he was crouching, Cosimo began to whistle at it and call, 'Here, come back here, Ottimo Massimo, come back here, where are you going?' but the dog did not obey, did not even turn; it ran on and on through the field, until nothing could be seen but a distant dot like a comma, its tail, and even that vanished.

On the ilex Cosimo was wringing his hands. He was used to the dog's escapes and absences, but now Ottimo Massimo was vanishing into this field where he could not follow, and the flight linked to the anxiety he had felt a short time ago and filled him with a vague sense of expectation, of waiting for something to appear in that field.

He was brooding over these thoughts when he heard steps under his oak tree, and saw a gamekeeper passing, whistling, hands in pockets. The man had a very careless distracted air for one of those terrible gamekeepers of the preserve, and yet the badge on his uniform was that of the ducal retainers, and Cosimo flattened himself against the trunk. Then the thought of the dog overcame his fear; he called down to the gamekeeper: 'Hey, you, sergeant, have you seen a dog around?'

The gamekeeper raised his face. 'Ah, it's you! The flying hunter with the sliding dog! No, I've not seen the dog. What have you caught this morning?'

Cosimo recognized one of his keenest adversaries, and said: 'Oh, nothing, the dog escaped from me and I had to follow it as far as this ... my gun's unloaded.'

The gamekeeper laughed. 'Oh, do load it, and fire it, too, whenever you like; it doesn't matter now!'

'Why not now?'

'Now that the Duke is dead, who cares about trespassing here?'

'Oh, he's dead, is he? I didn't know that.'

'He's been dead and buried for three months. And there's a row on between the heirs of his first two marriages and his new widow.'

'He'd a third wife, had he?'

'He married when he was eighty, a year before he died; she was a girl of twenty-one or that. It was a mad thing to do, a wife who never even spent a day with him, and is only now beginning to visit his estates, which she doesn't like.'

'What, she doesn't like them?'

'Oh, well, she installs herself in a palace, or a castle, and arrives with her whole court, as she always has a group of admirers around her, and after three days she finds everything ugly, everything sad, and sets off again. Then the other heirs come forward, rush into that estate and claim rights over it; she says "Oh, yes, take it if you like." Now she's come here to the hunting pavilion, but how long will she stay? Not long, I'd say.'

'And where's the hunting pavilion?'

'Down over the field beyond the oak trees.'

'Then my dog has gone there ...'

'It must have gone looking for bones ... Excuse me, but it makes me think your lordship keeps it on a lead!' – and he burst out laughing.

Cosimo did not reply, he looked at the uncrossable field, waiting for the dachshund to return.

The whole day long it never came. Next day Cosimo was again on the ilex tree looking at the field, as if forced by a turmoil within.

The dog reappeared towards evening, a little dot in the field under Cosimo's sharp eye, becoming more and more visible. 'Ottimo Massimo! Come here! Where have you been?' The dog stopped, wagging its tail and looking at its master, and seemed to be inviting him to follow; but then it realized the space he could not get over, turned back, made a few hesitating paces, and turned again. 'Ottimo Massimo! Come here! Ottimo Massimo!' But the dog was running off again and vanished into the distance of the field.

Later two gamekeepers passed. 'Still waiting for your dog, your lordship! But I saw it at the Pavilion, in good hands ...'

'What?'

'But yes, the Marchesa, or rather the widowed Duchess. We call her the Marchesa, as she was the little Marchesa as a girl. She's treating it as though it's been with her all the time. It's a lap-dog, that one, if you'll allow me to say so, your lordship. Now it's found a soft billet it's staying there ...'

And the two keepers went off grinning. Ottimo Massimo did not return any more. Day after day Cosimo spent on the ilex looking at the field as if he could read something in it that had been struggling inside him for a long time; the very idea of distance, of intangibility, of the waiting that can be prolonged beyond life.

21

One day Cosimo was looking out of the ilex tree. The sun was shining, a ray crossed the field and from pea-green went emerald. Down in the blackness of the oak wood there was a movement in the undergrowth, and a horse leapt out. On its saddle was a horseman dressed in black, in a cloak – no, a skirt; it wasn't a horseman, it was a horsewoman; she was galloping on a loose rein and she was fair!

Cosimo's heart gave a leap, and he found himself longing for the horsewoman to come near enough for him to see her face, and for that face to be very beautiful. But apart from this waiting of his for her to approach and to be beautiful, there was a third thing he was waiting for, a third branch of hope intwining with the other two, a longing that this evermore luminous beauty might respond to a need he felt to recapture some memory once known and now almost forgotten, a memory of which only a wispy line, a faint colour now remained, and that this would make all the rest emerge once more, or rather be rediscovered in something present and alive.

There he sat, yearning for her to come nearer his end of the field by the two towering pillars with the lions; but the wait was becoming agonizing, for now he realized that the horse-woman was not cutting through the field directly towards the lions, but across it diagonally, so that she would soon vanish into the wood again.

He was just about to lose sight of her, when she turned her horse brusquely and cut across the field in another diagonal, which would certainly bring her a little nearer, but would make her vanish just the same on the opposite side of the field.

And now, at that moment, Cosimo was annoyed to notice trotting into the field from the wood a couple of brown horses with men on them, but he quickly tried to eliminate his annoyance, and decided that these horsemen did not matter, one only had to see how they were tacking to and fro after her, he really must not let them bother him, and yet, he had to admit, they annoyed him.

And then the horsewoman, just before vanishing from the field, turned her horse round again, but in the other direction, farther away from Cosimo ... No, now the horse was swivelling and galloping this way, and the move seemed done on purpose to disorientate the two followers, who were now in fact galloping a long way off and had not yet realized that she was rushing in an opposite direction.

Now everything was going just as he wanted; the horsewoman was galloping along in the sun, getting more and more beautiful and corresponding more and more to Cosimo's lost memories; the only worrying thing was her continual zigzagging, which never gave him any idea of her intentions. The two horsemen did not understand where she was going either, and in trying to follow her evolutions covered a great deal of ground uselessly, though always with goodwill and dexterity.

Now, in less time than Cosimo expected, the woman on horseback reached the edge of the field near him, passed between the two pillars surmounted by lions which seemed almost to have been put there in her honour, turned towards the field and everything beyond it with a wide gesture of farewell, galloped on, and passed under the ilex; now Cosimo could see her clearly in face and body, sitting erect in the saddle, a haughty woman's and at the same time a child's face, a forehead happy to be above those eyes, eyes happy to be under that forehead, nose, mouth, chin, neck, everything about her happy to be with every other part of her, it all, yes all, reminded him of the little girl of twelve he had seen on the swing the first day he had spent on a tree; Viola Violante of Ondariva, the Sinforosa.

This discovery, or rather having brought it from an unconfessed suspicion in his mind to the point of being able to proclaim it to himself, filled Cosimo as if with a fever. He tried to call so that she would raise her eyes to the ilex tree and see him, but from his throat came only a hoarse gurgle and she did not turn.

Now the white horse was galloping into the chestnut grove, and the hoofs were beating on the cones scattered about the ground, splitting them open and exposing the shiny kernels of nut. The woman guided her horse first in one direction, then in another, with Cosimo at one moment thinking her away and unreachable, at another, as he jumped from tree to tree, seeing her with surprise reappear amid the perspective of trunks, and her way of moving fanned more and more the memory flaming up in his mind. He tried to reach her with a call, a sign of his presence, but the only sound that came to his lips was the crow of a pheasant, and she did not even hear.

The two cavaliers following her seemed to understand her intentions even less than her route and continued to take wrong directions, getting entangled in undergrowth and stuck in bog, while she arrowed her way ahead, safe and uncatchable. Every now and again she would give some order or encouragement to the horsemen by raising her arm with a whip or tearing off a carob nut and throwing it, as if to tell them to go that way. The horsemen would at once rush off in that direction, galloping over the fields and slopes, but she had turned another way and was no longer looking at them.

'It's her, it's her!' Cosimo was thinking, more and more inflamed with hope and trying to shout her name, but all that came from his lips was a long sad cry, like a plover's.

Now, this tacking to and fro, this deceiving of the cavaliers, and all the games seemed to be tending one way, however irregular and wavering. Guessing this goal, Cosimo abandoned the impossible task of following her, and said to himself, 'I'll go in a place she'll go to, if it's her. In fact, she can't be going anywhere else.' And leaping along by his own routes, he moved towards the abandoned park of the Ondarivas.

In that shade, in that scented air, in that place where even the leaves and twigs had another colour and another substance, he felt so carried away by memories of his childhood that he almost forgot the horsewoman, or if not forgot began telling himself it might not be her and that this waiting and hoping for her was yet so true that it was almost as if she were there.

Then he heard a sound. Horse's hoofs on the gravel. It was coming down the garden no longer at a gallop, as if the rider wanted to look at and recognize everything minutely. There was no sign of the cavaliers; they must have lost all trace of her.

He saw her; she was wandering round the fountains, urns and garden pavilions, looking at the plants which had now become huge, with hanging aerial roots, the magnolias grown into a copse. But she did not see him, who was trying to call at her together with the cooing of the doves, the trilling of the larks, with all the sounds merging into the close twitter of birds in the garden.

She had dismounted, and was leading the horse by the bridle. She reached the villa, left the horse, entered the portico. Then suddenly she broke into shouts of 'Ortensia! Gaetano! Tarquinio! This needs whitewashing, the shutters painting, the tapestries hung! And I want the big table here, the side ones there, the spinet in the middle, the pictures must all be re-hung.'

Cosimo realized then that the house which to his distracted eyes had seemed closed and empty as always, now on the other hand was open, full of people, servants cleaning and polishing and rearranging, opening windows, moving furniture, beating carpets. So it *was* Viola who was returning, Viola re-establishing herself at Ombrosa, taking possession once again of the villa she had left as a child! And the beating joy in Cosimo's heart was not very different from beating fear, for her return, the presence of her, unpredictable and proud, under his very eyes, might mean losing her for ever, even in his memory, even in that secret place of scented leaves and dappled green light, might mean that he would be forced to flee from her and so flee too from that first memory of her as a girl.

With this alternate beating of the heart Cosimo watched her swirling amid the servants, making them move sofas, clavichords and consoles, then passing hurriedly into the garden and remounting her horse, followed by groups waiting for more orders, then turning to the gardeners, and telling them how to arrange the abandoned flower-beds and rescatter on the paths gravel swept away by rain, and put back the wicker-chairs and the swing.

She pointed, with a wave of the arms, at the branch from which this had once been hanging and was now to be hung again, and indicated how long the ropes were to be, and how wide its course, and as she was saying all this, her gestures and glance went up to the magnolia tree on which Cosimo had once appeared. And there he was on the magnolia tree and she saw him again.

She was surprised. Very. No doubt of that, though her eyes were laughing through her surprise. But she recovered at once and pretended not to care, and smiled with her eyes and mouth and showed a tooth she had as a child.

'You!' and then, trying to use as natural a tone as she could, but not succeeding in hiding her interest and pleasure, she went on, 'Ah, so you've stayed up there without ever coming down?'

Cosimo succeeded in transforming a swallow's note in his throat into a 'Yes, Viola, it's me, d'you remember me?'

'You've never, really never once set a foot on the ground?'

'Never.'

Then she, as if she had already conceded too much: 'Ah, so you managed it, you see! It couldn't have been so difficult then.'

'I was awaiting your return ...'

'Excellent. Hey, you, where are you taking that curtain! Leave it all here and I'll see to it!' And she began looking at him again. Cosimo that day was dressed for hunting; hairy all over, with his cap of cat's fur and his musket. 'You look like Crusoe!'

'Have you read it?' he said at once, to show he was up to date.

Viola had already turned round. 'Gaetano! Ampelio! The dry leaves! It's full of dry leaves!' Then to him: 'In an hour, at the end of the park. Wait for me.' And she hurried away to give more orders, on horseback.

Cosimo threw himself into the thick of the wood; he would have liked it to be a thousand times thicker, a phalanx of branches and leaves and thorns and bracken and maidenhair, to plunge and replunge into and only after being completely immersed to understand if he was happy or if he was mad with fear.

On the big tree at the end of the park, with his knees tight against a branch, he looked at the time in a fob-watch that had belonged to his maternal grandfather General von Kurtewitz and said to himself: she won't come. Instead of which Donna Viola arrived almost punctually, on horseback. She stopped under the tree without even looking up; she was no longer wearing her rider's hat or jacket; her white blouse, decorated with lace on a black skirt, was almost nunlike. Raising herself on her stirrups she held out a hand to him on the branch; he helped her; she climbed on to the saddle and reached the branch, then still without looking at him, rapidly climbed up it, looked about for a comfortable fork, and sat down. Cosimo crouched at her feet, and could begin only by saying: 'So you're back?'

Viola gave him an ironical look. Her hair was fair as it had been as a child. 'How do you know that?' said she.

And he, without understanding her little joke: 'I saw you in that field of the Duke's preserve.'

'The preserve's mine. It can fill with weeds, for all I care! D'you know about it? About me, I mean?'

'No ... I've only just heard you're a widow now ...'

'Yes, of course I'm a widow,' and she hit her black skirt, smoothed it out, and began talking very quickly. 'You never know anything. There you are on the trees, all day long, putting your nose into other people's business, and yet you know nothing. I married old Tolemaico because my family made me, forced me. They said I was a flirt and must have a husband. For a year I've been the Duchess Tolemaico, and it was the most boring year of my life, though I never spent more than a week with the old man. I'll never set foot in any of their castles or ruins or topiary walks, may they fill with snakes! From now on I'm staying here, where I was as a child. I'll stay here as long as I feel like it, of course, then I'll go off; I'm a widow and can do what I like, finally. I've always done what I liked, to tell the truth; even Tolemaico I married because it suited me to marry him; it's not true they forced me to, they were determined to make a martyr of me, and so I chose the most decrepit suitor I could find. "Then I'll be a widow sooner," I said, and so I am, now.'

Cosimo sat there half stunned by this avalanche of information and peremptory affirmation, and Viola was further away than ever; flirt, widow, duchess, she was part of an unreachable world, and all he could find to say was: 'And whom d'you flirt with now?'

And she: 'There. You're jealous. Be careful, as I'll never let you be jealous.'

Cosimo did have a flash of jealousy provoked by this tiff, then thought at once: 'What? Jealous? Why admit that I could be jealous of her? Why say "I'll never let you"? It's as good as saying that she thinks that we ...'

Then, scarlet in the face, he felt a longing to tell her, to ask her, to hear her, instead of which it was she who asked him dryly: 'Tell me about you now. What have you done?'

'Oh, I've done things,' he began saying. 'I've hunted, boar too, but mostly foxes, hares, pheasants and then of course thrushes and blackbirds; and then pirates, Turkish pirates, we had a great fight, my uncle died in it; and I've read lots of books, for myself and a friend of mine, a brigand who was hanged; and I've got the whole Encyclopaedia of Diderot and have also written to him and he's replied, from Paris; and I've done lots of work, sown crops, saved a wood from fire ...'

'And will you always love me, absolutely, above all else, and will you do anything for me?'

At this remark of hers, Cosimo, with a catch at the heart, said: 'Yes.'

'You are a man who has lived on the trees for me alone, to learn to love me ...'

'Yes ... yes ...'

'Kiss me.'

He pressed her against the trunk, kissed her. Raising his face, he realized her beauty as if he had never seen it before. 'Say, how beautiful you are ...'

'For you ...' and she unbuttoned her white blouse. Her breast was young, the nipple rosy. Cosimo just grazed it with his lips, before Viola slid away over the branches as if she were flying, with him clambering after her, and that skirt of hers always in sight.

'But where are you taking me to?' asked Viola as if it were he leading her, not she him.

'This way,' exclaimed Cosimo, and began guiding her, and at every passage of branches he would take her by the hand or the waist and show her the way over.

'This way,' and they went on to certain olive trees, protruding from a cliff, and from the top of these was the sea, which till now they had glimpsed only in jagged bits and fragmentations between leaves and branches and now suddenly found there facing them, calm and limpid and vast as the sky. The horizon opened wide and high and the blue was taut and bare without a sail and they could count the scarcely perceptible crinkles of the waves. Only a very light rustle, like a sigh, ran over the pebbles on the beach.

With eyes half dazed, Cosimo and Viola moved back into the dark green shade of foliage. 'This way.'

In a nut tree, astride a trunk, was a hollow like a shell, formed from an old axe-wound, and this was one of Cosimo's refuges. Over it was stretched a boar-skin, and around set a flask, a tool or two, and a bowl.

Viola flung herself down on the boar-skin. 'Do you bring other women here?'

He hesitated. And Viola: 'If you haven't, you're not much of a man.'

'Yes ... One or two ...'

She slapped him full in the face. 'So that's how you awaited me?'

Cosimo passed his hand over his scarlet cheek and could

think of no word to say; but now she seemed to be in a good mood again. 'And what were they like? Tell me. What were they like?'

'Not like you, Viola, not like you ...'

'How d'you know what I'm like, eh, how d'you know?'

She was gentle now, and Cosimo never ceased to be surprised at these sudden changes of hers. He moved close to her. Viola was gold and honey.

'Say ...'

'Say ...'

They knew each other. He knew her and so himself, for in truth he had never known himself. And she knew him and so herself, for although she had always known herself she had never yet been able to recognize it as now.

22

The first pilgrimage they made was to the tree where, in a deep incision in the bark, now so old and deformed that it no longer seemed the work of human hands, were carved the big letters: *Cosimo, Viola*, and beneath; *Ottimo Massimo*.

'Up here? Who did it? When?'

'I; then.'

Viola was moved.

'And what does that mean?' and she pointed to the words, *Ottimo Massimo*.

'My dog. That is your dog. The dachshund.'

'Turcaret?'

'Ottimo Massimo, I called it.'

'Turcaret! How I sobbed for it, when I realized as I left that they hadn't put it in the carriage! ... Oh, I didn't care about not seeing you again, but was desperate at not having the dog any more!'

'If it hadn't been for the dog I wouldn't have found you again! It sniffed in the wind that you were near, and didn't rest until it found you.'

'I recognized it at once, as soon as I saw it arrive at the pavilion, panting fit to burst ... The others said, "And where's this come from?" I bent down to look at its colour, its markings. "But it's Turcaret! The dachshund I had as a child at Ombrosa!"'

Cosimo laughed. Suddenly she tweaked his nose. 'Ottimo Massimo! What an ugly name! Where d'you get such ugly names from?' And Cosimo's face clouded over.

But for Ottimo Massimo now there was no cloud on happiness. Its old dog's heart that had been divided between two masters was finally at peace, after having worked day after day to attract the Marchesa towards the borders of the game-preserve to the ilex on which Cosimo had been crouching. It had pulled her by the skirt, or skipped away with some object of hers, off towards the field so that she should follow, and she had exclaimed: 'But what do you want? Where *are* you dragging me? Turcaret! Stop it! What a *mad*dening little dog to find again!'

But already the sight of the dachshund had moved in her the memories of childhood, a nostalgia for Ombrosa. And she had at once begun preparing her move from the ducal pavilion and her return to the old villa with its strange vegetation.

She had returned, Viola had. For Cosimo now began the loveliest period of his life, and for her too, who would go galloping over the country on her white horse and when she caught sight of the Baron between branches and sky would dismount, climb up the slanting trees and branches, on which she soon became almost as expert as he and could reach him everywhere.

'Oh, Viola, I don't know, I don't know where I could still climb ...'

'To me ...' Viola would say quietly, and he felt himself seized by madness.

Love for her was heroic exercise; the pleasure of it was mingled with trials of courage and generosity and dedication and tension, of all the faculties of her soul. Theirs was a world of the most intricate and writhing and impenetrable trees.

'There!' she would exclaim, pointing to a fork high in the branches, and they would launch out together to reach it and start between them a competition in acrobatics culminating in new embraces. They made love suspended in the void, propping or gripping themselves on branches, she flinging herself on him almost flying.

Viola's stubbornness in love accorded with Cosimo's, and sometimes discorded too. Cosimo would flee from the inquiries, the byplay, the refined perversities; nothing in love pleased him that was not natural. The republican virtues were in the air; a period was coming both licentious and severe. Cosimo, insatiable lover, was a stoic, an ascetic, a puritan. Always in search of happiness in love, he would never be a mere voluptuary. He reached the point of distrusting kisses, caresses, verbal play, of everything that clouded or substituted the pure greeting of nature. It was Viola who revealed this in its fullness: and with her he never knew the sadness after love, preached by theologians; on this subject he even wrote a philosophic letter to Rousseau, who, perhaps disturbed by it, did not reply.

But Viola was also a subtle, sly, capricious woman, a catholic in blood and soul. Cosimo's love made her senses brim, but left her mind unsatisfied. From that came quarrels and cloudy resentments. But these did not last long, so varied was their life and the world around.

When tired, they would seek refuge in the thickest press of leaves: hammocks which enwrapped their bodies like rolls of paper, or hanging pavilions with curtains flapping in the breeze, or lairs of feathers. In such contrivances Donna Viola was a past-mistress: wherever she happened to be, the Marchesa had the gift of creating round herself comfort, luxury and complicated ease; complicated in appearance, but obtained by her with miraculous facility, for everything she wanted had to be carried out at once and at all costs.

On these aerial alcoves of theirs the robins would perch to sing, and between the curtains flutter butterflies in pairs, chasing each other. On summer afternoons, when sleep took the two lovers side by side, a squirrel would enter, looking for something to nibble, and stroke their faces with its feathery tail or plunge its teeth into a big toe. Then they would pull the curtains to more carefully; but a family of tree-mice began gnawing at the roof of the pavilion and fell down on their heads.

This was the time in which they were discovering each other, telling of their lives, questioning.

'And did you feel alone?'

'I hadn't you.'

'But alone with the rest of the world?'

'No. Why? I always had contacts with other people; I picked fruit, pruned trees, studied philosophy with the Abbé, fought the pirates. Isn't everyone like that?'

'You're the only one like that, that's why I love you.'

But the Baron had not yet realized what Viola would accept from him and what not. Sometimes a mere nothing, a word or a tone was enough to loose the fury of the Marchesa.

He might say for example: 'With Gian dei Brughi I used to read novels, with the Cavalier I made plans for irrigation ...'

'And with me?'

'With you I make love. Like picking, or pruning ...'

She would be silent, motionless. At once Cosimo realized he had unchained her anger; suddenly her eyes had become like ice.

'Why, what is it, Viola, what have I said?'

She was far away as if she did not see or hear, a hundred miles from him, her face like marble.

'But no, Viola, what is it, why, listen ...'

Viola got up; agile, with no need of help, she began climbing down the tree. Cosimo had not yet understood what his mistake could have been, had not had time to think it over, perhaps preferred not to think of it at all, not to understand it, the better to proclaim his innocence. 'No, no, you didn't understand, Viola, listen ...'

He followed her on to a branch lower down. 'Viola, don't go, please don't go, not like this, Viola . . .'

She spoke now, but to the horse, which she had reached and taken by the bridle. She mounted and off she went.

Cosimo began to despair, to jump from tree to tree. 'No, Viola, do say a word, Viola!'

She had galloped away. He followed her over the branches. '*Please*, Viola, I love you!' But he had lost sight of her. He flung himself on uncertain branches, made risky leaps. 'Viola! Viola!'

When he was sure of having lost her and could not retain his sobs, suddenly she reappeared at the trot, without raising her eyes.

'Look, do look, Viola, what I'll do?' and he began banging himself against a trunk with his bare head (which was, in truth, very hard).

She did not even look at him. She was already away.

Cosimo waited for her to return, zigzagging among the trees.

'Viola! I'm desperate!' and he flung himself into the void, head down, holding by the legs on to a branch and hitting himself all over head and face. Or he began to break branches in a fury of destruction, and a leafy elm was reduced in a few seconds to a bare stripped bark as if a hailstorm had passed.

But he never threatened to kill himself, indeed he never threatened anything, emotional blackmail was not in him. He did what he felt like doing and announced it while he was actually doing it, not before.

Then suddenly Donna Viola, unpredictable as her anger, reappeared. Of all Cosimo's follies which seemed never to have grazed her, one had suddenly refired her with pity and love. 'No, Cosimo, darling, wait for me!' And she jumped from her saddle and rushed to clamber up a trunk, and his arms were ready to raise her on high.

Love took over again with a fury equal to the quarrel. It was, really, the same thing, but Cosimo had not realized it.

'Why d'you make me suffer?'

'Because I love you.'

Now it was his turn to get angry. 'No, no, you don't love me! People in love want happiness, not pain!'

'People in love want only love, even at the cost of pain.'

'Then you're making me suffer on purpose.'

The Baron's philosophy refused to take him further.

'Pain is negative.'

'Love is all.'

'Pain should always be fought against.'

'Love refuses nothing.'

'Some things I'll never admit.'

'Oh yes, you do, now, for you love me and you suffer.'

Like his outbursts of despair, Cosimo's explosions of uncontainable joy were noisy. Sometimes his happiness reached such a point that he had to leave his love and go jumping off and shouting and proclaiming her wonders to the world.

'Yo quiero the most wonderful puellam de todo el mundo!'

Those sitting on the benches at Ombrosa, idlers or old mariners, got quite into the habit of these sudden apparitions of his. There he would come leaping through the ilexes, declaiming:

'Zu dir, zu dir, gunàika,
I search for mio ben,
On this isle of Jamaica
Du soir jusqu'au matin!'

or;

'Il y a un pré where the grass grows todo de oro
Take me away, take me away, che io ci moro!'

then he would vanish.

His studies of classic and modern languages, however little pursued, were enough to let himself go in this clamorous expression of his feelings, and the more he was shaken to the depths by intense emotion, the more his language became obscure. They remember here how once, at the Feast of the Patron Saint, when the people of Ombrosa were gathered in the square round the Tree of Plenty and the festoons and the flagpole, the

Baron appeared on the top of a plane tree and with one of those leaps of which only his acrobatic agility was capable, jumped on to the Tree of Plenty, clambered to the top, shouted '*Que viva die schöne Venus posterior!*' let himself slither down the pole almost to the ground, stopped, groped his way up to the top again, tore from the trophy a round rosy cheese, and with another of his jumps returned to the plane tree and fled, leaving the people of Ombrosa in a daze.

Nothing made the Marchesa happier than these exuberances, and moved her to repay them with demonstrations of love that were even more violent. The Ombrosians, when they saw her galloping along on a loose rein, her face almost buried in the white mane of the horse, knew that she was rushing to a meeting with the Baron. Even in her way of riding she expressed the strength of love, but here Cosimo could no longer follow her; and her equestrian passion, much as he admired it, was for him also a secret reason for jealousy and rancour, for he saw Viola dominated by a world vaster than his own and realized that he would never be able to have her for himself alone, to shut her in the confines of his kingdom. The Marchesa, on her side, suffered perhaps from her inability to be at once both lover and horsewoman; every now and again she was taken with a vague need for her love and Cosimo's to become a love on horseback, a feeling that running over trees was no longer enough for her, a yearning to race along at full gallop on the crupper of his charger.

And in fact her horse, with that racing over countryside all slopes and drops, was becoming like the tendril of a vine, and Viola now began urging it up certain trees, old olives, for example, with distorted trunks. Sometimes the horse would reach the first fork in the branches, and she got into the habit of tying it no longer on the ground, but up on the olive. Dismounting, she would leave it to munch leaves and twigs.

And so when some old gossip passing through the olive grove and raising curious eyes saw the Baron and the Marchesa up there in each other's arms, and went off and told people and added: 'The white horse was up on a branch too,' he was taken for a visionary and no one believed him. And once again that time the lovers' secret was saved.

23

This last story shows that the people of Ombrosa, who before had been teeming with gossip about my brother's love life, now, faced with this passion exploding as it were right above their heads, maintained a dignified reserve, as towards something bigger than themselves. Not that they did not criticize the Marchesa's conduct; but more for its exterior aspects, such as that breakneck galloping of hers ('Where can she be going, at such a pace?') and that continual hoisting of furniture on to tree-tops. There was already an air among them of considering it all just as one of the nobles' ways, one of their many extravaganzas. ('All up trees, nowadays; women, men. What'll they think of next?') In fact, times were coming that were to be more tolerant, but also more hypocritical.

Now the Baron would only show himself at rare intervals on the ilexes in the square, and when he did it was a sign that she had left. For Viola was sometimes away months seeing to her properties scattered all over Europe, though these departures of hers always corresponded to moments of shock in their relationship, when the Marchesa had been offended with Cosimo's not understanding what she wanted him to understand about love. Not that Viola left in this state of mind: they always managed to make it up before, though there remained the suspicion in him that she had decided on this particular journey from tiredness with him, because he could not prevent her going, perhaps she was already breaking away from him, perhaps some incident on the journey or a pause for reflection would decide her not to return. So my brother would live in a state of anxiety. He would try to go back to the habitual life he led before meeting her, to hunt and fish, follow the work in the fields, his studies, the gossip in the square, as if he had never done anything else (there persisted in him the stubborn youthful pride of refusing ever to admit himself under anyone else's influence); and at the same time he would congratulate himself on how much love was giving him, the alacrity, the pride; but on the other hand he noticed that so many things no longer mattered to him, that without Viola life had no savour, that his thoughts were always following her. The more he tried, away from the whirlwind of Viola's presence, to reacquire command of passions and pleasures in a wise economy of mind, the more he felt the void left by her or the fever for her return. In fact his love was just what Viola wanted it to be, not as he pretended it was; it was always the woman who triumphed, even from a distance, and Cosimo, in spite of himself, ended by enjoying it.

Suddenly the Marchesa would return. Once again the season of love on the trees began but also that of jealousy. Where had Viola been? What had she done? Cosimo was longing to know but at the same time afraid of how she answered his inquiries all by hints, and every hint seemed to insinuate itself as a suspicion and he realized that though she was doing this to torment him, it could all be quite true; and in this uncertain state of mind he would mask his jealousy at one moment then let it break out violently the next, and Viola would reply in a way that was always different and always unforeseeable, and at one moment seem more tied to him than ever, at another to be beyond any fanning of the flame.

What the Marchesa really did during her travels we at Ombrosa could not know, far as we were from capitals and their gossip. But I happened at that period to make my second journey to Paris in connection with certain contracts in lemons, for many nobles were already taking to commerce and I among the first.

One evening, at one of the most brilliant salons in Paris. I

met Donna Viola. Her headgear was so splendid and her robe
so sumptuous that if I recognized her at once, in fact gave a
start at first seeing her, it was because she was a woman who
could never be confused with any other. She greeted me with
indifference, but soon found a way of taking me aside and
asking me, without waiting for any reply between one question
and another: 'Have you news of your brother? Will you soon
be back at Ombrosa? Here, give him this to remember me by,'
and taking a silk handkerchief from her bosom she thrust it into
my hand. Then she quickly let herself be caught up in the court
of admirers who followed her everywhere.

'Do you know the Marchesa?' I was asked quietly by a Paris-
ian friend.

'Only slightly,' I replied, and it was true; when she stayed at
Ombrosa Donna Viola, under the influence of Cosimo's life in
the wilds, never bothered to see anything of the local nobility.

'Rarely has such beauty been allied to such a restless spirit,'
said my friend. 'Gossip has it that in Paris she passes from one
love to another, in such rapid succession that no one can call
her his own and consider himself privileged. But every now and
again she vanishes for months at a time and they say she retires
to a convent, to subdue herself with penance.'

I could scarcely avoid laughing, at finding the Marchesa's life
on the trees of Ombrosa being thought of by the Parisians as
periods of penance; but at the same time this gossip disturbed
me, and made me foresee times of sorrow for my brother.

To forestall ugly surprises I decided to warn him, and as soon
as I returned to Ombrosa went to search him out. He questioned
me at length about my journey and the news from France, but I
could not tell him anything of politics and literature about
which he was not already informed.

Eventually I drew Donna Viola's handkerchief from my
pocket. 'At Paris in a salon I met a lady who knows you, and
who gave me this for you, with her greetings.'

Quickly he dropped the basket attached to the rope, pulled
up the silk handkerchief and brought it to his face as if to inhale
its scent. 'Ah, you saw her? And how was she? Tell me, how was
she?'

'Very beautiful and very brilliant,' I answered slowly. 'But they say this scent is inhaled by many nostrils.'

He pushed the handkerchief into his chest as if fearing it might be torn away from him; then turned to me red in the face. 'And have you no sword to thrust those lies down the throat of the person who told you?'

I had to confess that it had not even crossed my mind.

He was silent a moment. Then he shrugged his shoulders. 'All lies. I alone know she's mine alone,' and he ran off on the branches without a greeting or farewell. I recognized his usual way of refusing to admit anything which would force him out of his own world.

From then on every time I saw him he was sad and impatient, jumping about here and there, without doing anything. If now and again I heard him whistling in competition with the blackbirds, his note was ever more restless and gloomy.

The Marchesa arrived. As always, his jealousy pleased her; she incited it a little, turned it a little into a joke. So back came the beautiful days of love and my brother was happy.

But now the Marchesa never let pass a chance to accuse Cosimo of having a narrow idea of love.

'What d'you mean? That I'm jealous?'

'You're right to be jealous. But you try to make jealousy submit to reason.'

'Of course; so I can do more about it.'

'You reason too much. Why should one ever reason about love?'

'To love you all the more. Everything done with reasoning grows in power.'

'You live on trees and have the mentality of a notary with gout.'

'The most arduous tasks are done in the simplest states of mind.'

He went on mouthing maxims, till she fled; then he followed, desperate, tearing his hair.

*

In those days a British flagship anchored in our port. The Admiral gave a fête to the notables of Ombrosa and the officers of other ships that happened to be in port; the Marchesa went; and from that evening Cosimo felt the pangs of jealousy start anew. Two officers of two different ships fell in love with Donna Viola and were seen continually on shore, courting the lady and trying to outdo each other in attentions. One was a flag-lieutenant on the Admiral's ship; the other was also a flag-lieutenant, but of the Neapolitan fleet. Hiring two sorrels, the two lieutenants would alternate beneath the Marchesa's balconies, and when they met the Neapolitan would roll at the Englishman an eye so fiery that it should have burnt him up on the spot, while between the half-shut lids of the Englishman glinted a glance like the point of a sword.

And Donna Viola? What should she do, the minx, but stay for hour on hour at home, leaning over the window-sill in her peignoir, as if she were newly widowed and just out of mourning! Cosimo, not having her on the trees with him any more, not hearing her white horse galloping towards him, went into a frenzy, and ended by settling (even he) before that window-sill, to keep an eye on her and the two flag-lieutenants.

He was thinking out a way of playing some trick on his rivals, to make them return fast to their respective ships, when he noticed that Viola showed signs of encouraging equally the courtship of both; he began hoping that she was only playing a game on them, and on him at the same time. Not that his surveillance diminished because of this; at the first sight she gave of preferring one of the two, he was ready to intervene.

Along, one morning, comes the Englishman. Viola is at the window. They smile at each other. The Marchesa lets fall a note. The officer catches it in the air, reads it, bows, blushes, and spurs away. A rendezvous! The Englishman was the lucky one! Cosimo swore he would never let him reach that night in calm.

At that moment along comes the Neapolitan. Viola throws him a note too. The officer reads it, puts it to his lips and kisses it. So he thought he was the chosen one, did he? What about the other, then? Against which was Cosimo to act? Donna Viola must surely have fixed an appointment with one of them; with the other she must have just played one of her jokes. Or did she want to make fun of them both?

As for the place of the meeting, Cosimo settled his suspicions on a pavilion at the end of the park. This had been done up and furnished by the Marchesa a short time before, and Cosimo was gnawed with jealousy at the thought of the times when she had loaded the tree-tops with sofas and curtains; now she was concentrating on places he could never enter. 'I'll watch the pavilion,' said Cosimo to himself. 'If she's arranged a meeting with one of the two lieutenants, it can only be there.' And he hid in the thickness of an Indian chestnut.

Shortly before dusk, the sound of a galloping horse is heard. It is the Neapolitan. 'Now I'll provoke him!' thinks Cosimo, takes his catapult and hits him on the neck with a handful of squirrel's dung. The officer shakes himself, looks around. Cosimo comes out on his branch, and as he appears in the open sees the English lieutenant dismounting beyond a hedge and tying his horse to a stake. 'Then it's him; perhaps the other was just passing here by chance.' And down comes a load of dung on the Englishman's nose.

'Who's there?' says the Englishman, and makes to cross the hedge, but finds himself face to face with his Neapolitan colleague who has also dismounted and is also saying, 'Who's there?'

'I beg your pardon, sir,' says the Englishman, 'but I must ask you to leave here at once!'

'I'm here with full right,' exclaims the Neapolitan. 'It's I who must ask your Lordship to leave!'

'No right can be more than mine,' replies the Englishman, 'I'm sorry, but I cannot allow you to stay.'

''Tis a question of honour,' says the other, 'and I rely upon that of my House: Salvatore di San Cataldo di Santa Maria Capua Vetere, of the Navy of His Majesty of the Two Sicilies!'

'Sir Osbert Castlefield, third of the name!' the Englishman introduces himself. ''Tis *my* honour to ask you to vacate the field.'

'Not before *I* have put you out with this trusty sword!' and he draws it from its sheath.

'Sir, you wish to fight!' exclaims Sir Osbert, and puts himself on guard.

They fight.

'This is where I wanted you, colleague, and for many a day,' and the Neapolitan makes a thrust.

And Sir Osbert, parrying: 'I've been following your movements for some time, lieutenant, and was awaiting this!'

Equals in skill, the two lieutenants threw themselves into assaults and feints. They were at the peak of their impetus when: 'Stop in heaven's name!' exclaimed a voice. On the steps of the pavilion had appeared Donna Viola.

'Marchesa, this man ...' said the two lieutenants in one voice, lowering their swords and pointing to each other.

And Donna Viola: 'My dear friends! Sheath your blades, I beg you! Is this the way to alarm a lady? I had chosen this pavilion as the most silent and most secret place in my park, and scarcely have I dozed off than I hear the clash of arms!'

'But, Milady,' said the Englishman, 'was I not invited by you?'

'You were here awaiting *me*, Signora ...' said the Neapolitan.

From Donna Viola's throat came a laugh light as a flutter of wings. 'Ah, yes, yes, I had invited you ... or you. Oh, I get so confused. Well, sirs, what are you waiting for? Do come in, please ...'

'Milady, I thought the invitation was for me alone. I am disappointed. May I offer my respects and request leave to withdraw.'

'I too wish to say the same, Signora, and bid farewell.'

The Marchesa laughed. 'My good friends ... My *good* friends ... I'm so scatter-brained ... I thought I had invited Sir Osbert at one time ... and Don Salvatore at another ... No, no, excuse me; at the same time, but in different places ... Oh, no, how can that be? ... Well, anyway, seeing that you are both here, why can we not sit down and hold civilized converse?'

The two lieutenants looked at each other, then looked at her. 'Are we to understand, Marchesa, that you are pretending to accept our attentions merely in order to make fun of both of us?'

'Why so, my good friends? On the contrary, quite on the contrary ... Your assiduity can scarcely leave me indifferent ... You are both such dear people ... And that is my worry ... If I choose the elegance of Sir Osbert I shall lose you, my passionate Don Salvatore ... And by choosing the fire of the Lieutenant of San Cataldo, I would have to renounce you, Sir. Oh, why ever ... why ever ...'

'Why ever what?' asked the two officers in one voice.

And Donna Viola, lowering her eyes: 'Why ever could it not be both at the same time?'

From the Indian chestnut above came a crash of branches. It was Cosimo who could retain his calm no longer.

But the two flag-lieutenants were too confused to hear this. They both stepped back a pace. 'That never, Madame.'

The Marchesa raised her lovely face with its most radiant smile. 'Well, then, I shall give myself to the first of you who, to please me in all things, declares himself ready to share me with his rival!'

'Signora.'

'Milady.'

The two lieutenants bowed coldly to Viola, then turned to face each other, held out their hands and clasped them.

'I was sure you were a gentleman, Signor Cataldo,' said the Englishman.

'I never doubted your honour, Mister Osberto,' exclaimed the Neapolitan.

They turned their backs on the Marchesa and marched off towards their horses.

'My friends ... Why so offended ... Silly boys ...' Viola was saying, but the two officers already had their feet in the stirrups.

It was the moment for which Cosimo had long been waiting, enjoying in anticipation the revenge he had prepared, when the two would get a most painful surprise. Now, however, seeing their virile attitude in bidding farewell to the immodest Marchesa, Cosimo suddenly felt reconciled with them. Too late! Now it was too late to remove his appalling devices for revenge! A second's thought, and Cosimo had generously decided to warn them. 'Stop!' he called from the tree. 'Don't mount!'

The two officers raised startled heads. 'What are you doing up there? What d'you mean by this? Come down!'

Behind them was heard Donna Viola's laugh, one of her bird's wing laughs.

The two were looking perplexed. So there was a third, who seemed to have been present at the whole scene! The situation was becoming more complicated than ever.

'Anyway,' said they to each other, 'we two remain in complete agreement!'

'On our honour!'

'Neither of us two will agree to share Milady with anyone else!'

'Never on our lives!'

'But if one of us two should decide to accept ...'

'In that case, still agreed! We would accept together!'

'That's a pact! And now, away!'

At this new dialogue, Cosimo began gnawing his thumb with rage for having tried to prevent his own revenge. 'Let it be, then!' he said, and drew back into the leaves. The two officers leapt into their saddles. 'Now they'll yell,' thought Cosimo, and stopped his ears. Double shrieks rang out. The two flag-lieutenants had sat on two porcupines hidden under the trappings of their saddles.

'Betrayed!' they flew to the ground in an explosion of shouts and skips and twists, and it looked for a moment as if they were going to revenge themselves on the Marchesa.

But Donna Viola, more indignant than they, shouted up: 'You malicious monstrous monkey!' rushed towards the trunk of the Indian chestnut and rapidly vanished from the sight of the two officers, who thought she had been swallowed up by the earth.

Up in the branches Viola was facing Cosimo. They looked at each other with flaming eyes, and their rage gave them a kind of purity, like archangels. They seemed just about to tear each other to pieces, when, 'Oh my darling!' exclaimed the woman. 'That's, yes, that's how I like you. Jealous, implacable! ...'

Already she had flung an arm round his neck and they were embracing and now Cosimo could remember nothing more.

She dangled him in her arms, took her face from his, as if some thought had struck her, and then: 'But that pair too, how much they love me. Did you see? They're even ready to share me between them ...'

Cosimo felt for a second like flinging himself at her, then he pulled himself up on the branches and banged his head against the trunk. 'They're vermin ...'

Viola had moved away with her face like a statue. 'You've a lot to learn from them!' She turned and climbed quickly down the tree.

The two suitors had quite forgotten their past differences and were now absorbed in patiently helping to pick out each other's quills. They were interrupted by Donna Viola. 'Quick! Into my carriage!' They all vanished behind the pavilion. The carriage moved off. Cosimo was left on the Indian chestnut, hiding his face in his hands.

Now began a time of torment for Cosimo, and also for the two ex-rivals. And for Viola, could it be called a time of joy? I believe the Marchesa tormented others because she wanted to torment herself. The two noble officers were always underfoot, inseparable, under her windows, or in her salon, or on long waits in the local tavern. She would flatter them both and ask them to compete in constant new proofs of love, which every time they declared themselves ready to do; and by now they were even ready to halve her with each other, not only that but to share her with anyone else, and once they had begun rolling down the slippery slopes of concessions they could no longer halt, each urged by the wish to succeed thus in moving her and obtaining the fulfilment of her promises, and each at the same time tied in a pact of solidarity with his rival, and devoured too by jealousy and by the hope of supplanting him, and, I fear, by the pull of the obscure degradation into which they felt themselves sinking.

At every new concession torn from the naval officers, Viola would mount her horse and go to tell Cosimo about it.

'Say, d'you know the Englishman is ready to do this and this

... And the Neapolitan too ...' She would shout as soon as she saw him gloomily perching on a tree.

Cosimo would not reply.

'This is absolute love,' she would insist.

'Absolute s—s, that's what you all are!' screamed Cosimo, and vanished.

This was now their cruel way of loving each other, and from it they could find no way out.

The English flagship was about to draw anchor. 'You're staying, aren't you?' said Viola to Sir Osbert. Sir Osbert did not report on board and was declared a deserter. In a spirit of solidarity and emulation, Don Salvatore did the same.

'They've deserted!' announced Viola triumphantly to Cosimo. 'For me! And you ...'

'And I?' screamed Cosimo with such a ferocious look that Viola did not dare say another word.

Sir Osbert and Salvatore di San Cataldo, deserters from the navies of their respective Majesties, now spent their days at the tavern, playing skittles, pale, restless, trying to encourage each other, while Viola was at the peak of her discontent with herself and with all around her.

She took her horse, went towards the wood. Cosimo was on an oak. She stopped underneath, in a field.

'I'm tired.'

'Of those?'

'Of you all.'

'Ah!'

'They've given me the greatest proofs of love ...'

Cosimo spat.

'... But that's not enough for me.'

Cosimo raised his eyes to hers.

And she: 'Don't you think that love should be an absolute dedication, a renunciation of self?'

There she was in the field, lovely as ever, and the coldness just touching her features and the haughtiness of her bearing would have dissolved at a touch, and he would have had her in his arms again ... Anything would have been enough for Cosimo to say, anything that was a concession: 'Tell me what you want me to do, I'm ready' ... and once more there would have been happiness for him, happiness without a shadow. Instead of which he said: 'There can be no love if one does not remain oneself with all one's strength.'

Viola made a movement of irritation which was a movement also of weariness. And yet she could have understood him still, as in fact she did understand him then and had on the tip of her tongue the words, 'You are as I want you,' and she would be back with him again ... She bit her lip. And said: 'Be yourself by yourself, then.'

'But being myself then has no sense.' That is what Cosimo wanted to say. Instead of which he said: 'If you prefer those vermin ...'

'I will not allow you to despise my friends!' she shouted, still thinking: 'All that matters to me is you, and it is only for you that I do all I do!'

'So, I'm the only one to be despised.'

'What a way you think!'

'It's part of me.'

'Then goodbye. I leave tonight. You won't see me again.'

She hurried to the house, packed her bags, left without even a word to the lieutenants. And she kept her word, never returned to Ombrosa. She went to France, and there historical events superimposed on her will when she was longing for nothing but to return. The Revolution broke out, then the war; first the Marchesa took an interest in the new course of events (she was in the *entourage* of Lafayette), then emigrated to Belgium and from there to England. In the London mists, during the long years of wars against Napoleon, she would dream of the trees of Ombrosa. Then she remarried, an English peer connected with the East India Company, and settled at Calcutta. From her terrace she would look out over the forests, the trees even stranger than those of the gardens of her childhood; every moment seemed to see Cosimo moving apart the leaves. But it would be the shadow of a monkey, or a jaguar.

Sir Osbert Castlefield and Salvatore di San Cataldo remained linked in life and death, and launched into a career of adventure. They were seen in the gaming-houses of Venice, in the Faculty of Theology at Göttingen, in Petersburg at the Court of Catherine II, then trace was lost.

Cosimo remained for a long time wandering aimlessly round the woods, weeping, ragged, refusing food. He would sob out loud, as do newborn babes, and the birds which had once fled in flight at the approach of this infallible marksman would now come near him, on the tops of nearby trees or flying over his head, and the swallow called, the goldfinch trilled, the dove cooed, the thrush whistled, the chaffinch chirped and so did the wren; and from their lairs on high issued the squirrels, the owls, the fieldmice, to join their squeals to the chorus, so that my brother moved amidst this cloud of lamentation.

Then a destructive violence came over him; every tree, beginning from the top, leaf by leaf, was quickly stripped till it was bare as winter, even if it usually shed no leaves at all. Then climbing back to the peaks he broke off all the smaller branches and twigs till he left nothing but the main wood, went farther up and with a penknife began to whittle off the shoots, and the stricken trees could be seen showing the whites of ghastly wounds.

In all this frenzy of his there was no resentment against Viola; only remorse at having lost her, at not having known how to keep her tied to him, at having wounded her with a pride unjust and stupid. For, he understood now, she had always been faithful to him, and if she took a pair of other men about with her it merely meant that it was Cosimo alone she considered worthy of being her only lover, and all her whims and dissatisfactions were but an insatiable urge for the increase of their love and the refusal to admit it could reach a limit, and it was he, he, he, who had understood nothing of this and had goaded her till he lost her.

For some weeks he kept to the woods, alone as never before; he had not even Ottimo Massimo, for Viola had taken the dog with her. When my brother showed himself at Ombrosa again, he had changed. Not even I could delude myself any longer; this time Cosimo really had gone mad.

24

It had always been said at Ombrosa that Cosimo was mad, ever since he had jumped on to the trees at the age of twelve and refused to come down. But later, as happens, this madness of his had been accepted by all, and I am not talking only of his determination to live up there, but of the various oddities of his character; and no one considered him other than an original. Then in the full spate of his love for Viola there were those burblings in incomprehensible languages, particularly the ones during the Feast of the Patron Saint which some considered as sacrilege, interpreting his words as heretical cries, perhaps in Punic, tongue of the Pelasgians, or as a profession of Socinianism in Polish. Since then began the rumour, 'The Baron's gone mad,' and the conventional added, 'How can someone go mad who's always been mad?'

In the midst of these contrasting judgements, Cosimo really had gone mad. If before he went about dressed in furs from head to foot, now he began to adorn his head with feathers, like the American aborigines, bright-coloured feathers of kingfisher or greenfinch, and apart from those on his head he scattered feathers all over his clothes. He ended by making himself jackets all covered in feathers, and imitating the habits of the various birds, such as the woodpecker, drawing worms and insects from the tree-trunks and boasting of what riches he had found.

He would also make speeches in defence of birds, to the people who gathered to listen and banter under the trees; and from marksman he became barrister to the feathered tribe, and declared himself now a tom-tit, now an owl, now a redbreast, and more suitable camouflaging and made long prosecution speeches against human beings, who did not know how to recognize birds as their real friends, speeches which were accusals of all human society in the form of parables. The birds also realized this change in his ideas, and came close to him, even if there were people listening beneath. Thus he was able to illustrate his speeches with living examples which he pointed out on the branches round.

Because of this particular quality of his, there was much talk among the shooting men of Ombrosa of using him as a decoy, but no one ever dared fire on the birds perching near him. For even now when he was more or less out of his senses the Baron still impressed them: they quizzed him, yes, and often under his trees he had a retinue of urchins and idlers jesting at his expense; yet he was also respected, and always heard with attention.

His trees were now hung all over with scrawled pieces of paper and bits of cardboard with maxims from Seneca and Shaftesbury, and with various objects; clusters of feathers, church candles, crowns of leaves, female busts, pistols, scales, tied to each other in a certain order. The Ombrosans used to spend hours trying to guess what those symbols meant; nobles, Pope, virtue, war? I think some of them had no meaning at all but just served to jog his memory and make him realize that even the most uncommon ideas could be the right ones.

Cosimo also began to write certain things himself, such as *The Song of the Blackbird, The Knock of the Woodpecker, The Dialogue of the Owls,* and to distribute them publicly. In fact, it was at this very period of dementia that he learnt the art of printing and began to print some pamphlets or gazettes (among them the *Magpie's Gazette*), later all collected under the title, the *Bipeds' Monitor.* He had brought on to a nut tree a carpenter's bench, a weaver's loom, a press, a case of letters, and a demijohn of ink, and he spent his days composing his pages and pulling his copies. Sometimes spiders and butterflies would get caught between loom and paper, and their marks would be printed on the page; sometimes a lizard would jump on the sheet while the ink was fresh and smear everything with its tail; sometimes the squirrels would take a letter of the alphabet and carry it off to their lair thinking it was something to eat, as happened with the letter Q, which because of its round shape and stalk they mistook for a fruit, so that Cosimo had to begin some of his articles with Cueer and end them with C.E.D.

All this was very fine, of course, but I had the impression that at the time my brother was not only quite mad, but getting imbecile too, which was more serious and sad, for madness is a force of nature, for good or evil, while imbecility is a weakness of nature, without any counterpart.

In winter, though, he seemed able to reduce himself to a kind of lethargy. He would hang on a bough in his lined sleeping-bag, with only his head out, as if from a huge nest, and it was rare if, in the warmest hours of the day, he made more than a few hops to reach the alder tree over the Merdanzo torrent for his daily duties. He would stay in the bag desultorily reading (lighting a little oil lamp in the dark), or muttering to himself, or humming. But most of the time he spent sleeping.

For eating he had certain mysterious arrangements of his own, but he would accept offerings of plates of soup or ravioli, when some kind soul brought these up to him, on a ladder. In fact, a kind of superstition had grown up among the local peasants, that an offering to the Baron brought luck; a sign that he aroused either fear or goodwill, and I think it was the latter. That the reigning Baron of Rondò should live on public charity seemed improper to me; and above all I thought of what our dead father would have said if he had known. As for myself till then I had nothing to reproach myself with, for my brother had always despised family comforts and had signed a power-of-attorney by which, after giving him a small allowance (which he spent nearly all on books) I had no more duties towards him. But now, seeing him incapable of getting himself food, I tried making one of our lackeys in livery and white wig go up a ladder to him with a quarter turkey and a glass of Bordeaux on a salver. I thought he would refuse from one of those mysterious principles of his, instead of which he accepted at once and most willingly; and from then on, every time it crossed my mind, we would send a portion of our viands up to him on the branches.

Yes, it was a sad decline. Then luckily there was an invasion of wolves, and that gave Cosimo a chance to show his best qualities again. It was an icy winter, snow had even fallen in our woods. Packs of wolves, pushed out of the Alps by famine, fell on to our coasts. Some woodman ran into them and rushed back in terror with the news. The people of Ombrosa, who from the days of the guardians against fires had learnt to unite in moments of danger, began to take turns as sentries round the town, to prevent the famished beasts from getting nearer. But no one dared go beyond the houses, particularly at night.

'What bad luck the Baron isn't what he was!' they were saying at Ombrosa.

That hard winter had not been without effect on Cosimo's health. He was dangling there crouched in his pelt like a chrysalis in its cocoon, his nose dribbling, looking muzzy and deaf. The alarm went up about the wolves and people passing beneath called up: 'Ah, Baron, once it would have been you keeping guard from your trees, and now it's we who are keeping guard on you.'

He remained with his eyes half-closed, as if he did not understand or did not care about anything. Then, suddenly he raised his head, blew his nose and said, hoarsely: 'Sheep. For the wolves. Put some on the trees. Tied.'

People were crowding about beneath to hear what nonsense he would bring out, and jeer at it. Instead he rose from the sack, puffing and coughing, and said : 'I'll show you where,' and moved off among the branches.

On to some nut trees or oaks between woods and cultivated land, in positions chosen with great care, Cosimo told them to bring sheep or lambs, which he himself tied to branches, alive, bleating, but so that they could not fall down. On each of these trees he hid a musketful of grapeshot. He then dressed himself up like a sheep: hood, jacket, breeches, all of curly sheepskin. And he began to wait out the night on the open trees. Everyone thought this was the maddest thing he had ever done.

That very night, though, down came the wolves. Sniffing the scent of sheep, hearing the bleating and then seeing them up there, the whole pack stopped at the foot of the trees and whinnied with famished fangs open to the air and clawed against the trunk. And now, bounding over the branches, along came Cosimo, and the wolves seeing that shape between sheep and man hopping up there like a bird were riveted open-mouthed. Until 'Boum! Boum!' and they got a couple of bullets in the throat. A couple – for Cosimo carried one gun with him (and recharged every time) and had another on every tree ready with a bullet in the barrel; so every time he fired two wolves were stretched on the frozen ground. He exterminated a great number like that and at every shot the pack tacked to and fro in confused flight, while the other men with guns ran to where they heard the cries and their shots did the rest.

Cosimo had many a tale in many a version to tell afterwards about this wolf-hunt, and I could not say which was the right one. For example: 'The battle was going quite well when, as I was moving towards the tree with the last sheep on it, I found three wolves which had managed to climb up on to the branches and were just killing it off. Half-blinded and stunned by fever as I was, I nearly got up to the wolves' snouts before they noticed me. Then, seeing this other sheep walking on two feet along the branches, they turned on it, baring fangs still red with blood. My gun was unloaded, as after all that firing I had run out of powder, and I could not reach the gun on that tree as the wolves were there. I was on a smaller, rather tender branch, but above me was a stronger one within arm's reach. I began walking backwards on my branch, retreating slowly away from the main trunk. And slowly, following me, came a wolf. But I was hanging on to the branch above by my hands, and moving my feet on that other one; really I was hanging from above. The wolf, deceived, moved forward and the branch bent beneath it, while with a jump I yanked myself on to the branch above. Down the wolf went with a little bark like a dog's, broke its back on the ground, and killed itself.'

'And what about the other two wolves?'

'... The other two were stock-still, staring at me. Then suddenly I took off my sheepskin jacket and hood and threw them at the wolves. One of the two, seeing this white ghost of a sheep flying towards them, tried to seize it in its teeth, but as it was expecting a heavy weight and that was just an empty skin, it lost its balance and also ended by breaking claws and neck on the ground.'

'There's still one left.'

'... There's still one left – but as my clothes had suddenly been so lightened by throwing away that jacket, a fit of sneezing came over me, to shake heaven and earth. At this sudden un-expected eruption, the wolf got such a shock that it fell from the tree and broke its neck too ...'

Thus my brother on his night of battle. What is certain is that the fever he caught as a result, ailing as he already was, very nearly proved fatal. For some days he lay between life and death, tended at the expense of the Commune of Ombrosa, in sign of gratitude. He was put into a hammock, and surrounded by doctors going up and down on ladders. The best doctors available were called into consultation, and some applied clys-ters, some leeches, some mustard plasters, some fomentations. None spoke any more of the Baron of Rondò as mad, but all as one of the greatest brains, one of the outstanding phenomena of the century.

That while he was ill. When he recovered, things changed. Once again, as always before, some said he was wise, some he was mad. But in fact he was never taken by these vagaries again. He went on printing a hebdomadary, no longer called the *Bipeds' Monitor* but the *Reasonable Vertebrate.*

25

I'm not sure if at that time a Lodge of Freemasons was already founded at Ombrosa; I myself was initiated into Masonry much later, after the first Napoleonic Campaign, together with a great part of the local upper bourgeoisie and petty nobility, and so I cannot tell when my brother's first relations were with the lodge. In this connection I will cite an episode which happened more or less at the time I am describing, and which various witnesses would confirm as true.

One day two Spaniards, passing travellers, arrived at Ombrosa. They went to the house of a certain Bartolomeo Cavagna, a pastrycook, a well-known freemason. They declared themselves, it seems, as brethren of the Lodge of Madrid, so that he took them one night to a meeting of the Ombrosian Masons, which then met by the light of torch and flare in a clearing in the middle of the woods. All this comes from hearsay and supposition; what is certain is that next day, as soon as the two Spaniards came out of their inn, they were followed by Cosimo, who had been watching them unseen from the trees above.

The two travellers entered the courtyard of a tavern outside the town gate. Cosimo perched himself in a liquorice tree. At a table was sitting a customer waiting for the pair; his face could not be seen, shaded as it was by a black hat with a wide brim. Their three heads, or rather their three hats, nodded over the white square of the tablecloth; and after some confabulation the hand of the unknown man began to write on a narrow piece of paper something dictated by the other two and which, from the order in which the words were set one below the other, appeared to be list of names.

'Gentlemen, good day to you,' said Cosimo. The three hats went up, showing three faces with eyes staring at the man on the liquorice tree. But one of the three, the one with the wide brim, dropped his at once, so low that he touched the table with the tip of his nose. My brother just had time to catch a glimpse of features which did not seem unknown to him.

'*Buenas dias a Usted!*' exclaimed the two. 'But is it a local habit here to introduce oneself to strangers by dropping from the sky like a pigeon? Perhaps you would be good enough to come down and explain!'

'Those high up are clearly seen,' said the Baron, 'though others trail in the dust to hide their faces.'

'May I say, *señor*, that none of us are under an obligation to show our faces, just as none of us are to show our rumps.'

'For certain kinds of persons, of course, it is a point of honour to hide the face.'

'Which, for instance?'

'Spies, to name one!'

The two companions started. The bent man remained motionless, but his voice was heard for the first time. 'Or, to name another, members of secret societies . . .' he said slowly.

This remark was open to various interpretations. So Cosimo thought and so he said out loud. 'That remark, sir, is open to various interpretations. Did you say "members of secret societies", hinting that I am one myself, or hinting that you are, or that we both are, or that neither of us are, or did you say it because whichever way it's taken the remark is useful in terms of my reply?'

'*Como, como, como?*' exclaimed the man with the wide-brimmed hat confusedly, and in his confusion he forgot to keep his head down, and raised it enough to look Cosimo in the eyes. And Cosimo recognized him; it was Don Sulpicio, the Jesuit, his enemy from the days at Olivabassa!

'Ah! So I was not mistaken. Down with the mask, Reverend Father!' exclaimed the Baron.

'You! I was sure of it!' exclaimed the Spaniard, and took off his hat and bowed, disclosing his tonsure. 'Don Sulpicio de Guadalete, *superior de la Compañia de Jesus.*'

'Cosimo di Rondò, Freemason!'

The two other Spaniards also introduced themselves with slight bows.

'Don Calisto!'

'Don Fulgencio!'

'Also Jesuits?'

'*Nos tambien!*'

'But has not your Order recently been dissolved by order of the Pope?'

'Not as a respite to libertines and heretics of your stamp!' exclaimed Don Sulpicio, baring his rapier.

They were Spanish Jesuits, who after the disbandment of the Order had gone into hiding and were trying to form an armed militia all over the countryside, to combat Theism and the new ideas.

Cosimo put his hand on the hilt of his sword. A number of people had formed a ring around. 'Be good enough to descend, if you wish to fight *caballerosamente*,' said the Spaniard.

Nearby was a wood of nut trees. It was the time of the crop and the peasants had hung sheets from one tree to another, to gather the nuts they beat down. Cosimo rushed on to a nut tree, jumped into the sheet, and managed to keep upright and prevent his feet from slipping on the cloth of this hammock-like support.

'You come up a span or two, Don Sulpicio, as I've come down farther than I usually do!' and he, too, drew his sword.

The Spaniard also jumped on to the outstretched sheet. It was difficult to keep upright, as the sheet tended to fold up like a sack round their bodies, but so heated were the two contestants that they managed to cross swords.

'To the Greater Glory of God!'

'To the Glory of the Great Architect of the Universe!'

And they set on each other.

'Before I plunge this blade into your gullet,' said Cosimo, 'give me news of the Señorita Ursula.'

'She died in a convent!'

Cosimo was disturbed by this news (which, however, I think was made up on the spot) and the ex-Jesuit profited by this for a left-hander. He swung out at one of the knots tied to the branches of the nut tree and sustaining the sheet on Cosimo's side, and cut it clean through. Cosimo would have fallen had he not quickly flung himself on to the sheet in Don Sulpicio's part and seized a rope. In his leap his sword pierced the Spaniard's guard and plunged into his stomach. Don Sulpicio slumped, slithered down the sheet on to the side where he had cut the knot, and fell to the ground. Cosimo pulled himself back on to the nut tree. The other two ex-Jesuits raised their companion – whether dead or just wounded was never known – hurried off and were never seen again.

A crowd formed round the blood-spattered sheet. And from that day my brother had the reputation of being a Freemason.

Due to the Society's secrecy I never got to know more. When I entered it, as I said, I heard Cosimo spoken of as an old-time brother whose relations with the Lodge were not quite clear, and whom some defined as 'sleeping', some as a heretic passed to another rite, some even as an apostate; but his past activities were always mentioned with great respect. He may even have been that legendary Master 'Woodpecker Mason', to whom was attributed the foundation of the Lodge called 'East of Ombrosa', and the description of the first rites of that Lodge seem to show his influence; suffice it to say that the neophytes were blindfolded, made to climb a tree, then dropped on the end of a rope.

It is certain that the first meetings of Freemasons with us took place at night in the midst of the woods. So Cosimo's presence would have been more than justified, whether he was the person who received from correspondence abroad the volumes of the Masonic Constitutions, or whether it was someone else who had been initiated possibly in France or England, who introduced the rites into Ombrosa too. It is possible, though, that Masonry had existed here for some time unknown to Cosimo, and that one night, moving about the trees in the wood, he happened by chance on a clearing where there was a reunion of men with strange vestments and instruments by the light of candles, and he stopped up there to listen and then intervened and confused them by some unexpected remark such as: 'If you put up a wall, think of what's left outside!' (a phrase which I often heard him repeat), or another of the kind, and the Masons, recognizing his superior insight, made him a member of their Lodge, with special duties, and he brought in a great number of new rites and symbols.

The fact is that for the whole period my brother had anything to do with it, the open-air Masonry (as I will call it to distinguish it from that which was later to meet in a closed building) had a much richer ritual, in which a part was played by owls, telescopes, pine cones, hydraulic pumps, mushrooms, Cartesian ovals, spiders, Pythagorean tables. There was also a certain show of skulls, not only of humans, but also of cows, wolves and eagles. Such objects and others such as the trowels, rulers and compasses of the normal Masonic liturgy, were found at that time hanging on to branches in strange juxtapositions, and also attributed to the Baron's madness. Only a few persons hinted that this rebus now had a more serious meaning; but anyway no one was ever able to trace a clear distinction between the earlier and later symbols, or exclude that from the first they had been esoteric symbols of some other secret society.

For long before Cosimo joined the Masons he had been in various associations and confraternities of trades and professions, such as St Crispin's or the Shoemakers', the Virtuous Coopers', the Just Armourers' or the Conscientious Capmakers'. As he made on his own nearly everything he needed to live with, he knew a great variety of trades, and could boast himself a member of many corporations, which on their part were pleased to have with them a member of a noble family, of freakish ingenuity and proved disinterest.

How this passion which Cosimo always showed for communal life fitted in with his perpetual flight from society, I have never properly understood, and it remains not the least of his singularities of character. One would say that the more determined he was to hide away in his den of branches, the more he felt the need to create new links with the human race. But although every now and again he flung himself, body and soul, into organizing a new fellowship, suggesting detailed rules and aims, choosing the aptest men for every job, his comrades never knew how far they could count on him, where they could meet him, and when he would be suddenly urged back into the bird-side of his nature and let himself be caught no more. Perhaps, if one tried, one could take these contradictory impulses back to a single impulse; one should remember that he was just as contrary to every kind of human organization flourishing at the time, and so he fled from them all and tried experiments with new ones; but none of these seemed right or different enough from the others; from this came his constant periods of utter wildness.

What he had in mind was an idea of a universal society. And every time he busied himself collecting people, either for a definite purpose such as guarding against fire or defending from wolves, or in confraternities of trades such as the Perfect Wheelwrights' or the Illuminated Skin Chandlers', since he always got them to meet in the woods, at night, round a tree from which he would preach, there was always an air of conspiracy, of sect, of heresy, and in that atmosphere his speeches also passed easily from particular to general, and from the simple rules of some manual trade moved far too easily to a plan for installing a world republic of men, equal, free and just.

So Cosimo did little more in Masonry than repeat what he had done in the other secret or semi-secret societies of which he had been part. And when a certain Lord Liverpluck, sent by the Grand Lodge of London to visit his brethren on the Continent, came to Ombrosa while my brother was Master, he was so scandalized by Cosimo's unorthodoxy that he wrote to tell London that this Ombrosa Masonry must be some new Masonry of the Scottish rite, financed by the Stuarts to do propaganda against the Hanoverian throne, for a Jacobite restoration.

After this came the incident I have described, of the two Spanish travellers who introduced themselves to Bartolomeo Cavagna as Masons. Invited to a meeting of the Lodge, they found it all quite normal, in fact they said it was just like the Orient of Madrid. It was this which roused the suspicions of Cosimo, who knew only too well how much of the ritual was his own invention; that is why he tracked down the spies, unmasked them and triumphed over his old enemy Don Sulpicio.

Anyway, my opinion is that these changes of liturgy were a personal need of his own, for he could equally well have taken the symbols of every trade, except that of mason, he who had never wanted nor built nor inhabited any houses with walls.

26

Ombrosa was also a land of vines. I have never mentioned this, as in following Cosimo I have always had to keep to vegetation with high trunks. But there were vast slopes of vines, and in August under the festooned leaves the rosy grapes swelled in clusters of dense juice that was already wine-coloured. Some vines were in pergolas. I mention this because as Cosimo became older he had got so small and light and learnt so well how to move without throwing all his weight in one place that the crossbars of the pergolas held him. He could thus pass on to the vines, and by supporting himself on the poles called *scarasse*, could do work such as pruning in winter, when the vines are bare hieroglyphics around barbed wire, or thin out the heavy foliage in summer, or look for insects, and then in September help with the vintage.

For the vintage the entire population of Ombrosa would come out for the day into the vineyards, and everywhere the green of vines was dappled with the bright colours of skirts and tasselled caps. Muleteers loaded basket after full basket on to the panniers and emptied them in the vats; other basketfuls were taken by the various tax-gatherers who came with squads of bailiffs to levy dues for the local nobles, the Government of the Republic of Genoa, the clergy and other tenths. Every year there was some row or other.

The question of what parts of crops to allot around were the major part of the protests set down in the 'books of complaints', during the revolution in France. Books like these were also filled up at Ombrosa, just as a try, even if here they were no use at all. This had been one of Cosimo's ideas, who at that time no longer felt any need to attend the meetings of the Lodge and hold discussions with those old stick-in-the-muds of Masons. He was on the trees in the square and all the people from the beaches and countryside around came crowding beneath to get him to explain the news, for he received newspapers by post and also had certain friends who wrote to him, among them the astronomer Bailly, who was later made mayor of Paris, and other club members. Every day there was something new; Necker, and the tennis court, and the Bastille, and Lafayette on his white horse, and King Louis disguised as a lackey. Cosimo would explain and act everything jumping from branch to branch, and on one branch he would be Mirabeau at the tribune, and on another Marat at the Jacobins, and on yet another King Louis at Versailles putting on a red bonnet to please the housewives who had come marching out from Paris.

To explain what 'books of complaints' were, Cosimo said: 'Let's try and make one.' He took a school notebook and hung it on the tree by a string; everyone came there and wrote down whatever they found wrong. All sorts of things came out; the fishermen wrote about the price of fish, and the vineyard men about those tenths, and the shepherds about the borders of pastures, and the woodmen about the commune's woods, and then there were all those who had relatives in prison, and those who had got lashes for some misdeed, and those who had it in for the nobles because of something to do with women; it was endless. Cosimo thought that even if it was a 'book of complaints' it need not be quite so glum, and he got the idea of asking everyone to write down what they would like most. And again everyone went to put down their ideas, sometimes rather well; one wrote of the local cakes, one of the local soup; one wanted a blonde, one a couple of brunettes; one would have liked to sleep the whole day through, one to go mushrooming all the year round; some wanted a carriage with four horses, some found a goat enough; some would have liked to see their dead mother again, some to meet the gods on Olympus; in fact all the good in the world was written down in the exercise book, or drawn as many did not know how to write, or even painted in colours. Cosimo wrote too; a name: Viola. The name he had been writing everywhere for years.

It was a fine exercise book full, and Cosimo called it 'Book of Complaints and Contents'. But when it was all written from cover to cover there was no assembly to send it to, so there it remained hanging on the tree by a string, and when it rained it began to blotch and fade, and the sight made the hearts of the Ombrosians tighten at their present plight, and filled them with desire to revolt.

In fact, all the causes of the French Revolution were present among us too. Only we were not in France, and there was no revolution. We live in a country where causes are always seen but never effects.

At Ombrosa, though, we had some exciting times all the same. The republican army warred against the Austrians almost under our noses. Massena at Collardente, Laharpe on the Nervia, Mouret on the coast road – and Napoleon was then only a general of artillery, so that those rumbles we heard fitfully reaching Ombrosa on the breeze were made by the man himself.

In September they began preparing for the vintage again. And now they seemed to be preparing something secret and terrible.

Counsels of war from door to door:

'The grapes are ripe!'

'Ripe! Yes, indeed!'

'Ripe as ripe! They need picking!'

'We'll go and get 'em!'

'We're all ready. Where will you be?'

'In the vineyard beyond the bridge. And you? And you?'

'In Count Pina's.'

'I in the vineyard by the mill.'

'Have you seen the number of bailiffs? They seem like blackbirds dropping to pick the grapes!'

'But they won't peck this year!'

'If there are so many blackbirds, we're just as many hunters!'

'Some of us daren't come! Some are running away.'

'Why is it so many people don't like the vintage this year?'

'They wanted to put it off here. But now the grapes are ripe!'

'They're ripe!'

Next day, though, the vintage began silently. The vineyards were crowded with chains of people under the festoons, but no song went up. A call or two, a shout of 'You here too? It's ripe!' a movement of groups, a touch of gloom, even in the sky, which was not entirely overcast, just rather cloudy, and if a voice struck up a song it soon faded off, not taken up by the chorus. The muleteers were taking the panniers full of grapes to the vats. In other years the dues for the nobles, the bishop and the government were set aside beforehand; this year, though, they seemed to have been forgotten.

The tax-gatherers, come to draw the tenths, were nervous, did not know quite what to do. The more time passed, the less happened, the more they felt something must happen, the more

the bailiffs realized they had to do something but the less they
understood what it was.

Cosimo was walking along the pergolas with his cat's tread.
He was carrying some scissors and cutting off a bunch here and
a bunch there, haphazard, offering them to the men and women
vintaging below, and saying something to each in a low voice.

The chief of the bailiffs could bear the tension no more. He
said: 'Eh, well, now, then, what about these tenths?' Scarcely
had he said this than he had already regretted it. Through the
vineyards rang a deep note, part bellow, part hiss; it was a
vintager blowing on a conch shell and sounding the alarm all
over the valley. From every hillock similar sounds replied, the
vintagers raised up their shells like trumpets, and Cosimo too,
from the top of a pergola.

A song went along the rows of vines; first broken, discordant,
so it was difficult to understand. Then the voices fused, har-
monized, took up the tune and sang as if they were running,
flying along, and the men and women standing stock-still half-
hidden among the vines and each pole's vine cluster seemed to
run, and the grapes to be vintaging themselves, flinging themselves into the vats and treading themselves down, and the air,
clouds, sun became all unfermented juice, and now the song
began to be understood, first the notes and then some of the
words, which went: 'Ça ira! Ça ira! Ça ira!' and the young
men pounded the grapes with their bare red feet, 'Ça ira!' and
the girls thrust their sharp dagger-like scissors into the thick
greenery wounding the twisted stalks of the grape-clusters; 'Ça
ira!' and clouds of gnats flew above the heaps of fruit ready for
the press! 'Ça ira!' and it was then that the bailiffs lost control
of themselves and called: 'Stop that! Silence! Enough of this
row! Who sings we shoot!' and they began firing rounds in the
air.

In reply came a rumble of gunfire that seemed to come from
regiments lined in battle order on the hills. All the muskets
of Ombrosa exploded, and from the top of a high fig tree
Cosimo sounded the charge on a conch shell. All over the hillsides people moved. It was impossible to distinguish now be-

tween vintage and crowd: men, grapes, women, sprigs, clippers, festoons, *scarasse*, muskets, baskets, horses, barbed wire, fists, mule's kicks, shins, teats, all singing '*Ça ira!*'

'Here are your tenths!' It ended by the bailiffs and tax-gatherers being thrust head over heels into the vats full of grapes, with their legs out waggling wildly. And they returned without having gathered a thing, smeared from head to foot with grape juice, and with pips, husks, stalks stuck all over their muskets, powder-pouches, and moustaches.

Then the vintage turned into a fête, with all convinced of their having abolished feudal privileges once for all. Meanwhile we nobles and petty squires had barricaded ourselves into our houses, armed to the teeth, and ready to sell our skins dear. (I, in truth, did no more than keep my nose inside our gates, above all to avoid giving the other nobles a chance to say I was in agreement with that Antichrist of a brother of mine, reputed the worst agitator and Jacobin in the whole area.) But that day, once the troops and tax-gatherers had been flung out, no one doffed a hat to anyone.

Everyone was deep in preparing celebrations. They even put up a Tree of Liberty, just to follow the mode from France; only they weren't quite sure what it was like, and then there were so many trees in our parts that it was scarcely worth while putting up a false one. So they adapted a real tree, an elm, with flowers, clusters of grapes, festoons and placards: '*Vive la Grande Nation!*' From the very tip my brother, in a tricolour cockade on his cat's cap, pronounced a lecture on Rousseau and Voltaire, of which not a single word could be heard, as the whole population was twirling round beneath singing '*Ça ira!*'

The gaiety was short-lived. Troops came in great strength. Genoese, to exact dues and guarantee territorial neutrality, and Austro-Sards too, as the rumour had got around that the Jacobins of Ombrosa intended to proclaim the place annexed to the 'Great Universal Nation', that is to the Republic of France. The rebels tried to resist, built a barricade or two, shut the town gates ... But no, more than that was needed! The troops passed into the place on every side, set up block-posts on every country lane, and those with the reputation of agitators were imprisoned, except for Cosimo, who would have taken a devil to catch, and a few others with him.

The trial of the revolutionaries was hastily mounted, but the accused succeeded in showing that they had nothing whatsoever to do with it and that the real leaders were the very ones who had decamped. So everyone was freed, particularly as with all those troops stationed at Ombrosa no more unrest was to be feared. A garrison of Austro-Sards stayed too, as a guarantee against any possible enemy infiltration, and in command of these was our brother-in-law, D'Estomac, the husband of Battista, emigrated from France in the suite of the Count of Provence.

So I found my sister Battista underfoot again, with what reaction I leave you to imagine. She installed herself in the house, with husband, horses, orderlies. And every evening she would spend describing the last executions in Paris; she even had a model of a guillotine, with a real blade, and to explain the end of all her friends and relations-in-law she would decapitate lizards, centipedes, worms and even mice. So we would spend our evenings. I envied Cosimo living his days and nights out in the open, hidden in some wood.

27

So many and so incredible were the tales Cosimo told about his activities in the woods during the war that I do not feel like throwing cold water on any one version. So I leave the word to him, and just faithfully report some of his stories.

'In the wood there used to patrol scouting parties from both the opposing armies. From up on the branches, at every step I heard crashing through the undergrowth, I would strain my ears to guess if they were Austro-Sards or French.

'A little Austrian lieutenant, with very fair hair, was in command of a patrol of soldiers in perfect uniforms, queues and tassels, tricornes and gaiters, crossed white bands, muskets and bayonets, and making them march along in double file, trying to keep them in step on the rough paths. Ignorant of what the wood was like, but certain of carrying out his orders punctiliously, the little officer was proceeding according to the lines traced on the map, banging his nose continually against tree trunks, the troops slipping with their hobnailed boots on the smooth stones or gouging their eyes out with brambles, but conscious always of the supremacy of the imperial arms.

'Magnificent soldiers they were. I waited for them at a clearing, hidden on a pine. In my hand I had a heavy pine cone which I dropped on the head of the leading file. The infantryman threw up his arms, his knees buckled and down he fell among the ferns of the undergrowth. No one noticed and the platoon continued its march.

'I caught them up again. This time I threw down a rolled-up porcupine on the head of a corporal. The corporal's head sagged and he fainted. This time the lieutenant saw what happened, sent two men to fetch a stretcher, and pressed on.

'The patrol, as if on purpose, went and got entangled in the thickest juniper bushes in the whole wood. And a new ambush was ready there too. I had collected some caterpillars in a piece of paper, the hairy, blue sort, whose touch makes the skin swell worse than a nettle, and poured a hundred or so down on them. The platoon passed, vanished in thick bushes, re-emerged scratching themselves, with hands and knees covered in little red bubbles, and marched on.

'Splendid troops, a splendid officer! The whole wood was so strange to him that he could not distinguish what was unusual about it, and proceeded with his decimated sections, but proud and indomitable as ever. Then I had recourse to a family of wildcats; I launched them by their tails, after swinging them in the air a bit, which goaded them to a frenzy. There was a lot of noise, specially feline, then silence and truce. The Austrians were tending their wounded. Then the patrol, white with bandages, started off on the march again.

"The only thing is to try and take them prisoners!" said I to myself, hurrying to get ahead of them, and hoping to find a French patrol to warn of the enemy approach. But the French had not been giving any sign of life on that front for some time.

'While I was getting over a slippery place, I saw something move. I stopped, and pricked up my ears. I heard a kind of bubbling stream which then ran on into a continual gurgle and I began distinguishing the words: *"Mais alors ... cré-nom-de ... foutez-moi-donc ... tu m'emmer ... quoi ..."* Squinting into the half-darkness, I saw that the soft vegetation below was composed chiefly of hairy busbies and flowing moustaches and beards. It was a squadron of French hussars. Havi..g been soaked with damp during the winter campaign, towards spring all their skin was sprouting with mildew and moss.

'In command of this outpost was Lieutenant Agrippa Papillon, of Rouen, poet, and volunteer in the republican army. Convinced of the general goodness of nature, Lieutenant Papillon told his soldiers not to crunch the pine needles, the chestnut cones, the twigs, the leaves, the snails which stuck on to his men as they crossed the wood. And the patrol was already so fused with surrounding nature that it needed my well-trained ear to spot them at all.

'Amid his bivouacking soldiers, the officer-poet, with long hair in ringlets framing his gaunt face under the cocked hat, was declaiming to the woods: "Oh Forest! Oh Night! Here I am in your power! Could a tender tendril of your maidenhair fern, clasped to the ankles of these doughty soldiers, not hold the destiny of France? Oh Valmy! How far away you are!"

'I came forward. *"Pardon, citoyen."*

' "Who is it? Who's there?"

' "A patriot of these woods, citizen officer."

' "Ah! Here? Where?"

' "Right over your nose, citizen officer."

' "So I see! Who is it? A birdman, progeny of the Harpies! Are you a creature of mythology?"

' "I am citizen Rondò, progeny of humans, I assure you, on father's and mother's side, citizen officer. In fact my mother was a brave soldier in the Wars of Succession."

' "I understand. Oh Times, oh Glory! I believe you, citizen, and I am anxious to hear the news which you appear to have come to announce."

' "An Austrian patrol is penetrating your lines!"

' "What d'you say? To battle then! 'Tis the hour! Oh stream, gentle stream, ah, soon you will be stained with blood! On, on! To arms!"

'At the lieutenant-poet's command the hussars began gathering up arms and equipment, but they moved in such a scatterbrained and placid way, stretching, spitting, swearing, that I began to have doubts of their military efficiency.

' "Citizen officer, have you a plan?"

' "A plan? To march on the enemy!"

' "Yes, but how?"

' "How? In closed ranks!"

' "Well, if you will allow me to give advice, I would keep the soldiers halted, in open order, and let the enemy patrol entrap itself!"

'Lieutenant Papillon was an accommodating fellow and made no objections to my plan. The hussars, scattered about the wood, could scarcely be distinguished from clumps of verdure, and the Austrian lieutenant was certainly the man least adapted to see the difference. The imperialist patrol was marching along according to the itinerary traced out on the map, with every now and again a brusque "by the right!" or "by the left!" So they passed under the noses of the French hussars without noticing them. Silently the hussars, producing only natural sounds such as the rustles of leaves and the flutter of wings, arranged themselves for an encircling manoeuvre. I kept sentry for them from above and made whistles and stoats' cries to signal the enemy troop movements, and the short cuts ours had to take. The Austrians, all unawares, were caught in a trap.

'Suddenly they heard a shout from a tree of "Halt there!

In the name of liberty, equality and fraternity. I declare you all prisoners!" And between the branches appeared a human ghost brandishing a long-barrelled hunting-gun.

'"*Urrah! Vive la Nation!*" And all the bushes around sprouted French hussars, with Lieutenant Papillon at their head.

'Deep oaths resounded from the Austro-Sards, but before they had a chance of reacting they had already been disarmed. The Austrian lieutenant, pale but head high consigned his sword to his enemy colleague.

'I became quite a useful auxiliary to the Republican Army, but preferred to go about things alone, with the help of the animals of the forest, like the time when I put an Austrian column to flight by tipping a nest of wasps on their heads.

'My reputation spread to the Austro-Sard camp, amplified to such a point that the woods were said to be pullulating with armed Jacobins, hidden on top of every tree. Wherever they went the royal and imperial troops were on the *qui-vive*; at the slightest plop of chestnuts dropping from their husks and the faintest squirrel's squeak they already felt themselves surrounded by Jacobins, and changed route. In this way, just by provoking almost imperceptible rustles and sounds, I caused the Piedmontese and Austrians' columns to deviate and succeeded in leading them by the nose wherever I wanted.

'One day I got one to a thick prickly copse and made them all lose their way. In the copse lived a family of wild boar; driven from the mountains by the boom of cannon, the boars were descending in droves to take refuge in the woods lower down. The lost Austrians were marching along without seeing a hand's breadth in front of their noses, and suddenly hairy boars sprung up everywhere under their feet, emitting piercing cries. Snouts thrust out, they flung themselves between the knees of every soldier, pushing them all head over heels and stamping on the fallen in an avalanche of pointed hoofs, and piercing their stomachs with tusks. The entire battalion was routed. I and my comrades, from our perch on the trees, followed them with musket-fire. Those who managed to get back to camp either said an earthquake had suddenly opened the thorny ground under their feet, or that they'd been attacked by a band of Jacobins sprung from the bowels of the earth, as these Jacobins were nothing but devils, half-man and half-beast, who lived on the trees or in the midst of bushes.

'As I said, I preferred to carry out my coups alone, or with a few comrades from Ombrosa who had taken refuge with me in the woods after that vintage. With the French army I tried to have as little to do as possible, as we know what armies are, every time they move there's some disaster. But I had taken rather a liking to that outpost of Lieutenant Papillon's and was rather worried about what might happen to them. For the immobility of the front threatened to be fatal to the squadron under the poet's command. Moss and lichen was growing on the troopers' uniforms, and sometimes even heather and fern; the tops of the busbies were nested in by screech owls, or sprouted and flowered with lilies of the valley; their thigh boots clotted with soil into compact clogs; the whole platoon was about to put down roots. Lieutenant Agrippa Papillon's yielding attitude towards nature was sinking that cohort of brave men into a fusion of animal and vegetable.

'They had to be woken up. How, though? I had an idea and went to Lieutenant Papillon to lobby it. The poet was declaiming to the moon:

' "Oh Moon! Round as a muzzle, like a cannonball whose thrust from gunpowder is exhausted and continues to rotate slowly and silently through the sky! When will you burst on us, oh moon, raising a high cloud of dust and sparks, submerging enemy armies and thrones, and opening a breach of glory for me in the compact wall of my fellow citizens' distrust of me! Oh Rouen! Oh moon! Oh fate! Oh Convention! Oh frogs! Oh girls! Oh life!"

'And I: *"Citoyen ..."*

'Papillon, annoyed at the constant interruptions, said sharply: "Well?"

' "I only wanted to suggest, citizen officer, a way of rousing your men from a lethargy which is getting dangerous."

' "I wish to heaven there were, citizen. Action is what I yearn for, as you see. And what might this way of yours be?"

' "Fleas, citizen officer."

' "I'm sorry to disillusion you, citizen. There are no fleas in the republican army. They've all died of famine as a result of the blockade and high cost of living."

' "I can supply some, citizen officer."

' "I don't know if it's sense or a joke you're making. Anyway I will report the matter to Higher Command, and we shall see. Citizen, my thanks for your help to the republican cause! Oh glory! Oh Rouen! Oh fleas! Oh moon!" and he went off raving.

'I realized I had to act on my own initiative. So I collected a lot of fleas, and as soon as I saw a French hussar I'd shoot one at him with a catapult, trying to aim accurately enough to get it into his collar. Then I began to sprinkle the whole unit, in handfuls. It was a dangerous mission, for had I been caught in the act, no reputation of mine as a patriot would have saved me: they would have taken me prisoner, dragged me off to France and guillotined me as an emissary of Pitt. Instead of which my intervention was providential; the itching of the fleas quickly kindled in the hussars a human and civilized need to scratch themselves, search themselves, delouse themselves; they flung away their mossy clothes, their packs and knapsacks covered with mushrooms and cobwebs, washed, shaved, combed, in fact reacquired a perception of their individual humanity and regained the sense of civilization, of enfranchisement from the ugly side of nature. They were spurred, too, by a stimulus to activity, a zeal a combativity, long forgotten. The attack, when it came, found them pervaded by this new zest: the Armies of the Republic overcame the enemy resistance, broke through the front, and advanced to the victories of Dego and Millesimo ...'

28

Our sister and the émigré D'Estomac escaped from Ombrosa just in time to avoid capture by the republican army. The people of Ombrosa seemed to have returned to those days of the vintage. They raised the Tree of Liberty, this time more in conformity to French examples, that is a little like a Tree of Plenty. Cosimo, it goes without saying, climbed on to it, with a Phrygian cap on his head; but he soon got tired and left.

There was a bit of fuss round the palaces of the nobles, a few cries of '*Aristó, aristó, string 'em up, Ça ira!*' Me, what with my being my brother's brother and our always having been nobles of little account, they left in peace; later on, in fact, they came to consider me as a patriot too (so that, at the next change, I was in trouble myself).

They set up a *municipalité*, a *maire*, all in French; my brother was nominated to the provisional junta, although many did not agree with this, considering him to be out of his wits. Those of the old régime laughed and said that the whole lot were a cageful of lunatics.

The sittings of the junta were held in the former palace of the Genoese governor. Cosimo would perch on a carob tree at the height of the windows and follow the discussion from there. Sometimes he intervened to protest and give his vote. It is an acknowledged fact that revolutionaries are greater sticklers for formality than conservatives; they found Cosimo laughable and his system of attendance unworkable, said that it lessened the decorum of the assembly and so on, and when the Ligurian Republic was set up in place of the oligarchic Republic of Genoa, my brother was not elected to the new administration.

Cosimo, by the way, had at that time written and published a *Constitutional Project for a Republican City with a Declaration of the Rights of Man, Women, Children, Domestic and Wild Animals, including Birds, Fishes and Insects, and all vegetation, whether Trees, Vegetables, or Grass.* It was a very fine work, which could have been a useful guide to any government;

but which no one took any notice of, and it remained a dead letter.

Most of his time, however, Cosimo still spent in the woods, where the sappers of the French Army were opening a road for the transport of artillery. With their long beards flowing under their busbies and merging into their leather aprons, the sappers were different from all the other troops. Perhaps this depended on the fact that they did not leave behind them all that trail of disaster and destruction (like other troops), but had the satisfaction of doing things that remained and the ambition to carry them out as best they could. Then they had so many stories to tell; they had crossed nations, seen sieges and battles; some of them had even been present at the recent great events in Paris, the breaching of the Bastille and the guillotinings; and Cosimo used to spend his evenings listening to them. On putting away their spades and stakes they would sit round a fire, smoking short pipes and reviving old memories.

By day, Cosimo used to help the surveyors mark out the track. No one was better fitted to do so than he; he knew all the places where the road could pass with the gentlest gradients and the least damage to plants. And he always bore in mind not so much the needs of the French artillery as of the population of those roadless parts. At least one advantage would come from all the passage of brutal and licentious soldiery; a road made at their expense.

This was no bad thing at the time, either; for by then the occupation troops, particularly since they had changed their name from Republican to Imperial, were a pain in the neck to all. And all went to the patriots to complain: 'Just see what your friends are doing!' And the patriots would fling up their arms and raise their eyes to the sky, and reply: 'Oh well! Soldiers! Let's hope it all blows over!'

The Napoleonic troops would requisition pigs, cows, even goats, from the stalls. And as for taxes and tithes – they were worse than before. With conscription on top. This having to go as a soldier, no one could understand round our way; and the called-up youths would take refuge in the woods.

Cosimo did what he could to help out: he would watch over cattle in the woods when the peasant owners sent them into the wilds for fear of a round-up; or he would guard clandestine loads of wheat on their way to the mill or olives to the press, so that the Napoleonic troops should not get a part; or show the youths called to the levies caves in the woods where they could hide. In fact he tried to defend people against hectoring, although he never made any attacks against the occupying troops, in spite of the armed bands beginning to wander round the woods making life difficult for the French. Cosimo, stubborn as he was, refused ever to give himself the lie, and having been a friend of the French before, went on thinking he must be loyal to them, even if so much had changed and all was so different from what he expected. Then one should also remember that he was no longer as young as he was, and did not put himself out much now, for either side.

Napoleon went to Milan to get himself crowned and then made a few journeys through Italy. Every town he passed people gave him a great welcome and took him to see the local sights. At Ombrosa they also put in the programme a visit to the 'patriot on the tree tops', for, as often happens, none of us bothered much about Cosimo, but he was very famous in the world outside, particularly abroad.

It was not a chance encounter. Everything was arranged beforehand by the municipal committee for the celebrations, so as to make a good impression. They chose a fine big tree: they wanted an oak, but the one most suitably placed was a walnut, so they tricked this up with a few oak branches, and hung it with ribbons in the French tricolour and the Lombard tricolour, cockades and frills. In the middle of all this they perched my brother, dressed in gala rig but wearing his characteristic cat's fur cap, with a squirrel on his shoulder.

Everything was set for ten o'clock and a big crowd was waiting round the tree, but of course Napoleon did not appear till half past eleven, to the great annoyance of my brother, who as he got older was beginning to suffer from bladder trouble and had to get behind the trunk every now and again to relieve nature.

Came the Emperor, with a suite all shimmering epaulettes. It was already midday. Napoleon looked up between the branch towards Cosimo and found the sun in his eyes. And he began to produce a few suitable phrases to Cosimo: *'Je sais très bien de vous, citoyen ...'* and he shaded his eyes, *'parmi les forêts ...'* and he gave a little skip to one side so that the sun did not come right into his eyes, *'parmi les frondaisons de notre luxuriante ...'* and he gave another skip the other way as Cosimo's bow of assent had bared the sun on him again.

Seeing Bonaparte so restless, Cosimo asked politely: 'Is there anything I can do for you, *mon Empereur?'*

'Yes, yes,' said Napoleon, 'keep over that side a bit, will you, to shade the sun off me, there, that's right, keep still now ...' Then he fell silent as if struck by some thought and turned to the Viceroy Eugène. 'All this reminds me of something ... something I've seen before.'

Cosimo came to his help. 'Not you, Majesty; it was Alexander the Great.'

'Ah, of course!' exclaimed Napoleon, 'the meeting of Alexander and Diogenes!'

'You never forget your Plutarch, *mon Empereur,'* said Beauharnais.

'Only that time,' added Cosimo, 'it was Alexander who asked Diogenes what he could do and Diogenes asked him to move ...'

Napoleon gave a flick of the fingers as if he had finally found the phrase he was looking for. Assuring himself with a glance that the dignitaries of his suite were listening, he said in excellent Italian: 'Were I not the Emperor Napoleon, I would like to be the Citizen Cosimo Rondò!'

And he turned and went. The suite followed with a great clinking of spurs.

That was all. One might have expected that within a week Cosimo would have been sent the cross of the Legion of Honour. My brother did not care a rap about that, but it would have given us pleasure in the family.

29

Youth soon passes on earth, so just think of the trees, where it is the fate of everything to fall: leaves, fruit. Cosimo was growing old. All the years, all the nights spent in the cold, the wind, the rain, under fragile shelters or nothing at all, surrounded by air, without ever a house, a fire, a warm dish ... he was getting to be a shrivelled old man, with bandy legs and long monkey-like arms, hunch-backed, sunk in a fur cloak topped by a hood, like a hairy friar. His face was baked by the sun, creased as a chestnut, with clear round eyes between the wrinkles.

The army of Napoleon was routed at the Beresina, the British fleet landed at Genoa, we spent the days waiting for news of reverses. Cosimo did not show himself at Ombrosa; he was crouching up on a pine tree in the woods overlooking the Sappers' road, where the guns had passed towards Marengo, and looking towards the east, over the deserted surface on which only shepherds with their goats or mules loaded with wood were to be seen. What was he waiting for? Napoleon he had seen, he knew how the Revolution had ended, there was nothing to expect now but the worst. And yet there he was, eyes fixed, as if at any moment the Imperial Army would appear round the bend, still covered with Russian icicles, and Bonaparte on horseback, his unshaven chin sunk in his chest, feverish, pale ... He would stop under the pine tree (behind him a confusion of smothered steps, a clattering of packs and rifles on the ground, exhausted soldiers taking off boots by the roadside, unwinding rags round their feet) and he would say: 'You were right, Citizen Rondò; give me the constitutions you wrote out, give me your advice to which neither the Directorate nor the Consulate nor the Empire would listen: let us begin again from the beginning, raise the Tree of Liberty once more, save the universal nation!' These were surely the dreams, the aspirations, of Cosimo.

Instead of which, one day, three figures came limping along the Sappers' Road from the east. One, lame, was supporting himself on a crutch, another's head was wrapped in a turban of bandages, the third was the halest as he only had a black patch over one eye. The filthy rags they wore, the tattered braid hanging from their chests, the cocked hats without cockades but with a plume still on one of them, the high boots rent all the way up the leg, seemed to have belonged to uniforms of the Napoleonic Guard. But they had no arms; or rather one was brandishing an empty scabbard, another had a gun-barrel on his shoulder like a stick, with a bundle on it. They came on singing: *'De mon pays ... De mon pays ... De mon pays ...'* like a trio of drunks.

'Hey, strangers,' shouted my brother at them, 'who are you?'

'What an odd bird! What are you doing up there? Eating pine kernels?'

And another: 'Who wants pine kernels? Famished as we are, d'you expect us to eat pine kernels?'

'And the thirst! We got that from eating snow!'

'We are the Third Regiment of Hussars!'

'To a man!'

'All that's left!'

'Three out of three hundred; not bad!'

'Well, I've made it and that's enough for me!'

'Ah, it's too early to say that, you're not home yet with a whole skin!'

'A plague on you!'

'We are the victors of Austerlitz!'

'And the botched of Vilna! Hurrah!'

'Hey talking bird, tell us where there's a tavern round here!'

'We've emptied the wine barrels of half Europe but can't get rid of our thirst!'

'That's because we're riddled with bullets, and the wine never sticks.'

'You know where you're riddled!'

'A tavern that would give us credit!'

'We'll come back and pay another time!'

'Napoleon will pay!'

'Prrr ...'

'The Czar will pay! He's coming along behind, hand him the bills!'

Cosimo said: 'There's no wine round here, but farther on there's a stream and you can slake your thirst.'

'May you drown in the stream, you owl!'

'If I hadn't lost my musket at the Vistula I'd have shot you down by now and cooked you on the spit like a thrush!'

'Wait a bit, will you: I'm going to get my feet in that stream, they're burning.'

'You can wash your — in it, for all I care.'

But all three of them went to the stream, to take off their boots, bathe their feet, wash their faces and clothes. Soap they got from Cosimo, who was one of those people who get cleaner as they get older, as they are seized by a self-disgust which they did not notice in youth; so he always took soap round with him. The cool water cleared the fumes of alcohol a little in the three. And as the drunkenness passed they were overwhelmed by the gloom of their state and heaved a sigh; but in their dejection the limpid water became a joy, and they splashed about in it, singing: *'De mon pays ... De mon pays ...'*

Cosimo had returned to his look-out post on the edge of the road. He heard galloping and a squadron of light horse appeared, raising dust. They were in uniforms he had never seen before; and under their heavy busbies could be seen fair-skinned faces, bearded and rather gaunt with half-closed green eyes. Cosimo doffed off his cap to them. 'What good wind, sirs?'

They stopped. *'Sdrastvuy!* Say, *batjuska,* how long more before we get there?'

'Sdrastvujte, soldiers,' said Cosimo, who had learned a bit of every language and Russian too. *'Kudà vam?* to get where?'

'To get wherever this road goes to ...'

'Oh, this road goes to so many places. Where are you going?'

'V Pariž'

'Well, there are better routes to Paris.'

'Niet, nie Pariž. Vo Frantsiu, za Napoleonom. Kudà vedjòt eta doroga?'

'Oh to so many places: Olivabassa, Sassocorto, Trappa ...'

'Kay? Aliviabasse? *Niet, niet.'*

'Well, if you want to you can get to Marseilles ...'

'*V Marsel ... da, da, Marsel ... Frantsia ...*'

'And what are you going to do in France?'

'Napoleon came to war on our Czar, and now our Czar is chasing Napoleon.'

'And where do you come from?'

'*Iz Charkova. Iz Kieva. Iz Rostova.*'

'What nice places you must have seen! And which d'you like more, here or in Russia?'

'Nice places, ugly places, all the same to us, we like Russia!'

A gallop, a cloud of dust, and a horse pulled up, ridden by an officer, who shouted at the Cossacks: '*Von! Marš! Kto vam pozvolil ostanoĭtsja?*'

'*Do svidanja, batjuska!*' said the troopers to Cosimo, '*Nam porà ...*' and spurred away.

The officer had remained there at the foot of the pine tree. He was tall, slim, with a noble and sad air; he was holding his bare head raised towards a sky veined with clouds.

'*Bonjour, monsieur,*' he said to Cosimo. 'So you know our language?'

'*Da, gospodin ofitsèr,*' replied my brother, 'but not more than you do French, all the same.'

'Are you an inhabitant of this country? Were you here while Napoleon was about?'

'Yes, *monsieur l'officier.*'

'How did that go?'

'You know, *monsieur,* armies always loot, whatever the ideas they bring.'

'Yes, we too do a lot of looting ... but we don't bring ideas ...'

He was sad and worried, though a victor. Cosimo liked him and tried to console him. 'You have won!'

'Yes. We fought well. Very well. But perhaps ...'

Suddenly yells broke out, rifle fire, a clash of arms. '*Kto tam?*' exclaimed the officer. The Cossacks returned, dragging over the ground some half-naked corpses, and holding something in their hands, their left hands (the right were grasping wide curved scimitars, bared and – yes – dripping with blood) and this something was the hairy heads of those three drunken hussars. '*Frantsuzy! Napoleon!* All dead!'

The young officer barked out a sharp order, and made them take the things away.

'You see ... War ... For years now I've been dealing as best I can with a thing that in itself is appalling; war ... and all this for ideals which I shall never, perhaps, be able to explain fully to myself ...'

'I too,' replied Cosimo, 'have lived many years for ideals which I would never be able to explain to myself; but I do something entirely good; I live on trees.'

The officer's mood had suddenly changed from melancholy to nervous. 'Well,' he said, 'I must be moving on.' He gave a military salute. *'Adieu, monsieur ... What is your name?'*

'Le Baron Cosme de Rondeau,' Cosimo shouted after his departing figure. *'Proščajte, gospodin ... And yours?'*

'Je suis le Prince Andréj ...' and the galloping horse carried off the surname.

30

I have no idea what this nineteenth century of ours will bring, starting so badly and getting so much worse. The shadow of the Restoration hangs over Europe; all the innovators – whether Jacobins or Bonapartists – defeated; once more absolutism and Jesuitry has the field; the ideals of youth, the lights, the hopes of our eighteenth century, all are dust.

Such thoughts I confide to this notebook, nor would I know how to express them otherwise; I have always been a balanced man, without great impetus or yearnings, a father, a noble by birth, enlightened in ideas, observant of the laws. The excesses of politics have never shocked me much, and I hope never will. And yet within how sad I feel!

It was different before, my brother was there; I used to say to myself 'That's his business' and get on with my life. For me the sign of changes has not been the arrival of the Austro-Russians or our annexation to Piedmont or the new taxes or anything of that kind, but just the fact of never, when I open the window, seeing him balancing there up above. Now that he is no longer here I seem to have to worry about so many things, philosophy, politics, history; I follow the news, read books, but they fuzz me, what he meant to say is not there, for he understood something else, something that was all embracing, and he could not say it in words but only by living as he did. Only by being so frankly himself as he was till his death could he give something to all men.

I remember when he fell ill. We realized it because he brought his sleeping-bag on to the great nut tree in the middle of the square. Before, the places where he slept he had always kept hidden, with his wild beast's instinct. Now he felt the need to be always seen by others. It gave me a catch at the heart; I had always thought that he would not like to die alone, and perhaps this was a first sign. We sent a doctor up on a ladder; when he came down he made a grimace and raised both arms.

I went up the ladder myself. 'Cosimo,' I began, 'you're past sixty-five now, can you stay up here any longer? What you wanted to say you've said now, we've understood, it's meant a great effort of will on your part, but you've done it, and now you can come down. For those who have spent all their lives on the sea too there comes a time for landing.'

No use. He made a sign of disagreement with one hand. Now he could scarcely speak. Every now and again he would get up, wrapped in a blanket to the top of his head, and sit on a branch to sun himself a little. More than that he did not move. An old peasant woman, an old mistress of his perhaps, went up and did for him, and brought him hot food. We kept the ladder leaning against the trunk, since there was constant need of going up to help him, and also since some still hoped that he might suddenly take it into his head to come down. (It was others who hoped so; I knew what he was like.) On the square below there was always a circle of people who kept him company, chatting among themselves and sometimes making a remark to him too, though they knew that he no longer wanted to talk.

He got worse. We hoisted a bed on to the tree, and succeeded in fixing it in balance; he got into it quite willingly. We felt a twinge of remorse at not having thought of it before; but in truth he had never rejected comfort; though on trees, he had always tried to live the best he could. So we hurriedly took up other comforts; screens to keep the draught off, a canopy, a brazier. He improved a bit, and we brought him an armchair and lashed it between two branches; he began to spend his days on it, wrapped in his blankets.

One morning, though, we saw him neither in bed nor in the armchair; alarmed, we raised our eyes; he had climbed on to the top of the tree and was sitting astride a very high branch, wearing only a shirt.

'What are you doing up there?'

No reply. He was half rigid, and seemed to stay up there by a miracle. We got out a big sheet of the kind used to gather olives, and twenty or so of us held it taut beneath, as we were expecting him to fall.

Meanwhile the doctor went up; it was a difficult climb, and two ladders had to be tied together end to end. When he came down he said: 'Let the priest go up.'

We had already agreed to try a certain Don Pericle, a friend of his, a priest of the Constitutional Church at the time of the French, a Freemason before it was forbidden to the clergy, and readmitted to his offices by the Bishop a short time before, after many ups and downs. He went up with his vestments and ciborium, followed by an acolyte. He spent a short time up there, they seemed to confabulate, then he came down. 'Has he taken the Sacraments then, Don Pericle?'

'No, no, but he says it's all right, for him it's all right.' And I never managed to get more out of him.

The men holding the sheet were tired. Cosimo was still up there, motionless. The wind came up, it was westerly, the tip of the tree quivered, we stood ready. At that moment in the sky appeared a balloon.

Some English aeronauts were experimenting with balloon

flights along the coast. It was a fine big balloon, decorated with fringes and flounces and tassels, with a wickerwork basket attached, inside which were two officers in gilt epaulettes and peaked caps, gazing through telescopes at the landscape beneath, watching the man on the tree, the outstretched sheet, the crowd, strange aspects of the world. Cosimo had raised his head too and was looking fixedly at the balloon.

And then suddenly the balloon was caught in a gust of westerly wind; it began running before the wind, twisting like a trout and going out to sea. The aeronauts, undaunted, busied themselves reducing – I think – the pressure in the balloon, and at the same time unrolled the anchor to try and grip some support. The anchor flew silvery in the sky attached to a long rope, and following the balloon's course obliquely it began passing right over the square, more or less at the height of the top of the nut tree, so that we were afraid it would hit Cosimo. But little did we guess what we were to see with our own eyes a second later.

The dying Cosimo, at the second when the anchor rope passed near him, gave one of those leaps he used so often to do in his youth, gripped the rope, with his feet on the anchor and his body in a hunch, and so we saw him fly away, taken by the wind, scarce braking the course of the balloon, and vanish out to sea ...

The balloon, having crossed the gulf, managed to land on the other side. On the rope was nothing but the anchor. The aeronauts, too busy at the time trying to keep a lookout, had noticed nothing. It was presumed that the dying old man had disappeared while the balloon was flying over the bay.

So vanished Cosimo, without giving us even the satisfaction of seeing him return to earth a corpse. On the family tomb there is a plaque in commemoration of him, with the inscription: 'Cosimo Piovasco di Rondò – Lived on trees – Ever loved earth – Went into sky.'

Every now and again as I write I interrupt myself and go to the window. The sky is empty, and for us old folk of Ombrosa, used to living under those green domes, it hurts the eyes to look out now. Trees seem almost to have no right here since my

brother left them or since men have been swept by this frenzy
for the axe. And the species have changed too; no longer are
there ilexes, elms, oaks; nowadays Africa, Australia, the Americas, the Indies, reach out roots and branches as far as here.
What old trees exist are tucked away on the heights; olives on
the hills, pines and chestnuts in the mountain woods; the coast
below is a red Antipodes of eucalyptus, of swollen convolvulus,
huge and isolated garden growths, and the whole of the rest is
palms, with their scraggy tufts, inhospitable trees from the
desert.

Ombrosa no longer exists. Looking at the empty sky, I ask
myself if it ever did really exist. That mesh of leaves and twigs
of fork and froth, minute and endless, with the sky glimpsed
only in sudden specks and splinters, perhaps it was only there
so that my brother could pass through it with his tom-tit's tread,
was embroidered on nothing, like this thread of ink which I
have let run on for page after page, swarming with cancella-
tions, corrections, doodles, blots and gaps, bursting at times into
clear big berries, coagulating at others into piles of tiny starry
seeds, then twisting away, forking off, surrounding buds of
phrases with frameworks of leaves and clouds, then interweaving again, and so running on and on and on until it splutters
and bursts into a last senseless cluster of words, ideas, dreams,
and so ends.

The Non-Existent Knight

I

Beneath the red ramparts of Paris lay marshalled the army of France. Charlemagne was due to review his paladins. They had been waiting for more than three hours already; it was a hot, early summer afternoon, misty, a bit cloudy; the men inside the armour felt as if they were broiling in pots over a slow fire. Along that motionless row of knights one or two might even have gone off in a daze or a doze but were kept stiff in their saddles by their armour like everyone else. Suddenly there came three trumpet calls; plumes swayed in the still air as if at a gust of wind, and silence replaced a surf-like sound which must have come from warriors snoring inside the metal throats of their helmets. Finally along came Charlemagne from the end of the line, on a horse that looked over lifesize, beard on chest, hands on the pommel of his saddle. With all his warring and ruling, ruling and warring, he seemed slightly aged since the last time those warriors had seen him.

At every officer he stopped his horse and turned to look him up and down. 'And who are you, paladin of France?'

'Solomon of Brittany, sire!' boomed the knight's reply, as he raised his visor, showing a flushed face; then he added a few practical details such as: 'Five thousand mounted knights, three thousand five hundred foot-soldiers, one thousand eight hundred service troops, five years' campaigning.'

'Up with the Bretons, paladin!' said Charlemagne, and toc-toc, toc-toc, on he trotted till he reached another squadron commander.

'Andwhoareyou, paladin of France?' he asked again.

'Oliver of Vienna, sire!' lilted lips as soon as the grille was up. Then, 'Three thousand chosen knights, seven thousand troops, twenty siege-machines. Conqueror of Proudarm the pagan, by the Grace of God and for the glory of Charles, King of the Franks.'

'Well done, my fine Viennese,' said Charlemagne; then to the officers of his suite, 'Rather thin, those horses, they need more fodder.' And on he went, 'Andwhoareyou, paladin of France?' he repeated, always in the same rhythm: 'Tatatata-tatata-tata ...'

'Bernard of Mompolier, sire! Winner of Brunamonte and Galiferno.'

'A fine town, Mompolier! A town of lovely women!' and to his suite, 'See he's put up in rank.' All these remarks, said by a king, give pleasure, but they had been the same for years.

'Andwhoareyou, with that coat of arms I know?'

He knew all armorial bearings on their shields without needing to be told, but it was usage for names to be proffered and faces shown. Otherwise, maybe one with better things to do than be reviewed might send his armour on parade with another inside.

'Alard of Dordogne, son of Duke Amone ...'

'Good man, Alard, how's your dad?' and on he went. 'Tatatata-tatata-tata ...'

'Godfrey of Mountjoy! Knights, eight thousand, not counting dead!'

Crests waved. 'Hugh the Dane!' 'Namo of Bavaria!' 'Palmerin of England!'

Evening was coming on. In the wind and dusk faces could not be made out clearly. But by now every word, every gesture was foreseeable, as all else in that war which lasted so many years, its every skirmish, every duel, conducted according to rules, so that it was always known beforehand who would win or lose, be heroic or cowardly, get gutted or merely unhorsed and thumped. Each night by torchlight the blacksmiths hammered out the same dents on cuirasses.

'And you?' The king had reached a knight entirely in white armour; only a thin black line ran round the seams, the rest was light and gleaming, without a scratch, well finished at every joint, with a helmet surmounted by a plume of some oriental cock, changing with every colour in the rainbow. On the shield was painted a coat of arms between two draped sides of a wide cloak, within which opened another cloak on a small shield, containing yet another even smaller coat of arms. In faint clear outline were drawn a series of cloaks opening inside each other, with something in the centre that could not be made out, so minutely was it drawn. 'Well, you there, looking so clean ...' said Charlemagne, who the longer war lasted had less respect for cleanliness among his paladins.

'I' came a metallic voice from inside the closed helmet, with a slight echo as if it were not a throat but the very armour itself vibrating, 'am Agilulf Emo Bertrandin of the Guildivern and of the Others of Corbentraz and Sura, Knight of Selimpia Citeriore and Fez!'

'Aha! ...' exclaimed Charlemagne, and from his lower lip, pushed forward, came a faint whistle as if to say, 'You don't expect me to remember all those names, do you?' Then he frowned at once. 'And why don't you raise your visor and show your face?'

The knight made no gesture; his right hand, gloved in close-webbed chain mail, gripped the crupper firmer than ever, while a quiver seemed to shake the other arm holding the shield.

'I'm talking to you, paladin!' insisted Charlemagne. 'How come you don't show your face to your king?'

A voice came clearly through the gorge-piece, 'Sire, because I do not exist!'

'This is too much!' exclaimed the emperor. 'We've even on strength a knight who doesn't exist! Let's just have a look now.'

Agilulf seemed to hesitate a moment, then raised his visor with a slow but firm hand. The helmet was empty. No one was inside the white armour with its iridescent crest.

'Well, well! Who'd have thought it!' exclaimed Charlemagne. 'How d'you do your job, then, if you don't exist?'

'By will power,' said Agilulf, 'and faith in our holy cause!'

'Oh yes, yes, well said, that is how one does one's duty. Well, for someone who doesn't exist you seem in fine form!'

Agilulf was last in the rank. The emperor had now passed everyone in review; he turned his horse and moved away towards the royal tents. He was old and apt to put complicated questions from his mind.

A bugle sounded 'Fall out'. Amid the usual confusion of horses, the forest of lances rippled into waves like a corn field when wind passes. The knights dismounted, moved their legs, stretched, while squires led off their horses by bridles. Then the paladins drew apart from the rabble and the dust, gathering in lopped clumps of coloured crests, easing themselves after all those hours of forced immobility, jesting, boasting, gossiping of women and honour.

Agilulf moved a few steps to mingle in one of these groups, then without any particular reason moved on to another, but did not press inside and no one took notice of him. He stood uncertainly behind one of the knights without taking part in their talk, then moved aside. Night was falling; the iridescent plumes on his crest now seemed all merged into a single indeterminate colour; but the white armour stood out isolated on the field. Agilulf, as if feeling suddenly naked, made a gesture of crossing his arms and hugging his shoulders.

Then he shook himself and moved off with long strides towards the stabling area. On reaching it he found that the horses were not being groomed properly; he shouted at grooms, meted out punishments to stable-boys, went his rounds of inspection, redistributed duties, explaining in detail to each man what he was to do and making him repeat the instructions to see if they were properly understood. And as more and more signs of negligence by his paladin brother officers showed up, he called them over one by one, dragging them from their sweet languid evening chatter, pointed out discreetly but firmly when they were at fault, and made them go out one by one on picket, sentry duty or patrol. He was always right, the paladins had to admit, but they did not hide their discontent. Agilulf Emo Bertrandin of the Guildivern and of the Others of Corbentraz and Sura, Knight of Selimpia Citeriore and Fez was certainly a model soldier; but disliked by all.

2

Night, for armies in the field, is regular as the starry sky; guard duty, sentry-go, patrols. All the rest, the constant confusion of an army in war, the daily bustle in which the unexpected can suddenly start up like a restive horse, was now quiet; for sleep had conquered all warriors and quadrupeds of the Christian array, the latter standing in rows, at times pawing a hoof or letting out a brief whinny or bray, the former finally loosed from helmets and cuirasses, and snoring away content at being distinct and differentiated human beings once again.

On the other side, in the Infidels' camp, all was the same; the same march of sentinels to and fro, the guard-commander watching a last grain of sand pass through his hour-glass before waking a new turn, the duty officer writing to his wife in the night watch. And both Christian and Infidel patrols went out half a mile, nearly reached the wood then turned, each in opposite directions, without ever meeting, back to the camp to report all calm and go to bed. Over both enemy camps stars and moon flowed silently on. Nowhere is sleep so deep as in the army.

Only Agilulf found no relief. In his white armour, still clamped up, he tried to stretch out in his tent, one of the most ordered and comfortable in the Christian camp; and he continued to think; not the lazy meandering of one about to fall asleep, but exact and definite reasoning. Shortly afterwards he raised himself on an elbow; he felt a need of doing some manual job, such as shining his sword, which was already resplendent, or smearing the joints of his armour with grease. This impulse did not last long; soon he was on his feet and moving out of the tent, taking up lance and shield; and his whitish shadow began wandering over the camp. From cone-shaped tents rose a concert of heavy breathing. Agilulf could not know what it was like to shut the eyes, lose consciousness, plunge into emptiness for a few hours and then wake and find oneself the same as before, link up with the threads of one's life again: and his envy for the faculty of sleeping possessed by people who existed was vague, as of something he could not even conceive. What disquieted him more was the sight of bare feet showing here and there from under tents, with toes up-turned; the camp in sleep was a realm of bodies, a stretch of Adam's old flesh, emanating the reek of wine and the sweat of the warriors' day. On the threshold of pavilions lay messy heaps of empty armour which squires and retainers would shine and order in the morning. Agilulf passed by, attentive, nervy, proud; the bodies of people with bodies gave him a sense of unease not unlike envy, but also a stab of pride, of contemptuous superiority. These famous fellow officers of his, these glorious paladins, what were they? Here was their armour, proof of rank and name, of feats, of power and worth, all reduced to a shell, to empty iron; and there lay the men them-selves, snoring away, faces thrust in pillows, with a thread of spittle dribbling from open lips. But he could not even be taken into pieces or dismembered; he was and remained every moment of the day and night Agilulf Bertrandin of the Guild-ivern and of the Others of Corbentraz and Sura, armed Knight of Selimpia Citeriore and Fez, on such and such a day, having carried out such and such actions to the glory of the Christian arms, and assumed in the Emperor Charlemagne's army the command of such and such troops: possessor of the finest whit-est armour, inseparable from him, in the whole camp; a better officer than many who vaunted themselves illustrious; the best of all officers in fact. Yet there he was, walking unhappily in the night.

He heard a voice. 'Sir officer, excuse me, but when does the guard change? They've left me here for three hours already!' It was a sentry, leaning on a lance as if he had stomach ache.

Agilulf did not even turn; he said, 'You're mistaken, I'm not the guard officer,' and passed on.

'I'm sorry, sir officer. Seeing you walking round here I thought ...'

The slightest failure on duty gave Agilulf a mania to inspect everything and search out other errors and negligences elsewhere, a sharp reaction to things ill-done, out of place ... But having no authority to carry out such an inspection at that hour, this attitude of his could seem improper, even ill-disciplined. Agilulf tried to control himself, to limit his interest to particular matters which would fall to his duties next day, such as ordering arms racks for pikes, or arranging for hay to be kept dry ... But his white shadow was continually getting entangled with the guard commander, the duty officer, a patrol wandering into a cellar looking for a demijohn of wine from the night before ... Every time Agilulf had a moment's uncertainty whether to behave like someone who could impose a respect for authority by his presence alone, or like one who was where he has no right to be so steps back discreetly and pretends not to be there at all. In his uncertainty he stopped, thought, but did not succeed in taking up either attitude; he just felt himself a nuisance all round and longed for any contact with his neighbour, even by shouting orders or curses, or grunting swear words like comrades did in a tavern. But instead he mumbled a few incomprehensible words of greeting, shyly, and moved on; still thinking they might say a word to him he would turn round slightly with a 'Yes?', then realize at once no one was talking to him, and go off as if escaping.

He moved away towards the verges of the camp, solitary places, up a bare rise. The calm night was ruffled only by a soft flutter of formless little shadows with silent wings, moving around with no direction, however momentary; bats. Even their wretched bodies, rat or bird, were tangible and definite, could flutter openmouthed swallowing mosquitoes, while Agilulf with all his armour was pierced through every chink by gusts of wind, flights of mosquitoes, moon rays. A vague rancour growing inside him suddenly exploded; he drew his sword from his sheath, seized it in both hands and waved it wildly against every low flying bat. No result; they continued their flight without beginning or end, scarce shaken by the movement of air. Agilulf swung blow after blow at them, not even trying to hit the bats any more; his lunges followed more regular trajectories, ordered themselves according to the rules of sabre fencing; now Agilulf was beginning to do his exercises as if training for the next battle, and testing the theory of parry, transverse, and feint.

Suddenly he stopped. A youth had appeared from behind a bush up on the slope and was looking at him. He was armed only with a sword and had a light cuirass strapped to his chest.

'Oh, knight!' he exclaimed. 'I didn't want to interrupt! Are you exercising for the battle? Because there's to be a battle at dawn tomorrow isn't there? May I exercise with you?' And after a silence, 'I reached the camp yesterday ... It will be my first battle ... It's all so different from what I expected ...'

Agilulf was standing sideways, sword close to his chest, arms crossed, all behind his shield. 'Arrangements for armed encounters decided by headquarters are communicated to officers and troops one hour before the start of operations,' said he.

The youth looked a little dismayed, as if checked in his course, but, overcoming a slight stutter he went on with his former warmth, 'Well, you see, I've only just got here ... to avenge my father ... And I wish you experienced old soldiers would please tell me, how I can get into battle right opposite that pagan dog Isohar, and break my lance on his ribs, as he did to my heroic father, whom may God hold ever in glory, the late Marquis Gerard of Roussillon!'

'That's quite simple, my lad,' said Agilulf, and there was a certain warmth in his voice too, the warmth of one who knows rules and regulations by heart and enjoys showing his own competence and confusing others' ignorance, 'You must put in a request to the Superintendency of Duels, Feuds and Besmirched Honour, specify the motives for your request, and means will then be considered how best to place you in a position to attain the satisfaction you desire.'

The youth, expecting at least a sign of surprised reverence at the sound of his father's name, was mortified more by the tone than the sense of this speech. Then he tried to reflect on the words used by the knight, but kept his conclusion alive to contradict them to himself. 'But, sir knight, it's not the superintendents who're worrying me, please don't think that, what I'm asking myself is whether in actual battle the courage I feel now, the excitement which seems enough to gut not one but a hundred infidels, and my skill in arms too, as I'm well trained, you know, I mean if in all that confusion before getting my bearings ... Suppose I don't find that dog, suppose he escapes me? I'd like to know just what you do in such a case, sir knight, can you tell me that? When a personal matter is at stake in battle, a matter concerning yourself and yourself alone...'

Agilulf replied dryly, 'I keep to the rules. Do so too and you will not make a mistake.'

'Oh I'm so sorry,' exclaimed the youth, looking crestfallen, 'I didn't want to be a nuisance. I should have so liked to try a little fencing exercise with you, with a paladin! I'm good at fencing, you know, but sometimes in the early morning my muscles feel slack and cold and don't respond as I'd like. D'you find that too?'

'No, I do not,' said Agilulf, and, turning his back, he walked away.

The youth wandered into the camp. It was the uncertain hour preceding dawn. Among the pavilions could be seen signs of early movement. The headquarters was already astir before the rising bugle. Torches were being lit in staff and orderly tents, contesting with the half light filtering in from the sky. Was it really a day of battle, this one beginning, as rumour went the night before? The new arrival was a prey to excitement, but a different excitement from what he had expected or felt till then; rather it was an anxiety to feel ground under his feet again, now that all he touched seemed to ring empty.

He met paladins already locked into their gleaming armour and plumed round helmets, their faces covered by visors. The youth turned round to look at them and longed to imitate their bearing, the proud way they swung on hips, breastplate, helmet and shoulder-plates as if made all in one piece! Here he was among the invincible paladins, here he was ready to emulate them in battle, arms in hand, to become like them! But the pair he was following, instead of mounting their horses, sat down behind a table covered with papers; they must be important commanders. The youth rushed forward to introduce himself; 'I am Raimbaud of Roussillon, squire, son of the late Marquis Gerard! I've come to enrol so as to avenge my father, who died a heroic death beneath the ramparts of Seville!'

The two raised hands to their plumed helmets, lifted them by unfastening the beavers, and put them on the table. And from under the helmets appeared two bald yellowish heads, two faces with softy pouchy skin and straggly moustaches; the faces of old clerks after a lifetime of scribbling. 'Roussillon, Roussillon,' they exclaimed, turning over rolls with saliva-damped thumbs. 'But we've already matriculated you once yesterday! What d'you want? Why aren't you with your unit?'

'Oh, I don't know, last night I couldn't sleep at the thought of battle, I must avenge my father you know, I must kill the Argalif Isohar and so find ... Oh yes: the Superintendency of Duels, Feuds and Besmirched Honour, where's that?'

'He's only just arrived, this fellow, and comes out with this! How d'you know of the Superintendency, may I ask?'

'I was told by that knight, I don't know his name, the one in all-white armour ...'

'Oh not him again! He puts that nose he hasn't got in any-where!'

'What? Not got a nose?'

'Since he can't have the itch!' said the other of the two from behind the table, 'he finds nothing better to do than scratch the itches of others.'

'Why can't he have the itch?'

'Where d'you think he could have the itch if he's got no place to itch? That's a non-existent knight, that is ...'

'Non-existent? How d'you mean? I saw him myself! There he was!'

'What did you see? Mere ironwork ... He exists without existing, d'you understand that, recruit?'

Never could young Raimbaud have imagined appearances to be so deceptive; from the moment of his reaching the camp he had found everything quite different from what it seemed...

'So in Charlemagne's army one can be a knight with lots

of names and titles and what's more a bold warrior and zealous officer, without needing to exist!'

'Come! No one said that in Charlemagne's army one can etc., etc. All we said was, in our regiment there is a knight who's so and so. That's all. What can or can't be as a matter of general practice is of no interest to us. D'you understand?'

Raimbaud moved off towards the pavilion of the Superintendency of Duels, Vendettas and Besmirched Honour. Now he did not let casques and plumed helmets deceive him; he knew that the armour behind those tables merely hid dusty wrinkled little old men. He felt thankful there was *some*one inside.

'So you wish to avenge your father, the Marquis of Roussillon, by rank a general! Let's see, now! The best procedure to avenge a general is to kill off three majors. We can assign you three easy ones, then you're in the clear.'

'I don't think I've explained properly. It's Isohar the Argalif I must kill. It was he in person felled my glorious father!'

'Yes yes, we realize that, but to fell an argalif is not so simple, believe me ... What about four captains? We can guarantee you four infidel captains in a morning. Four captains, you know, are equal to an army commander, and your father only commanded a brigade!'

'I'll search out Isohar and gut him! Him and him alone!'

'You'll end in the guardhouse, not in battle, you can be sure of that! Just think a little before speaking, won't you? If we make difficulties for you about Isohar, there'll be reasons ... Suppose our emperor, for instance, is in the middle of negotiations with Isohar ...'

But one of the officials whose head had been buried in papers till then now raised it jubilantly. 'All solved! All solved! No need to do a thing! No point in a vendetta here! The other day Oliver thought two of his uncles were killed in battle and avenged them! But they'd stayed behind and got drunk under a table! We have these two extra uncles' vendettas on our hands, an awful nuisance. Now it can all be settled; we count an uncle's vendetta as half a father's; it's as if we had a father's vendetta clear, already carried out.'

'Oh, Father!' Raimbaud began to rave.

'What's up?'

Reveille had sounded. The camp, in first light, pullulated with armed men. Raimbaud would have liked to mingle with that jostling mob gradually taking shape as squadrons and companies, but the clanking armour sounded to him like a vibrating swarm of insects abuzz, like dry husks crackling. Many warriors were shut in their helmet and breastplates to the waist, and under their hip and kidney-guards appeared their legs in breeks and stockings, because they were waiting to put on thigh-pieces and leg-pieces and knee-pieces when they were in the saddle. Under those steel chests the legs seemed thin as crickets' and their way of moving and speaking, their round eyeless heads, arms folded hugging forearms and wrists were also like crickets' or ants'; so the whole bustling throng seemed a senseless clustering of insects. Amid them all, Raimbaud's eyes were searching for something; the white armour of Agilulf whom he was hoping to meet again, maybe because his appearance could make the rest of the army seem more concrete, or because the most solid presence he had yet met was the non-existent knight's.

He found him under a pine tree, sitting on the ground, arranging fallen pine cones in a regular design, right angled triangle. At that hour of dawn Agilulf always needed some precise exercise to which to apply himself; counting objects, arranging them in geometric patterns, resolving problems of arithmetic. It was the hour in which objects lose the consistency of shadow that accompanies them during the night, and gradually reacquire colours, but seem to cross meanwhile an uncertain limbo, faintly touched, just breathed on by light; the hour in which one is least certain of the world's existence. He, Agilulf, always needed to feel himself facing things as if they were a massive wall against which he could pit the tension of his will, for only so did he manage to keep a sure consciousness of himself. But if the world around was melting instead into the vague and ambiguous, he would feel himself drowning in that morbid half-light, incapable of allowing any clear thought or act of decision or punctilio to flower in that void. In such moments he felt bad, faint, and sometimes only at the cost of an extreme effort did he feel himself avoid melting away completely. It was then he began to count; trees, leaves, stones, lances, pine cones, anything in front of him. Or to put them in rows and arrange them in squares and pyramids. Applying himself in this exact occupation helped him to overcome his malaise, absorb his discontent and disquiet, reacquire his usual lucidity and composure.

So Raimbaud saw him, as with quick assured movements he arranged the pine cones in a triangle, then in squares on the sides of the triangle, and compared obstinately the pine cones on the shorter sides of the triangle with those of the square of the hypotenuse. Raimbaud realized that all this moved by ritual, convention, formulae, and beneath it there was ... what? And he felt a vague sense of discomfort come over him at knowing himself to be outside all these rules of a game ... But then his wanting to avenge his father's death, his ardour to fight, to enrol himself among Charlemagne's warriors, were those too not also a ritual to avoid plunging into the void, like this raising and setting of pine cones by Sir Agilulf? And oppressed by the turmoil of such unexpected questions, young Raimbaud flung himself on the ground and burst into tears.

He felt something on his head, a hand, an iron hand, lightly though. Agilulf was kneeling beside him. 'What's the matter, lad? Why are you crying?'

States of confusion or despair or fury in other human beings immediately gave perfect calm and security to Agilulf. His immunity from the shocks and agonies to which people who exist are subject made him take on a superior and protective attitude.

'I'm sorry,' exclaimed Raimbaud, 'it's weariness maybe. I've not managed to shut an eye all night, and now I'm bewildered. If I could only doze off a minute ... But now it's day. And you, who have been awake too, how d'you do it?'

'I would feel bewildered if I dozed off for even a second,' said Agilulf slowly, 'in fact I'd never come round at all but be lost for ever. So I keep wide awake every second of the day and night.'

'It must be awful ...'

'No!' The voice was sharp and firm again.

'And don't you ever doff your armour?'

The murmuring began again. 'For me there's no doffing. Doff or dress has no sense to me.'

Raimbaud had raised his head and was looking into the cracks of the visor, as if searching in that darkness for the glimmer of a glance.

'How's that?'

'How d'you mean how's that?'

The iron gauntlet of white armour had settled on the young man's hair again. Raimbaud felt it scarcely weighing on his head, a mere object, without communicating any warmth of human propinquity, consoling or bothersome, though he felt a kind of tense obstinacy spreading over him.

3

Charlemagne trotted along at the head of the Frankish army. It was the approach march; there was no hurry, and they were not moving fast. Around the emperor were grouped his paladins, reigning impetuous mounts by the bit; in the trotting and jostling their gleaming shields rose and fell like fishes' gills. Behind, the army looked like a long gleaming fish; an eel.

Peasants, shepherds, villagers gathered at the corners of the track. 'That's the king, that is, our Charles!' and they bowed to the ground at the sight, not so much of his unfamiliar crown, as his beard. Then they straightened up at once to spot the warriors; 'That's Roland! No, that's Oliver!' Never once did they guess right but that did not really matter, as the paladins were all somewhere there, so they could always swear to have seen the one they wanted.

· Agilulf trotted with the group, every now and again spurting ahead, then halting and waiting for the others, twisting round to check that the troops were following in compact order, or turning towards the sun as if calculating the time from its height above the horizon. He was impatient. He alone among them all had clear in his mind the order of march, halting places, the staging post to be reached before nightfall. As for the other paladins, well, they thought, an approach march was all right by them and fast or slow they were anyway approaching; and with the excuse of the emperor's age and weariness they were ready to stop for a drink at every tavern. The road seemed lined with tavern signs and tavern maids; apart from that, they might have been travelling sealed in a wagon.

Charlemagne was even more curious than anyone else at all the things to be seen around. 'Oh, ducks, ducks!' he exclaimed. A flock of them was moving through the fields beside the track. In the middle of them was a man, walking crouched, his hands behind his back, plopping up and down on flat feet like web-toes, his neck out, and repeating, 'Qua ... qua ... qua ...' The ducks were taking no notice of him, as if they considered him one of them. Really there was not all that much difference between man and ducks, as the rags he wore, of earthen-colour (they seemed mostly sacking) had big greenish-grey bits the same colour as feathers and there were also patches and rents and marks of varied colours like the iridescent streakings on ducks.

'Hey you, that's not the way to greet your emperor!' cried the paladins, always ready to make nuisances of themselves.

The man did not turn at their voices, but the ducks took alarm and all fluttered into flight together. The man waited a moment, watching them rise, beaks outstretched, then splayed out his arms and began skipping, and so jumping and skipping and waving splayed rag-hung arms, with little yelps of laughter and 'Quaa! ... Quaa! ...' full of joy, he tried to follow the flock.

There was a pond. The ducks flew on to the surface of the water and swam off lightly, with closed wings. On reaching the pond the man flung himself on his belly into the water, raising huge splashes and thrashing his arms about. Then he tried another 'Qua! Qua!' which ended in gurgles because he was sinking to the bottom, he re-emerged, tried to swim and sank again.

'Is that the duck-keeper, that man?' the warriors asked a peasant girl wandering along holding a reed.

'No, I keep the ducks, they're mine, he's nothing to do with 'em, he's Gurduloo,' said the little peasant girl.

'Then what was he doing with your ducks?'

'Oh nothing, every now and again he gets taken that way, d'y'see, and mistakes himself for one of them ...'

'Does he think he's a duck too?'

'He thinks the ducks are him ... Gurduloo's like that; a bit careless ...'

'Where's he gone to now though?'

The paladins neared the pond. There was no sign of Gurduloo. The ducks, having crossed the piece of water, now began waddling along the grass on their webbed feet. Around the pool, from among the reeds, rose a croak of frogs. Suddenly the man pulled his head out of the water as if he had that moment remembered he had to breathe. He looked round in a daze, not understanding this fringe of reeds reflected in the water a few inches from his nose. On each reed leaf was sitting a small smooth green creature, looking at him and calling as loud as it could: 'Gra! Gra! Gra!'

'Gra! Gra! Gra!' replied Gurduloo, pleased; and at this voice from every reed came a leaping of frogs into the water from water to bank. Gurduloo yelled, 'Gra!' gave a leap out too and reached the bank, soaking wet, muddy from head to foot, crouching like a frog and yelling such a loud 'Gra!' that with a crash of bamboo and reeds he fell back into the pond.

'Won't he drown?' the paladins asked a fisherman.

'Oh, sometimes Omoboo forgets himself, loses himself ... No, not drown ... The trouble is he's apt to end in our net with the fishes ... One day it came over him when he'd started fishing ... He flung the nets in the water, saw a fish just about to enter, and got so much into the part of the fish that he plunged into the water and then into the net himself ... You know what Omoboo's like ...'

'Omoboo? Isn't his name Gurduloo?'

'Omoboo, we call him.'

'But that girl there ...'

'She doesn't come from our parts, maybe she calls him that.'

'From what part is he?'

'Oh, he goes round ...'

The cavalcade was now skirting an orchard of pear trees. The fruit was ripe. The warriors pierced the pears with their lances, making them vanish into the beaks of their helmets, then spitting out the cores. And there in the middle of a pear tree who should they see but Gurduloo-Omoboo! He was sitting with raised arms twisted about like branches, and in his hands and mouth and on his head and in the rents of his clothes were pears.

'Look, he's being a pear!' chortled Charlemagne.

'I'll give him a shake!' said Roland, and swung him a blow.

Gurduloo let fall the pears all together, which rolled down the slope, and on seeing them roll he could not prevent himself rolling round and round down the field like a pear, and so vanished from sight.

'Forgive him, majesty!' said an old gardener. 'Martinzool sometimes doesn't understand that his place is not amid trees or inanimate fruits but your majesty's devoted subjects!'

'What on earth's got into this madman you call Martinzool?' asked the Emperor graciously. 'He doesn't seem to me to know what's going through that pate of his.'

'Who are we to understand, majesty?' The old peasant was speaking with the modest wisdom of one who had seen a good deal of life. 'Maybe mad's not quite the right word for him: he's just a person who exists and doesn't realize he exists.'

'That's a good one! We have a subject who exists but doesn't realize he does and there's my paladin who thinks he exists but actually doesn't. What a fine pair they'd make!'

Charlemagne was tired now from the saddle. Leaning on his grooms, panting into his beard, puffing, 'Poor old France,' he dismounted. As soon as the emperor set foot to the ground, at a signal the whole army stopped and bivouacked. Cooking pots were put on the fires.

'Bring me that Gurgur ... What's his name?' exclaimed the king.

'It varies according to the place he's in,' said the wise gardener. 'And to the Christian or Infidel armies he attaches himself to. He's Gurduloo or Gudi-Ussuf or Ben-Ya-Ussuf or Ben-Stanbúl or Pestanzool or Bertinzool or Martinbon or Omoboo or Omobestia or even the Wild Man of the Valley or Gian Paciasso or Pier Paciugo. Maybe in out-of-the-way parts they give him quite a different name from the others; I've also noticed that his name changes from season to season everywhere. I'd say every name flows over him without sticking. Whatever he's called it's the same to him. Call him and he thinks you're calling a goat; say "cheese" or "torrent" and he answers "Here I am." '

The paladins Sansonet and Dudone came up dragging Gurduloo along as if he were a sack. They yanked him to his feet before Charlemagne. 'Bare your head, poltroon! Do you not see you are before your king?'

Gurduloo's face lit up; it was broad and flushed, mingling Frankish and Moorish characteristics; red freckles scattered on olive skin; liquid blue eyes with blood veins above a snub nose and thick lips; fairish curly hair and a shaggy speckled beard. The hair was stuck all over with chestnut and corn husks.

He began doubling into bows and talking very quickly. The noblemen around, who had only heard him produce animal sounds till then, were astounded. He spoke very hurriedly, eating his words and getting all entangled; sometimes passing, it seemed, without interruption from one dialect to another or even one language to another, Christian or Moorish. Amid incomprehensible words and mistakes the meaning of what he said was more or less, 'I touch my nose with the earth, I fall to my feet at your knees, I declare myself an august servant of your most humble majesty, order and I will obey myself!'

He brandished a spoon tied to his belt ... 'And when your majesty says, "I order command and desire," and do this with your sceptre, as I do, with this, d'you see? And when you shout as I shout, "I orderrr commanddd and desirrrre!" you subjects must all obey me or I'll have you strung up, you first there with that beard and silly old face.'

'Shall I cut off his head at a stroke, sire?' asked Roland unsheathing his sword.

'I implore grace for him, majesty,' said the gardener. 'It's just one of his vagaries; when talking to the king he's confused and can't remember who is king, he or the person he's talking to.'

From smoking vats came the smell of food.

'Give him a mess tin of soup!' said clement Charlemagne.

With grimaces, bows and incomprehensible speeches, Gurduloo retired under a tree to eat.

'What on earth's he doing now?'

He was thrusting his head into the mess tin which he had put on the ground, as if he were trying to get into it. The good gardener went to shake him by a shoulder. 'When will you understand, Martinzool, that it's you who is to eat the soup, and not the soup you! Don't you remember? You must put it to your mouth with a spoon.'

Gurduloo began lapping up spoonful after spoonful. So eagerly did he brandish the spoon that sometimes he missed his aim. In the tree under which he was sitting there was a cavity just by his head. Gurduloo now began to fling spoonfuls of soup into the hole in the tree.

'That's not your mouth! It's the tree's!'

From the beginning Agilulf had followed with attention, mingled with distress the movements of the man's heavy fleshy body, which seemed to wallow in existing as naturally as a chick scratches; and he felt something like vertigo.

'Agilulf!' exclaimed Charlemagne. 'You know what? I assign you this man here as your squire! Eh? Isn't that a good idea?'

The paladins grinned ironically. But Agilulf, who took everything seriously (particularly any expression of the im-

perial will) turned to his new squire in order to impart his
first orders, only to find Gurduloo, after gulping down the
soup, had fallen asleep in the shadow of that tree. He lay
stretched out on the grass, snoring with open mouth, his chest
and belly rising and falling like a blacksmith's bellows. The
dirty mess tin had rolled near one of his big bare feet. In the
grass a hedgehog, attracted maybe by the smell, went up to the
mess tin and began licking the last traces of soup. In doing
this its prickles got up against the bare sole of Gurduloo's
foot and the more it licked up the last trickles of soup the
more its prickles pressed on the bare foot. Eventually the
vagabond opened his eyes and rolled them round, without
realizing whence came that sensation of pain which had awo-
ken him. He saw his bare foot standing upright in the grass
like an Indian fig tree, and the prickle against his foot.

'Oh foot!' Gurduloo began to say. 'Hey foot, I'm talking to
you! What are you doing there like an idiot? Don't you see
that creature is tickling you? Oh foot! Oh fool! Why not
pull yourself away? Don't you feel it hurting? Fool of a foot!
You need do so little, you need only move a tiny inch! Why
ever are you so silly? Foot! Just listen! Can't you see you're
being taken advantage of? Pull over there foot! Watch carefully now: see what I'm doing. I'll show you ...' So saying
bent his knee, pulled his foot towards him and moved it
away from the hedgehog. 'There, it was quite easy, as soon
as I showed you what to do you did it by yourself. Silly foot,
why did you stay there so long and get yourself pricked?'

He rubbed the aching part, jumped up, began whistling,
broke into a run, flung himself into the bushes, let out a fart,
another, then vanished.

Agilulf began moving to try and find him, but where had
he gone? The valley was striped with thickly sown fields of
oats and clumps of arbutus and privet, and swept by breezes
laden with pollen and butterflies and, above, with clusters of
white clouds. Gurduloo had vanished amid it all, down that
slope where the sun was drawing mobile patterns of shadow
and light; he might be in any part of this or that hillside.

From somewhere came a faint discordant song:

'*De sur les ponts de Bayonne ...*'

The white armour of tall Agilulf stood high on the edge of the valley, arms crossed on chest.

'Well, when does the new squire begin his duties?' asked his colleagues.

Mechanically, in a voice without intonation, came Agilulf's declaration. 'A verbal statement by the emperor has the validity of an immediate decree.'

'*De sur les ponts de Bayonne ...*'
came the voice still farther away.

4

World conditions were still confused in the era when this took place. It was not rare then to find names and thoughts and forms and institutions that corresponded to nothing in existence. But at the same time the world was pullulating with objects and capacities and persons who lacked any name or distinguishing mark. It was a period when the will and determination to exist, to leave a trace, to rub up against all that existed, was not wholly used up since there were many who did nothing about it – from poverty or ignorance or simply from finding things bearable as they were – and so a certain amount was lost into the void. Maybe too there came a point when this diluted will and consciousness of self was condensed, turned to sediment, as imperceptible watery particles condense into banks or clouds; and then maybe this sediment merged, by chance or instinct, with some name or family or military rank or duties or regulations particularly in empty armour, for in times when armour was necessary even for a man who existed, how much more was it for one who didn't ... Thus it was that

Agilulf of the Guildivern had begun to act and acquire glory for himself.

I who recount this tale am Sister Theodora, nun of the order of Saint Columba. I am writing in a convent, from old papers unearthed or talk heard in our parlour here or a few rare accounts by people who were actually present. We nuns have few occasions to speak with soldiery, so what I don't know I try to imagine; how else could I set about it? Not all the story is clear to me yet. I must crave indulgence: we country girls, however noble, have always led retired lives in remote castles and convents; apart from religious ceremonies, triduums, novenas, gardening, harvesting, vintaging, whippings, slavery, incest, fires, hangings, invasions, sacking, rape and pestilence, we have had no experience. What can a poor nun know of the world? So I proceed laboriously with this tale whose narration I have undertaken as a penance. God alone knows how I shall describe the battle, I who by God's grace, have always been apart from such matters, except for half a dozen or so rustic skirmishes in the plain beneath our castle or which we followed as children from the battlements amid cauldrons of boiling pitch (the unburied bodies remained to rot afterwards in the fields and we would come upon them in our games next summer, beneath a cloud of hornets!) – of battles, as I say, I know nothing.

Nor did Raimbaud; though he had thought of little else in all his young life, this was his baptism of arms. He sat on horseback in line awaiting the signal for attack, but did not enjoy it. He was wearing too much. The coat of mail with its standard, the cuirass with gorget and pauldrons, the hounskul helmet from which he could scarcely see out, a robe over the armour, a shield taller than himself, a lance which he banged on comrades' heads every time he swung it, and beneath him a horse of which he could see nothing such was the iron bard covering it.

The desire to avenge the killing of his father with the blood of Argalif Isohar had almost left him. They had told him, looking at papers on which all the formations were set down, 'When the trumpet sounds you gallop ahead in a straight line with set lance until you pierce him. Isohar always fights in that point of the line. If you keep straight you're bound to run into him, unless the whole enemy army folds up, which never happens at the first impact. Of course there can always be some little deviation, but if you don't pierce him your neighbour's sure to.'

If such was the case Raimbaud cared no more about it. Coughing was the signal that the battle had started. In the distance he saw a cloud of yellow dust advancing, and another cloud rising from the ground as the Christian horses too broke into a canter. Raimbaud began coughing: the whole imperial army coughed and shook in its armour, quivering and shaking as it raced towards the infidel dust, hearing more coughing coming nearer and nearer. The two dusts fused: and the whole plain rang with the echo of coughs and the clang of lances.

The aim of the first encounter was not so much to pierce the enemy (as one risked breaking one's lance against his shield and what's more getting flung flat on one's face from the shock) as to unhorse him by thrusting a lance between his saddle and arse at the moment of wheeling. This was a risky business, as a lance pointing downwards can easily get entangled in some obstacle or even stick in the ground and jerk a rider right out of the saddle like a catapult. So the first contact was full of warriors flying through the air gripping their lances. And side movement being difficult, since lances could not be waved far without getting into a friend's or enemy's ribs, there was soon such a bottleneck that it was difficult to understand a thing. Then up galloped the champions and began clearing a way through the mêlée.

Then they too found themselves facing the enemy champions, shield to shield. Duels started, but already the ground was so covered with carcasses and corpses that it was difficult to move, and when they could not reach each other they yelled insults. Here rank and intensity of insult was decisive, for according to whether offence given was mortal – to be wiped out in blood – medium or light, various reparations were laid down or even implacable hatreds transmitted to descendants. So the important thing then was to understand each other, not an easy matter between Moors and Christians and with the various Moorish and Christian languages too; what did one do if along came an insult one just couldn't understand? One might find oneself swallowing it and being dishonoured for life! So interpreters took part in this phase of the battle, light-armed men swiftly mounted on fast horses which swivelled around, catching insults on the wing and translating them there and then into the language of destination.

'Khar as-Sus!'

'Worms' excrement!'

Mushrik! Sozo! Mozo! Esclavao! Marrano! Hijo de puta! Za'alkan! Merde!'

These interpreters, by tacit agreement on both sides, were not to be killed. Anyway they galloped swiftly away and if it wasn't easy in that confusion to kill a heavy warrior mounted on a charger which could scarcely move for its encrustation of armour, imagine how difficult it was with these grasshoppers. But war is war, as the saying goes, and every now and again one did catch it. Anyway, even with the excuse of knowing how to say 'Son of a whore' in a couple of languages, they had to expect some risk. On a battlefield anyone with a quick hand can get good results, particularly at the right moment before the hordes of infantry swarm over and confuse all they touch.

Infantry, being short little men, pick things up easily, but knights from up on their saddles are apt to stun them with the flats of their swords and haul up the best loot for themselves. 'Loot' does not mean things torn off the backs of the dead, as it takes special concentration to strip a corpse, but all that gets dropped. With knights going into battle loaded with supplementary harness, at the first clash a mess of disparate objects falls to the ground. After that no one can think of fighting, can they? The struggle now is to gather all the things up; and in the evening on returning to camp bargain and traffick in them. On the whole nearly always the same things pass from camp to camp and regiment to regiment in the same camp; what is war, after all, but this passing of ever-more dented objects from hand to hand?

Raimbaud found all that happened quite different from what he had been told. On he rushed, lance forward, in tense expectation of the meeting between the two ranks. Meet they did: but all seemed calculated for each knight to pass through the space between the two enemies without their even grazing each other. For a time the two ranks continued to rush on, each in their own direction, each turning their backs to the other, then they turned and tried to come to grips. But by now impetus was lost. Who could ever find the Argalif in the middle of all that? Raimbaud found himself clashing shields with a man hard as dried fish. Neither of the two seemed to have any intention of giving way to the other; they pushed against their shields, while the horses stuck their hooves in the ground.

The Moor, who had a face pale as putty, spoke.

'Interpreter!' yelled Raimbaud. 'What's he saying?'

Up trotted one of those lazybones. 'He's saying you must give way to him!'

'Oh, not by my throat.'

The interpreter translated; the other replied.

'He says he's got to go and get a certain job done, or the battle won't work out according to plan ...'

'I'll let him pass if he tells me where I can find Isohar the Argalif!'

The Moor waved towards a hillock and shouted. The interpreter said, 'Over there on that rise to the left!' Raimbaud turned and galloped off.

The Argalif, draped in green, was staring at the horizon.

'Interpreter!'

'Here I am.'

'Tell him I'm son of the Marquis of Roussillon, come to avenge my father.'

The interpreter translated. The Argalif raised a hand with fingers clenched.

'Who's he?'

'Who's my father? That's the final insult!' Raimbaud bared his sword. The Argalif imitated him. He was a good swordsman. Raimbaud was already hard pressed when up came rushing the Moor with the putty face, panting hard and shouting something.

'Stop sir!' translated the interpreter hurriedly. 'I'm so sorry I got confused; the Argalif Isohar is on the hillock to the right! This is the Argalif Abdul!'

'Thank you! You're a man of honour!' said Raimbaud, then moved his horse, saluted the Argalif with his sword and galloped off towards the other slope.

On being told that Raimbaud was the marquis's son, the Argalif Isohar said, 'What's that?' It had to be repeated more than once in his ear, very loud.

Eventually he yawned and raised his sword. Raimbaud rushed at him. And as their swords crossed doubt came over him whether this was Isohar either, and his impetus was rather blunted. He tried to work himself into a frenzy, but the more he hit out the less he felt sure of his enemy's identity.

This uncertainty was nearly fatal. The Moor was pressing closer and closer when a great row went up nearby. A Moorish officer in the press of the battle suddenly let out a cry.

At this shout Raimbaud's adversary raised his visor as if asking for a truce, and called out in reply.

'What's he say?' Raimbaud asked the interpreter.

'He said, "Yes, Argalif Isohar, I'll bring your spectacles at once!"'

'So it's not him!'

'I am the Argalif Isohar's spectacle bearer,' exclaimed his adversary. 'Spectacles are instruments as yet unknown to you Christians, and are lenses to correct the sight. Isohar, being short-sighted, is forced to wear them in battle, but as they're glass a pair gets broken at every fight. I'm attached to him to supply new ones. May I therefore request that we interrupt our duel, otherwise the Argalif, weak of sight as he is, will get the worst of it?'

'Ah, the spectacle bearer!' roared Raimbaud, not knowing whether to gut him in a rage or rush at the real Isohar. But what merit would there be in fighting a blind adversary?

'Do let me go, sir,' went on the optician, 'as the plan of

battle depends on his keeping in good health, and if he doesn't see he's lost!' and brandishing the spectacles he shouted back, 'Here, Argalif, here are the glasses!'

'No!' said Raimbaud, and slashed at the bits of glass, shattering them.

At the same instant, as if the sound of lenses in smithereens had been a sign of his end, Isohar was pierced by a Christian lance.

'Now,' said the optician, 'he needs no lenses to gaze at the houris in Paradise,' and off he spurred.

The corpse of the Argalif, lurched over the saddle, remained hitched to the stirrups by the legs, and the horse dragged it up to Raimbaud's feet.

Emotion at seeing Isohar dead on the ground, contradictory thoughts assailing him – of triumph at being able finally to say his father's blood was avenged, of doubt whether he had actually himself killed the Argalif by fracturing his spectacles and so considered the vendetta duly consummated, of confusion at finding himself suddenly deprived of the aim which had brought him so far – all lasted only a moment. Then he felt a wonderful sense of lightness at finding himself rid of that nagging thought in the midst of battle, and able to rush about, look round, fight, as if his feet had wings.

In his fixation about killing the Argalif he had paid no attention to the order of battle, and did not even think there was any. Everything seemed new to him, and only exaltation and horror seemed to touch him now. The earth already had its crop of dead. Fallen in their armour, they lay in awkward postures, according to how their greaves and poleyns or other iron accoutrements had settled in a heap, sometimes with arms or legs in the air. At points the heavy armour had been breached and spread its contents, as if the armour was filled not with whole bodies but with stuffed guts which spilled out of every gash. Such ghastly sights filled Raimbaud with horror: had he perhaps forgotten that it was warm human blood had moved and given vigour to all those wrappings? To all except one; or did the unseizable nature of the knight in white armour seem extended over the whole field of battle?

On he spurred, anxious to face living presences, friends or foes.

He found himself in a valley, deserted, apart from dead and flies buzzing over them. The battle had reached a moment of truce, or was raging on some quite other part of the field. Raimbaud was gazing around as he rode. There was a clatter of hoofs; on the crest of a hill appeared a mounted warrior. A Moor! He looked around, reined in, then spurred his horse and galloped off. Raimbaud spurred too and followed. Now he was on the hill too; there in the plain he saw the Moor galloping off and vanishing among the nut trees. Raimbaud's horse was like an arrow; it seemed longing for the chance of a race. The youth was pleased: under those inanimate shells at last a horse was a horse, a man a man. The Moor veered off to the right. Why? Now Raimbaud felt certain of catching up. But from the right now appeared another Moor who jumped out of the undergrowth and barred his way. Then both infidels turned and came at him; an ambush! Raimbaud flung himself forward with raised sword and cried, 'Cowards!'

One came at him, his black two-horned helmet like a hornet. The youth parried and banged the other's shield, but his horse shied; now the first Moor began pressing him, and Raimbaud had to make play with shield and sword and get his horse to twist round on its tracks by pressing his knees to its sides. 'Cowards!' he cried, and his rage was real, and his fight was a real fight, and the effort to hold at bay two enemies was agonizingly exhausting both in bone and blood, and maybe Raimbaud must die now he is sure that the world exists, and does not know if dying is more sad or less.

Both were on him now. He backed, seizing the hilt of his sword as if stuck to it; if he lost it he was done. At that extreme moment he heard a gallop. At the sound, as at a roll of drums, both his enemies broke away. They backed, protecting themselves with raised shields. Raimbaud turned too; beside him he saw a knight of the Christian armies with a robe of periwinkle blue over his armour. A crest of long feathers also periwinkle in colour waved from his helmet. Swiftly turning a light lance round the warrior kept the Moors at bay.

Now they were side by side, Raimbaud and the unknown knight. The latter was still brandishing his lance. Of the two enemies one tried to feint and bounce the lance out of his hand. But the periwinkle knight at that moment put his lance into its socket on his saddle, bared his sword, and flung himself on the infidel; they duelled. Raimbaud, seeing how lightly the unknown helper handled his sword, almost forgot everything else to sit still there and look. But it was only a moment; soon the other enemy launched himself with a great clash of shields.

So he went on fighting side by side with the periwinkle knight. Every time the enemy after a useless new assault found themselves backing, one took on the other's adversary with a rapid exchange, so confusing them with their different techniques. Fighting side by side with a companion is far nicer than fighting alone; each encourages the other, and the feeling of having an enemy and of having a friend fuse in similar warmth.

Raimbaud often shouted incitement to the other; but the warrior was silent. The young man realized that in battle one must save one's breath and was also silent, though rather sorry not to hear his comrade's voice.

The tussle grew fiercer. Then the periwinkle knight unhorsed his Moor; the latter escaped on foot into the undergrowth. The other rushed at Raimbaud but in the clash broke his sword; afraid of falling prisoner he too turned his horse and fled.

'Thanks, brother,' exclaimed Raimbaud to his helper, opening his visor. 'You've saved my life!' and he held out his hand. 'My name is Raimbaud son of the Marquis de Roussillon, squire.'

The periwinkle knight did not reply; nor did he give his own name or shake Raimbaud's extended right hand or uncover his face. The youth flushed. 'Why don't you answer me?' And at that moment what should the other do but turn his horse and gallop off! 'Hey, knight, even if I do owe you my life, I consider this a mortal insult!' yelled Raimbaud, but the periwinkle knight was already far away.

In gratitude to his unknown helper, mute community borne in battle, anger at that unexpected rebuff, curiosity at that mystery, excitement temporarily appeased by victory and immediately on the look-out for any other objective, and there was Raimbaud spurring his horse after the periwinkle warrior. 'You'll pay for this insult, whoever you are!'

He spurred and spurred but his horse did not budge. He pulled its bit, and its snout dropped. He shook himself in the saddle. The horse gave a quiver as if made of wood. Then he dismounted, raised its iron chamfron and saw its white eye; it was dead. A blow from a Moor's sword had penetrated the chinks of the bard and pierced the heart. The animal would have crashed to the ground long before had not the iron pieces round flank and legs kept it rigid as if rooted to the spot. Sorrow for a valorous charger killed on its feet after serving him faithfully till then conquered Raimbaud's rage a moment; he threw his arms round the horse's neck standing there like a statue, and kissed it on its cold snout. Then he shook himself, dried his tears and ran off on foot.

But where could he go? He found himself running over vaguely marked paths, beside a stream deep in woods, with no more sign of battle around him. All trace of the unknown warrior had vanished. Raimbaud meandered on, resigned now to losing him, but still thinking, 'I'll find him again, though it's at the very end of the world!'

What tormented him most now, after that blazing morning, was thirst. As he climbed down towards the surface of the stream to drink he heard branches moving; tied to a nut tree by a loose bridle rein was a horse cropping at the grass, relieved of its biggest pieces of armour which were lying nearby. There was no doubt; it was the horse of the unknown warrior, and the knight could not be very far away! Raimbaud flung himself among the reeds to find him.

He reached the river bank, put his head between the leaves: there was the warrior. Head and torso were still enclosed in armour and in the impenetrable helmet like a crab; but the poleyns and cuisses had been taken off, and the warrior was naked from the waist downwards and running barefoot over rocks in the stream.

Raimbaud could not believe his eyes. For the naked flesh was a woman's; a smooth gold-flecked belly, round rosy hips, long straight girl's legs. This half of a girl (the crab half now had an even more inhuman and expressionless aspect than ever) turning round and looking for a suitable spot, set one foot on one side, one on the other, of a trickle of water, bent knees slightly, leant on the ground arms covered with iron plates, pushed her head forward, her behind back and began quietly and proudly to pee. She was a woman of harmonious moons, tender plumage, gentle flow. Raimbaud fell head over heels in love with her on the spot.

The young Amazon went down to the stream, lowered herself into the water again, made quick ablutions, shivering slightly, then ran up again with little skips of her bare pink feet. It was then that she noticed Raimbaud peering at her between the reeds. '*Schweine Hund!*' she cried, pulled a dagger from her waist and threw it at him, not with the gesture of a perfect manager of weapons that she was, but the impetus of a furious woman throwing at a man's head a plate or brush or whatever else she happens to have in her hand.

Anyway she missed Raimbaud's forehead by a hairbreadth. The youth, ashamed, drew back. But a moment later he longed to reappear before her and reveal his feelings to her in some way. He heard a clatter, rushed to the field, the horse was no longer there; she had vanished. The sun was declining; only now did he realize that the entire day had gone by.

Tired, on foot, too stunned by so many things that had happened to feel happy, too happy to understand that he had exchanged his former preoccupation for even more burning anxieties, he returned to the camp.

'I've avenged my father, you know, I've won, Isohar has fallen, I ...' but he told his tale confusedly, over hurriedly, since the point he wanted to reach was another ... 'And I was fighting against two of them, and a knight came to help me, and then I found out it wasn't a soldier, it was a woman, lovely, the face I don't know, in armour she wore a periwinkle blue robe ...'

'Ha, ha, ha,' roared his companions in the tent, intent on spreading grease on bruises all over chests and arms, amid the great stink of sweat every time armour comes off after battle. 'So you want to go with Bradamante, do you, chicklet? If she likes you! Bradamante only takes on generals or grooms! You won't get her, not if you put salt on her tail!'

Raimbaud could not bring out a word. He left the tent; the sun was setting red. Only the day before, when seeing the sun go down, he had asked himself, 'Where will I be at tomorrow's sunset? Will I have passed the test? Will I be confirmed as a man? Making a mark in the world?' And now here he was at the next day's dusk, and the first tests were over, but now nothing counted any longer, and the new test was difficult and unexpected and could be confirmed only there. In this state of uncertainty Raimbaud would have liked to confide in the knight with white armour, as the only one who might understand him, he had no idea why.

5

Beneath my cell is the convent kitchen. As I write I can hear the clatter of copper and earthenware as the sisters wash platters from our meagre refectory. To me the abbess has assigned a different task, the writing of this tale; but all our labours in the convent have, as it were, one aim and purpose alone – the health of the soul. Yesterday when I was writing of the battle, I seemed to hear in the sink's din the clash of lances against shields and armour plate, and the clang of heavy swords on helmets; from beyond the courtyard came the thudding of looms as nuns wove and to me it seemed like the pounding of galloping horses' hoofs; thus was what reached my ears transformed by my half-closed eyes into visions and by my silent lips into words and words and words, and on my pen rushed over the white sheet to catch up.

Today perhaps the air is hotter, the smell of cabbage stronger, my mind lazier, and the hubbub of nuns washing up can transport me no farther than the field kitchens of the Frankish army; I see warriors in rows before steaming vats amid a constant clatter of mess tins and tinkle of spoons, of ladles on edges or scraping the bottom of empty encrusted cooking pots; and this sight and smell of cabbage is repeated in every regiment, Norman, Burgundian and Angevin.

If an army's power is measured by the din it makes, then the resounding array of the Franks can best be known at mealtimes. The sound echoes over valleys and plains, till eventually it joins and merges with a similar echo, from infidel pots. For the enemy too are intent at the very same time on gulping foul cabbage soup. Yesterday's battle never made so much noise – nor such a stink.

All I have to do next is imagine the heroes of my tale at the kitchens. I see Agilulf appear amid the smoke and bend over a vat, insensible to the smell of cabbage, making suggestions to the cooks of the regiment of Auvergne. Now up comes young Raimbaud, at a run.

'Knight,' says he panting, 'at last I've found you! Now I want to be a paladin too! During yesterday's battle I had my revenge ... in the mêlée ... then I was all alone against two ... an ambush ... then ... now I know what fighting is, in fact. And I want to be given the riskiest place in battle . . . or to set off on some adventure that will gain glory ... for our holy faith ... to save women and sick and weak and old ... you can tell me ...'

Agilulf, before turning round, stood there for a moment with his back to him, in sign of annoyance at being interrupted in the course of duty; then, when he did turn, began to talk in rapid polished phrases which betrayed enjoyment at his own masterly grasp of a subject put to him at a moment's notice and of the competence of his exposé.

'From what you say, apprentice, you appear to consider our rank as paladins to comport exclusively the covering of ourselves with glory, whether in battle at the head of troops, or in bold individual tasks, the latter either in defence of our holy faith or in assistance of women aged and sick. Have I taken your meaning well?'

'Yes.'

'Well then; what you have suggested are in fact activities particularly recommended to our corps of chosen officers but ...' and here Agilulf gave a little laugh, the first Raimbaud had heard from the white helmet, a laugh courteous and ironic at the same time '... but those are not the sole ones. If you so desire, it would be easy for me to list one by one duties allotted to Simple Paladins, Paladins First Class, Paladins of the General Staff ...'

Raimbaud interrupted him. 'All I need is to follow you and take you as an example, sir.'

'You prefer to set experience before doctrine then: that's admissible. Yet today you see me doing my turn of inspection as I do every Wednesday, on behalf of the quartermaster's department. As such I am about to inspect the kitchens of the regiments of Auvergne and Poitiers. If you follow me, you can gain some experience in this difficult branch of service.'

This was not what Raimbaud had expected, and he felt rather put out. But not wanting to contradict himself he pretended to pay attention to what Agilulf did and said with cooks, vintners and scullions, still hoping that this was but a preparatory ritual before rushing into some dashing feat of arms.

Agilulf counted and recounted allocations of food, rations of soup, numbers of mess tins to be filled, contents of vats. 'Even more difficult than commanding an army, you know,' he explained to Raimbaud, 'is calculating how many tins of soup one of these vats contains. It never works out in any regiment. Either there are rations in excess which can't be traced or put on returns or – if allocations are reduced – there are not enough to go round, and discontent flares up among the troops. Of course every military kitchen always has hangers-on of different kinds, old women, cripples and so on, who come for what's left over. But that's all very irregular, of course. To clear things up, I have arranged for every regiment to make a return of its strength including even the names of such poor as usually queue for rations. We can then know exactly where every mess tin of soup goes. Now to get practice in your paladin's duties, you can go and make a tour of regimental kitchens, with the lists, and check that all is in order. Then you will report back to me.'

What was Raimbaud to do? To refuse, demand glory or nothing? If he did he risked ruining his career for a nonsense. He went.

He returned bored, no clearer minded. 'Oh, yes, it seems to be all right,' he said to Agilulf, 'though it's certainly all very confused. And those poor folk who come for soup, are they all brothers by any chance?'

'Why brothers?'

'Oh, they're so alike ... In fact they might be mistaken for each other. Every regiment has its own, just like those of the others. At first I thought it was the same man moving from kitchen to kitchen. But on the list there were different names: Boamoluz, Carotun, Balingaccio, Bertel ... then I asked the sergeants, and checked; yes, he always corresponded. Though surely that similarity ...'

'I'll go and see for myself.'

They moved towards the lines of Lorraine. 'There, that man over there,' and Raimbaud pointed as if someone was there. There was, in fact; but at first sight, what with green and yellow rags faded and patched all over, and a face covered with freckles and ragged beard, the eye was apt to pass him over and confuse him with the colour of earth and leaves.

'But that's Gurduloo!'

'Gurduloo? Yet another name! D'you know him?'

'He's a man without a name and with every possible name.

Thank you, apprentice; not only have you laid bare an ir-regularity in our organization, but you have given me the chance of refinding the squire assigned to me by the emperor's order, and lost at once.'

The Lorrainer cooks, having finished distributing rations to the troops, now left the vat to Gurduloo. 'Here, all this soup's for you!'

'All is soup!' exclaimed Gurduloo, bending over the pot as if leaning over a window sill, and taking great sweeps with his spoon to bring off the most delicious part of the contents, the crust stuck to the sides.

'All is soup!' resounded his voice from inside the vat, which tipped over at his onslaught.

Gurduloo was now imprisoned in the overturned pot. His spoon could be heard banging like a cracked bell, and his voice moaning, 'All is soup!' Then the vat moved like a tor-toise, turned over again, and Gurduloo reappeared.

He had cabbage soup spattered, smeared, all over him from head to toe, and was stained with blacking. With liquid stick-ing up his eyes he felt blind and came on crying, 'All is soup!' with his hands forward as if swimming, seeing nothing but the soup covering eyes and face. 'All is soup!' brandishing the spoon in one hand as if wanting to draw to himself spoonfuls of everything around. 'All is soup!'

Raimbaud found this so worrying it made his head go round; not so much with disgust though, as doubt at the possibility of that man in front of him being right and the world being nothing but a vast shapeless mass of soup in which all things dissolved and tinged all else with itself. 'Help! I don't want to become soup,' he was about to shout, but Agilulf was stand-ing impassively near him with arms crossed, as if quite remote and untouched by the squalid scene; and Raimbaud felt that he could never understand his apprehension. The anguish which the sight of the warrior in white armour always made him feel was now counterbalanced by this new anguish caused by Gurduloo; and this thought saved his balance and made him calm again.

'Why don't you make him realize that all *isn't* soup and put an end to this saraband of his?' he said to Agilulf, managing to speak in a tone without trace of annoyance.

'The only way to cope with him is to give him a clear-cut job to do,' said Agilulf; and to Gurduloo, 'You are my squire, by order of Charles King of the Franks and Holy Roman Emperor. From now on you must obey me in all things. And as I am charged by the Superintendency for Inhumation and Compassionate Duties to provide for the burial of those killed in yesterday's battle, I will provide you with stake and spade and we will proceed on to the field to bury the baptized flesh of our brethren whom God now has in glory.'

He also asked Raimbaud to follow him and so take note of this other delicate task of a paladin.

All three walked towards the field, Agilulf with his step which was intended to be loose but was actually like walking on nails, Raimbaud with eyes staring all round, impatient to see again the places he had passed the day before beneath a hail of darts and blows, Gurduloo with spade and stake on his shoulder, not at all impressed by the solemnity of his duties, singing and whistling.

From a rise could be seen the plain where the cruellest fighting had taken place. The soil was covered with corpses. Vultures sat with talons grappling the shoulders or the faces of the dead, and bent their beaks to peck in gutted bellies.

The behaviour of these vultures can scarcely be called appealing. Down they swoop as a battle nears its end, when the field is already strewn with dead lying about like Roman soldiers in their steel breastplates, which the birds' beaks tap without even scratching. Scarcely has evening fallen when, silently, from opposite camps, crawling on all fours, come the corpse despoilers. The vultures rise and begin wheeling in the sky waiting for them to finish. First light glimmers on a battlefield whitish with naked corpses. Down the vultures come again and begin their great meal. But they have to hurry, as gravediggers are soon coming to deny the birds what they concede to the worms.

Agilulf and Raimbaud with blows of their swords, Gurduloo with his pole, thrashed off the black visitors and made them fly away. Then they set to their sorry task; each of the three chose a corpse, took it by the feet and dragged it up the hill to a place suitable for scooping a grave.

As Agilulf dragged a corpse along he thought, 'Oh corpse, you have what I never had or will have: a carcass. Or rather you *have*; you *are* this carcass, that which at times, in moments of despondency, I find myself envying in men who exist. Fine! I can truly call myself privileged, I who can live without it and do all; all, of course, which seems most important to me; many things I manage to do better than those who exist, since I lack their usual defects of coarseness, carelessness, incoherence, smell. It's true that someone who exists always has a particular attitude of his own to things, which I never manage to have. But if their secret is merely here, in this bag of guts, then I can do without it. This valley of disintegrating naked corpses disgusts me no more than does the flesh of living human beings.'

As Gurduloo dragged a corpse along he thought, 'Corpsy, your farts stink even more than mine. I don't know why everyone mourns you so. What's it you lack? Before you used to move, now your movement is passed on to the worms you nourish. Once you grew nails and hair; now you'll ooze slime which will make grass in the fields grow higher towards the sun. You will became grass, then milk for cows which will eat the grass, blood of the baby that drinks their milk, and so on. Don't you see you get more out of life than I do, corpsy?'

As Raimbaud dragged a dead man along he thought, 'Oh corpse, I have come rushing here only to be dragged along by the heels like you. What is this frenzy that drives me, this mania for battle and for love, when seen from the place where your staring eyes gaze and your flung-back head knocks over stones? It's that I think of, oh corpse, it's that you make me think of: but does anything change? Nothing. No other days exist but these of ours before the tomb, both for us the living and for you the dead. May it be granted me not to waste them, not to waste anything of what I am, of what I could be: to do deeds helpful to the Frankish cause: to embrace, to be embraced by, proud Bradamante. I hope you spent your days no worse, oh corpse. Anyway to you the dice have already shown their numbers. For me they are still whirling in the box. And I love my own disquiet, corpse, not your peace.'

Gurduloo, singing, began arranging to scoop out his corpse's grave. He stretched it on the ground to take its measurement, marked the edges with his spade, moved it, and began digging at full speed. 'Corpsy, maybe you'll get bored waiting there.' He turned it over on a side, towards the grave, so as to keep it in view as he dug. 'Corpsy, you might help with a spadeful or two yourself.' He straightened it up, tried to put in its hand a spade, which fell. 'Enough. You're not capable. I see I'll have to dig it out myself, then you can fill the grave up.'

The grave was dug, but so messy was Gurduloo's work that it turned out a strange irregular concave shape. Then Gurduloo decided to try it out. In he got and lay down. 'Oh, how cosy it is, how comfy! What soft earth! How nice to turn over! Corpsy, do come and feel this lovely grave I've dug for you!' Then he thought a bit. 'Let's make a pact, though, as you fill the grave I'd better stay down here, and you shovel the earth down on me with the stake!' He waited a little, then, 'Come on! Quick! It's nothing! This is the way!' And from where he was lying down in the grave he began shovelling earth down by raising his spade. And the whole heap of earth fell down on top of him.

Agilulf and Raimbaud heard a muffled cry, whether of alarm or satisfaction at finding himself so well buried they did not know. They were just in time to extract Gurduloo, all covered with earth, before he died of suffocation.

The knight found Gurduloo's work ill-done and Raimbaud's insufficient. He himself had traced out a whole little cemetery, marking the verges of rectangular graves, parallel to the two sides of an alley.

On their return in the evening they passed a clearing in the woods where carpenters of the Frankish army were cutting tree trunks for war machines and fires.

'Now, Gurduloo, cut wood.'

But Gurduloo swung blows in all directions with his axe

and put together kindling twigs and green wood and saplings of maidenhair fern and shrub of arbutus and bits of bark covered with mould.

The knight inspected the carpenters' axe work, their tools and stacks and explained to Raimbaud the duties of a paladin for provisioning wood. Raimbaud was not listening; all that time a question had been burning in his throat, and now that his outing with Agilulf was near its end he had not put it to him yet. 'Sir Agilulf!' he interrupted.

'What d'you want?' asked Agilulf, fingering an axe.

The youth did not know where to begin, did not know how to approach the only subject close to his heart. So he flushed and said, 'D'you know Bradamante?'

At this name Gurduloo, just coming up clutching one of his composite bundles, gave a start. In the air scattered a flight of twigs, honeysuckle tendrils, of juniper bunches, privet branches.

Agilulf was holding a sharp two-edged axe. He brandished it, and buried it in the trunk of an oak tree. The axe passed right through the tree and cut it neatly, but the tree did not move from its trunk, so clean had been the blow.

'What's the matter, Sir Agilulf?' exclaimed Raimbaud with a start of alarm. 'What's come over you?'

Agilulf with crossed arms was now examining all round the trunk. 'D'you see?' he said to the young man, 'A clean blow, without the slightest waver. Observe how straight the cut.'

6

This tale I have undertaken is even harder to write than I thought. Now it is my duty to describe that greatest of mortal follies, the passion of love, from which my vow, the cloister and my natural shyness have saved me till now. I do not say I have not heard it spoken of; in fact here in the convent, so as to keep on guard against temptations, we sometimes discuss it as best we can with the vague notions we have, particularly whenever any of our poor inexperienced girls is made pregnant or raped by some powerful godless man and returns and tells us all that was done to her. So of love as of war I shall give a picture as best I can imagine it; the art of writing tales consists in an ability to draw the rest of life from the little one has understood of it: but life begins again at the end of the page, and one realizes that one knew nothing whatsoever.

Did Bradamante know more? After all that Amazon's life of hers, a deep disquiet was growing within her. She had taken to the life of chivalry due to her love for all that was strict, exact, severe, conforming to moral rule and – in the management of arms and horses – to exact precision of movement. But whom was she surrounded by now? Sweating louts who seemed to wage war in a very slack and slovenly manner, and who after duty hours were always mooning around after her like boobies to see which of them she would decide to take back to her tent that night. For knightly chivalry is a fine thing, but knights themselves are coarse, accustomed to doing great deeds in a slapdash way, only just keeping within the sacrosanct rules which they had sworn to follow and which being so firmly fixed take away any bother of thought. War anyway is made up of part slaughter and part routine and doesn't bear being looked into too closely.

Bradamante was no different from them at heart; maybe she had got those ideas about severity and rigour into her head as contrast to her real nature. For instance if ever there was a slattern in the whole army of France, it was she. To start with, her tent was the untidiest in the whole camp. While poor menfolk had to get down to work they considered womanish, such as washing clothes, mending, sweeping floors, tidying up, she being brought up a princess, was spoilt and refused to touch a thing; had it not been for those old washerwomen and dish washers who always hang round troops – procuresses the lot of them – her tent would have been worse than a kennel. Anyway, she was never in it; her day began when she put on her armour and mounted her saddle; in fact no sooner was she armed than she became another person, gleaming from the tip of her helmet to her greaves, each piece of armour more perfect than the last, with the periwinkle tassels all over the robe covering her cuirass, each carefully in place. Her wish to be the most resplendent figure on the battlefield was an expression not so much of feminine vanity as of her constant challenge to the paladins, her superiority over them, her pride. In a warrior, friend or foe, she expected a perfection of turnout and weapon management as a reflection of similar perfection of soul. And if she happened to meet a champion who seemed to respond in some measure to her expectations, then the woman of strong amorous appetites awoke in her. But there again, so it was said, she gave the lie to her own rigid ideals; for as a lover she was at one and the same time furious and tender. But if a man followed her in utter abandon, lost his self-control, at once she fell out of love or went searching for a temperament more adamantine. Whom could she find now though? Not one of the Christian or enemy champions had ascendancy over her any more; she knew the weaknesses and fatuity of them all.

She was exercising at archery, in the space before her tent, when Raimbaud, who was wandering anxiously in search of her, looked her for the first time in the face. She was dressed in a short tunic; her bare arms were holding the bow, her face a little strained with the effort; her hair was tied on the nape of her neck then spread in a big fantail. But Raimbaud's look did not pause on details: he saw the woman as a whole, her person, her colours, and felt it could only be she, she whom without having yet seen he desperately desired; for him from now on she could never be different.

The arrow winged from the bow, and pierced the target in an exact line with the other three which she had already put there. 'I challenge you to an archery competition!' cried Raimbaud, hurrying towards her.

Thus does a young man always hurry towards his woman. But is he truly urged by love for her and not by love for himself, the search for a certainty of existing that only a woman can give him? A young man hurries, falls in love, uncertain of himself, happy, desperate, and for him his woman is the person who certainly exists, of which only she can give the proof. But the woman too either exists or not; there she is before him, also trembling and uncertain. How is it the young man does not understand that? What does it matter which of the two is strong and which weak? They are equals. But that the young man does not know, because he does not want to; what he yearns for is a woman who exists, a woman who is definite. She on the other hand knows more; or less; anyway things that are different: what she is in search of is another way of existing; and together they have a competition in archery; she shouts at him, does not appreciate him; he does not know that is part of her game. Around are pavilions of the Frankish army, pennants in the wind, rows of horses eating fodder at last. Retainers prepare the paladins' meals. The latter, waiting for the dinner hour, are grouped around watching Bradamante at archery with the boy. Says Bradamante, 'You hit the target all right, but it's always by chance!'

'By chance? But I don't put an arrow wrong!'

'If you didn't put a hundred arrows wrong it would still be by chance!'

'What isn't by chance then? Who can do anything but by chance?'

On the edge of the field Agilulf was slowly passing; on his white armour hung a long black mantle: he was walking along like one who wants to avoid looking but knows he is being looked at himself, and thinks he should show that he does not care while on the other hand he does, though in a different way than others may think.

'Sir knight, come and show him how ...' Bradamante's voice had lost its usual contemptuous tone and her bearing its arrogance. She took two paces towards Agilulf and offered him the bow with an arrow already set in it.

Slowly Agilulf came closer, took the bow, drew back his cloak, put one foot behind the other and moved arms and bow forward. His movements were not those of muscles and nerves concentrating on a good aim: he was ordering his forces by will power, setting the tip of the arrow at the invisible line of the target; he moved the bow very slightly and no more, and let fly. The arrow was bound to hit the target. Bradamante cried, 'A fine shot!'

Agilulf did not care, he held tight in his iron fist the still quivering bow; then he let it fall and gathered his mantle around him, holding it close in both fists against his breastplate; and so he moved off. He had nothing to say and had said nothing.

Bradamante set her bow again, raised it with taut arms, shook the ends of her hair on her shoulders. 'Who or who else could shoot such a neat bow? Whoever else could be so exact and perfect as he in his every act?' So saying she kicked away the grassy tufts and broke her arrows against palisades. Agilulf was already far off and did not turn; his iridescent crest was bent forward as if he were walking bent, arms tight across his steel chest, black cloak dragging.

Of the warriors gathered around one or two sat on the grass to enjoy the scene of Bradamante's frenzy. 'Since she's fallen in love with Agilulf like this the poor girl hasn't had a moment's peace ...'

'What? What's that you say?' Raimbaud had caught the phrase, and gripped the arm of the man who had spoken.

'Hey you, my chicklet, puff out your chest for our little paladiness if you like! Now she only likes armour that's clean inside and out! Don't you know she's head over heels in love with Agilulf?'

'But how can that be ... Agilulf ... Bradamante ... How?'

'How? Well, if a girl has had her fill of every man who exists, her one remaining desire could be for a man who doesn't exist at all ...'

Raimbaud was now finding it a kind of natural instinct, in every moment of doubt and discouragement, to feel he wanted to consult the knight in the white armour. He felt this now, but did not know if he should ask his advice again or face him as a rival.

'Hey, blondie, isn't he a bit of a lightweight for bed?' her fellow warriors called. Now Bradamante must be in real deca-

dence; as if once upon a time anyone would have dared talk
to her in that tone!

'Say,' insisted the cheeky voices, 'suppose you strip him, what
d'you get?' and they roared with laughter.

Raimbaud felt a double anguish at hearing Bradamante
and the knight spoken of so, and rage at realizing that he did
not come into it at all and that no one considered him in the
least connected with it mingled to discourage him.

Bradamante had now armed herself with a whip and was
swirling it in the air to disperse standers-by, Raimbaud among
them. 'Don't you think I'm woman enough to make any man
do whatever I want him to?'

Off they ran shouting, 'Uh! Uh! If you'd like us to lend
'im a bit of something, Bradamà, don't hesitate to ask!'

Raimbaud, urged on by the others, followed the group of
jeering warriors until they dispersed. Now he had no desire to
return to Bradamante; even Agilulf's company would have
made him ill at ease. By chance he found himself walking beside another youth called Torrismund, younger son of the
Duke of Cornwall, who was mooching along and staring
glumly at the ground and whistling. Raimbaud walked on with
this youth who was almost unknown to him, and feeling a need
to express himself began talking, 'I'm new here, I don't know,
it's not like I thought, I can't catch it, one never seems to get
anywhere, it all seems quite incomprehensible.'

Torrismund did not raise his eyes, just interrupted his glum
whistling for a moment and said, 'It's all quite foul.'

'Well, you know,' answered Raimbaud. 'I wouldn't be so
pessimistic, there are moments when I feel full of enthusiasm,
even of admiration, as if I understand everything at last; and
eventually I say to myself, if I've now found the right view-
point from which to see things, if war in the Frankish army is
all like this, then this is really what I dreamt of. But one can
never be quite sure of things ...

'What d'you expect to be sure of?' interrupted Torrismund.
'Insignia, ranks, titles ... All mere show. These paladins'
shields with armorial bearings and mottoes are not made of
iron; they're just paper, you can put your finger through them.'

They had reached a well. On the stone verge frogs were leaping and croaking. Torrismund turned towards the camp and pointed at the high pennants above the palisades with a gesture as if wanting to blot it all out.

'But the Imperial army,' objected Raimbaud, his outburst of bitterness suffocated by the other's frenzy of negation, and trying not to lose his sense of proportion and to find a place again for his own sorrows, 'the Imperial army, one must admit, is still fighting for a holy cause and defending Christianity against the infidel.'

'There's no defence or offence about it, or sense in anything at all,' said Torrismund. 'The war will last for centuries, and nobody will win or lose, we'll all sit here face to face for ever. Without one or the other there'd be nothing, and yet both we and they have forgotten by now why we're fighting ... D'you hear those frogs? What we are all doing has as much sense and order as their croaks, their leaps from water to bank and from bank to water ...'

'To me it's not like that,' said Raimbaud, 'to me, in fact, everything is too pigeon-holed, too regulated ... I see the virtue and value, but it's all so cold ... A knight who doesn't exist, though, that does rather frighten me, I must confess ... Yet I admire him, he's so perfect in all he does, he makes one more confident than if he did exist, and almost' – he blushed – 'I can sympathize with Bradamante ... Agilulf is surely the best knight in our army ...'

'Puah!'

'What d'you mean, puah!'

'He's a made-up job, worse than the others!'

'What d'you mean, a made-up job? All he does he takes seriously.'

'Nonsense! All tales ... Neither he exists nor the things he does nor what he says, nothing, nothing at all ...'

'How then, with the disadvantage he is at compared to others, can he do in the army the job he does? By his name alone?'

Torrismund stood a moment in silence, then said slowly, 'Here the names are false too. If I could I'd blow the lot up.

There wouldn't even be earth on which to rest the feet.'

'Is there nothing savable, then?'

'Maybe. But not here.'

'Who? Where?'

'The knights of the Holy Grail.'

'And where are they?'

'In the forests of Scotland.'

'Have you seen them?'

'No!'

'Then how d'you know about them?'

'I know.'

They were silent. Only the croak of frogs could be heard. Raimbaud began to feel a fear coming over him that this croaking might drown everything else, drown him too in a green slimy blind pulsation of gills. But he remembered Bradamante, how she had appeared in battle with raised sword, and all his unease was forgotten; he longed for a chance to fight and do doughty deeds before her emerald eyes.

7

Here in the convent each nun is given her own penance, her own way of gaining eternal salvation. Mine is this of writing tales: and a hard penance it is. Outside it is high summer, from the valley rises a murmur of voices and a movement of water; my cell is high up and through its slit of a window I can see a bend of the river with naked peasant youths bathing, and farther on, beyond a clump of willows, girls too have taken off their dresses and are going down to bathe. Now one of the youths has swum underwater and surfaced to look at them and they are pointing at him with cries. I might be there too, in gay company, with young folk of my own condition, and servants and retainers. But our holy vocation leads us to set before the fleeting joys of the world something which remains. Which remains ... that is if this book, and all our acts of piety carried out with ashen hearts, are not already ashes too ... even more ashes than the sensual frolics down at the river, which tremble with life and propagate like circles in water ... One starts off writing with a certain zest; but a time comes when the pen merely grates in dusty ink and not a drop of life flows, and life is all outside, outside the window, outside oneself, and it seems that never more can one escape into a page one is writing, open out another world, leap the gap. Maybe it's better so; maybe the time when one wrote with delight was neither a miracle nor grace but a sin, of idolatry, of pride. Am I rid of such now? No, writing has not changed me for the better at all; I have merely used up part of my restless, conscienceless youth. What value to me will these discontented pages be? The book, the vow, are worth no more than one is worth oneself. One can never be sure of saving one's soul by writing. One may go writing on and on with a soul already lost.

Then do you think I ought to go to the Mother Abbess and beg her to change my task, send me to draw water from the well, thread flax, shell chick-peas? There'd be no point in that. I'll go on with my scribe's duties as best I can. My next job is to describe the paladins' banquet.

Against all imperial rules of etiquette, Charlemagne settled at table before the proper time, when no one else had reached the board. Down he sat and began to pick at bread or cheese or olives or peppers, everything on the tables in fact. Not only that, but he also used his hands. Absolute power often slackens all controls, generates arbitrary actions, even in the most temperate of sovereigns.

One by one the paladins arrived, in their grand gala robes which, between laced brocades, still showed chain mail cuirasses, the kind with a very wide mesh, worn with dress armour gleaming like a mirror but splintering at a mere rapier's blow. First came Roland who sat down on his uncle the emperor's right, and then Rinaldo of Montalbano, Astolf, Anjouline of

Bayonne, Richard of Normandy and all the others.

At the very end of the table went to sit Agilulf, still in his stainless battle armour. What had he come to do at table, he who had not and never would have any appetite, nor stomach to fill, nor mouth to bring his fork to, nor palate to sprinkle with Bordeaux wine? Yet he never failed to appear at these banquets, which lasted for hours, though the time would surely have been better employed in operations connected with his duties. But no: he had the right like all the others to a place at the imperial table, and he occupied it; and he carried out the banquet ceremonial with the same meticulous care that he put into every other ceremonial act of the day.

The courses were the usual ones at a military mess; stuffed turkey roasted on the spit, braised oxen, sucking pig, eels, goldfish. Scarcely had the lackeys offered the platters than the paladins flung themselves on them, rummaged about with their hands and tore the food apart, smearing their cuirasses and squirting sauce everywhere. The confusion was worse than battle; soup tureens overturning, roast chickens flying, and lackeys yanking away platters before a greedy paladin emptied them into his porringer.

At the corner of the table where Agilulf sat, on the other hand, all proceeded cleanly, calmly and in an orderly way. But he who ate nothing needed more attendance by servers than the whole of the rest of the table. Firstly – while there was such a confusion of dirty plates everywhere that there was no chance of changing them between courses and each ate as best he could, even on the tablecloth – Agilulf went on asking to have put in front of him fresh crockery and cutlery, plates big and small, porringers, beakers of every size and shape, endless forks and spoons and knives that had to be well sharpened; and so exigent was he about cleanliness that a shadow on beaker or plate was enough for him to send it back. And he served himself with everything; little, but of everything; not a single dish did he let pass. For example he peeled off a sliver of roast boar, put meat on one plate, sauce on another smaller plate, then with a very sharp knife chopped the meat into tiny cubes which he then passed one by one on to yet another plate, where he flavoured them with sauce until they were soaked in it, those with sauce he then put in a new dish and every now and again called a lackey to take away the last plate and bring him a new one; thus he busied himself for half-hours at a time. Not to mention chickens, pheasants, thrushes; at them he worked for whole hours without ever touching them except with the point of little knives which he asked for specially and which he very often had changed in order to strip the last little bone of its finest and most recalcitrant shred of flesh. He also had wine served, continuously pouring and repouring it among the many beakers and vessels in front of him, and goblets in which he mingled one wine with the other, every now and again handing one to a lackey to take away and change for a new one. He used a great deal of bread, constantly crushing it into tiny round pellets all of the same size which he arranged on the tablecloth in neat rows; the crust he pared down into crumbs, and with them made little pyramids; eventually he would get tired of them and order the lackeys to brush down the table. Then he started all over again.

With all this on, he never lost the thread of talk weaving to and fro across the table, and always intervened in time.

What do paladins talk of at dinner? They boast, as usual.

Said Roland, 'I must tell you that the battle of Aspramonte was going badly before I challenged King Agolante to a duel and bore off Excalibur. So attached to it was he that when I cut off his right arm at a blow his fist remained tight around its hilt and I had to use pliers to detach 'em.'

Said Agilulf, 'I do not wish to contradict, but in the interests of accuracy I must record that Excalibur was surrendered by our enemies in accord with the armistice treaties five days after the battle of Aspramonte. It figures in fact in a list of light weapons handed over to the Frankish army among the conditions of the treaty.'

Exclaimed Rinaldo, 'Anyway that's nothing compared with my sword Fusberta. When I met that dragon passing over the Pyrenees I cut it in two with one blow and, d'you know that a dragon's skin is harder than a diamond?'

Interrupted Agilulf, 'Let's just get this clear; the passage of the Pyrenees took place in April, and in April, as everyone knows, dragons slough their skins and are soft and tender as new born babes.'

The paladins cried, 'Yes, it was that day or another, if not there it was somewhere else, that's what happened, there's no point in splitting hairs ...'

But they were put out. This Agilulf always remembered everything, cited chapter and verse even for a feat-of-arms accepted by all and piously described by those who had never seen it, tried to reduce it to a normal incident of service to be mentioned in a routine evening's report to a regimental commander. Since the world began there has always been a difference between what actually happens in war and what is told afterwards; but if certain events actually happen or not in a warrior's life matters little; his person, his power, his bearing guarantees that if things did not happen just like that in every petty detail, they might have and could still on a similar occasion. But someone like Agilulf has nothing to sustain his own actions, whether true or false; either they are set down day by day in verbal reports and taken down in registers, or there's emptiness, blankness. To this he wanted to reduce his colleagues, sponges of Bordeaux wine, full of boasts or projects winging into the past without ever having been in the present, of legends attributed to different people and eventually hitched to a suitable protagonist.

Every now and again someone would call Charlemagne in testimony. But the emperor had done so many wars that he always got confused between one and another and did not really even remember which he was fighting now. His job was to wage war, and at most think of what would come after; wars of the past were neither here nor there to him: everyone knew that the tales of chroniclers and bards were to be taken with a grain of salt: the emperor could not be expected to rectify them all. Only when some matter came up with repercussions on military organization, on ranks, for instance, or attribution of titles of nobility or estates, did the king give an opinion. An opinion of a sort, of course; in such matters Charlemagne's wishes counted for little, he had to stick to the issues on hand, judge by such proofs as were given and see that laws and customs were respected. So when asked his opinion he would shrug his shoulders, keep to generalities, and sometimes get out of it with some such quip as, 'Oh! Who knows? War is war, as they say!' Now Charlemagne felt like setting some heavy task on this Sir Agilulf of the Guildivern who kept crumbling bread and contradicting every feat which – even if not told in versions accurate in every detail – were genuine glories of Frankish arms; but he had been told that the knight treated the most tiresome duties as tests of zeal so there was no point.

'I don't see why you must niggle so, Agilulf,' said Oliver. 'The glory of our feats tends to amplify in the popular memory, thus proving it to be genuine glory, basis of the titles and ranks we have won.'

'Not of mine,' rebutted Agilulf, 'every title and predicate of mine I got for deeds well asserted and supported by incontrovertible documentary evidence!'

'So *you* say!' cried a voice.

'Who spoke will answer to me!' said Agilulf, rising to his feet.

'Calm down, now, be good,' said the others, 'you who are always picking at others' feats must expect someone to say a word about yours ...'

'I offend no one; I limit myself to detailing facts, with place, date and proofs!'

'It was I who spoke. I will detail too—' A young warrior had got up, pale in the face.

'I'd like to see what you can find contestable in my past, Torrismund,' said Agilulf to the youth, who was in fact Torrismund of Cornwall. 'Would you deny, for instance, that I was granted my knighthood because, exactly fifteen years ago, I saved from rape by two brigands the King of Scotland's virgin daughter, Sophronia?'

'Yes, I do contest that; fifteen years ago Sophronia, the King of Scotland's daughter, was no virgin.'

A bustle went the whole length of the table. The code of chivalry then holding prescribed that whoever saved from certain danger the virginity of a damsel of noble lineage was immediately dubbed knight; but saving from rape a noble-woman no longer a virgin only brought a mention in des-patches and three months' double pay.

'How can you sustain that, which is an affront not only to my dignity as knight but to the lady whom I took under the protection of my sword?'

'I do sustain it.'

'Your proof?'

'Sophronia is my mother.'

A cry of surprise rose from all the paladins' chests. Was young Torrismund then no son of the Duke and Duchess of Cornwall?

'Yes, Sophronia bore me twenty years ago, when she was thirteen years of age,' explained Torrismund. 'Here is the medal of the royal house of Scotland,' and rummaging in his breast he took out a seal on a golden chain.

Charlemagne, who till then had kept his face and beard bent over a dish of river prawns, judged that the moment had come to raise his eyes. 'Young knight,' said he, giving his voice the major imperial authority, 'do you realize the gravity of your words?'

'Fully,' said Torrismund, 'for me even more than for others.'

There was silence all round; Torrismund was denying a connection to the Duke of Cornwall which bore with it, as a cadet, the title of knight. By declaring himself a bastard, even of a princess of blood royal, he risked dismissal from the army.

But much more serious was Agilulf's position. Before battl-ing for Sophronia when she was attacked by bandits and sav-ing her virtue he had been a simple nameless warrior in white armour wandering round the world at a venture: or rather (as was soon known) empty white armour, with no warrior inside. His deed in defence of Sophronia had given him the right to be an armed knight; the knighthood of Selimpia Citeriore being vacant just then, he had assumed that title. His entry into service, all ranks and titles added later, were a consequence of that episode. If Sophronia's virginity which he had saved was proved non-existent, then his knighthood went up in smoke too, and nothing that he had done afterwards could be recognized as valid at all, and his names and titles would be annulled so that each of his attributions would become as non-existent as his person.

'When still a child, my mother became pregnant of me,' narrated Torrismund, 'and fearing the ire of her parents when they knew her state, fled from the royal castle of Scotland and wandered throughout the Highlands. She gave birth to me in the open air, on a heath, and raised me while wandering over fields and woods of England till the age of five. Those first memories are of the loveliest period of my life, interrupted by this intruder. I remember the day. My mother had left me to guard our cave, while she went off as usual to rob fruit from the orchards. She met two roving brigands who wanted to abuse her. They might have made friends in the end; who knows, for my mother often lamented her solitude. Then along came this empty armour in search of glory, and routed the brigands. Recognizing my mother as of royal blood, he took her under his protection and brought her to the nearest castle, that of Cornwall, where he consigned her to the duke and duchess. Meanwhile I had remained in the cave hungry and alone. As soon as my mother could she confessed to the duke and duchess the existence of her son whom she had been forced to abandon. Servants bearing torches were sent out to search for me and I was brought to the castle. To save the honour of the royal family of Scotland, linked to that of Cornwall by bonds of kinship, I was adopted and recognized as son of the duke and duchess. My life was tedious and burdened with restriction as are always those of cadets of noble houses. No longer was I allowed to see my mother, who took the veil in a distant convent. This mountain of falsehood has weighed me down till now and distorted the natural course of my life. Now finally I have succeeded in telling the truth. Whatever happens to me now must be better than the past.'

At table meanwhile the pudding had been served, a sponge in various delicately coloured layers, but such was the general amazement at this series of revelations that not a fork was raised towards speechless mouths.

'And you, what have you to say about this story?' Charlemagne asked Agilulf. All noted that he had not said, 'Knight'.

'Lies. Sophronia was a virgin. On the flower of her purity reposes my honour and my name.'

'Can you prove it?'

'I will search out Sophronia.'

'Do you expect to find her the same fifteen years later?' said Astolf, maliciously. 'Breastplates of beaten iron have lasted less.'

'She took the veil immediately after I had consigned her to that pious family.'

'In fifteen years, in times like these, no convent in Christendom has been saved from dispersal and sack, and every nun has had time to de-nun and re-nun herself at least four or five times over.'

'Anyway violated chastity presupposes a violator. I will find him and obtain proof from him of the date when Sophronia could be considered a virgin.'

'I give your permission to leave this instant, should you so desire,' said the emperor. 'I feel that nothing at this moment can be closer to your heart than the right to wear a name and arms now contested. If what this young man says is true I cannot keep you in my service, in fact I can take no account of you, even to make good arrears of pay,' and here Charlemagne could not prevent giving a touch of passing satisfaction to his little speech as if to say, 'At last we've found a way of getting rid of this bore, d'you see!'

The white armour now leant forward, and never till that moment had it shown itself so empty. The voice issuing from it was scarcely audible, 'Yes, my emperor, I will go.'

'And you?' Charlemagne turned to Torrismund. 'Do you realize that by declaring yourself born out of wedlock you cannot bear the rank due to your birth? Do you at least know who was your father? And have you any hope of his recognizing you?'

'I can never be recognized ...'

'One never knows. Every man, when growing older, tends to make out a balance sheet of his whole life. I too have recognized all my children by concubines, and there were many, some certainly not mine at all.'

'My father was no man.'

'And who was he? Beelzebub?'

'No, sire,' said Torrismund calmly.

'Who then?'

Torrismund moved to the middle of the hall, put a knee to the ground, raised his eyes to the sky and said, "Tis the Sacred Order of the Knights of the Holy Grail!'

A murmur rustled over the banqueting table. One or two of the paladins crossed themselves.

'My mother was a bold lass,' explained Torrismund, 'and always ran into the deepest woods around the castle. One day in the thick of the forest she met the Knights of the Holy Grail, encamped there to fortify their spirit in isolation from the world. The child began playing with those warriors and from that day she went to their camp every time she could elude family surveillance. But in a short time she returned pregnant from those childish games.'

Charlemagne remained in thought a moment, then said, 'The Knights of the Holy Grail have all made a vow of chastity and none of them can ever recognize you as a son.'

'Nor would I wish them to,' said Torrismund. 'My mother has never spoken of any knight in particular, but brought me up to respect as a father the Sacred Order as a whole.'

'Then,' added Charlemagne, 'the Order as a whole is not bound by any vow of the kind. Nothing therefore prevents it from being recognized as a person's father. If you succeed in finding the Knights of the Holy Grail and get them to recognize you as son of the whole Order collectively, then your military rights, in view of the Order's prerogatives, would be no different from those you had as scion of a noble house.'

'I go,' said Torrismund.

It was an evening of departure, that night, in the Frankish camp. Agilulf prepared his baggage and horse meticulously, and his squire Gurduloo rolled up in knapsacks, blankets, curry-combs, cauldrons, made such a heap they prevented him seeing where he was riding, took the opposite direction to his master, and galloped off losing everything on the way.

No one had come to greet Agilulf as he left, except a few poor ostlers and blacksmiths who did not make too many distinctions and realized this officer might be fussier but was also unhappier than others. The paladins did not come, with the excuse that they did not know the time of his departure; and anyway there was no reason to: Agilulf had not said a word to any of them since coming from the banquet. His departure aroused no comment; when his duties were distributed in such a way that none remained unaccounted for, the absence of the non-existent knight was thought best left in silence by general consent.

The only one to be moved, indeed overwhelmed, was Bradamante. She hurried to her tent. 'Quick!' she called to her maids and retainers. 'Quick!' and flung into the air clothes, armour, lances and ornaments. 'Quick!' doing this not as usual when undressing or angry but to have all put in order, make an inventory and leave. 'Prepare everything, I'm leaving, leaving, not staying here another minute; he's gone. The only one who made any sense in this whole army, the only one who can give any sense to my life and my war, and now there's nothing left but a bunch of louts and nincompoops who don't understand me, and life is just a constant rolling between bed and battle; he alone knew the secret geometry, the order, the rule, by which to understand its beginning and end!' So saying she put on her country armour piece by piece and over it her periwinkle robe: soon she was in the saddle, male in all except the proud way certain true women have of looking virile, spurred her horse to the gallop, dragging down palisades and tents and sausage stalls, and soon vanished in a high cloud of dust.

That dust was seen by Raimbaud as he ran about on foot looking for her, crying, 'Where are you going, oh, where, Bradamante, here am I for you, for you, and you go away!' with a lover's stubborn indignation which means, 'I'm here, girl, loaded with love, how can you not want it, what *can* a girl want that she doesn't take me, doesn't love me, what can she want more than what I feel I can and ought to give her?' So he rages, incapable of accepting, and at a certain moment love for her is also love for himself, love of himself is love for her and love for what could be them both together and is not. And in his frenzy Raimbaud ran into his tent, prepared horse, arms and knapsack, and left too; for war can be well fought where there's a glimpse of a woman's mouth between lance points, when nothing, wounds, dust, horses' stink, means anything, but that smile.

Torrismund also left that evening, sad and hopeful too. He wanted to find the wood again, the damp dark wood of his infancy, his mother, his days in that cave, and even more the pure comradeship of his fathers, armed and watching around a hidden bivouac fire, robed in white, silent in the thick of a forest, with low branches almost touching bracken and mushrooms sprouting from rich earth which never saw sun.

Charlemagne, as he rose from the banquet rather shaky on his legs, heard of all these sudden departures and moved towards the royal pavilion thinking of days when the departures were of Astolf, Rinaldo, Guidon the Wild One, Roland, to do deeds which later entered the epics of poets, while now the same veterans would never move a step unless forced by duty. 'Let them go, they're young, let them get on with it,' said Charlemagne with the habit, usual to men of action, of considering movement always good, but already with the bitterness of the old who suffer at losing things of the past more than they enjoy greeting those of the future.

8

Book, evening is here, and I have begun to write more rapidly; no sound rises from the river but the rumble of the cascade, bats fly mutely by the window, a dog bays, voices ring from the haystacks. Maybe this penance of mine has not been so ill-chosen by the Mother Abbess; every now and again I notice my pen beginning to hurry over the paper as if by itself, with me hurrying along after it. 'Tis towards the truth we hurry, my pen and I, the truth which I am constantly expecting to meet deep in a white page, and which I can reach only when my pen strokes have succeeded in burying all the disgust and dissatisfaction and rancour which I am here enclosed to expiate.

Then at a mere scamper of a mouse (the convent attics are full of them), or a sudden gust of wind banging the shutter (always apt to distract me, and I hurry to reopen it), or at the end of some episode in this tale and the start of another, or maybe just at the repetition of a line, there, my pen is heavy as a cross once again and my race towards truth wavers in its course.

Now I must show the lands crossed by Agilulf and his squire on their journey; I must set it all down on this page, a dusty main road, a river, a bridge, and Agilulf passing on his light hooved horse, tock-tock, tock-tock, for this knight without a body weighs little, and the horse can do many a mile without tiring and its master is quite untirable. Next a heavy gallop passes over the bridge: tututum! It's Gurduloo clutching the neck of his horse, their two heads so close it's impossible to tell if the horse is thinking with the squire's head or the squire with the horse's. On my paper I trace a straight line with occasional angles, and this is Agilulf's route. This other line all twirls and zigzags is Gurduloo's. When he sees a butterfly flutter by Gurduloo at once urges his horse after it, thinking himself astride not the horse but the butterfly, and so wanders off the road and into the fields. Meanwhile Agilulf goes straight ahead, following his course. Every now and again Gurduloo's route off the road coincides with invisible short cuts (or maybe the horse is following a path of its own choice, with no guidance from its rider) and after many a twist and turn the vagabond finds himself again beside his master on the main road.

Here on the river's bank I will set a mill. Agilulf stops to ask the way. The miller woman replies courteously and offers wine and bread, which he refuses. He accepts only fodder for the horse. The road is dusty and sun swept; the good millers are amazed at the knight not being thirsty.

When he has just left up gallops Gurduloo, with the sound of a regiment at full tilt. 'Have you seen my master?'

'And who may your master be?'

'A knight ... no, a horse ...'

'Are you in a horse's service then?'

'No ... it's my horse that's in a horse's service ...'

'Who's riding that horse?'

'Eh ... no one knows ...'

'Who is riding your own horse, then?'

'Oh, ask it!'

'Don't you want any food or drink either?'

'Yes, yes! Eat! Drink!' and he gulps it all down.

Now I am drawing a town girt with walls. Agilulf has to pass through it. The guards at the gate ask him to show his face; they have orders to let no one pass with closed visor, lest he be a ferocious brigand infesting the local countryside. Agilulf refuses, comes to blows with the guard, forces his passage, escapes.

Beyond the town I now trace out a wood. Agilulf scours it through and through until he finds the dreadful bandit. He disarms him, chains him up, and drags him before the guards who had refused him passage. 'Here is the man you so much feared!'

'Ah blessings on you, white knight! But tell us who you are, and why you keep your helmet shut?'

'My name is at my journey's end,' said Agilulf, and flees away.

Around the town goes a rumour that he is an archangel or soul from purgatory. 'The horse moved so lightly,' says one, 'there might have been no one in the saddle at all.'

Here by the edge of the wood verges passes another road also leading to the town. Along this road is riding Bradamante. To those in the town she says, 'I am looking for a knight in white armour. I know him to be here.'

'No. No, he's not,' is the reply.

'If he's not, then it must be him.'

'Go and find where he is, then. He's rushed away from here.'

'Have you really seen him? White armour which seems to have a man inside?'

'Who's inside if not a man?'

'One who is more than all other men!'

'There's devil's work in this,' says an old man, 'and in you too, O knight of the gentle voice!'

Away spurs Bradamante.

A little later, Raimbaud reins his horse in the town square. 'Have you seen a knight pass?'

'Which? Two have passed and you're the third.'

'One rushing after the other.'

'Is it true one isn't a man?'

'The second is a woman.'

'And the first?'

'Nothing.'

'What about you?'

'Me? I'm ... I'm a man.'

'Thanks be to God!'

Along Agilulf was riding, followed by Gurduloo. A damsel, with flowing hair and tattered dress, ran on to the road, and flung herself on her knees. Agilulf stopped his horse. 'Help, noble cavalier,' she invoked. 'Half a mile from here a flock of wild bears is besieging the castle of my lady, the noble widow Priscilla. Only a few helpless women inhabit the castle. Nobody can get in or out. I was dropped by a rope from the battlements and escaped the claws of those beasts by a miracle. Oh knight, come and free us, do!'

'My sword is always at the service of widows and helpless creatures,' said Agilulf. 'Gurduloo, take on your crupper this damsel who will guide us to the castle of her mistress.'

They began climbing a rocky path. The squire was not even looking at the way as he rode; the breast of the woman sitting in his arms showed pink and plump through the tears in her dress, and Gurduloo felt lost.

The damsel turned to look at Agilulf. 'What a noble bearing

your master has!' she said.

'Uh, uh,' replied Gurduloo, reaching out a hand towards that warm breast.

'He's so sure and proud in every word and gesture ...' said she, still with eyes on Agilulf.

'Uh,' exclaimed Gurduloo, and his rein slung on his wrist, he tried with both hands to ascertain how a creature could be so firm and so soft at the same time.

'And his voice,' said she, 'so sharp and metallic ...'

From Gurduloo's mouth came only a faint whine, for he had buried it between the young woman's neck and shoulder and was lost in their scent.

'How happy my mistress will be to find herself freed from the bears by such a man ... Oh I do envy her ... But hey, we're going off the track! What is it, squire, are you distracted?'

At a turn in the path was a hermit, holding out a hand for alms. Agilulf, who gave to every beggar he met the regular sum of three centimes, drew in his horse and rummaged in his purse.

'Blessings on you, knight,' said the hermit, pocketing the money and signing for him to bend down so as to speak in his ear, 'I will reward you at once by telling you to beware of the widow Priscilla! This tale of the bears is all a trap; she herself raises them, so as to be freed by the most valiant knights passing on the road below and draw them up to the castle to feed her insatiable lust.'

'It may be as you say, brother,' replied Agilulf, 'but I am a knight and it would be discourteous to reject a formal request for help made by a female in tears.'

'Are you not afraid of the flames of lust?'

Agilulf was slightly embarrassed. 'Well, we'll see ...'

'Do you know what remains of a knight after a sojourn in that castle?'

'What?'

'You see it before your eyes. I too was a knight, I too saved Priscilla from the bears, and now here I am!' And he really was in rather bad shape.

'I will take note of your experience, brother, but I affront the trial,' said Agilulf, spurred away and up to Gurduloo and the girl.

'I don't know what these hermits always find to gossip about,' said the girl to the knight. 'No group of religious or lay folk chatter so much and so maliciously.'

'Are there many hermits round here?'

'It's full of 'em. And new ones are constantly being added.'

'I will not be one of those,' exclaimed Agilulf. 'Let's hurry!'

'I hear the snarl of bears,' exclaimed the girl. 'I'm afraid! Let me get down and hide behind that bush!'

Agilulf came out on to the open space before the castle. All around was black with bears. At the sight of horse and knight they bared their teeth and lined up side by side to bar his way. Agilulf set his lance and charged. One or two he pierced, others he stunned, others he bruised. Gurduloo came riding up and chased them with a kitchen spit. In ten minutes those not stretched on the ground like so many carpets had gone to hide in the forest depths.

The castle gate opened. 'Noble night, can hospitality repay what I owe you?' On the threshold had appeared Priscilla, surrounded by her ladies and maids. Among these was the young woman who had accompanied the pair till then; inexplicably, she was already home and no longer dressed in rags but a nice clean apron.

Agilulf, followed by Gurduloo, made his entry into the castle. The widow Priscilla was not particularly tall nor plump but well cared for, with a bosom not large but well in view, and sparkling black eyes, in fact a woman with something to say for herself. There she stood, before Agilulf's white armour, looking pleased. The knight was grave but reserved.

'Sir Agilulf Emo Bertrandin of the Guildivern,' said Priscilla, 'I know your name already and know who you are and who you are *not*.'

At this announcement Agilulf, as if freed from a discomfort, put aside his shyness and looked more at ease. Even so he bowed, dropped on one knee, said, 'At your service,' then snapped back on his feet.

'I have heard you much spoken of,' said Priscilla, 'and it has been for long my ardent wish to meet you. What miracle has brought you along this remote road?'

'I am travelling,' said Agilulf, 'to trace before it be too late a virginity of fifteen years ago.'

'Never have I heard a knightly enterprise with so fleeting an aim,' said Priscilla. 'But as fifteen years have passed I have no scruples in retarding you another night and requesting you to be a guest in my castle,' and off she moved beside him.

The other women all stood there with eyes fixed on him until he vanished with the châtelaine into a series of withdrawing chambers. Then they turned to Gurduloo.

'Aha, what a fine figure of a squire,' they cried, clapping their hands. He stood there like an ape, scratching himself. 'A pity he has so many fleas and stinks so,' they said. 'Quick, let's wash him!' They bore him to their quarters and stripped him naked.

Priscilla had led Agilulf to a table laid for two. 'I know your habitual temperance, knight,' said she, 'but how else can I begin to do you honour but by inviting you to sit at my board? Certainly,' she added slyly, 'the signs of gratitude which I intend to offer do not stop there!'

Agilulf thanked her, sat down facing the châtelaine, broke a few pieces of bread in his fingers, and after a moment or two of silence, cleared his voice and began to speak fluently.

'How truly strange and eventful, lady, are the adventures which befall a knight errant. These can be grouped under various headings. First ...' And so he conversed, affably, clearly, informatively, at times arousing a suspicion of over meticulousness, soon banished by the volubility with which he went on to other subjects, interlarding serious phrases with jests in excellent taste, expressing about matters and persons opinions neither too favourable nor too contrary and always such as to offer his partner opportunities to put her own opinion, and encouraging her with gracious questions.

'Oh, what delicious talk is this!' exclaimed Priscilla, all abeam.

Then just as suddenly as he had begun talking Agilulf went silent.

'Let the singing begin,' cried Priscilla and clapped her hands. Lute girls entered the chamber. One intoned the song which starts, ' 'Tis the unicorn gathers the rose,' then another, *Jasmin, veuillez embellir le beau coussin.*'

Agilulf had words of appreciation for both music and voices.

Now a cluster of maidens entered dancing. They wore light robes and had garlands in their hair. Agilulf accompanied their dance by banging his iron gloves on the table in rhythm.

No less festive were the dances taking place in another wing of the castle, in the quarters of the maidens-in-waiting. Half-clothed, the young women were playing at ball and drawing Gurduloo into the game. The squire, dressed in a short tunic which the ladies had lent him, never kept to his place or waited for the ball to be thrown but ran after it and tried to grasp it in any way he could, flinging himself headlong at one or other damsel, then amid his struggles being often struck by another inspiration and rolling with the girl on one of the soft cushions scattered around.

'Oh, what *are* you doing? Oh no, no, you great big camel! Oh, see what he's doing to me. No, I want to play ball. Ah! ah! ah!'

Gurduloo was quite beside himself now. What with the warm bath they had given him, the scents and all that pink and white flesh, his only desire now was to merge into the general fragrance.

'Oh oh, here again, Oh *Mama Mia*! Oh really, aah ... !'

The others went on playing ball as if noticing nothing, jesting, laughing and singing. 'Oho! Ohi! The morn does fly on high...'

A girl whom Gurduloo had whisked away, after a long last cry, returned to her companions rather flushed, rather stunned, then laughing and clapping her hands cried, 'Over here, here to me!' and began to play again.

Before long Gurduloo was rolling on another girl.

'Come on, come on, oh what a bore, oh what a thruster, no, you're hurting ...' and she succumbed.

Other women and maidens not participating in the game were sitting on benches and chattering away ... 'Since Philomena, you know, was jealous of Clara, but—' then one would suddenly feel herself seized round the waist by Gurduloo – 'Oh, what a fright! ... well, as I was saying, William seems to have gone with Euphemia ... where *are* you taking me?' Gurduloo had loaded her on to a shoulder ... 'D'you understand? Meanwhile that other silly with her usual jealousy ...' the girl was continuing to chatter and gesticulate, as dangling on Gurduloo's shoulder, she vanished.

Not long after back she came, rather dishevelled, a shoulder strap torn, and settled it back, still gabbling away, 'Well, as I was saying, Philomena made such a scene with Clara and the other on the other hand ...'

In the banqueting chamber dancers and songsters had withdrawn. Agilulf was giving the châtelaine a long list of compositions often played by the Emperor Charlemagne's musicians.

'The sky darkens,' observed Priscilla.

' 'Tis night, deep night,' admitted Agilulf.

'The room which I have reserved for you ...'

'Thanks. Listen to the nightingale out there in the park.'

'The room which I have reserved for you ... is my own ...'

'Your hospitality is exquisite ... 'Tis from that oak the nightingale sings. Let us draw close to the window.'

He got up, offered her his iron arm, moved to the window. The gurgle of nightingales was a cue for him to launch out on a series of poetic and mythological references.

But Priscilla cut this off short. 'What the nightingale sings about is love. And we ...'

'Ah love!' cried Agilulf with such a brusque change of tone that Priscilla was alarmed. Then, without a break, he plunged into a dissertation of the passion of love. Priscilla was tenderly excited; leaning on his arm, she urged him towards a room dominated by a big four-poster bed.

'Among the ancients, as love was considered a god ...' was pouring out Agilulf.

Priscilla closed the door with a double bolt, went up to him, bowed her head on his armour and said, 'I'm a little cold, the fire is spent ...'

'The opinion of the ancients,' said Agilulf, 'as to whether it be better to make love in cold rooms rather than in hot is a controversial one. But the advice of most ...'

'Oh, you do know all about love,' whispered Priscilla.

'The advice of most is against stiflingly hot rooms and in favour of a certain natural warmth.'

'Shall I call my maid to light the fire?'

'I will light it myself.' He examined the wood in the fire-place, praised the flame of this or that type of wood, enumerated the various ways of lighting fires in the open or in enclosed places. A sigh from Priscilla interrupted him; as if realizing that this new subject was dispersing the amorous trepidation being created, Agilulf quickly began smattering his speech with references and allusions and comparisons to warmth of emotions and senses.

Priscilla, smiling now with half-closed eyes, stretching out a hand towards the flames which were beginning to crackle, said, 'How lovely and warm ... how sweet it would be to be warm between sheets, prone ...'

The mention of bed suggested a series of new observations to Agilulf; according to him the difficult art of bed making was unknown to the serving maids of France, and in nobles' palaces could be found only ill-stretched sheets.

'Oh no, do tell me, my bed too ... ?' asked the widow.

'Certainly yours is a queen's bed, superior to all others in the imperial dominions, but my desire to see you surrounded only with things worthy of you in every detail makes me eye that fold there with some apprehension ...'

'Oh, a fold!' cried Priscilla, also swept by the passion for perfection communicated to her by Agilulf.

They undid the bed, finding and deploring little folds and puckers, portions too stretched or too loose, and this search gave moments of stabbing anguish and others of ascent to ever higher skies.

Having upset the whole bed as far as the mattress, Agilulf began to remake it according to the rules. This was an elaborate operation; nothing was to be left to chance, and secret expedients were put to work; all this with diffuse explanations to the widow. But every now and again something left him dissatisfied, when he would begin all over again.

From the other wings of the castle rang a cry, or rather a moan or bray, forced out unwillingly.

'What's that?' started Priscilla.

'Nothing, it's my squire's voice,' said he.

With that shout mingled others more acute, like strident sighs soaring to the sky.

'What's that now?' asked Agilulf.

'Oh, just the girls,' said Priscilla. 'Playing ... youth, you know.'

And they went on remaking the bed, listening every now and again to the sounds of the night.

'Gurduloo's shouting ...'

'What a noise those girls do make ...'

'The nightingale.'

'The cicadas ...'

The bed was now ready, puckerless. Agilulf turned towards the widow. She was naked. Her robes had fallen chastely to the floor.

'Naked ladies are advised,' declared Agilulf, 'that the most sublime of sensual emotions is embracing a warrior in full armour.'

'You don't need to teach me that!' exclaimed Priscilla, 'I wasn't born yesterday!' So saying she took a leap and clamped herself to Agilulf, entwining her legs and arms around his greaves.

One after the other she tried all the ways in which armour can be embraced, then, all languor, entered the bed.

Agilulf knelt down beside her pillow. 'Your hair,' he said.

Priscilla when disrobing had not undone the high array of her brown mane of hair. Agilulf began illustrating the place of loose hair in the transport of the senses. 'Let us try.'

With firm delicate movements of his iron hands he loosened her castle of tresses and made her hair fall down over her breast and shoulders.

'But,' he added, 'it is certainly more subtle for the man to prefer a woman whose body is naked but hair elaborately dressed, even covered with veils and diadems.'

'Shall we try again?'

'I will dress your hair myself.' He dressed it and showed his capacity at weaving tresses, winding and twisting them round and fixing them with big pins. Then he made an elaborate arrangement of veils and jewels. So an hour passed; but Priscilla, on his handing her the mirror, had never seen herself so lovely.

She invited him to lie down by her side. 'They say,' said he, 'that every night Cleopatra dreamt she had an armed warrior in her bed.'

'I've never tried,' she confessed, 'they usually take it off beforehand.'

'Well, try now.' And slowly, without soiling the sheets, he entered the bed fully armed from head to foot and stretched out taut as if on a tomb.

'Don't you even loosen the sword from its scabbard?'

'Amorous passion knows no half measures.'

Priscilla shut her eyes in ecstacy.

Agilulf raised himself on an elbow. 'The fire is smoking. I will get up to see why the flue does not draw.'

The moon was just showing at the window. On his way back from fireplace to bed Agilulf paused. 'Lady, let us go out on to the battlements and enjoy this late moonlit eve.'

He wrapped her in his cloak. Entwined, they climbed the tower. The moon silvered the forest. A horned owl sang. Some windows of the castle were still alight and from them every now and again came cries or laughs or groans or a bray from the squire.

'All nature is love ...'

They returned to the room. The fire was almost out. They crouched down to puff on the embers. Close to each other, with Priscilla's pink knee grazing his metallic greave, grew a new, more innocent intimacy.

When Priscilla went to bed again the window was already touched by first light. 'Nothing disfigures a woman's face like the first ray of dawn,' said Agilulf; but to get her face to appear in the best light he had to move bed and all.

'How do I look?' asked the widow.

'Most lovely.'

Priscilla was happy. But the sun was rising fast and to follow its rays Agilulf continually had to move the bed.

' 'Tis dawn,' said he. His voice had already changed. 'My duty as knight requires me to set out on my road at this hour.'

'Already!' moaned Priscilla. 'Now as ever is?'

'I regret, gentle lady, but 'tis a graver duty urges me.'

'Oh how lovely it was . . .'

Agilulf bent his knee. 'Bless me, Priscilla.' He rose, called his squire. He had to wander all over the castle before he finally spied him, exhausted, asleep like a log in a kind of dog kennel. 'Quick, saddle up!' but he had to carry Gurduloo himself. The sun in its continuing ascent outlined the two figures on horseback against golden leaves in the woods; the squire balanced like a sack, the knight straight, pollarded like the slim shadow of a poplar.

Maidens and servant maids had hurried around Priscilla. 'How was it, mistress, how was it?'

'Oh, if you only knew! What a man, what a man . . .'

'But do tell, do describe, how was it? Tell us.'

'A man . . . a man . . . a knight . . . a continuous . . . a paradise . . .'

'But what did he *do*? What did he *do*?'

'How can one tell that? Oh, lovely, how lovely it was . . .'

'But has he got everything? Yet . . . Do tell . . .'

'I simply wouldn't know how . . . So much . . . But what about you, with that squire . . . ?'

'Oh nothing, no, did you? No; you? I really forget . . .'

'What? I could hear you, my dears . . .'

'Oh well, poor boy, I don't remember, I don't remember either, maybe you . . . what, me? Mistress, do tell us about him, about the knight, eh? What was Agilulf like?'

'Oh, Agilulf!'

9

As I write this book, following a tale told in an ancient almost illegible chronicle, I realize only now that I have filled page after page and am still at the very start: for now begin the real ramifications of the plot, Agilulf's and his squire's intrepid journeys for proof of Sophronia's virginity, interwoven with Bradamante's pursuit and flight, Raimbaud's love, and Torrismund's search for the Knights of the Grail. But this thread, instead of running swiftly through my fingers, is apt to sag or stick; and when I think of all the journeys and obstacles and flights and deceits and duels and jousts that I still have to put on paper I feel rather dazed. How this discipline as convent scribe and my assiduous penance of seeking words and all my meditations on ultimate truths have changed me! What the vulgar – and I too till now – considered as the greatest of delights, the interweaving adventures which make up every knightly tale, now seem to me pointless decorations, mere fringes, the hardest part of my task.

I long to hurry on with my story, tell it quickly, embellish every page with enough duels and battles for a poem; but when I pause and start rereading I realize that my pen has left no mark on the paper and the pages are blank.

To tell it as I would like this blank page would have to bristle with reddish rocks, flake with pebbly sand, sprout sparse juniper trees. In the midst, on a twisting ill-marked track, I would set Agilulf, passing erect on his saddle, lance at rest. But this page would have to be not only a rocky slope but the dome of sky above, slung so low that there is room only for a flight of cawing rooks in between. With my pen I should also trace faint dents in the paper to represent the slither of an invisible snake through grass or a hare crossing a heath, suddenly coming into the clear, stopping, sniffing around through its short whiskers, then vanishing again.

Everything moves on this bare page with no sign, no change on its surface, as after all everything moves and nothing changes on the earth's crinkly crust; for there is but one single expanse of the same material, as there is with the sheet on which I write, an expanse which in spite of contractions and congealings in different forms and consistencies and various subtle colourings can still seem smeared over a flat surface; and even when hairy or feathery or wobbly bits seem at times to move, that is but the change between the relations of various qualities distributed over the expanse of uniform matter around, without anything changing in fact. The only person whc can be said definitely to be on the move is Agilulf, by which I do not mean his horse or armour, but that lonely self-preoccupied impatient something jogging along on horseback inside the armour. Around him pine cones fall from branches, streams gurgle over pebbles, fish swim in streams, maggots gnaw at leaves tortoises rub their hard bellies on the ground; but all this is mere illusion of movement, perpetual revolving to and fro like waves. And in this wave Gurduloo is revolving to and fro, prisoner of the material world, he too smeared like the pine cones, fish, maggots, stones and leaves, a mere excrescence on the earth's crust.

How much more difficult it is for me to plot on my paper Bradamante's course or Raimbaud's or glum Torrismund's! There would have to be some such very faint pucker on the surface as can be got by pricking paper from below with a pin; and this pucker would always have to be impregnated with the general matter of the world and this itself constitutes its sense and beauty and sorrow, its true attrition and movement.

But how can I get on with my tale if I begin to torture over the white page like this, scoop out valleys and clefts in it, score it with creases and scratches, reading into it the paladin's progress? To help tell my tale it would be better if I drew a map. the gentle countryside of France, and proud Brittany, and the English Channel surging with black billows, and high Scotland up there and harsh Pyrenees down here, and Spain still in infidel hands, and Africa mother of serpents. Then with arrows and crosses and numbers I could plot the journey of one or other of our heroes. Here, for instance, with a rapid line in spite of a few twists, I can make Agilulf land in England

and direct him towards the convent where Sophronia has lived retired for fifteen years.

He arrives, and finds the convent a mass of ruins.

'You come too late, noble knight,' said an old man. 'These valleys still resound with the cries of those poor women. A short while ago a fleet of Moorish pirates landed on this coast and sacked the convent, bore off the nuns as slaves and set fire to the walls.'

'Bore off, where to?'

'As slaves to be sold in Morocco, m'lord.'

'Was there among those nuns one Sophronia, who in the world was the King of Scotland's daughter?'

'Ah, you mean Sister Palmyra! There was indeed! They loaded her up on their shoulders straight away, the rascals! Though no longer a girl she was still attractive. I remember as if it were now her shouts and groans at those ugly faces.'

'Were you present at the sack?'

'Well, we who live here, you know, are always out on the village green.'

'And you didn't help?'

'Help who? Well m'lord, you know, so suddenly ... we had no orders, or experience ... Between doing a thing and doing it badly we thought it best to do nothing at all.'

'Tell me, did this Sophronia lead a pious life in the convent?'

'These days there are nuns of all kinds, but Sister Palmyra was the holiest and most chaste in the entire diocese.'

'Quick, Gurduloo, down to the port we go and embark for Morocco.'

All this part I am now scoring with wavy lines is the sea, or rather the ocean. Now I draw the ship on which Agilulf makes his journey, and farther on I draw an enormous whale, with an ornamental scroll and the words 'Ocean Sea.' This arrow indicates the ship's route. I do another arrow showing the whale's course: there, they met. So at this point of the ocean will take place an encounter between whale and ship, and as I've drawn the whale in bigger, the ship will get the worst of it. Now I'm drawing in a criss-cross of arrows to show that at this point there was a savage battle between whale and ship. Agilulf fights peerlessly and plunges his lance into the creature's side. Over him squirts a nauseating jet of whale oil, which I show by these divergent lines. Gurduloo leaps on the whale and forgets all about the ship, which at a whisk from the whale's tail overturns. Agilulf with his iron armour of course sinks like a stone. Before the waves entirely submerge him he cries to his squire, 'We'll meet in Morocco! I'm walking there!'

In fact, after dropping mile after mile into the depths, Agilulf lands on his feet on the sand at the bottom of the sea and begins walking briskly. Often he meets marine monsters and defends himself against them with his sword. The only bother about armour at the bottom of the sea is rust. But having been squirted from head to foot in whale oil, the white armour had a layer of grease which kept it intact.

On the ocean I now draw a turtle. Gurduloo had gulped down a pint of salty water before realizing that the sea is not supposed to be inside him but he inside the sea; eventually he seizes the shell of a big sea turtle. Partly letting himself be drawn along, partly guiding it by pinches and prods, they near the coast of Africa. Here they became entangled in the nets of some Moorish fishermen.

When the nets are drawn on board the fishermen see appear amid a wriggling school of mullet a man in soaking wet clothes covered with seaweed. 'The merman! The merman!' they cry.

'Merman? Nonsense! It's Gudi-Ussuf,' cried the head fisherman. 'It's Gudi-Ussuf, I know him!'

Gudi-Ussuf was in fact one of the names by which Gurduloo was known in the Moslem field kitchens when unrealizing he crossed the lines and found himself in the Moorish army in Spain; so knowing Gurduloo to have a strong body and docile mind, he took him on as an oyster fisher.

One evening the fishermen, and Gurduloo among them, were sitting on the rocky Moroccan shore opening the oysters they'd fished one by one, when from the water appeared a helmet, a breastplate, and then a complete suit of armour walking step by step up the beach. 'A lobster-man! A lobster-man!' cried the fishermen – running away in terror to hide among the rocks.

'A lobster-man! Nonsense!' said Gurduloo. 'It's my master! You must be exhausted, sir, after walking all that way!'

'I'm not the least tired,' replied Agilulf. 'And you? What are you doing here?'

'Finding pearls for the sultan,' intervened the ex-soldier, 'as he has to give a new pearl to a different wife every night.'

Having three hundred and sixty-five wives, the sultan visited one a night, so every wife was only visited once a year. To the one visited it was his custom to give a pearl, so that every day merchants had exhausted their supplies they had to recourse to the fishermen to procure a pearl at all costs.

'You who've managed to walk so well on the sea bottom,' the ex-soldier said to Agilulf, 'why don't you join our enterprise?'

'A knight does not join enterprises with lucre as their aim, particularly if conducted by enemies of his religion. I thank you, O pagan, for having saved and fed this squire of mine, but I don't care a jot if your sultan cannot present a pearl to his three hundred and sixty-fifth wife tonight.'

'We care a lot though, as we shall all be whipped,' exclaimed the fisherman. 'Tonight is no ordinary wife's night. It's the turn of a new one, whom the sultan is visiting for the first time. She was bought almost a year ago from some pirates, and has awaited her turn till now. 'Tis improper that the sultan should present himself to her with empty hands, particularly as she is a co-religionist of yours, Sophronia of Scotland, of royal blood, brought to Morocco as a slave and immediately destined for our sovereign's harem.'

Agilulf did not betray his emotion. 'I will show you how to get out of your difficulty,' said he, 'let the merchants suggest that the sultan bring his new wife not the usual pearl but a present to soothe her homesickness; the complete armour of a Christian warrior.'

'Where can we find such armour?'

'Mine!' said Agilulf.

Sophronia was awaiting nightfall in her quarters of the palace harem. From the grating of the cuspid window she looked out over garden palms, fountains, alleys. The sun was setting, the muezzin launching his cry, and in the garden were opening the scented flowers of dusk.

A knock. 'Tis time! No, the usual eunuchs. They are bearing a present from the sultan. A suit of armour. Of white armour. What can it mean? Sophronia, alone again, remains at the window. She has been there for almost a year. When bought as a wife she had been assigned the turn of a wife recently repudiated, a turn which would fall due again more than eleven months later. Living in the harem doing nothing, one day after the other, was even more boring than the convent.

'Do not fear, noble Sophronia,' said a voice behind her. She turned. It was the armour talking. 'I am Agilulf of the Guildivern who saved your immaculate virtue once before.'

'Help!' screamed the sultan's wife. Then, recomposing herself, 'Ah yes, I thought I knew that white armour. It was you who arrived just in time, years ago, to prevent me being abused by a brigand ...'

'Now I arrive just in time to save you from the horror of pagan nuptials.'

'Oh yes ... always you ... you are ...'

'Now, protected by this sword, I will accompany you forth from the sultan's domains.'

'Yes ... indeed ... of course.'

When the eunuchs came to announce the sultan's arrival they were put to the sword one by one. Wrapped in a cloak, Sophronia ran through the gardens by the knight's side. The dragomen gave the alarm. But their heavy scimitars could do little against the agile sword of the warrior in white armour. And his shield sustained well the assault of a whole picket's lances. Gurduloo was waiting behind a cactus tree with horses. In the port a felucca was ready to leave for Christian lands. From the prow Sophronia watched the palms of the beach drawing further away.

Now I am drawing the felucca here in the sea. I'm doing a rather bigger one than the ship before, so that if it does meet a whale there'll be no disaster. With this curved line I mark the passage of the felucca which I want to reach the port of St Malo. The trouble is that here in the Bay of Biscay there's such a mess of criss-crossing lines already that it's better to let the felucca pass a little farther out, over here, yes, over here; then what should it go and do but hit the Breton rocks! It's wrecked, sinks, and Agilulf and Gurduloo just manage to bear Sophronia in safety to the shore.

Sophronia is weary. Agilulf decides to put her for refuge in a cave and then together with his squire go to Charlemagne's camp and announce her virginity to be still intact and so also the legitimacy of his name. Now I'm marking the cave with a small cross at this point of the Breton coast so as to be able to find it again later. I can't think what this line is doing passing the same place; by now my paper is such a mess of lines going in all directions. Ah yes, here's a line corresponding to Torrismund's journey. So the thought-laden youth is passing right here, while Sophronia lies in the cave. He too approaches the cave, enters, sees her.

10

However had Torrismund got there? While Agilulf was moving from France to England, England to Africa, and Africa to Brittany, the putative cadet of the House of Cornwall had wandered far and wide over forests of Christian lands in search of the secret camp of the Knights of the Holy Grail. As the Holy Order has a habit of changing its headquarters from year to year and never makes a show of its presence to the profane, Torrismund could find no indications to follow in his journey. He wandered about at a venture, chasing a remote sensation which was the same for him as the name of the Grail; but was it the order of the pious Knights he was searching for, or the memory of his childhood on Scottish heather? Sometimes the sudden opening of a valley black with larches or a cleft of grey rocks at the end of which boomed a torrent white with spray filled him with an inexplicable emotion which he took for a warning. 'Perhaps they're here, nearby.' And if from nearby rose the faint and distant sound of a hunting horn then Torrismund lost all doubts and began searching every crevice yard by yard for trace of them. But at most he would run into some lost huntsman or shepherd with his flock.

On reaching the remote land of Kurwalden he stopped in a village and asked the local rustics to be so good as to give him some goat's cheese and grey bread.

'Willingly would we give you some, sir,' said a goatherd, 'but see how I, my wife and children are reduced to skeletons! We have to make so many offerings to the knights! This wood is crawling with colleagues of yours, though differently dressed. There's a whole troop of 'em, and for supplies you know, they all come down on us!'

'Knights living in the wood? How are they dressed?'

'In white cloaks and golden helmets with two white swans' wings on the sides.'

'Are they very holy?'

'Oh, yes they're holy enough. And they certainly never soil their hands with money, as they haven't a cent. But they expect a lot and we have to obey. Now we're stripped clean, and there's a famine. What shall we give them when they come next time?'

But the young man was already hurrying towards the wood.

Amid the fields, on the calm waters of a brook, slowly passed a flock of swans. Torrismund followed them along the bank. From among the bushes resounded an arpeggio, 'Flin, flin, flin!' The youth walked on and the sound seemed at times to be following him and at others preceding him, 'Flin, flin, flin!' Where the bushes thinned out appeared a human figure. It was a warrior in a helmet decorated with white wings, carrying both a lance and a small harp on which now and again he struck that chord, 'Flin, flin, flin!' He said nothing; his eyes did not avoid Torrismund but passed over him as if not perceiving him, although they seemed to be following him; when tree trunks and branches separated them, he got him back on the right track again by calling with one of his arpeggios, 'Flin, flin, flin!' Torrismund longed to talk to him, ask him questions, but he followed silent and intimidated.

They came into a clearing. On every side were warriors armed with lances, in golden cuirasses, wrapped in long white cloaks, motionless, each turned in a different direction with his eyes staring into a void. One was feeding a swan with grains of corn, his eyes turned elsewhere. At a new arpeggio from the player, a warrior on horseback answered by raising his horn and sending out a long call. When he was silent all the warriors moved, each made a few steps in his direction and stopped again.

'Knights ...' Torrismund plucked up courage to say, 'excuse me, I may be mistaken, but are you not the Knights of the Grai—?'

'Never pronounce the name!' interrupted a voice behind him. A knight with white hair had halted near him. 'Is it not enough for you to come disturbing our holy recollection?'

'Oh do forgive me.' The youth turned to him, 'I'm so happy to be among you! If you knew how long I've looked for you!'

'Why?'

'Why ... ?' and his longing to proclaim his secret was stronger than his fear of committing sacrilege ... 'Because I'm your son!'

The old knight remained impassive. 'Here neither fathers nor sons are acknowledged,' said he after a moment of silence, 'whoever enters the Sacred Order leaves behind him all earthly relationships.'

Torrismund felt more disappointed than repudiated; he would have preferred an angry reply from his chaste fathers, which he could have contradicted or argued with by giving proofs and invoking the voice of blood; but this calm reply, which did not deny the possibility of the facts but excluded all discussion on a matter of principle, was discouraging.

'My only other aspiration is to be recognized as a son of the Sacred Order,' he tried to insist, 'for which I bear a limitless admiration.'

'If you admire our Order so much,' said the old man, 'you should have one sole aspiration, to be admitted as part of it.'

'Would that be possible, d'you think?' exclaimed Torrismund, immediately attracted by the new prospect.

'When you have made yourself worthy.'

'What must one do?'

'Purify oneself gradually from every passion and let oneself be possessed by love of the Grail.'

'Oh, you do pronounce that name then?'

'We knights can; you profane no.'

'But tell me, why are all here silent and you the only one to talk?'

'I am charged with the duty of relations with the profane. Words being often impure the Knights prefer to abstain from them, and also to let the Grail speak through their lips.'

'Tell me, what must I do to begin?'

'D'you see that maple leaf? A drop of dew has formed on it. Try and stand quite still and stare at the drop on that leaf, identify yourself with it, forget all the world in that drop, until you feel you have lost yourself and are pervaded by the infinite strength of the Grail.'

And he left him. Torrismund stared fixedly at the drop, stared and stared, began thinking of his own affairs, saw a frog jumping on the leaf, stared and stared at the frog, and then at the drop again, moved a foot which had gone numb, and then suddenly felt bored. Around in the woods knights appeared and disappeared, moving very slowly, their mouths open and eyes staring, accompanied by swans whose soft plumage they caressed every now and again. One suddenly threw wide his arms and with a hoarse cry broke into a little run.

'That one over there,' Torrismund could not prevent himself asking the old man, who had reappeared nearby, 'what's up with him?'

'Ecstasy!' said the old man. 'That is something you will never know, who are so distracted and curious. Those brothers have finally reached complete communion with the all.'

'And what about those?' asked the youth. Some knights were swaying about as if taken by slight shivers, and yawning.

'They're still at an intermediate stage. Before feeling one with the sun and stars the novice feels as if he has the nearest objects within himself, very intensely. This has an effect, particularly on the youngest. Those brothers of ours whom you see are feeling a pleasant gentle tickle from the running brook, the rustling leaves, the mushrooms growing underground.'

'And don't they tire of it in the long run?'

'Gradually they reach the higher states in which no longer the nearest vibrations occupy them but the great sweep of the skies, and very slowly they detach themselves from the senses.'

'Does that happen to all?'

'To few. And completely only to one of us, the Elect, the King of the Grail.'

They had reached a glade where a large number of knights were exercising their arms before a canopied tribunal. Under that canopy was sitting, or rather crouching, motionless, someone who seemed to be more mummy than man, dressed too in the uniform of the Grail, but more sumptuously. His eyes were open, indeed staring, in a face dried up as a chestnut.

'Is he alive?' asked the youth.

'He's alive, but now he's so rapt by love of the Grail that he no longer needs to eat or move or do his daily needs, or scarcely to breathe. He neither feels nor sees. No one knows his thoughts; they certainly reflect the movements of distant planets.'

'But why do they make him preside over military parades, if he doesn't see?'

' 'Tis a rite of the Grail.'

The knights were fencing among themselves. They were moving their swords in jerks, looking in the void, and taking sharp sudden steps as if they could never foresee what they would do a second later. And yet they never missed a blow.

'How can they fight with that air of being half asleep?'

' 'Tis the Grail in us moving our swords. Love of the universe can take the form of great frenzy and urge us lovingly to pierce our enemies. Our Order is invincible in war just because we fight without making any effort or choice but letting the sacred frenzy flow through our bodies.'

'And does it always turn out all right?'

'Yes, with whoever has lost all residues of human will and only lets the Grail direct his slightest gesture.'

'Slightest gesture? Even now when you're walking?'

The old man was walking like a somnambulist. 'Certainly. It's not I who am moving my feet; I am letting them be moved. Try. 'Tis the start of all.'

Torrismund tried, but at first he just could not succeed, and secondly – he did not enjoy it. There were the woods, green and leafy, all aflutter and achirp, where he longed to run and let himself go and put up game, to set against that shadow, that mystery, that extraneous nature, himself, his strength, his effort, his courage. Instead of which he had to stand there swaying like a paralytic.

'Let yourself be possessed,' the old man was warning him, 'let yourself be possessed entirely.'

'But really, you know,' burst out Torrismund, 'what I long for is to possess, not be possessed.'

The old man crossed his elbows over his face so as to stop up eyes and ears. 'You still have a long way to go, my boy.'

Torrismund remained in the encampment of the Grail. He tried hard to learn and imitate his fathers or brothers (he didn't know which to call them), tried to suffocate every motion of the mind which seemed too individual, to fuse himself in communion with the infinite love of the Grail, attentive for any indication of those ineffable sensations which sent the knights into ecstasies. But days passed and his purification made no progress. Everything they most liked bored him utterly; those voices, that music, their constant aptness to vibrate. And above all the continual proximity of the brethren, dressed like that, half naked, with golden breastplates and helmets, their flesh very white, some old, others fussy, touchy youths, all this became more and more antipathetic to him. With their story about the Grail always moving them they indulged in all sorts of loose habits while pretending to be ever pure.

The thought that he could have been generated like that by people with eyes staring in the void without even thinking of what they were up to, forgetting right away, he found quite unbearable.

The day came for handing over tribute. All the villagers around the wood, in carefully arranged order, were to hand over to the Knights of the Grail a certain number of goats' cheeses, baskets of carrots, sacks of millet and young lambs.

A delegation of peasants advanced. 'We wish to put forward the fact that the year has been a very bad one over the whole land of Kurwalden. We are at our wits' end even to feed our children. Famine touches rich and poor. Pious knights, we have come humbly to ask you to forgo our tribute just this time.'

The King of the Grail, under the canopy, sat silent and still as ever. But at a certain moment, slowly, he unjoined his hands, which he had crossed over his stomach, raised them to the sky (he had very long nails), and from his mouth came, 'Iiiih...'

At that sound all the Knights advanced with set lances towards the poor peasants. 'Help! Let's defend ourselves!' they cried. 'We'll hurry off and arm ourselves with axes and pitchforks!' and they dispersed.

The Knights, their eyes turned to the sky, marched during the night on the local villages, to the sound of horns and timbrels. From hop rows and bushes leapt villagers armed with pitchforks and billhooks, trying to contest their passage. But they could do little against the Knights' inexorable lances. Breaking the scattered defences they flung their heavy chargers against the huts of stone and straw and mud, grinding them under their hooves, deaf to the shout of women, calves, children. Other Knights bore lit torches and set fire to roofs, haystacks, stalls and a few poor granaries, until the villages were reduced to wailing screeching bonfires.

Torrismund, in the wake of the Knights, was horrified.

'Why, tell me, why?' he cried to the old man, keeping

behind him as the only one who could listen to him. 'So it's not true you are pervaded by love of all! Hey, be careful, you're trampling down that old woman! How have you the hearts to attack these poor folk? Help, the flames are licking that cradle! What're you doing?'

'Do not scrutinize the designs of the Grail, novice!' warned the old man. 'We are here but for this: 'tis the Grail moving us! Abandon yourself to its burning love.'

But Torrismund had dismounted, rushed to the help of a mother and gave her back a fallen baby.

'No! Don't take my crop! I've worked so hard for it!' yelled an old man.

Torrismund was beside him. 'Drop that sack, you brigand!' and he rushed at a Knight and tore the bag from him.

'Blessings on you! Stay with us!' cried some of the poor wretches, trying with pitchforks and knives to defend themselves behind a wall.

'Get into a semicircle, and we'll attack 'em together,' shouted Torrismund at them, and so put himself at the head of the local militia.

Now he ejected the Knights from the house. At one moment he found himself face to face with the old Knight and another two armed with torches. 'He's a traitor, take him!'

A fierce struggle rose. The locals used spits and their women and children stones. Suddenly a horn sounded 'Retreat!' Before the peasant counterattack the Knights had fallen back at many points and were now clearing out of the village.

The group pressing Torrismund had retired too. 'Away brothers!' shouted the old man, 'let us be led where the Grail takes us.'

'The Grail will triumph,' chorused the others, turning their bridles.

'Hurrah! You've saved us!' The peasants crowded round Torrismund. 'You're a knight, but you're generous! At last one who is! Stay with us! Tell us what you want; we'll give it to you.'

'Well ... what I want ... Now I don't know,' stuttered Torrismund.

'We knew nothing either, even if we were human, before this battle ... And now we seem to be able ... to want ... to need to do things ... however difficult ...' and they turned to mourn their dead.

'I can't stay with you ... I don't know who I am ... Farewell!' and away he galloped.

'Come back!' cried the peasants, but Torrismund was already far from the village, from the wood of the Grail, from Kurwalden.

Again he began his wandering among nations. Till now he had despised every honour and pleasure, his sole ideal being the Sacred Order of the Knights of the Grail. And now that ideal had vanished, to what aim could he set his disquiet?

He fed on wild fruit in the woods, on bean soup in monasteries he met on the way, on shellfish along rocky coasts. And on the shores of Brittany, seeking for shellfish in a cave, what should he find but a sleeping woman.

The desire which had moved him over the world, for places of soft velvety vegetation swept by low searing wind, for tense sunless days, now at the sight of those long black lashes lowered over full pale cheeks, and that tender relaxed body, and the hand on the full-formed bosom, the soft loose hair, the lip, the hip, the toe, the breath, finally his desire seemed assuaged.

He was leaning over her, looking, when Sophronia opened her eyes. 'You'll do me no hurt,' she said gently, 'what do you seek amid these deserted rocks?'

'I seek something which I have always lacked and only now that I see you know what it is. How did you reach this shore?'

'Though a nun, I was forced to marry a follower of Mohammed; but the nuptials were never consummated as I was the three hundred and sixty-fifth wife and Christian arms intervened and brought me here, victim of a shipwreck on my return voyage, as I was of ferocious pirates on my way out.'

'I understand. And are you alone?'

'My deliverer has gone to the Imperial camp to make certain arrangements, as far as I understand.'

'I yearn to offer the protection of my sword, but fear that the emotion firing me at sight of you may turn to suggestions which you might not consider honest.'

'Oh, have no scruples, you know, I've seen so much. Though every time, just at the very moment, arrives that deliverer, always the same one.'

'Will he arrive this time too?'

'Oh well, one never knows.'

'What is your name?'

'Azira; or Sister Palmyra. According to whether I'm in a Sultan's harem or a convent.'

'Azira, I seemed always to have loved you ... already to have lost myself in you ...'

11

Charlemagne was prancing along towards the coast of Brittany. 'We'll soon see, we'll soon see, Agilulf of the Guildivern, calm yourself. If what you tell me is true, if this woman still bears the same virginity as she had fifteen years ago, then there's no more to be said, and you have been an armed knight by full right, and that young man was just trying to deceive us. To make certain I have brought along in our suite an old woman who's an expert in such matters; we soldiers haven't quite got the touch for these things, eh ...'

The old midwife, on the crupper of Gurduloo's saddle, was twittering away, 'Yes, yes, majesty, I'll be most careful, even if it's twins ...' She was deaf and had not yet understood what it was all about.

Into the grotto first went two officers of the suite, bearing torches. They returned in some confusion. 'Sire, the virgin is lying in the embrace of a young soldier.'

The lovers were brought before the emperor.

'You, Sophronia!' cried Agilulf.

Charlemagne had the young man's face raised. 'Torrismund!'

Torrismund started towards Sophronia. 'Are you Sophronia? Ah, my own mother!'

'Do you know this young man, Sophronia?' asked the emperor.

The woman bent her head, pale-faced, 'If it's Torrismund, I brought him up myself,' said she in a faint voice.

Torrismund leapt into his saddle. 'I've committed foul incest! Never will you see me more!' He spurred and galloped off into the woods to the right.

Agilulf spurred off in his turn. 'Nor will you see me again!' said he. 'I have no longer a name! Farewell!' And he rode off deep into the woods on the left.

All remained in consternation. Sophronia hid her head between her hands.

Suddenly came a thud of hooves from the right. It was Torrismund cantering back out of the wood at full tilt. He shouted, 'Hey! She was a virgin until a short time ago! Why didn't I think of that at once? She was a virgin! She can't be my mother!'

'Would you explain?' asked Charlemagne.

'In truth, Torrismund is not my son, but my brother or rather half-brother,' said Sophronia. 'Our mother the Queen of Scotland, my father the king having been at the wars for a year, bore him after a chance encounter – it seems – with the Sacred Order of the Knights of the Grail. On the king announcing his return, that perfidious woman (as am I forced to consider our mother) with the excuse of my taking my little brother for a walk, let us loose in the woods. And she arranged a foul deceit for her husband on his arrival. She said that I, then aged thirteen, had run away to bear a little bastard. Held back by ill-conceived respect, I never betrayed our mother's secret. I lived on the heaths with my infant half-brother; and they were free and happy years for me, compared with those awaiting in the convent which I was forced to enter by the Duke of Cornwall. Never until this morning at the age of thirty-three have I known man, and my first experience turns out to be incestuous ...'

'Let's think it all over calmly,' said Charlemagne, conciliatingly. 'It is incest, of course, but that between half-brother and sister is not the most serious.'

' 'Tis not incest, Sacred Majesty! Rejoice, Sophronia!' exclaimed Torrismund, radiant. 'In my researches on my origin I learnt a secret which I wished to keep for ever; she whom I thought my mother, that is you, Sophronia, was not born of the Queen of Scotland but is the king's natural daughter by a farmer's wife. The king had you adopted by his wife, that is, by her whom I now learn from you was my mother and your stepmother. Now I understand how she, obliged by the king to pretend herself your mother against her wish, longed for a chance to be rid of you; and she did so by attributing to you the result of a passing adventure of her own, myself. You are the daughter of the King of Scotland and of a peasant woman, I of the queen and of the Sacred Order, we have no blood tie, only the link of love forged freely here a short time ago and which I ardently hope you will be willing to reforge.'

'All seems to be working out for the best ...' said Charlemagne, rubbing his hands. 'Let us hasten to trace our fine knight Agilulf and reassure him that his name and title are no longer in danger.'

'I will go myself, Majesty!' cried a knight, running forward. It was Raimbaud.

He entered the woods, crying, 'Knight! Sir Agilulf! Knight of the Guildiveeeern ... Agilulf Emo Bertrandin of the Guildivern and of the Others of Corbentraz and Sura, Knight of Selimpia Citeriore and Feeeez! ... All's in oooorder! ... Come baaack!'

Only the echo replied.

Raimbaud began to search the woods track by track, and off the tracks over crags and torrents, calling, ears stretched, seeking a sign, a trace. He saw the marks of horse's hooves. At a certain point they were stamped deeper, as if the animal had stopped. From there on the trail of hooves grew lighter, as if the horse had been let loose. But at the same point diverged another trail, a trail of iron footsteps. Raimbaud followed that.

On reaching a clearing he held his breath. At the foot of an oak tree, scattered over the ground, were an overturned helmet with a crest of iridescent plumes, a white breastplate, greaves, vambraces, bascinet, gauntlets, in fact all the pieces of Agilulf's armour, some disposed as if in an attempt at an ordered pyramid, others rolled haphazard on the ground. On the hilt of the sword was a note, 'I leave this armour to Sir Raimbaud of Roussillon.' Beneath was a half-squiggle, as of a signature begun and soon interrupted.

'Knight!' called Raimbaud, turning towards the helmet, the breastplate, the oak tree, the sky. 'Knight! Take back your armour! Your rank in the army and the nobility of France is assured!' and he tried to put the armour together, to stand it on its feet, continuing to shout, 'You're all set, sir, no one can deny it now!' No voice replied. The armour would not stand, the helmet rolled on the ground. 'Knight, you have resisted so long by your will power alone, and succeeded in doing all things as if you existed; why suddenly surrender?' But he did not know in which direction to turn; the armour was empty, not empty like before, but empty of that something going by the name of Sir Agilulf which was now dissolved like a drop in the sea.

Raimbaud then unstrapped his own armour, stripped, put on the white armour, donned Agilulf's helmet, grasped his shield and sword, leapt on his horse. Thus accoutred he appeared before the emperor and his retinue.

'Ah, Agilulf, so you're back, are you, and all's settled, eh?'

But another voice replied from the helmet. 'I'm not Agilulf, majesty!' The visor was raised and Raimbaud's face appeared. 'All that remains of the Knight of the Guildivern is his white armour and this paper assigning me its possession. Now my one longing is to fling myself into battle!'

The trumpets sounded the alarm. A fleet of feluccas had just landed a Saracen host in Brittany. The Frankish army hurried to arms. 'Your desire is granted!' cried Charlemagne.

'Now is the hour of battle. Do honour to the arms you bear! Although Agilulf had a difficult character, he was a fine soldier.'

The Frankish army held the invaders at bay, opened a breach in the Saracen ranks through which young Raimbaud was the first to rush. He laid about him, giving blows and taking them. Many a Moor bit the dust. On Raimbaud's lance were spitted as many as it could take. Already the invading hordes were falling back on their moored feluccas. Hard pressed by Frankish arms the defeated invaders took off from the shore, except those who remained to soak the grey Breton soil with Moorish blood.

Raimbaud issued from battle victorious and untouched: but his armour, Agilulf's intact impeccable white armour, was now all encrusted with earth, bespattered with enemy blood, covered with dents, scratches and slashes, the helmet askew, the shield gashed in the very midst of that mysterious coat of arms. Now the youth felt it to be truly his own armour, his, Raimbaud of Roussillon's; his first discomfort on donning it was gone; now it fitted him like a glove.

He was galloping, all alone, on the edge of a hill. A voice rang from the bottom of the valley, 'Hey, up there! Agilulf!'

A knight was coursing towards him, in armour covered with a mantle of periwinkle blue. It was Bradamante following him. 'At last I've found you, white knight!'

'Bradamante, I'm not Agilulf, I'm Raimbaud!' he was on the point of calling in reply, but thought it better to say so from nearby, and turned his horse to reach her.

'At last 'tis you coursing to meet me, oh unseizable warrior!' exclaimed Bradamante. 'Oh, that it should be granted me to see you rushing so after me, you the only man whose actions are not mere impulse, shallow caprice, like those of the usual rabble who follow me!' And so saying, she wheeled her horse and tried to escape him, though turning her head every now and again to see if he were playing her game and following her.

Raimbaud was impatient to say to her, 'Don't you notice how I too move awkwardly, how my every gesture betrays desire, dissatisfaction, disquiet? All I wish is to be one who knows what he wants!' And to tell her so he galloped after her, as she laughed and called, 'This is the day I've always dreamt of!'

He lost sight of her. There was a grassy solitary vale. Her horse was tied to a mulberry tree. It was like that first time he had followed her when still not suspecting her to be a woman. Raimbaud dismounted. There she was, lying down on a mossy slope. She had taken off her armour, was dressed in a short topaz-coloured tunic. As she lay there she opened her arms to him. Raimbaud went forward in his white armour. This was the moment to say, 'I'm not Agilulf, the armour with which you fell in love is now filled out with the weight of a body, a young agile one like mine. Don't you see how this armour has lost its inhuman whiteness and become a covering for battle exposed to every blow, a tool patient and useful?' This was what he wanted to say, instead of which he stood there with trembling hands, taking hesitant steps towards her. Perhaps the best thing would have been to show himself, take off his armour, make it clear that he was Raimbaud, particularly now as she closed her eyes and lay there with a smile of expectation. Tensely the young man tore off his armour, now Bradamante would open her eyes and recognize him ... No; she had put a hand over her face as if not wanting to be disturbed by the sight of the non-existent knight's invisible approach. Raimbaud flings himself on her.

'Yes, I was sure of it!' exclaims Bradamante, with closed eyes. 'I was always sure it would be possible!' and she hugs him close, and in a fever of which both partook they are united. 'Yes, oh yes, I was sure of it!'

Now it's over and the moment comes to look each other in the eyes.

'She'll see me,' Raimbaud thinks in a flash of pride and hope. 'She'll understand all, she'll understand it's been right and fine and love me for ever!'

Bradamante opens her eyes.

'You!'

She leaps from her couch, pushes Raimbaud back.

'You! You!' she cries, her mouth enraged, her eyes starting with tears. 'You! Imposter!'

And on foot she brandishes her sword, raises it against Raimbaud and hits him, but with the flat, on his head, stunning him, and all he can bring out as he raises unarmed hands either to defend himself or embrace her is, 'But, but ... say ... wasn't it good ... ?', Then he loses his senses and hears only vaguely the clatter of her departing horse.

If a lover is wretched who invokes kisses of which he knows not the flavour, a thousand times more wretched is he who has had a taste of the flavour and then had it denied him.

Raimbaud continued his intrepid warrior's life. Wherever the fight was thickest, there his lance cleft. If in the turmoil of swords he spied a glint of periwinkle blue, he would rush towards it. 'Bradamante!' he would shout, but always in vain.

The only person to whom he wanted to confess his troubles had vanished. Sometimes, wandering around the bivouacs, the way some armour stood erect on its side-pieces made him quiver, for it reminded him of Agilulf. Suppose the knight had not dissolved but found some other armour? Raimbaud would go up and say, 'Don't think me offensive, colleague, but would you mind raising the visor of your helmet?'

Every time he hoped to find himself facing an emptiness: instead of which there was always a nose above a pair of twisted moustachios. 'I'm sorry,' he would murmur, and turn away.

Another was also searching for Agilulf; Gurduloo, who every time he saw an empty pot, cauldron or tub would stop and exclaim, 'Oh sir master! At your orders, sir master.'

Sitting in a field on the verge of a road, he was making a long speech into the mouth of a wine flask when a voice interrupted him, 'What are you seeking inside there, Gurduloo?'

It was Torrismund, who having celebrated his solemn nuptials with Sophronia in the presence of Charlemagne, was riding off with his bride and a rich suite to Kurwalden, of which the emperor had named him Count.

'It's my master I'm looking for,' says Gurduloo.

'In that flask?'

'My master is a person who doesn't exist; so he cannot exist as much in a flask as in a suit of armour.'

'But your master has dissolved into thin air!'

'Then am I squire to the air?'

'You will be my squire, if you follow me.'

They reached Kurwalden. The country was unrecognizable. Instead of villages now rose towns and houses of stone, and mills, and canals.

'I have returned, good folk to stay among you ...'

'Hurrah! Fine! Hurrah! Long live the bride!'

'Wait and show your joy at the news I bring you; the Emperor Charlemagne, bow to his sacred name, has invested me with the title of Count of Kurwalden.'

'Ah ... But ... Charlemagne? ... Well ...'

'Don't you understand? You have a count now! I will defend you against the incursions of the Knights of the Grail.'

'Oh we've thrust all those out of the whole of Kurwalden some time ago! You see, we've always obeyed for so long ... But now we've seen one can live quite well without having truck with either knights or counts ... We cultivate the land, have put up artisan shops, and mills, and try to get our laws respected by ourselves, to defend our borders, in fact we're going ahead and don't complain. You're a generous young man and we'll not forget what you've done for us ... Stay here if you wish ... but as equals ...'

'As equals? You don't want me as count? But don't you understand it's the emperor's order? It's impossible for you to refuse!'

'Oh, people are always saying that! Impossible! ... To get rid of those Grail people seemed impossible ... and then we only had pitchforks and billhooks ... We wish no ill to anyone, young sir, and to you least of all ... You're a fine young man, and know many things which we don't ... If you stay here as equals with us and do no bullying, maybe you will become the first among us just the same ...'

'Torrismund, I am weary of so many mishaps,' said Sophronia, raising her veil. 'These good people seem reasonable and courteous and the town pleasanter and in better state than many ... Why should we not try to come to an arrangement?'

'What about our suite?'

'They can all become citizens of Kurwalden,' replied the inhabitants, 'and will be given to each according to their worth.'

'Am I to consider myself an equal to this squire of mine, Gurduloo, who doesn't even know if he exists or not?'

'He too will learn ... We ourselves did not know we existed ... One can also learn to be ...'

12

Book, now you have reached your end. Those last pages I found myself writing away at breakneck speed. From one line to another I have leapt about among nations and seas and continents. What is this frenzy which has seized me, this impatience? It's as if I were waiting for something. But what can nuns await, withdrawn here so as to be outside the ever changing happenings of the world? What else can I await except new pages to cover and the routine ringing of convent bells?

There, I hear a horse come up the narrow track; now it stops right at the convent gates. The rider knocks. I can't stretch far enough out of my little window to see him, but I can hear his voice. 'Hey, good sisters, listen!'

But is that his voice, or am I mistaken? Yes, 'tis Raimbaud's voice which I have so long made resound over these pages! What can Raimbaud want here?

'Hey, good sisters, can you please tell me if an Amazon has found refuge in this convent, the famous Bradamante?'

Yes, searching for Bradamante throughout the world, Raimbaud was bound to reach here one day.

I hear the Sister Guardian's voice reply, 'No, soldier, there are no Amazons here; only poor holy women praying for your sins.'

But now I run to the window and cry, 'Yes, Raimbaud, I'm here, wait for me, I knew you'd come, I'll be down, I'll leave with you.'

And hurriedly I tear off my wimple, my cloistral bands, my nun's skirt, pull out of a drawer my little topaz-coloured tunic, my cuirass, my helmet, my spurs, my periwinkle blue robe. 'Wait for me, Raimbaud, I'm here, I'm here, I, Bradamante!'

Yes, book. Sister Theodora who tells this tale and the amazon Bradamante are one and the same. Sometimes I gallop for a time over battlefields between duels and loves, sometimes shut myself in convents, meditating and jotting down the adventures that have happened to me, so as to try and understand them. When I came to shut myself in here I was desperate with love for Agilulf, now I burn for the young and passionate Raimbaud.

That is why my pen at a certain point began running on so. I rushed to meet him; I knew he would not be long in coming. A page is good only when we turn it and find life surging along and confusing every passage in the book. The pen rushes on urged by the same joy that makes me course the open road. A chapter started when one doesn't know which tale to tell is like a corner turned on leaving a convent, when one might come face to face with a dragon, a Saracen gang, an enchanted isle or a new love.

I'm hurrying to you, Raimbaud. I'm not even bidding the abbess goodbye. They know me already and realize that after affrays and affairs and blighted hopes I always return to this cloister. But it will be different now ... It will be ...

From describing the past, from the present which seized my hand in its excited grasps, here I am, oh future, now mounting the crupper of thy horse. What new pennants wilt thou unfurl before me from towers of cities not yet founded? What rivers of devastation set flowing over castles and gardens I have loved? What unforeseeable golden ages art thou preparing, ill-mastered, indomitable harbinger of treasures dearly paid for, my kingdom to be conquered, the future ...